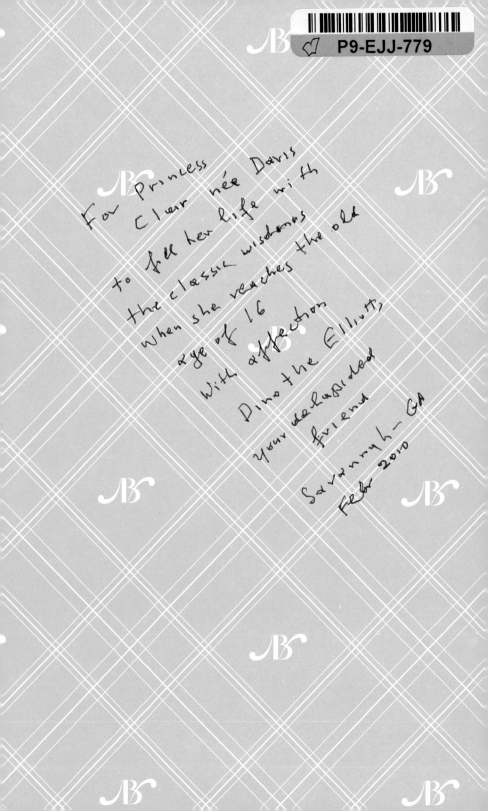

For Princess
Clear née Davis
to fill her life with
the classic wisdoms
when she reaches the old
age of 16
With affection
Dino the Elliott,
your devoted
friend

Savannah – GA
Febr 2010

From the Pages of
Utopia
and The Life of Sir Thomas More

'The way to heaven out of all places is of like length and distance.'
(from Utopia, page 18)

One man to live in pleasure and wealth, whiles all other weep and smart for it, that is the part not of a king, but of a jailor.
(from Utopia, page 49)

"If you had been with me in Utopia and had presently seen their fashions and laws, as I did, which lived there five years and more, . . . then doubtless you would grant that you never saw people well ordered, but only there."
(from Utopia, page 56)

Now you see how little liberty they have to loiter; how they can have no cloak or pretense to idleness. There be neither wine taverns, nor alehouses, nor any occasion of vice or wickedness, no lurking corners, no places of wicked councils, or unlawful assemblies. But they be in the present sight and under the eyes of every man, so that of necessity they must either apply their accustomed labors, or else recreate themselves with honest and laudable pastimes.
(from Utopia, page 83)

To gold and silver nature hath given no use that we may not well lack, if that the folly of men had not set it in higher estimation for the rareness sake. But of the contrary part, nature, as a most tender and loving mother, hath placed the best and most necessary things open abroad, as the air, the water, and the earth itself, and hath removed and hid farthest from us vain and unprofitable things.
(from Utopia, page 86)

The wits, therefore, of the Utopians, inured and exercised in learning, be marvelous quick in the invention of feats helping anything to the advantage and wealth of life.
(from Utopia, page 105)

They have but few laws, for to people so instruct and institute very few do suffice.   (from *Utopia*, page 112)

When I consider and weigh in my mind all these commonwealths which nowadays anywhere do flourish, so God help me, I can perceive nothing but a certain conspiracy of rich men procuring their own commodities under the name and title of the commonwealth. They invent and devise all means and crafts, first how to keep safely, without fear of losing, that which they have unjustly gathered together, and next how to hire and abuse the work and labor of the poor for as little money as may be.   (from *Utopia*, page 143)

> My king and conqueror, Utopus by name,
> A prince of much renown and immortal fame,
> Hath made me an isle that erst no island was,
> Full fraught with worldly wealth, with pleasure and solace.
>   (from an untitled poem by More, page 151)

Forasmuch as Sir Thomas More, Knight, sometime Lord Chancellor of England, a man of singular virtue and of a clear unspotted conscience, as witnesseth Erasmus, more pure and white than the whitest snow, and of such an angelical wit, as England, he saith, never had the like before, nor never shall again, universally, as well in the laws of our realm, a study in effect able to occupy the whole life of a man, as in all other sciences right well studied, was in his days accounted a man worthy famous memory.
         (from William Roper's *Life of Sir Thomas More*, page 163)

And so was he by Master Lieutenant brought out of the Tower and from thence led towards the place of execution, where, going up the scaffold, which was so weak that it was ready to fall, he said merrily to Master Lieutenant: "I pray you, Master Lieutenant, see me safe up, and for my coming down, let me shift for myself."
         (from William Roper's *Life of Sir Thomas More*, page 214)

He turned to the executioner and with a cheerful countenance spake thus unto him: "Pluck up thy spirits, man, and be not afraid to do thine office. My neck is very short. Take heed therefore thou strike not awry, for saving of thine honesty."
         (from William Roper's *Life of Sir Thomas More*, page 214)

UTOPIA

Sir Thomas More

Translated by Ralph Robinson

With *The Life of Sir Thomas More* by William Roper

*Edited with an Introduction and Notes
by Wayne A. Rebhorn*

George Stade
Consulting Editorial Director

JB

BARNES & NOBLE CLASSICS
NEW YORK

$\mathcal{B}$

BARNES & NOBLE CLASSICS
NEW YORK

Published by Barnes & Noble Books
122 Fifth Avenue
New York, NY 10011

www.barnesandnoble.com/classics

Utopia was first published in Latin in 1516. Ralph Robinson's English translation first appeared in 1551. William Roper's *Life of Sir Thomas More* was first published in 1626.

Originally published in trade paperback format in 2005 by Barnes & Noble Classics with new Introduction, Notes, Biography, Chronology, Inspired By, Comments & Questions, and For Further Reading. This hardcover edition published in 2005.

Introduction, Notes, and For Further Reading Copyright © 2005 by Wayne A. Rebhorn.

Note on Sir Thomas More, The World of Sir Thomas More and *Utopia*, Inspired by *Utopia*, and Comments & Questions Copyright © 2005 by Barnes & Noble, Inc.

Utopia
ISBN-13: 978-1-59308-369-4
ISBN-10: 1-59308-369-6
LC Control Number 2005931383

Produced and published in conjunction with:
Fine Creative Media, Inc.
322 Eighth Avenue
New York, NY 10001

Michael J. Fine, President and Publisher

Printed in the United States of America
1 3 5 7 9 10 8 6 4 2
FIRST PRINTING

Sir Thomas More

When philosopher Desiderius Erasmus was asked to describe his close friend Thomas More, he obliged with intimate details regarding More's quick wit and humor, his piety, his good looks and winning way with women, his loyal friendship, and his love of corned beef and eggs. While such details could apply to many men, the subject in question was also the most famous philosopher in England, author of the masterpiece *Utopia*, and the right-hand man of King Henry VIII. But it was the cruel fate that followed hard on this glorious career that made More a political martyr and canonized saint in the Catholic Church.

More was born in London in 1478. His father, Sir John More, was a respected judge with connections to Cardinal John Morton, the lord chancellor of England and second most powerful figure in the country. In the early 1490s More worked as a page in the Cardinal's house, and the boy's keen mind motivated Morton to sponsor More at Oxford University, where he studied classical languages, French, mathematics, and history. His professors were favorably impressed by their brilliant, charismatic student; indeed, scholar Thomas Linacre provided More with introductions to the renowned intellects of Europe.

Following in his father's footsteps, More went on to study law. A concomitant spiritual quest led him to consider the priesthood; he moved into a monastery, donned a painful hair shirt, and lived like a devout monk while pursuing his legal studies. More finally opted to forgo the priesthood and in 1502 began the legal career that would earn him a place in King Henry VIII's court. A successful tenure in Parliament defending London merchants followed, as did an appointment as under-sheriff of London. In 1515 the King's lord chancellor, Cardinal Thomas Wolsey, selected More for an ambassadorial mission to Flanders; while there he began writing *Utopia*.

The publication of *Utopia* in 1516 spread More's fame throughout Europe. At home, he was elected speaker of the House of Commons (1523) and appointed high steward of both Oxford (1524) and Cambridge Universities (1525); in 1529 King Henry VIII appointed him lord chancellor of England. By this time Martin Luther and other reformers had begun to strongly criticize the Catholic Church and call for reform. More strongly defended the King and Catholicism with such texts as *A Dialogue Concerning Heresies* (1529).

More's devout faith ultimately proved to be his downfall. In 1533 the Pope excommunicated Henry VIII for his marriage to Anne Boleyn, and the following year More refused to endorse the legitimacy of Henry's subsequent heirs. For this supposed treason, the King's former favorite was sent to the Tower of London to await trial. More was found guilty and sentenced to death. On July 6, 1535, he was executed and his head placed on a spear on London Bridge. For the steadfastness of his faith, he was beatified in 1886 and canonized in 1935.

Table of Contents

The World of Sir Thomas More and Utopia

1478	Thomas More is born on February 7 in London to Sir John More, an influential lawyer and judge, and Agnes Graunger.
c.1482–1490	Sir John sends his son to one of England's best schools, Saint Anthony's in Threadneedle Street.
c.1490–1492	Thomas works as a page in the household of England's second most powerful figure, Cardinal John Morton, archbishop of Canterbury and lord chancellor of England. The Cardinal is so taken with the young man's sharp mind and engaging personality that he sends him to Oxford University.
c.1492–1494	Thomas enters Oxford. Sir John gives him a scant allowance, hoping that if he has meager means, he will stay away from tempting distractions and focus on his studies. Thomas proves to be a superior student, excelling in Latin, Greek, history, French, and mathematics. His mentor, Thomas Linacre, will be instrumental in introducing More to the many eminent scholars with whom he will correspond in the coming years.
1494	His father brings More back to London to study law. He enrolls at New Inn.
1496	For additional legal studies, he enters Lincoln's Inn in London's Inns of Court.
1499	More is introduced to celebrated Dutch philosopher Desiderius Erasmus. The two form a close, lifelong friendship, maintained in part through a lively, witty, and intellectually rigorous correspondence.
1500	More lives as a guest in a Carthusian monastery and considers becoming a priest in the Catholic Church. His strict piety compels him to rise early, pray often, fast, and wear a hair shirt.
1502	Having decided to forego a religious vocation, More becomes an "utter barrister," a full member of the legal profession.
1504	He is elected to Parliament, where he advocates on behalf of London merchants. His persuasive style and positions place

him in conflict with King Henry VII, who briefly imprisons Sir John as retribution for More's Parliamentary speeches.

1505 More marries Jane Colt, with whom he will have four children; he is a devoted family man.

1505– Amerigo Vespucci's accounts of his voyages to the New
1507 World are published.

1509 Henry VII dies, and Henry VIII becomes king. More demonstrates his skill as a negotiator and interpreter in dealings with a group of merchants from Antwerp.

1510 More becomes one of two under-sheriffs of London, a position he will hold until 1518.

1511 When Jane Colt, More's wife, dies, he marries the widow Alice Middleton; their home is a happy refuge from More's hectic life. Erasmus publishes *Moriae encomium* (*The Praise of Folly*), which he says was written with More's encouragement.

1512 Henry VIII and France go to war.

1513 Niccolò Machiavelli writes *The Prince*. Around this time More begins writing *The History of King Richard III* in Latin and English.

1515 The King's council sends More on an important ambassadorial mission to Flanders; while there, More begins his masterpiece, *Utopia*.

1516 *Utopia* is published at Louvain (in today's Belgium); its success makes More one of the best-known intellectuals in Europe. Henry VIII appoints More to his court; he is awarded a life pension and a number of governmental responsibilities. He becomes a member of the Council of the Star Chamber under Cardinal Wolsey.

1517 More travels to Calais to negotiate suits following the war with France. He is appointed master of requests and becomes a member of the King's Privy Council. The second edition of *Utopia* is published in Paris. Martin Luther's Ninety-five Theses, attacking the papal authority to grant indulgences, herald the Reformation.

1518 Further editions of *Utopia* are published in Basel.

1521 More is knighted and made the King's under-treasurer. His daughter Margaret marries William Roper, a lawyer.

1523   More is elected speaker of the House of Commons on Cardinal Wolsey's recommendation. His relationship with Henry VIII deepens; the King dines at the More household.

1524   More is appointed high steward of Oxford University.

1525   The leading intellectual in England, More is appointed high steward of Cambridge University as well as chancellor of the Duchy of Lancaster, with administrative and judicial responsibility for a large area of northern England.

1527   Henry VIII, desperate to have a male heir, seeks from the Pope an annulment of his marriage to Catherine of Aragon so that he may marry Anne Boleyn.

1528   Bishop Cuthbert Tunstall commissions More to write against the new Protestant texts.

1529   The King appoints More lord chancellor of England; the first layman to assume the position, he is now the second most powerful man in the nation. He publishes *A Dialogue Concerning Heresies*, a refutation of the ideas of religious reformers Martin Luther and William Tyndale; several similar works will follow through 1533.

1532   When Henry demands that all clerical legislation have royal approval and the bishops agree, More resigns the chancellorship.

1533   When Henry divorces Catherine and marries Anne Boleyn, the Catholic Church excommunicates him. More does not attend Anne's coronation.

1534   More declines to support the Act of Succession, which would legitimize Boleyn's children as heirs to the throne and reject the Pope as head of the Church. When he also refuses to support Henry's claims to be supreme head of the English Church, he is imprisoned in the Tower of London. He conducts correspondence and writes *A Dialogue of Comfort Against Tribulation* before his writing materials are taken away.

1535   More is tried and convicted of treason at Westminster Hall. He is beheaded on July 6. His head is displayed on London Bridge, where it remains for a month until his family has it removed and buried in the family plot.

1886   More is beatified by Pope Leo XIII.

1935   More is canonized by Pope Pius XI.

Introduction

Omnium horarum homo: a "man for all hours." That's what Desiderius Erasmus calls his friend Thomas More. The phrase appears in the letter that serves as the preface for Erasmus's masterpiece, *The Praise of Folly*, and is also the source of Robert Bolt's title for his play and movie about More, *A Man for All Seasons*. Bolt's title transforms More into a secular saint, a model of individual integrity, a man "for all seasons"—that is, for all of history. Indeed, the French translated the title of Bolt's film as *Un Homme pour l'éternité*, making More into "A Man for Eternity." This is not, however, what Erasmus meant by the words he penned in 1511, long before More achieved martyrdom, suffering death rather than accept Henry VIII as the head of the Church. Erasmus is actually praising More for being able "to play the man for all hours with everyone." More is an ideal figure, in other words, because he is adaptable, able to get along with all sorts of people in all sorts of situations and as circumstances change from hour to hour, what Erasmus means by "folly"—that is, a supreme versatility in living life in this world. The historical More certainly possessed such versatility, so that when Erasmus decided to praise "Folly," or *Moria* in Greek, it is not surprising that the name of More, *Morus* in Latin, should have popped into his head not just as an appropriate dedicatee, but as someone who epitomized all the best meanings he attributed to folly in his work.

Erasmus's compliment to More makes More into a *player*, someone who knows how "to play—or act—the man" (*hominem agere*) in every situation. Indeed, in his biography of More, almost the very first thing his son-in-law William Roper does is to praise More's success at improvisational acting when he was still a young page in the household of the learned John Cardinal Morton: "Though he was young of years, yet would he at Christmastide suddenly sometimes step in among the players, and never studying for the matter, make a part of his own there presently among them, which made the lookers-on more sport than all the players beside" (see, in this edition, pp. 163–164). Even a cursory review of More's life and works reveals his ability to play many incredibly varied roles, some of which were even opposed to one another. For example, More was a faithful husband and devoted father, but also an ascetic who seriously considered entering a monastery. He was a learned humanist scholar and translator of the classics, but also a propagandist for the Tudor regime and a mud-slinging critic of Luther. More won cases as a clever lawyer and fought to preserve his economic, social, and political status, but he was also a deeply religious devotional writer who looked down on attachments to this world. An impartial and fair-minded negotiator, civil servant, and magistrate, he became an implacable opponent and persecutor of heretics; best known for his role as a lord chancellor who willingly implemented Henry's policies and paid his royal master almost servile deference, he was also, at the end, a defender of his own conscience against monarchical tyranny. Finally, More stands on the world stage as an unfettered genius capable of imagining brave new worlds in his greatest literary and philosophical achievement, even though he was also an uncompromising defender of received traditions and of an ancient, long-established institution that was deeply opposed to change. Luther once said of Erasmus, complaining of the Dutch humanist's mutability and contradictoriness, "Erasmus of Rotterdam, where will you stand fast?" He could almost have said the same thing about Thomas More.

More's complexities and contradictions go to the heart of the Renaissance and the Reformation, the two great cultural upheavals England, like the rest of Europe, experienced in the early decades of the sixteenth century—and would continue to experience for many years after More's death in 1535. In these two social transformations More played a key role both in what he did and in what he said or wrote. Nor was More merely an important English figure; he was also well known on the European continent, respected everywhere as a humanist writer and political thinker, and, finally, either admired as a martyr for the true faith or disparaged as a fool for not seeing the insufficiency of the Catholic Church.

More's reputation in the last century has been equally complex and contradictory. The Catholic Church finally beatified him in 1886 and made him a saint in 1935, and many scholars and historians, some Catholic and some not, have admired his deep commitment to his religious faith. His *Utopia* has been celebrated by others for its relatively egalitarian social structure, its religious tolerance, and its economic system—a system in which all things are held in common and which thus seems to anticipate the ideals of socialism and communism. Indeed, *Utopia* was one of the first books authorized for translation into Russian after the Communist Revolution in 1917. By contrast, in Bolt's 1960 *A Man for All Seasons*, More has turned into a secular saint who defends his "self," not his "soul," against tyrannical political authority. Finally, More has been attacked by others as a mediocre statesman and condemned for his servile relationship to Henry, a servility best seen in the exaggerated expressions of deference he made to the King, as recorded in Roper's *Life*, while Protestant polemicists have objected to the largely popular press he has enjoyed and have stressed his persecution of heretics, instead.

There is perhaps no way to resolve all the contradictions that characterize More, for they reflect both his complexity and that of the age he was living through. What we can do, however, is to make them somewhat more comprehensible by placing them in the context of his times. Indeed, it may well be that More's enduring attraction for us derives precisely from his contradictoriness, his ability to be so many different Thomas Mores to so many different people. In a sense, his being Erasmus's man of all hours is really what ensures he will always be Robert Bolt's man for all seasons.

Born in 1478 into what we would call a middle-class family—his father John More was a barrister—Thomas More grew up just as the Renaissance was arriving in England. That cultural shift had begun in Italy in the late fourteenth century and had reached full bloom in the fifteenth. The "Renaissance," as the name implies, sought nothing less than the *rebirth* of classical antiquity in its own time. That rebirth focused primarily on the replacement of late medieval Latin with a revived classical Latin based on Roman writers such as Cicero and Vergil. This seemingly trivial concern with language was actually crucial for European culture, for Latin was the language of education as well as the professions, diplomacy, and the Church. Latin was, in short, the *lingua franca* of the educated, and they not only read it as trained classicists do now, but wrote it and spoke it in both public forums and private conversations. To this revived classical Latin scholars added the study of ancient Greek, a language that had been generally unknown in western Europe during the Middle Ages and that was given a substantial boost after the fall of Constantinople and the Byzantine Empire to the Turks in 1453—which led many Greek scholars to flee to Italy, bearing with them their knowledge of the ancient language as well as countless manuscripts. Enthusiasm for the study of classical Latin and Greek, what soon became known as the New Learning, began to spread outside of Italy in the late fifteenth century, thanks in part to the recent invention of printing with movable type and in part to the fact that scholars from the rest of Europe began to come to Italy to study. Two of those scholars, the Englishmen William Grocyn (c.1446–1519) and Thomas Linacre (c.1460–1524), came to Florence to hear lectures by Italian Neo-Platonist Angelo Poliziano (1454–1494), and on their return home they spread their knowledge of and commitment to the New Learning through their teaching, thus becoming the leading figures in a group that included John Colet (1466/67–1519) and William Lyly (1468?–1522). Colet went on to found Saint Paul's School in London to teach the new disciplines, and together with Lyly and Erasmus, he produced what would become the standard Latin grammar in England for several decades. These scholars as well as their students have generally been referred to as "humanists" since the early nineteenth century because they were committed to what they called "humane letters"—that is, the *artes liberales*, or liberal arts, which were centered on the teaching of classical Latin and Greek, of rhetoric, literature, and history, what we now call the humanities. Note that they are not called humanists because they wished to replace religion with some set of secular values. Indeed, although the New Learning did have an important secular dimension, especially in Italy, it was generally thought to be fully compatible with Christianity, and many of the leading humanists in northern Europe, such as Colet and Erasmus—and More—were deeply religious men.

More was initially educated at Saint Anthony's school in London, one of the best in England, and then spent about two years from 1490 to 1492 in the household of John Morton, the archbishop of Canterbury and lord chancellor of England. Morton recognized More's abilities and sent him to Oxford, where he studied either at Canterbury College (now Christ Church) or at Magdalen College School. Oxford was divided for several decades about the New Learning, as many professors rejected the humanist program of studies and continued to teach logic, or dialectic, which had been the Queen of the Sciences in the Middle Ages. As late as 1518 More was writing to the university defending the study of Greek there. Nevertheless, Grocyn did teach Greek at Oxford in the early 1490s, and John Holt, the master of Magdalen College while More was at the university, produced a new classical Latin grammar to which More contributed a prologue and dedicatory epistle. Even while he was training to become a lawyer in the late 1490s, More continued his classical education; he achieved recognition for his learning when, in 1501, he was invited to lecture on Saint Augustine's *City of God* at Saint Lawrence Jewry—whose rector at the time just happened to be Grocyn. Attaching himself to the distinguished humanist, More began the study of classical Greek, which he mastered sufficiently over the next few years so that by 1506 he could embark on the project with his friend Erasmus of translating some of the dialogues of the ancient Greek satirist Lucian into Latin. Crowning his achievements, his publication of *Utopia* in 1516 established More's European reputation as a classical scholar and writer. Not surprisingly, he hired a tutor to give a thorough classical education to his children, including his daughters, to all of whom he was especially devoted. More wrote to his children practically on a daily basis, and he expected their replies, like his letters, to be written in the choicest classical Latin.

More valued and could clearly play the role of the scholar. Indeed, in *Utopia* he makes the learned exempt from the universal work requirement imposed on everyone else, revealing just how important the life of the mind was for him as a humanist intellectual. Nevertheless, More chose to pursue a career in the law, a career that engaged him deeply in the world of practical affairs and that quickly led him into politics and royal service. Consequently, after just two years in Oxford, he returned to London in 1494 to begin his legal studies at New Inn, one of the Inns of Chancery, where one was taught how to compose legal documents. Then, on February 12, 1496, he was accepted as a student at Lincoln's Inn, one of the Inns of Court, an institution that took the place of universities in England in providing legal training. Finally, some six years later, in 1502, he was admitted to the bar, and within two years was elected to Parliament. More's political rise after that was sure and steady: an under-sheriff of London in 1510; a member of the Council of the Star Chamber under Cardinal Wolsey in 1516; master of requests (one of the heads of a court that heard the complaints of the poor) and a member of the Privy Council in 1517; knighthood in 1521; under-treasurer of the Exchequer in 1521; speaker of the House of Commons in 1523; chancellor of the duchy of Lancaster in 1525; high steward of Oxford in 1524 and of Cambridge in 1525; and lord chancellor from 1529 to 1532. Starting in 1509, More was sent on various important commercial and diplomatic missions to the continent, activity that climaxed in 1520 when he accompanied Henry VIII to meet Francis I of France and later helped to conclude a peace treaty between Henry and the Holy Roman Emperor Charles V. More's political ascent may have had something to do, especially at first, with his legal training, but it also depended on his intellectual vigor, moral rectitude, and skills as a diplomat and a courtier. His wit especially endeared him to the King, as Roper's *Life* amply documents. More's political rise would have been impossible without his ability to read, write, and converse fluently in classical Latin, for he had to make use of that language not only on diplomatic missions, but even in trade negotiations both in England and abroad. Thus, his scholarly education, though clearly attractive to him on its own terms, also helped transform a skilled lawyer and judge into a dependable royal servant, a transformation that brought More considerable wealth and worldly status. It effectively made More into a New Man, a *novus homo*, a term applied, sometimes with praise and sometimes with contempt, to commoners who rose to prominence because of their intellectual ability and training and who were thus put on the same plane, or even above, those whose social rank depended on their inherited wealth and titles. After almost a century of civil war driven by the ambitions of powerful noblemen that culminated in the War of the Roses and the bloody reign of Richard III, Tudor monarchs, such as Henry VIII and his father, Henry VII, who came to power by defeating Richard in 1485, were determined to consolidate their power by diminishing that of the nobility. To that end, they gave well-educated, talented commoners often newly created legal and political positions of importance; such New Men were beholden to royal authority in a way that dukes and earls seldom were. The Middle Ages saw relatively few commoners rise in this fashion. Those who did so were invariably churchmen since education was exclusively in the hands of the Church and the Church itself offered the surest possibility of meritocratic advancement for those it educated. Secular advancement became increasingly possible for laymen in the Renaissance, and one of those laymen was Thomas More, who would be the first non-churchman in almost a hundred years to be named lord chancellor of England.

Although More's training as a lawyer was a first step toward politics, his acceptance of royal service was by no means inevitable. Indeed, More was at something of a crossroads in the middle of the second decade of the sixteenth century. He had been earning a good living as a lawyer, had served in Parliament, and was working as a judge as one of the under-sheriffs of London. Then, in June 1515 his situation changed dramatically: He was asked by the King's council to join a mission being sent to Flanders to negotiate commercial and political treaties there. This would be his first entry into royal service, albeit at some remove from the King himself. That he was hesitant to embrace such a career path is evident from the literary work that he composed during the long months he spent in Flanders and then completed upon his return to London in 1516. That work was, of course, *Utopia*. Although the second book of *Utopia* and the introductory pages of the first were written during More's stay in Bruges and Antwerp in the fall of 1515, he added the bulk of the first book during the following spring and summer. In this two-book form, the work finally appeared in November 1516 at Louvain. The history of its creation raises a question: Why did More not publish what he had completed while abroad, but instead wait to add the material that became the first book? One answer—an answer relevant to More's life situation—is that book 1 is intensely concerned with one simple question: Should a learned humanist, such as the fictional Raphael Hythloday, who tells the story of Utopia in book 2, remain a kind of unattached intellectual, or should he enter the service of a monarch in order to better the state he lives in? Significantly, More introduces himself as a fully developed character into the debate of book 1, arguing in favor of such service, while Hythloday voices a series of powerful arguments against it. However one judges the final outcome of their debate—and scholars are divided as to whether More or Hythloday "wins"—the issues they consider must reflect what the real More was actually pondering in the first half of 1516. Thomas Cardinal Wolsey had just consolidated his own political position as lord chancellor, and it is possible that More felt the Cardinal would be receptive to some of the reforming ideas that he has Hythloday offer. Thus, since More himself had just taken the first steps toward full participation in governmental service, it is easy to imagine that the arguments of his character "More" in the work reflect his own more positive responses to governmental service: One has a public duty to engage in it; there is hope for some good to be done; people in power may well listen to sound arguments. On the other hand, More doubtless felt there was a serious downside involved in such a move, a downside he gives voice to in Hythloday's objections: One will accomplish little because of the irrationality and limited vision of people in power; one will be forced to compromise basic principles; one may even be forced to place one's immortal soul in jeopardy as one carries out governmental policies. We can see, with the benefit of hindsight, that More must have accepted "More's" arguments since he went on to embrace a career of royal service. Nevertheless, Hythloday's arguments are substantial, and they suggest that More must have been actively thinking about the attractions of a life free from service to the crown. He would have remained a lawyer, working as an under-sheriff or in other comparable positions, and he would have thus kept a certain independence, preserved a space within which he could have maintained his personal integrity while still serving the commonwealth, not as a member of the King's council, to be sure, but as a thinker and writer who would produce works such as _Utopia_ in order to persuade people to make fundamental reforms. Ironically, although he chose to serve Henry first by becoming part of the Court of the Star Chamber in 1516 and then by joining Henry's Privy Council in 1517, it was precisely that personal integrity that would eventually lead More to the scaffold fewer than twenty years later. With the benefit of yet more hindsight we can see that if More had remained a lawyer in 1516, he might have avoided not just royal service, but martyrdom as well.

Further complicating More's life choices was his Christian piety. Between 1500 and 1504, More resided as a guest in a Carthusian monastery located just outside the walls of London. The Carthusians, an order founded at the end of the eleventh century, were known for their learning, but even more for their austerity and their discipline. Their daily regimen of seclusion and solitude, work and prayer appealed to More, but he was probably drawn to them even more because of their fervent piety. This piety was also embodied in one of his favorite books, Thomas à Kempis's *Imitation of Christ*, which stressed the vanity of worldly existence, saw death as the gateway to a better life, and urged close imitation of Christ in one's daily behavior. According to Erasmus, the young More even contemplated becoming a priest. Although he married in 1504 and was elected to Parliament that same year, his deep religiosity remained with him for the rest of his life. He always wore a hair shirt next to his skin, allowing only his favorite daughter, Margaret, to wash it for him. He had a private chapel built when he was having a house constructed on his estate in Chelsea, where he moved with his family in 1525 or 1526. Moreover, his first public lectures, in 1501, were on Saint Augustine's *City of God*, a work that opposes the heavenly city to the earthly one. More also helped Henry VIII give final shape to his *Assertion of the Seven Sacraments Against Martin Luther* (1521), and More himself wrote polemical, often vitriolic works against Luther and other Protestants, such as William Tyndale, in the 1520s. His last work, *A Dialogue of Comfort Against Tribulation*, was written while he was imprisoned in the Tower and expresses his piety most directly as he meditates on painful death and explores various kinds of religious consolation. Most famously, of course, More died for his faith in 1535 rather than acknowledge the King as the head of the Church.

If More's learning and worldly ambition mark him as a man of the Renaissance, his piety and engagement in religious controversy mark him as a man of the Reformation. More was not just pious, but also critical of the worldliness and idleness of many of the clergy. This condemnation appeared, for instance, in his letters and satirical verse condemning the laziness of monks, and it also surfaces in the first book of *Utopia*, which attacks the idleness of the clergy and satirizes a foolish friar in the entourage of Cardinal Morton. The idleness of the clergy was not the only source of discontent with the Church in the late fifteenth and early sixteenth centuries, however. The authority of the papacy had been shaken in the fourteenth century when it was removed from Rome to Avignon in southern France and even more when two popes reigned simultaneously in Rome and Avignon between 1378 and 1417. The Great Schism, as it was called, ended in 1417 when the Council of Constance placed the authority of Church councils above that of the pope. By the end of the fifteenth century, popes in Italy were behaving more like secular princes than like spiritual leaders, and their worldliness and venality, like those of the clergy more generally, were widely condemned. The nadir was the pontificate of Alexander VI (1492–1503), who was rumored to have slept with his own daughter and who sought to rule Italy thanks to the military conquests of his son Cesare Borgia, a figure celebrated for his political ruthlessness in Machiavelli's *The Prince*.

But most people were upset with the Church less because of what was going on in Rome than because of what was happening at home, particularly the selling of indulgences. Theoretically, an indulgence was a partial remission of the temporal punishment for sin and was granted by the Church only after the sin was forgiven through the sacrament of penance. By More's time, however, the Church had long been selling indulgences without requiring penance, and in 1476 the pope proclaimed that indulgences could even cancel the sufferings sinners had to undergo in purgatory. Moreover, selling indulgences took money from the poor at the local level in order to support the temporal ambitions of the papacy; it lined the pockets of various clergymen and lay middlemen along the way. In 1517 Pope Leo X proclaimed yet another indulgence, hoping to use the proceeds to rebuild Saint Peter's. In response, on October 31 of that year, an Augustinian monk in Germany named Martin Luther nailed his Ninety-five Theses— that is, propositions for debate—on the door of the Schlosskirche (Castle Church) in Wittenberg. Those theses primarily attacked papal authority to grant indulgences, but as Luther was required to defend himself, his position became more radical until, in 1520, he was writing treatises that reduced the number of sacraments from seven to two, denied the mass, rejected papal authority, proclaimed the preeminence of scripture and individual conscience, and argued that salvation could not be achieved through good works of any sort—including the purchasing of indulgences—but *sola fide*, through faith alone. His radical stance forced many reformers, who otherwise shared much of his discontent with the Church, to oppose him. Among them was Desiderius Erasmus, who reluctantly agreed to write against Luther in 1525 and produced a brief treatise on the issue of the freedom of the will. Among those who took up arms against the Reformers was also Thomas More.

More did not just write against Luther and his followers, however. When he became lord chancellor, he actively sought to root out what he considered heresy. He had heretical books banned, ordered their confiscation and burning, and conducted investigations into suspected persons, setting up something like a spy network in order to find them. Those arrested were questioned and sometimes tortured, and if they refused to recant, or relapsed later after they had recanted, they were condemned to be burnt at the stake. During More's chancellorship, six men were so executed, and More himself was personally involved in three of the cases. He has been faulted for the severity of this response to religious dissent, both in absolute moral terms and because his actions seem to contradict the relative tolerance extended to such dissent in his own Utopia. This second criticism merits a more detailed consideration.

One of the most fundamental principles of Utopian society in More's work is "that no man shall be blamed for reasoning in the maintenance of his own religion" (p. 129). Utopus, the founder of Utopia, uncertain about what sort of belief and worship people should have, and fearing that violence and force might lead to the triumph of false rather than true religion, left the choice of belief up to the individual. So far then, More seems quite close to advocating a principle of religious tolerance that would have to include the Protestants he would later persecute. However, Utopus's rejection of the use of force in religious matters sprang from his belief that "the truth of [its] own power would at the last issue out and come to light" (p. 130). In other words, since the Utopians' religion, while differing from Christianity, shares much with it, such as a belief in divine providence and in the immortality of the soul, when Utopus says that truth will come out in debate, what More may be implying is that the good, rational people of Utopia will debate their way to the conclusion that the only true religion is Christianity. In fact, Hythloday explains that once he had unfolded the Christian religion to the Utopians, "you will not believe with how glad minds they agreed unto the same" (p. 128). Moreover, although Utopus's fundamental principle seems to guarantee religious tolerance in Utopia, the kind of debate he envisages is limited: It must be a fairly restrained discussion that goes on in private, for anyone who expresses his or her views too vehemently in public is condemned by Utopian law "as a seditious person and a raiser-up of dissension among the people" (p. 129) and can be punished with exile or enslavement. In short, in his vision of Utopian society More is not really espousing complete religious toleration, both because he thought Christianity would triumph handily over all other religions and because he really tolerated toleration only if it did not threaten to create public disorder. Thus, More might well have pursued heretics in the late 1520s because of the threat he believed they posed to public order.

Nonetheless, what he did went well beyond what happens in Utopia, where proselytizers are merely exiled or enslaved. More's zeal against Luther and the Protestants arose from a deep fear that the sacred institution of the Church, with all its rituals and traditions and the sense of community it provided, things from which More derived important aspects of his own identity, was being placed in jeopardy by the reformers. Nor did More make any apologies for his harsh treatment of heretics, arguing, for instance, in his *Dialogue Concerning Heresies* (1529) that they must be stopped lest they infect others with their disease. He saw their burning as normal, something that had been meted out to such sinners for centuries, as indeed it had been, and he even expressed a grim satisfaction in seeing it carried out. We might prefer to think of More as the kindly husband, father, and master of Bolt's play, the passionate defender of individual conscience against tyranny, but he was also the implacable foe of the Lutheran reformers and was neither kind nor a respecter of *their* conscience as he carried out what he saw as his duty to act against them.

Lord Chancellor Thomas Wolsey fell from grace in early October 1529, having failed in his diplomatic efforts to get the Pope to grant Henry a divorce from Catherine, since her nephew, the Holy Roman Emperor Charles V, controlled the papacy. Henry's elevation of More to the position of lord chancellor on October 25 of that year is something of a mystery, for More had made it perfectly clear well before then that he could not support the King's "great matter"—that is, his desire for a divorce from Catherine so that he could marry Anne Boleyn. Perhaps Henry felt More could be brought round over time, despite the King's assurances that More would not have to take a public stand on the matter. Perhaps Henry valued More's loyalty and good judgment more than he worried about More's opposition to the divorce. But whatever Henry's motives, why did More accept the appointment, knowing he might have to deny his royal master? He may have felt he had no choice but to accept, since Henry's will allowed for no denials. Perhaps he actually embraced it, seeing his elevation to the chancellorship as a fitting climax to a career of service and the logical last step in an ascent that began when he was a mere page in the court of Cardinal Morton. Because the King was preoccupied with his divorce, More did, in fact, have a relatively free hand to run his office as he saw fit, something that included prosecuting Protestants for heresy. Nevertheless, the King's "great matter" would not be denied. In March 1531 More presented to Parliament the opinion of the universities—a largely favorable opinion—about the divorce, while refusing to take a position himself on the matter, a tactic that would remain his crucial defense until the very end. However, when Henry demanded in May 1532 that all clerical legislation needed royal assent and the bishops gave in on May 15, More resigned his office the next day.

By now More was simply too famous in Europe for Henry to permit him to take refuge in silence. Sometime in January 1533, Henry married Anne in secret, and in May, after Thomas Cranmer, archbishop of Canterbury, had annulled Henry's marriage to Catherine, the union with Anne was made public, and she was crowned queen a month later. More was conspicuously absent from the ceremony. Then, in March 1534, Parliament passed the Act of Succession declaring Henry's marriage to Catherine null and void while fixing the succession on Anne's offspring, and More, like the rest of Henry's subjects, was required to swear an oath to uphold the act. More refused to do so, but said he would not deny the succession, thus making a subtle distinction between Parliament's right to name an heir to the throne and its right to invalidate Henry's marriage, something, in More's view, only the Church could do. In November, Parliament then raised the stakes by passing the Act of Supremacy declaring Henry the head of the Church and making it treasonous for anyone to attempt to deprive the King of his title. An Act of Attainder was passed against More, declaring that he was attempting to sow sedition by refusing the oath of succession, and as a result, he was condemned to imprisonment for life and had his property confiscated. Were he, in addition, to deny Royal Supremacy outright, he could be condemned to death. More was repeatedly asked to swear an oath affirming the King as the head of the Church, and he steadfastly refused to do so, although he repeatedly insisted that his refusal, his silence, should not be construed as denying the King's title. On April 30, 1535, More was called before the Privy Council and asked to swear the oath of supremacy. He once more refused, but said he did not dispute the King's title. In retaliation, the authorities made the conditions of More's imprisonment much harsher, taking away all his books and writing materials. As they were doing so, the Solicitor General, Richard Rich, engaged More in conversation, attempting to trick him into denying the King's supremacy. Although More outmaneuvered his opponent, a special commission was appointed to try him, and he was hauled before them on July 1. Lacking any real evidence that More was guilty of denying the King's supremacy, Rich perjured himself and swore that More had done so. Although More argued brilliantly that if he had refused to say anything on the subject before, it was unlikely he would have done so before such a man as Rich, the court condemned him to death. Finally, More felt free to speak his conscience and declared that Parliament had no authority to make a law against the Church. Five days later he was executed, the King showing his mercy by allowing More to suffer decapitation rather than the more gruesome drawing and quartering usually visited on those condemned of high treason.

In the drama of his last years, most people see More as a hero of conscience resisting the desires of an autocratic king. That is certainly the way Bolt presents him in his play. But Henry's concern to divorce his wife in order to marry someone with whom he might sire a son was not a mere tyrannical whim. Like virtually all of his contemporaries, Henry was convinced that only a male heir could safely inherit the throne, and with the War of the Roses just fifty years behind him, he must have feared that a female heir could create political chaos and lead to a reprise of the civil war his father had ended. History, of course, in the person of Elizabeth, was to prove him wrong. Moreover, popes had, in fact, granted annulments and divorces to monarchs before, so Henry's failure to succeed with his "great matter" seemed—and was—essentially a matter of international politics, not one of violating a basic religious doctrine. Nevertheless, even if one is tempted to see things from Henry's perspective, it is still hard to avoid condemning him for not at least allowing More to end his days in the silence he clung to as his best defense.

Although the circumstances of More's life and death have led many to see him as a martyr, he himself resisted the impulse to become one. He refused to deny the oath of supremacy not because he accepted it, but because he feared his denying it would amount to an expression of a desire for martyrdom, a wish for a kind of suicide, almost an expression of pride. To avoid courting martyrdom, More never denounced Henry as a tyrant or attacked him for breaking with the Church of Rome. Only when More had been condemned to death could he embrace this one last role, the martyr's role, which allowed him to transcend all the other, often contradictory roles he played throughout his life. He died, as he put it, "the King's good servant, but God's first." In the unfinished biography of Richard III, which More wrote as a piece of Tudor propaganda, he identified the executioner's scaffold with the players' stage. Thus, he must have seen the scaffold on which he would be beheaded as the final stage on which to perform his final part—and perform it he did, to the hilt. Wearing a coarse gown and carrying a red cross, he verbally identified himself with Christ as he was led to the place of execution, refusing a cup of wine offered to him by explaining that Christ had been given vinegar to drink on the cross. He consistently presented himself not merely as unafraid to die, but as looking forward to the death that was about to come. His confidence is conveyed by the joking, ironic manner he adopted at the end. In his biography, Roper reports that More, seeing the rickety steps of the scaffold, asked for help: "I pray you, Master Lieutenant, see me safe up, and for my coming down, let me shift for myself" (p. 214). Then, not only did he forgive the executioner, as was the custom, but he kissed him and, according to Roper, made one final joke: "My neck is very short. Take heed therefore thou strike not awry, for saving of thine honesty" (p. 214). Although it took the Catholic Church until 1935 to declare More a martyr and a saint, in his last, magnificent performance More had already acted that part to perfection.

Utopia was written as a dialogue from the start: Even book 2 and the opening section of book 1 represent a supposed conversation in Antwerp involving More himself, Peter Giles (or Gillis), a prominent humanist and the chief clerk of the court of justice in Antwerp, and the fictional Raphael Hythloday. More's choosing to present his ideas in dialogue form arose from his humanist—and legal—education. The center of that education was rhetoric, which taught students not just how to present and defend cases, but how to see them from multiple points of view, how to argue *in utramque partem*, "from either side," of a question. Rhetoric thus taught a certain kind of skepticism that assumed one could never arrive at certainty and forced one to see issues from the perspective of many different "truths." Moreover, More translated some of Lucian's dialogues with his friend Erasmus and honed his Latin style by reading Cicero's dialogues on philosophy and rhetoric. *Utopia* also shows that he had read and admired the greatest writer of dialogues in antiquity, Plato. In fact, Plato's *Republic* served as a model for More's work. Not only does he refer to it explicitly in several places during the debate in book 1, but his very project of describing an ideal state would have been virtually unthinkable without the precedent established by Plato's work. There are differences between the two, to be sure: More wrestles with such practical questions as how to eliminate theft and how to distribute the wealth of the state in an equitable fashion, while Plato explores the abstract notion of justice. Nevertheless, justice is also a fundamental concern in More's work, and the preliminary debate in book 1 of *Utopia* mimics the *Republic*, which likewise begins with a lengthy debate between Socrates and his opponents.

More chose the dialogue form for political reasons as well. Since many of the ideas he was offering in his work contradicted conventional wisdom and customary arrangements, he was at risk of reprisals by authorities, both secular and religious, who might feel that what he said was subversive. By writing a dialogue, More could hide behind his characters, claiming that this or that idea was not his, but merely belonged to one of them. More put yet further distance between himself and his ideas by naming the spokesman for the most radical views "Hythloday," a word that can be translated as "speaker of nonsense," and by calling his ideal state Utopia, "nowhere" (although the word may also be a pun on "Eutopia"—that is, "beautiful place"). Moreover, More includes customs in Utopia that would have raised eyebrows in Renaissance England, such as having couples inspect one another naked before marriage, thus suggesting that we should take this description of a supposedly ideal place with a grain of salt. Finally, by adding the dialogue of book 1 to his work, More made it into a more genuine debate between the character "More" and Hythloday, thus inviting readers to see the ideal described in book 2 as possibly flawed by its association with Hythloday's possibly flawed character. Nevertheless, the beauty of dialogue as a literary form is that it protects its author while permitting the expression of sometimes quite radical ideas—and More knew it. Thus, in book 1, he has Hythloday recount how he once argued in Cardinal Morton's house that thieves should not be put to death, but instead condemned to hard labor and made to repay their victims. Several of those present objected to his views, but the Cardinal finally cut them off and tentatively embraced Hythloday's ideas. Here More shows us how dialogue works: It offers multiple points of view, some admittedly more persuasive and more fully developed than others, although none unambiguously right, and allows the auditor, like Cardinal Morton, to choose among them. In this scene More is offering a model of how the radical ideas contained in *Utopia* should be received: They should be listened to attentively and dispassionately by those in authority, and then, should they prove persuasive, they should be used as a basis for experiments in social reform. Thus, by writing *Utopia* as dialogue, More can have his cake and eat it, too: He can protect himself from charges of directly advocating subversive ideas, while still managing to present those ideas to the public and even showing them, through the model situation in Cardinal Morton's home, how to respond to what they are reading.

Can either one of the opposed speakers in *Utopia*, the fictional Hythloday or the historically real "More," be said to be the more persuasive—that is, to be the winner in their debates? This question leads to others: Does Hythloday represent More's views, with "More" serving merely to help create a protective smokescreen of dialogue for the author; or does "More" represent More's views, while Hythloday and his ideas are the objects of satire; or, finally, do both characters somehow represent their author, and if so, what does that mean?

Let us consider the arguments made by the two speakers in book 1 about serving a monarch. "More" takes the position that philosophers like Hythloday have a duty to serve and to do as much good as possible, while Hythloday argues that such efforts would be futile in a world where most people are simply not open to new ideas. The debate between the two speakers reaches its climax when Hythloday proposes a hypothetical situation, asking "More" to imagine what would happen in a king's council if Hythloday were to oppose the king's other advisers who were urging the monarch to pile up wealth at the people's expense in order to be able live a life of luxury and to engage in the true sport of kings at the time—namely, warfare. Hythloday concludes that his speech would be directed to "deaf hearers" (p. 50). "More's" response is immediate and intense: He attacks Hythloday for spouting a "school [academic] philosophy," something completely out of place in a king's council. "More" argues that one has to adapt oneself and one's discourse to the social and political context using the kind of philosophy with the king that statesmen employ, the kind of philosophy that "knoweth, as ye would say, her own stage, and thereafter ordering and behaving herself in the play that she hath in hand, playeth her part accordingly with comeliness, uttering nothing out of due order and fashion" (p. 51). Here, "More" approaches the world much as the real More did—that is, as a stage play, or perhaps several different plays, in which one is required to perform different parts at different times. And he drives the point home by then complaining that what Hythloday imagined he would be doing in a king's council would be equivalent to coming onstage in the middle of a comedy by Plautus and reciting a serious speech out of a tragedy by Seneca. "More" stresses the need for tact and indirection; he insists that what one cannot make good should at least be made as little bad as possible.

Hythloday responds to "More" by setting up a rigorous opposition between an absolute "truth," on the one hand, and the madness of most human beings, on the other, insisting he will never betray the former by joining everyone else in the latter. Hythloday then raises the stakes: The statesman's philosophy advocated by "More," says Hythloday, would force him to "wink at the most part of all those things which Christ taught us" (p. 52) since they differ so much from men's normal values and behavior. In Hythloday's view, one can be a statesman-philosopher or one can be a Christian; no middle way is admitted. In fact, Hythloday fears he would actually wind up having to approve the worst advice offered by others. Borrowing from Plato, Hythloday argues that the philosopher is like the person who sees others getting wet outside in the street, cannot persuade them to come inside where he is, and knows that if he goes out, too, he "should nothing prevail nor win ought by it, but with them be wet also in the rain" (p. 53). In other words, he will run the risk of actively abetting evil and thereby putting his immortal soul at risk. At this point the debate on counsel more or less ends, as Hythloday responds to "More's" disbelief (that men could ever be made good) by offering to describe Utopia, that "best state of a commonwealth," in which all people, he claims, have indeed been made into paragons of virtue.

How is one to decide between these two speakers and their views? Hythloday certainly seems right about the values of contemporary rulers, including Henry VIII, who squandered the enormous fortune his father left him on extravagant living at court and futile wars abroad. Hythloday also seems right about the counselor's risk of being made to acquiesce in evil, something More himself would have later had to do, as he saw it, had he acknowledged Henry as the head of the Church. By staying silent on the oath of supremacy, More did not rush out into the rain with the others and get himself wet for his pains. Finally, his life and death suggest that the "play" of the court was not what "More's" words implied: It was more like a tragedy by Seneca than a farce by Plautus. If Hythloday's reasoning thus leads many to see him as the real More's mouthpiece, others argue that "More" has that honor. After all, he bears his creator's name and champions the values of tact and diplomacy, for which More was famous. Moreover, Hythloday's all-or-nothing idealism, based on his belief in human perfectibility, may seem extreme to some readers, who prefer "More's" half a loaf—making the state a little better—rather than have no loaf at all with Hythloday. Finally, More the author goes out of his way to undercut Hythloday's argument that people would not be receptive to new ideas. When Hythloday recounts what happened at Cardinal Morton's court, he reveals that the Cardinal did, in fact, think Hythloday's views on punishing theft worth serious consideration.

Clearly, there is no easy way to judge between the two men. Both Hythloday and "More" are "right," and hence, both are "wrong." Both offer powerful, even compelling arguments to support their positions. And since both speak for aspects of their creator's personality and for some of his firmest beliefs, it seems almost impossible to decide the question. Perhaps the most we can say is that More's work represents an attempt to give voice to various important issues, to explore their implications, and then to leave it up to the reader to reach whatever conclusion seems possible. Perhaps, in other words, More's work is even more of a dialogue than it has seemed so far: It is an unresolved and irresolvable debate presenting irreconcilable contrary viewpoints.

How one responds to the debate in book 1 affects how one interprets More's utopian fantasy in book 2. If one feels Hythloday wins the debate, or even if one concludes that it remains unresolved and open-ended, then one may well conclude that More is setting the reader up to take most of what he proposes in book 2 seriously. Hythloday thus becomes More's spokesman, or at least the spokesman for a certain part of him. By contrast, if one sees Hythloday as an inflexible ideologue who undercuts his own argument at Cardinal Morton's house, and if one prefers "More" as a more humanly attractive character who embraces the more reasonable principles, then one might conclude that "More," not Hythloday, represents his creator's views. Utopia might then appear more like a satirical work designed to ridicule not just such things as the Utopians' lack of fashion sense, their facile belief in psychological conditioning, and their strange marriage customs, but the utopian project in general. This line of reasoning, taken to its logical conclusion, means that More was being completely ironic when he invented his Utopia, his "no place," and called it the "best state of a commonwealth." In this view, More did not want his readers to see it as "Eutopia," the "beautiful place," but rather as "Dystopia," the "bad place," not the best of all possible worlds, but the worst. Such a "logical conclusion," however, is less than fully persuasive, for it ignores almost all of the positive features of Utopia that a man like More would have found attractive, such as its meritocratic political order, its positive evaluation of scholarship, its hatred and subversion of war, its genuine concern for the common good, its serious attempt to eliminate poverty, and the general religiosity of its people. Indeed, it is hard to believe that More would have written dozens and dozens of pages to elaborate an ideal state only to hold it up to ridicule.

Nevertheless, seeing Utopia as Dystopia did gain a certain currency in mid- and late-twentieth-century interpretations of More's work. Up until that time, virtually all readers had taken Utopia to be an expression of More's idealism, a serious, if not perfect blueprint for a better society, something that made him a hero to socialists and communists and reformers of every stripe. Starting in the 1960s, however, some scholars began stressing the ironies of More's work, the many absurd or unattractive features of his Utopia, and the inflexibility of its idealistic defender Hythloday. Such a rejection of many aspects of Utopia's society, including its communism, and the attacks on Hythloday as a misguided idealist—almost all of them from American scholars—may well have arisen from the Cold War that then dominated international politics. Critics who fault Utopia because there are strict governmental controls on travel and because everyone is dressed in the same gray clothing are reacting to the totalitarianism of states such as Stalin's Soviet Union, not to mention Mao's China, where millions and millions of people literally did all wear the same gray uniforms. Such critics essentially want to save More for modern liberalism by pronouncing *Utopia* a satire and identifying More with "More," the political pragmatist, kindly friend, and loving father and husband in the book. But More, the earnest Christian humanist reformer, really did believe in many of the things he described. The problem is that More does not just endorse things we might desire, such as choosing leaders according to their merits, but also those we might find repellent, such as the communal raising of children. We must, however reluctantly, accept the fact that More's idealism may not be identical with ours, just as we have to accept the fact that the admirable defender of the rights of individual conscience was also willing to have Protestant proselytizers burned at the stake.

The society of Utopia is based on a fairly radical and innovative assumption in its time, namely that social engineering is both possible and desirable. Utopia assumes that human beings are malleable and can be shaped by their education and social environment to have practically any set of values and beliefs and to behave in just about any way one desires. Hythloday, for example, explains that Utopian educators take the greatest pains from the very start "to put into the heads of their children, whiles they be yet tender and pliant, good opinions and profitable" opinions that, once implanted, "remain with them all their life after" (p. 135). Or think of the Utopian response to gold. By making such things as chamber pots out of the precious metal, Utopians are taught from birth to despise it, and their scorn leads to one of the more humorous anecdotes in the book involving foreign ambassadors who arrive on their shores decked out in gold and precious jewels in order to impress their hosts. More shared this belief in the malleability of human beings both with ancient writers, such as Plutarch, and with contemporary humanists, such as Erasmus. The latter summed up the matter in one of his treatises on education: *homines non nascuntur, sed finguntur*—that is, "men are not born, but made." Clearly, More shared Erasmus's sentiment.

Perhaps more important, Utopia denies the notion that the social order is God-given, eternal, and unchangeable, as most medieval and Renaissance people in Europe were taught to believe. On the contrary, in Utopia, the social order is seen as an arrangement that could be transformed in order to improve, if not perfect, both it and the humans who belonged to it. For example, Hythloday recounts how the "ideal" policy of toleration practiced by the Utopians came about. Before Utopus conquered the country, its inhabitants were divided into a host of different religious sects, all of which were fighting with one another. Consequently, once he had conquered them, he "made a decree that it should be lawful for every man to favor and follow what religion he would" (p. 129), and that he could seek to convert others, but only if he did so in a restrained and modest manner that did not create public strife. Hythloday does not recount how Utopus's decree was received at the time, although the inhabitants must have found it attractive and reasonable, since they put it in place. Thus, by the time of Hythloday's visit, it has become a fundamental institution, so that when one of his companions attempts to convert the people to Christianity by violent denunciations of their religion, he is arrested, charged with trying to cause a riot, and sent into exile. The social engineering that makes Utopia possible was paralleled by a feat of real engineering. When Utopus first conquered the land, it was not initially surrounded by the sea, so he ordered that a fifteen-mile-wide ditch be excavated to separate it from the rest of the continent. Since he had all of the native inhabitants as well as his own soldiers do the digging, the labor was completed so quickly that it filled the skeptical neighbors who were watching with "marvel" and "fear" (p. 63). In other words, Utopia as a separate—indeed, a separated—country comes into being through a literal act of engineering that demonstrates dramatically the triumph of culture over nature. Similarly, the Utopians themselves have been transformed from a "rude and wild people" into models of "good fashions, humanity, and civil gentleness" (p. 62). Even the physical environment reflects Utopian ideals. There are fifty-four cities, all roughly equidistant from one another, all square in shape like their capital Amaurote, which is situated at the very center of the island, and all surrounded by cultivated fields and pastureland, with very little space left over for wastelands, deserts, and the wilds of nature. Moreover, those cities are made up of regular blocks of houses, all enclosing the gardens, by which the people "set great store" (p. 67). Thus, seen from the air, Utopia is a farmer's paradise; it celebrates the ability of human culture and cultivation to transform whatever nature has to offer. Since almost all the citizens are required to work at least six hours every day in the fields, in a sense everyone in Utopia is a farmer. They are, to use More's Latin, *agricolae* or *coloni*, both words deriving from the verb *colere*, which means "to farm," "to till or cultivate fields," and "to settle in an area or colonize it." Furthermore, the past participle of *colere*, *cultus*, means "tilled or cultivated" and, by extension, "neat, well-dressed, refined, and civilized," while the noun *cultus* means "tilling (of fields)," "tending (of flocks)," "refinement," "care (of the body)," "education," "style," and "worship" or "reverence." In short, Utopia is a celebration of "cultivation" in every conceivable sense of the term.

People are cultivated in Utopia for the specific end of making them morally good. Indeed, although More's work starts out as a discussion of the problems of theft and poverty, which Utopia "solves" by means of communism, the holding of all goods in common, the ultimate reason for the elimination of private property is not the secular one of achieving an equitable distribution of wealth and eliminating crime. Rather, More's real goal is the more traditional, Christian one, namely, the elimination of pride. Pride requires an unequal distribution of wealth so that the rich can hold themselves up above the poor, for it "measureth not wealth and prosperity by her own commodities, but by the misery and incommodities of other" (p. 145). Pride thus generates poverty and the crimes, such as theft, fraud, and murder, that accompany it as well as leading to the idleness and self-indulgence of both the rich and their retainers. It produces ambition and factionalism in the state, creating both civil unrest and wars among nations. If one remembers how Utopians love their gardens and how they live on an island that looks like a garden from one side to the other, then their social engineering acquires a decidedly Christian character in this context, for it leads to something like a self-generated form of salvation in which they achieve redemption—a return to the paradisal garden humanity once lost, and now has recovered—not through divine mercy, but through their education and discipline and social institutions. More never claims that his Utopians can save themselves by their own efforts, but he certainly seems to flirt with the idea, and that flirtation may help to explain why the Catholic Church took until 1935 to declare the man who died a martyr for his faith to be a saint.

So far, More seems to have a fairly optimistic view of human nature, believing that humans are educable and that a social system can be designed in which any impulse they have toward pride can be eliminated. That optimism also seems to inform the Utopians' philosophy of pleasure. Although an embracing of pleasure might seem to open the floodgates to all sorts of vices, Utopians have been taught to avoid this problem by arranging pleasures in a hierarchy. First, although bodily pleasures, from scratching an itch to sex, are said to be good, they are placed on the lowest level because they are related to pain or deprivation. By contrast, good health is higher, and such things as eating and drinking are considered less as ends than as means to it. Finally, mental pleasures, and particularly those associated with the practice of virtue, occupy the highest position. Since Utopians have been taught to prefer higher pleasures to lower ones, they would thus never place scratching an itch above reading a good book. Moreover, their philosophy includes several other principles: No pleasure is valuable if it involves the loss of something more pleasurable; and no pleasure is good if it is followed by pain. And they have learned that because of our natural fellowship with other human beings, we get the greatest pleasure of all from aiding them, nor can anything be considered pleasurable if it is sought through doing them wrong. Thus, by the time he is through, More's Utopian philosophy of pleasure looks less like an invitation to sybaritic hedonism than like a confirmation of the central teachings of the Judeo-Christian tradition.

However, the Utopian philosophy of pleasure is actually a bit more complicated than that. Utopians believe that human beings are drawn to pleasures that are good and decent *by nature;* we are called by it not merely to pursue the pleasures of the body and the mind, but also to help one another to a better life. In other words, Utopian philosophy assumes that people *naturally* want pleasures that are good in themselves and are consistent with what is morally good. But what about those individuals who prefer scratching and sex to reading good books, something the Utopians—and More—admit does happen? Indeed, the Utopians concede that such spurious pleasures may seem good to some people, may come to possess their minds so that there will be "no place left for true and natural delectations" (p. 95). Hythloday identifies such "foolish pleasures" (p. 97) in familiar terms; they include: pride in having a better suit of clothes than someone else, having others bow before you, the possession of gold and jewels, gambling, and the vicious destruction of animals in hunting. But if all these things are not "true" pleasures, then how can human beings convince themselves that they are? How can they make such obvious mistakes? More's answer reveals less optimism about human beings than has appeared so far. After having opposed true delights to these false pleasures, Hythloday declares:

> There be many things which of their own nature contain no pleasantness—yea, the most part of them much grief and sorrow—and yet, *through the perverse and malicious flickering enticements of lewd and unhonest desires*, be taken not only for special and sovereign pleasures, but also be counted among the chief causes of life (pp. 95–96, emphasis added).

The italicized phrase above lets the cat out of the bag: If humans are attracted to good pleasures by nature, then they also appear to be equally attracted to bad ones, illusory ones, by their "unhonest desires"—in other words, by something else that is also within them and that must thus be as "natural" to them as is their desire for the good. In short, if More believes that human beings still have within them the ability to pursue the good, he also believes they feel the "perverse . . . enticements of lewd and unhonest desires," which can only mean that they have not escaped the taint of original sin.

In actuality, Utopian society seems to be based as much on a distrust of our potential evil as on a belief in our potential goodness. To be sure, the availability of education to everyone, the meritocratic political system, and such specific practices as the erection of statues for those individuals who "have been great and bountiful benefactors to the commonwealth" (p. 112)—all of these things point to a definite confidence in humanity. However, many of the features of Utopia—in fact, most of the things modern readers have found most objectionable about it—can be explained as aiming to make Utopians good in spite of themselves, in spite of their "natural" inclinations to behave otherwise. The restrictions on religious proselytizing, for example, would not continue to exist if the Utopians' education had been able to eliminate their capacity for the intolerance, violence, and abuse that led Utopus to institute those restrictions in the first place. Similarly, despite the rational manner in which Utopians go about choosing their marriage partners, including their inspection of one another naked, they cannot be counted on to remain content in monogamous relationships.

Consequently, Utopia passed a law that those who violate the marriage tie are to be "punished with most grievous bondage" (p. 110)—that is, slavery—and if they are forgiven and allowed to have their liberty back, they are actually punished with death should they slip again. Moreover, those who have intercourse before marriage are also severely punished, because all know that "unless they be diligently kept from the liberty of this vice, few will join together in the love of marriage" (p. 108). One of subtlest indications that human nature is not to be trusted, even in Utopia, is that Utopians are not allowed to butcher their own animals. Hythloday gives this a positive spin: "They permit not their free citizens to accustom themselves to the killing of beasts, through the use whereof they think clemency, the gentlest affection of our nature, by little and little to decay and perish" (pp. 78–79). If clemency dies, what remains is the unfettered human aggressiveness that would destroy the harmony of life in Utopia. Hence, slaves do all the butchering. Since Hythloday never suggests that the Utopians look forward to a vegetarian future, they will always have to have slaves. And this means there will always be at least a few Utopians who will fail to reach perfection and will become slaves because of their failings.

The Utopians' distrust of human nature can also be seen in their requirement that everyone must work at agriculture, a craft, or some other pursuit. Obviously, this rule guarantees the prosperity of the island and ensures that everyone contributes to the common good. However, Utopians justify it primarily on the grounds that it prevents idleness. For instance, the chief function of the syphogrants, elected officials who oversee thirty households apiece, is not to make sure everyone works his or her fair share, but "to see and take heed that no man sit idle" (p. 71). In this context, the Utopians' right to a certain amount of leisure time could create a problem, since it could lead to idleness. However, they have been taught how to deal with the danger involved: "All the void [empty] time that is between the hours of work, sleep, and meat [food] that they be suffered to bestow, every man as he liketh best himself, not to the intent that they should misspend this time in riot or slothfulness, but, being then licensed from the labor of their own occupations, to bestow the time well and thriftily upon some other science [learning], as shall please them" (p. 71). What begins by granting the Utopians the freedom to relax however they wish is immediately qualified here by the prohibition that free time is not to be wasted "in riot or slothfulness," but rather should be devoted to an occupation identified as some intellectual pursuit. Since "idle hands are the devil's workshop," according to the proverb, Utopians must become complete workaholics: They must work even when they are at leisure, though they do so not to fatten some corporate bottom line, but to save themselves from evil.

The communal nature of the Utopians' institutions reflects their notion that the state is the common possession of all its citizens, their belief in the ideal of community, and their sense that the citizens of the state should constitute something like a great family. But those institutions also ensure that everyone will always behave properly, because everyone will be constantly under the surveillance of everyone else. As Hythloday puts it, "They be in the present sight and under the eyes of every man, so that of necessity they must either apply their accustomed labors, or else recreate themselves with honest and laudable pastimes" (p. 83). Utopia is a shame culture in which everyone is always on display. Even at times of leisure, Utopians cannot escape the eyes of all of their fellows, for there are "neither wine taverns, nor alehouses, nor any occasion of vice or wickedness, no lurking corners, no places of wicked councils, or unlawful assemblies" (p. 83) for them to retreat into. The practice of constant surveillance explains the special restrictions placed on Utopian travel. Although Hythloday says that citizens can easily obtain a written permit from the authorities to visit people in other towns, those who stray out of their territory without such leave are brought back as runaways, shamed, and punished. If they repeat their offense, they are made into slaves. Utopia does not have Big Brother watching its citizens, but rather, lots of big brothers—and big sisters, too—although they engage in surveillance not for the sake of power, as Big Brother does in Orwell's dystopian fantasy, but in order to make all the citizens good, whether they want to be good or not.

Although some Utopian practices may be repugnant to people today, they are, in fact, consistent with More's own values. From his other writings, it is clear that he hated idleness and valued work, and that he saw the state as having a legitimate function in making people morally good. In fact, Hythloday and "More" seem to agree about many such matters in More's dialogue. Thus, "More" may be critical of Utopia and think many things in it to be "instituted and founded of no good reason" (p. 145), but in book 1, when Hythloday unfolds his criticisms of the enclosure of land by greedy landowners to raise sheep, the idleness of the retainers of great lords, and the injustice of capital punishment for theft, "More" voices no dissent and even compliments Hythloday, telling him, "all things that you said were spoken so wittily [intelligently] and so pleasantly" (p. 42).

So, how are we to "take" Utopia? Perhaps the best answer may be that More is not offering it as a blueprint for a brave new world or a practical model for immediate implementation. Rather, he may be conducting something like a thought experiment—that is, setting up Utopia as the kind of society one would wind up with if one started with the premises that human beings have the potential to be morally good and that the institutions of the state can be re-fashioned in order to achieve that end. Once that moral goodness has been defined both positively as involving a commitment to others and their well-being, and negatively as the removal of pride and the other vices or sins that flow from it, then the Utopians' institutions and practices, such as their elimination of money, their communal life together, and their emphasis on work as a way to avoid idleness, can be seen as possessing a kind of logic, if not an inevitability. It is as though More were saying: If you accept the goals that Utopia is designed to reach, then these means are legitimate and necessary insofar as they are designed to reach those goals. To be sure, "More" does attack Utopia's communism at the end of book 1, saying that without the motive of gain, no one would want to work, but his objection here is a stock response, and it is so brief that one can legitimately wonder how seriously More expects us to take it. What happens at the end of book 2 is even more revealing. There, when "More" declares that many things in Utopia have been "instituted and founded of no good reason" (p. 145) and goes on to name the country's religious practices as an example, this is an objection we can imagine the real More might have made. However, "More's" main objection to Utopia is to its communism and elimination of money, for they overthrow, he declares, "all nobility, magnificence, worship, honor, and majesty, the true ornaments and honors, as the common opinion is, of a commonwealth" (p. 146). It seems very unlikely that the serious and deeply religious More would have thought that magnificent displays of wealth—as opposed to good citizens—were the true ornaments of the commonwealth. And in case we miss the point, he notes that such things are a matter of "common opinion"—that is, the opinion of the common people—and More, as Erasmus said clearly in the prefatory letter to his *Praise of Folly*, was a man who typically dissented from the crowd. Clearly, More is being ironic here; he is making a joke, and the joke is at "More's" expense.

More's thought experiment—if that is what Utopia is—leads him in some directions that make us particularly uncomfortable nowadays. One involves the Utopians' attitude toward mercenaries. Although Utopia differs from most European states in the Renaissance, including England, by not having imperial ambitions, its citizens are trained to defend themselves from the attack of other states. But not only do they try to buy off the enemy; they willingly use mercenaries if and when they can, because they wish to spare their own citizens' lives. This might seem like a reasonable position that does not contradict the kind of humanity that Hythloday displays, for instance, when he argues against capital punishment for theft, or that is built into Utopia's concern to educate and care for all of its inhabitants. Moreover, mercenaries embrace a life of warfare, and those who live by the sword must accept the risk that they may die by it, too. However, the deaths of these mercenaries, the so-called Zapoletans—a satirical dig at the Swiss, who were feared throughout Europe for their savagery in battle—actually make the Utopians rejoice, for they think that "they should do a very good deed for all mankind, if they could rid out of the world all that foul stinking den of that most wicked and cursed people" (p. 122). One might well ask why the Utopians, who refuse to butcher their own meat lest they harden themselves to killing, should rejoice in the death of other human beings. The answer is simple: because mercenaries are not thought of as really being human. Hythloday describes them as "hideous, savage, and fierce," of a "hard nature . . . born only to war"; they are animals that will forget "both kindred and friendship" for the sake of money (pp. 120–121). The Utopians have what might be called a qualitative definition of humanity. Humans there are not defined in some descriptive, nonjudgmental way as, say, featherless bipeds or tool-making animals, but as rational beings whose beliefs and moral behavior must conform to the ideals found in Utopia. If human beings fail to meet such a standard, then they simply stop being human. The Utopians' qualitative conception of humanity helps to explain several features of their culture that might otherwise appear strange. For instance, Utopus forbids anyone to believe that the soul perishes with the body or that the world is not governed by divine providence. Individuals holding such views are not punished, but are made to defend themselves at frequent intervals before the priests until their "madness" finally gives way to "reason" (p. 131), for until such a person has seen reason, "they count [him] not in the number of men" (p. 130). Moreover, the death penalty imposed on slaves who rebel clearly does not bother Hythloday, for by rebelling, they have turned into "desperate and wild beasts, whom neither prison nor chain could restrain and keep under" (pp. 110–111). The "best state of a commonwealth" assumes that most human beings are tameable, capable of being educated into their humanity and kept in that condition by safeguards and manifold controls. Should they violate Utopia's laws or resist its punishments, then they drop out of the category of the human and either join the ranks of the insane until they can be brought back to reason, or reveal themselves as "desperate and wild beasts" who, ipso facto, deserve to be put out of their misery.

Finally, the Utopians' ideal of "cultivated" humans helps explain why these farmers, these *coloni*, to use More's Latin word for them, are, in fact, willing to colonize other countries. Hythloday explains that when the population of Utopia outgrows the ability of the land to sustain it, colonists are sent to the mainland, "where the inhabitants have much waste [uncultivated] and unoccupied ground" (p. 77). If the natives are willing, then they are incorporated into the Utopian colony, and the land, "which before was neither good nor profitable for the one nor for the other" (p. 77), is now cultivated to the point that it can support both groups. But if the natives should resist the Utopians' invasion, then the Utopians wage war against them, to drive them out. For they consider it a just war "when any people holdeth a piece of ground void and vacant to no good nor profitable use, keeping others from the use and possession of it, which notwithstanding by the law of nature ought thereof to be nourished and relieved" (p. 77). The Utopians clearly judge land just as they do people: If cultivated, it is valued; if uncultivated, it is not. Those who get in the way of its cultivation, who keep land waste and wild, must either be removed or eliminated since they are denying the principle of cultivation, the very principle on which the Utopians' culture is based and on which their definition of the human is founded. To be sure, the Utopians colonize only to find a place for their surplus population, not for the glory of empire, and they bring their colonists home when the population of their own island declines. Moreover, their "rule of nature," dictating that unused land should be cultivated, particularly when people are in need, is not necessarily entirely wrong. However, we cannot forget that More was writing during the first phase of Europe's imperial expansion into the "Third World," and particularly into the Americas, where Utopia is, in fact, located. The past five centuries of colonialism, with all its attendant horrors, make the Utopians' breezy determination to oust natives from ground that is "void and vacant" seem deeply culpable.

There is one final, troubling contradiction transcending all the others that characterize More's complicated and contradictory masterpiece: If it begins with an act of imaginative freedom, it ends by insisting on something close to mindless conformity. The imagining of Utopia, whether as sheer fantasy, thought experiment, or blueprint for reality, depends on the ability to think differently, to entertain the possibility of discrete social systems based on different assumptions about human nature. The imagining of Utopia, in other words, requires a fundamental social, intellectual, and ethical freedom, a freedom More certainly displays as he dreams up no fewer than four different societies in his book as alternatives to those of Europe: the states of the Polylerites, the Achorians, the Macarians, and the Utopians. However, the great contradiction of More's *Utopia*—and perhaps of all utopian thinking—is that once he has freed himself to imagine alternatives to the status quo, the seemingly inevitable next step is to turn it into "Eutopia," the "beautiful place," the "best state of a commonwealth," from which any deviation is unthinkable. In other words, More begins with complete freedom and ends with a world marked by complete control and restriction, a world in which real change is impossible. To be sure, More's Utopians welcome technical advances such as the lodestone and Greek books, but those things do not really promise to change the institutions and practices of their state in any fundamental way. Nor does Christianity. Utopia's religion is clearly moving in that direction already, so that the conversion of the island would merely bring to perfection that which is only a step away. Essentially, the freedom to think differently is irrelevant, if not downright dangerous, to Utopia. No wonder, then, that the Utopians do not permit idleness or tolerate wine shops or alehouses, for there the imagination might find release from normal social and ethical constraints and have the freedom both to critique the established order and to conjure up alternatives to it. The keenest irony of this very ironic book is that, once More has arrived at his conclusion, once he arrives in the safe harbor of Utopia, his "no place" really leaves him no place else to go.

This volume contains two Renaissance English classics, Ralph Robinson's translation of More's *Utopia* and William Roper's *Life of Sir Thomas More*. Both works have been edited and annotated to clarify allusions and provide relevant contextual information, and unfamiliar and difficult words and expressions have fully been glossed. Both Robinson and Roper were living in an age when Latin was the standard against which the vernacular was measured, and both consequently strove to produce an English with the heft and density of that ancient language. This means that they often translated or simply imported Latin words into English, and they composed long and elaborate sentences to imitate the syntax of Latin. Since these sentences can sometimes be difficult to follow, I have re-punctuated many of them, often dividing them into two or more short sentences, in order to help readers sort them out. In fact, on occasion in the notes, I have "translated" what they said into modern English. And in Roper's *Life of More* I have inserted names in square brackets into the text in order to clarify pronoun referents. Nevertheless, despite their Latinate quality and occasional opacities, both texts are remarkable for their vigor, and both have the virtue of being close in time and space to More and his work.

Two words that occur frequently in Robinson's translation deserve special comment. The first is "weal," which appears by itself and in the phrase "the weal public." The word means the "riches, well-being, and prosperity" of an individual, but also of a community. Thus, the phrase "weal public" means the "general good" and is a synonym for "commonwealth"—that is, "state." "Weal public," like the word "commonwealth," is essentially the equivalent of the Latin *respublica*, or *res publica*, the "public (or common) wealth," although it is also a rendering of the Latin *bonum publicum*, the "public good." The second word is "bondman," which Robinson uses to translate both *servus* and *famulus*, which would be more accurately translated in modern terms as "slave." His translation is misleading in that we now think of a bondman, or bondsman, as someone who freely offers himself or herself as surety ("bond"). In the Renaissance, the word meant "serf" or "slave"; freedom of choice was never involved, as it was not for those to whom More's terms refer in his work.

Relatively little is known about the life of Ralph Robinson (or Robynson). He was born in 1521 in Lincolnshire to poor parents, attended grammar school there with William Cecil, who would eventually become Elizabeth's chief minister, and studied at Corpus Christi College, Oxford, where he took a B.A. degree in 1540, was made a fellow in 1542, and applied for an M.A. in 1544. At some point after that he went to London, where he became a member of the Goldsmiths' Company and obtained the post of clerk from Cecil, to whom he applied for additional financial support in 1551, to whom he dedicated his translation of *Utopia*, and to whom he applied for money again in 1572, the last year for which there is any record of his activities. He was urged to publish his *Utopia* by George Tadlowe, a prominent member of London's Company of Haberdashers, who sat on the city council in the 1550s. Despite his voiced misgivings about its supposedly crude style—something of a conventional posture many writers adopt—Robinson published his work in 1551, during the last few years of the short reign of Edward VI and under the Protectorship of the staunchly Protestant Edward Seymour, duke of Somerset.

Robinson's connections to Cecil place him squarely in the Protestant camp, a conclusion that is supported by the slight intensifying he gives to More's anti-clerical satire in the first book of *Utopia*. It is also supported more fully by the critical view he offers of More's Catholicism in the dedicatory letter to Cecil, where, although Robinson praises *Utopia* for its fruitful matter, he accuses More of having been "blinded, rather with obstinacy than with ignorance" (p. 157), to certain principal points of Christianity, an obstinacy he persisted in until his death. Revealingly, Robinson dropped the dedicatory letter to Cecil in the second edition, which appeared in 1556 during the reign of Mary (1553–1558), who had restored England to Catholicism and whose favor Cecil did not enjoy. The translation was published again in 1597 and 1624, times of agricultural depression and hardship in England, so one might speculate that it had a particular resonance at those times and was being read as a text about social and agrarian problems more than as a philosophical work addressed to a learned, international audience. Indeed, Robinson's decision in his first edition to eliminate most of the commendatory and other ancillary material written by humanists that was published in the Latin editions of *Utopia* underscores the more domestic focus of his translation. Robinson's work reveals its Englishness in yet another way, for he consistently refers to Utopus, the supposed founder of Utopia, as King Utopus, whereas More never assigns him any such rank in the Latin original. Robinson thus imposes an English monarchical structure on More's imaginary country that is actually distinguished by its republican and meritocratic form of government. Finally, it must be noted that Robinson's translation suffers from a tendency toward redundancy in that he frequently translates one of More's Latin words with two or more English ones. His reason for doing so is, one suspects, his desire to render the original as accurately and completely as possible.

The version of More's *Utopia* printed here is based on Robinson's second edition of the work, although the dedication to Cecil from the first edition has been retained and is printed after the text of *Utopia*. In its place in the second edition Robinson put a dedication to the "Gentle Reader," in which he eliminated the potentially dangerous criticism of More's religion contained in the dedication to Cecil. In his second edition Robinson also corrected some of the mistakes in translation that had been brought to his attention, and he included some of the prefatory material that accompanied the Latin editions of More's work. In addition, he supplied a series of marginal comments on the text that imitate, but do not directly translate, the marginal comments in More's Latin text that were written by Peter Giles and Erasmus. The prefatory material and marginal comments were designed to make the Latin *Utopia* into a learned document that would be accepted as such by the humanist community to which it was addressed. Robinson initially dispensed with this material, since his translation of the work into English focused it on a more general, less learned reading public. However, his second edition moves the work back toward the humanist community a bit, without making it speak any less to that more general English reading public.

If Robinson started out near the bottom of society, William Roper (1496–1578) was born into a well-to-do family with landed estates. He was the eldest son of John Roper, who was sheriff of Kent in 1521 and held the office of prothonotary (chief clerk) of the Court of the King's Bench, a position he later shared with his son, who continued to hold it until the year of his death. Although Roper flirted briefly with Lutheranism in his youth, he was an ardent Catholic most of his life. Despite his Catholicism, he managed to retain his judicial post under Protestant monarchs, perhaps because he was willing to go along with whatever government was in power. For example, he and his wife Margaret, More's eldest daughter and his favorite, both swore the oath of supremacy that made Henry VIII the head of the Church. During Mary's reign, Roper served in Parliament on several occasions but dropped out of political life permanently when Elizabeth came to the throne. Roper was called before the Privy Council in 1568 to answer charges that he had aided Catholic exiles with money and had printed books against the Queen's government. He made his submission to the council the next year and was allowed to go free. Roper married More's daughter in 1521 and lived in More's home for the next sixteen years. His biography of his father-in-law, which was written sometime in the middle of the sixteenth century and circulated in manuscript then, was finally published only in 1626 in an edition that lists Paris as the place of publication, although it was probably brought out in England. (That edition is the basis of the text included in this volume.)

Throughout, Roper's *Life* testifies to the genuine intimacy between the two men and contains important information about More's personal history that is available nowhere else. It does not discuss More's work as a writer at all, but focuses instead on him as a family man, a public servant, and a devout Catholic who felt guilt that he had not chosen a life in holy orders and who wore a hair shirt continually as an act of penance. From start to finish it stresses the importance of conscience for More, for it was conscience that led him at the beginning of his career to speak against a measure before Parliament that Henry VII desired, thereby earning him the enmity of that king, and it was conscience that made him refuse to swear the oath of supremacy and eventually led him to the executioner's block. Roper's biography also reveals More's extraordinary warmth and capacity for friendship, qualities that attracted others to him, including Henry VIII and his first wife, Catherine. While Roper presents his biography as a simple, artless record, it is nevertheless a carefully calculated work of art whose ultimate purpose is to make the More who goes to death at the end rather than submit to Henry into a martyr for his faith. In doing so, Roper beat the Catholic Church to that conclusion by four hundred years.

Wayne A. Rebhorn is Celanese Centennial Professor of English at the University of Texas at Austin. A graduate of the University of Pennsylvania and Yale University, he has also taught at the Bread Loaf School of English, the Université Paul Valéry in Montpellier, and the Université de Paris, and he has won many awards, including a Fulbright and fellowships from the American Council of Learned Societies and the Guggenheim Foundation. He has written extensively on

Renaissance literature in English, Italian, French, Spanish, and Latin, on authors from Boccaccio through More and Shakespeare down to Milton. Among his recent books are *The Emperor of Men's Minds: Literature and the Renaissance Discourse of Rhetoric* (1995) and *Renaissance Debates on Rhetoric* (2000), both published by Cornell University Press. His *Foxes and Lions: Machiavelli's Confidence Men* (Cornell University Press, 1988) won the Howard R. Marraro Prize of the Modern Language Association of America in 1990. Rebhorn translated and wrote the Introduction and Notes to the Barnes & Noble Classics edition of *The Prince and Other Writings*, by Niccolò Machiavelli.

UTOPIA

A FRUITFUL,

PLEASANT, AND WITTY WORK,

OF THE BEST STATE OF A PUBLIC

WEAL, AND OF THE NEW ISLE CALLED UTOPIA,

WRITTEN IN LATIN BY THE RIGHT WORTHY

AND FAMOUS SIR THOMAS MORE,

KNIGHT, AND TRANSLATED INTO ENGLISH BY

RALPH ROBYNSON, SOMETIME FELLOW

OF CORPUS CHRISTI COLLEGE IN

OXFORD, AND NOW BY HIM AT THIS

SECOND EDITION NEWLY PERUSED

AND CORRECTED, AND

ALSO WITH DIVERS NOTES

IN THE MARGIN

AUGMENTED.

The Translator to the Gentle Reader

Thou shalt understand, gentle reader, that though this work of *Utopia* in English come now the second time forth in print, yet was it never my mind nor intent that it should ever have been imprinted at all, as who for no such purpose took upon me at the first the translation thereof, but did it only at the request of a friend for his own private use,[1] upon hope that he would have kept it secret to himself alone. Whom though I knew to be a man indeed both very witty* and also skillful, yet was I certain that in the knowledge of the Latin tongue, he was not so well seen† as to be able to judge of the fineness or coarseness of my translation. Wherefore I went the more slightly through with it, propounding to myself therein, rather to please my said friend's judgment than my own, to the meanness of whose learning I thought it my part to submit and attemper my style. Lightly, therefore, I overran the whole work, and in short time, with more haste than good speed,‡ I brought it to an end. But as the Latin proverb saith: the hasty bitch bringeth forth blind whelps. For, when this my work was finished, the rudeness thereof showed it to be done in posthaste. Howbeit, rude and base though it were, yet fortune so ruled the matter that to imprinting it came, and that partly against my will. Howbeit, not being able in this behalf to resist the pithy persuasions of my friends, and perceiving therefore none other remedy but that forth it should, I comforted myself for the time only with this notable saying of Terence:

> Ita vita est hominum, quasi quum ludas tesseris.
> Si illud, quod est maxime opus, iactu non cadit,
> Illud, quod cecidit forte, id arte ut corrigas.[2]

---

*Intelligent, knowledgeable.
†Well instructed.
‡Success.

3

In which verses the poet likeneth or compareth the life of man to a dice playing or a game at the tables,* meaning therein, if that chance rise not, which is most for the player's advantage, that then the chance, which fortune hath sent, ought so cunningly to be played, as may be to the player least damage. By the which worthy similitude surely the witty poet giveth us to understand that, though in any of our acts and doings, as it oft chanceth, we happen to fail and miss of our good pretensed[†] purpose, so that the success[‡] and our intent prove things far odd, yet so we ought with witty circumspection to handle the matter that no evil or incommodity, as far forth as may be and as in us lieth, do thereof ensue. According to the which counsel, though I am indeed in comparison of an expert gamester and a cunning player but a very bungler, yet have I in this by chance, that on my side unawares hath fallen, so (I suppose) behaved myself that, as doubtless it might have been of me much more cunningly handled, had I forethought so much, or doubted[§] any such sequel at the beginning of my play, so I am sure it had been much worse than it is, if I had not in the end looked somewhat earnestly to my game. For though this work came not from me so fine, so perfect, and so exact at the first, as surely for my small learning it should have done, if I had then meant the publishing thereof in print, yet I trust I have now in this second edition taken about it such pains that very few great faults and notable errors are in it to be found. Now, therefore, most gentle reader, the meanness of this simple translation, and the faults that be therein (as I fear much there be some) I doubt not but thou wilt, in just consideration of the premises, gently and favorably wink at them. So doing, thou shalt minister unto me good cause to think my labor and pains herein not altogether bestowed in vain. *Vale.*[‖]

---

*Backgammon.
[†]Intended.
[‡]Outcome.
[§]Feared.
[‖]Farewell (Latin).

Letter of Thomas More
to Peter Giles

Thomas More to Peter Giles sendeth greeting.

I am almost ashamed, right well-beloved Peter Giles, to send unto you this book of the Utopian commonwealth well nigh after a year's space, which I am sure you looked for within a month and a half.[1] And no marvel. For you knew well enough that I was already disburdened of all the labor and study belonging to the invention of this work, and that I had no need at all to trouble my brains about the disposition or conveyance of the matter, and therefore had herein nothing else to do, but only to rehearse those things which you and I together heard Master Raphael tell and declare. Wherefore, there was no cause why I should study to set forth the matter with eloquence, forasmuch as his talk could not be fine and eloquent, being first not studied for, but sudden and unpremeditate, and then, as you know, of a man better seen in the Greek language than in the Latin tongue. And my writing, the nigher* it should approach to his homely, plain and simple speech, so much the nigher should it go to the truth, which is the only mark whereunto I do and ought to direct all my travail and study herein.

Truth loveth simplicity and plainness.

I grant and confess, friend Peter, myself discharged of so much labor, having all these things ready done to my hand, that almost there was nothing left for me to do. Else either the invention or the disposition of this matter might have required of a wit neither base, neither at all unlearned, both some time and leisure, and also some study. But if it were

---

*Nearer.

requisite and necessary that the matter should also have been written eloquently, and not alone* truly, of a surety that thing could I have performed by no time nor study. But now, seeing all these cares, stays, and lets† were taken away, wherein else so much labor and study should have been employed, and that there remained no other thing for me to do but only to write plainly the matter as I heard it spoken—that, indeed, was a thing light and easy to be done.

Howbeit, to the dispatching of this so little business my other cares and troubles did leave almost less than no leisure. *The author's business and lets.* Whiles I do daily bestow my time about law matters, some to plead, some to hear, some as an arbitrator with mine award to determine, some as an umpire or a judge with my sentence to discuss; whiles I go one way to see and visit my friend, another way about mine own private affairs; whiles I spend almost all the day abroad among others and the residue at home among mine own, I leave to myself, I mean to my book, no time. For when I am come home, I must common‡ with my wife, chat with my children, and talk with my servants, all the which things I reckon and account among business, for as much as they must of necessity be done, and done must they needs be, unless a man will be stranger in his own house. And in any wise, a man must so fashion and order his conditions and so appoint and dispose himself that he be merry, jocund, and pleasant among them whom either nature hath provided, or chance hath made, or he himself hath chosen to be the fellows and companions of his life. So that with too much gentle behavior and familiarity he do not mar them, and by too much sufferance of his servants maketh them his masters. Among these things now rehearsed stealeth away the day, the month, the year. When do I write then? And all this while have I spoken no word of sleep, neither yet of meat,§ which among a great number doth waste no less time

---

*Only.
†Hindrances.
‡Commune.
§Food.

than doth sleep, wherein almost half the lifetime of man creepeth away. I therefore do win and get only that time which I steal from sleep and meat. Which time, because it is very little, and yet somewhat it is, therefore have I once at the last, though it be long first, finished *Utopia* and have sent it to you, friend Peter, to read and peruse, to the intent that if anything have escaped me, you might put me in remembrance of it.

Meat & sleep: great wasters of time.

For though in this behalf I do not greatly mistrust myself (which would God I were somewhat in wit and learning, as I am not all of the worst and dullest memory), yet have I not so great trust and confidence in it that I think nothing could fall out of my mind. For John Clement,[2] my boy, who as you know was there, present with us, whom I suffer to be away from no talk wherein may be any profit or goodness—for out of this young-bladed and new-shot-up corn, which hath already begun to spring up both in Latin and Greek learning, I look for plentiful increase at length of goodly ripe grain—he, I say, hath brought me into a great doubt. For whereas Hythloday (unless my memory fail me) said that the bridge of Amaurote, which goeth over the river of Anyder, is 500 paces, that is to say half a mile, in length, my John saith that 200 of those paces must be plucked away, for that the river containeth there not above 300 paces in breadth.[3] I pray you heartily call the matter to your remembrance. For if you agree with him, I also will say as you say and confess myself deceived. But if you cannot remember the thing, then surely I will write as I have done and as mine own remembrance serveth me. For as I will take good heed that there be in my book nothing false, so if there be anything doubtful, I will rather tell a lie than make a lie, because I had rather be good than wily.[4]

John Clement.

A diversity between making a lie and telling a lie.

Howbeit, this matter may easily be remedied, if you will take the pains to ask the question of Raphael himself by word of mouth, if he be now with you, or else by your letters, which you must needs do for another doubt also that hath chanced, through whose fault I cannot tell, whether through mine or yours or Raphael's. For neither we remembered to inquire of him, nor he to tell us in what part of the new world Utopia

In what part of the world Utopia standeth it is unknown.

It is thought of some that here is unfeignedly meant the late famous vicar of Croydon in Surrey.

A godly suit.

is situate. The which thing I had rather have spent no small sum of money than that it should thus have escaped us, as well for that I am ashamed to be ignorant in what sea that island standeth, whereof I write so long a treatise, as also because there be with us certain men, and especially one virtuous and godly man and a professor of divinity, who is exceeding desirous to go unto Utopia, not for a vain and curious desire to see news,* but to the intent he may further and increase our religion, which is there already luckily begun. And that he may the better accomplish and perform this his good intent, he is minded to procure that he may be sent thither by the high bishop; yea, and that he himself may be made Bishop of Utopia, being nothing scrupulous herein, that he must obtain this bishopric with suit.[5] For he counteth that a godly suit which proceedeth not of the desire of honor or lucre, but only of a godly zeal.

Wherefore I most earnestly desire you, friend Peter, to talk with Hythloday, if you can, face to face, or else to write your letters to him, and so to work in this matter that in this my book there may neither anything be found which is untrue, neither anything be lacking which is true. And I think, verily, it shall be well done that you show unto him the book itself. For if I have missed or failed in any point, or if any fault have escaped me, no man can so well correct and amend it as he can; and yet, that can he not do, unless he peruse and read over my book written. Moreover, by this means shall you perceive whether he be well willing and content that I should undertake to put this work in writing. For if he be minded to publish and put forth his own labors and travails† himself, perchance he would be loathe, and so would I also, that in publishing the Utopian weal public‡ I should prevent§ him and take from him the flower and grace of the novelty of this his history.

---

*Something new.
†Efforts, work.
‡Commonwealth (Latin: *respublica*).
§Anticipate.

Howbeit, to say the very truth, I am not yet fully determined with myself whether I will put forth my book or no.
For the natures of men be so divers, the fantasies of some so
wayward, their minds so unkind, their judgments so corrupt   *The unkind*
that they which lead a merry and a jocund life, following their   *judgments of*
own sensual pleasures and carnal lusts, may seem to be in a   *men.*
much better state or case than they that vex and disquiet
themselves with cares and study for the putting forth and
publishing of something that may be either profit or pleasure
to others, which others nevertheless will disdainfully, scorn-
fully, and unkindly accept the same. The most part of all be
unlearned, and a great number hath learning in contempt.
The rude and barbarous alloweth nothing but that which is
very barbarous indeed. If it be one that hath a little smack of
learning, he rejecteth as homely gear and common ware
whatsoever is not stuffed full of old, moth-eaten terms and
that be worn out of use. Some there be that have pleasure only
in old, rusty antiquities, and some only in their own doings.
One is so sour, so crabbed, and so unpleasant that he can away
with* no mirth nor sport. Another is so narrow between the
shoulders that he can bear no jests nor taunts. Some silly poor
souls be so afraid that at every snappish word their nose shall
be bitten off that they stand in no less dread of every quick
and sharp word than he that is bitten of a mad dog feareth
water. Some be so mutable and wavering that every hour they
be in a new mind, saying one thing sitting and another thing
standing. Another sort sitteth upon their ale benches, and
there among their cups they give judgment of the wits of
writers, and with great authority they condemn, even as
pleaseth them, every writer according to his writing, in most
spiteful manner mocking, louting, and flouting† them—being
themselves in the mean season safe and, as saith the proverb,
out of all danger of gunshot.[6] For why they be so smug and
smooth that they have not so much as one hair of an honest

---

*Go along with—that is, tolerate.
†Mocking, and jeering at.

man whereby one may take hold of them. There be, moreover, some so unkind and ungentle, that though they take great pleasure and delectation in the work, yet for all that they cannot find in their hearts to love the author thereof, nor to afford him a good word, being much like uncourteous, un-

*A fit simili-
tude.*

thankful, and churlish guests which, when they have with good and dainty meats well-filled their bellies, depart home, giving no thanks to the feast maker. Go your ways now and make a costly feast at your own charges for guests so dainty-mouthed, so divers in taste, and besides that of so unkind and unthankful natures.

But nevertheless, friend Peter, do, I pray you, with Hythloday as I willed you before. And as for this matter, I shall be at my liberty afterwards to take new advisement. Howbeit, seeing I have taken great pains and labor in writing this matter, if it may stand with his mind and pleasure, I will, as touching the edition or publishing of the book, follow the counsel and advice of my friends, and especially yours. Thus, fare you well, right heartily, beloved friend Peter, with your gentle wife, and love me as you have ever done, for I love you better than ever I did.

Contents for Utopia

THE FIRST BOOK OF UTOPIA.

THE FIRST BOOK
OF THE

Communication of
Raphael Hythloday Concerning the Best
State of a Commonwealth.

THE MOST VICTORIOUS AND triumphant King of England, Henry the Eighth of that name, in all royal virtues a prince most peerless, had of late in controversy with Charles, the right high and mighty King of Castile,[1] weighty matters and of great importance. For the debatement and final determination whereof, the King's Majesty sent me ambassador into Flanders, joined in commission with Cuthbert Tunstall,[2] a *Cuthbert* man doubtless out of comparison and whom the King's *Tunstall.* Majesty of late, to the great rejoicing of all men, did prefer to the office of Master of the Rolls. But of this man's praises I will say nothing, not because I do fear that small credence shall be given to the testimony that cometh out of a friend's mouth, but because his virtue and learning be greater and of more excellency than that I am able to praise them, and also in all places so famous and so perfectly well known that they need not nor ought not of me to be praised, unless I would seem to show and set forth the brightness of the sun with a candle, as the proverb saith.

There met us at Bruges (for thus it was before agreed) they whom their Prince had for that matter appointed commissioners, excellent men all. The chief and the head of them was the Margrave (as they call him) of Bruges, a right honorable man, but the wisest and the best spoken of them was George Temsice,[3] provost of Cassel, a man, not only by learning but also by nature of singular eloquence, and in the laws profoundly learned. But in reasoning and debating of matters, what by his natural wit, and what by daily exercise, surely he had few fellows. After that we had once or twice met, and upon certain points or articles could not fully and thoroughly

15

agree, they for a certain space took their leave of us and departed to Brussels, there to know their Prince's pleasure. I in the meantime (for so my business lay) went straight thence to Antwerp.

Whiles I was there abiding, oftentimes among other, but which to me was more welcome than any other, did visit me one Peter Giles, a citizen of Antwerp, a man there in his country of honest reputation and also preferred to high promotions, worthy truly of the highest, for it is hard to say whether the young man be in learning or in honesty more excellent. For he is both of wonderful virtuous conditions, and also singularly well learned, and towards all sorts of people exceeding gentle, but towards his friends so kindhearted, so loving, so faithful, so trusty, and of so earnest affection that it were very hard in any place to find a man that with him in all points of friendship may be compared. No man can be more lowly or courteous; no man useth less simulation or dissimulation; in no man is more prudent simplicity. Besides this, he is in his talk and communication so merry and pleasant, yea, and that without harm, that through his gentle entertainment and his sweet and delectable communication, in me was greatly abated and diminished the fervent desire that I had to see my native country, my wife, and my children, whom then I did much long and covet to see, because that at that time I had been more than four months from them.

Upon a certain day, when I had heard the divine service in Our Lady's Church,[4] which is the fairest, the most gorgeous and curious* church of building in all the city and also most frequented of people, and the service being done, was ready to go home to my lodging, I chanced to espy this foresaid Peter talking with a certain stranger, a man well stricken in age, with a black sunburned face, a long beard, and a cloak cast homely† about his shoulders, whom, by his

Peter Giles. (margin)

---

*Skillfully constructed, beautiful.
†Casually (More's Latin: *neglectim*).

favor* and apparel, forthwith I judged to be a mariner. But the said Peter, seeing me, came unto me and saluted me.

And as I was about to answer him, "See you this man?" saith he (and therewith he pointed to the man that I saw him talking with before). "I was minded," quoth he, "to bring him straight home to you."

"He should have been very welcome to me," said I, "for your sake."

"Nay," quoth he, "for his own sake, if you knew him, for there is no man this day living that can tell you of so many strange and unknown peoples and countries as this man can. And I know well that you be very desirous to hear of such news."

"Then I conjectured not far amiss," quoth I, "for even at the first sight I judged him to be a mariner."

"Nay," quoth he, "there ye were greatly deceived: he hath sailed indeed, not as the mariner Palinurus, but as the expert and prudent prince Ulysses; yea, rather as the ancient and sage philosopher Plato.[5] For this same Raphael Hythloday (for this is his name) is very well learned in the Latin tongue, but profound and excellent in the Greek language, wherein he ever bestowed more study than in the Latin, because he had given himself wholly to the study of philosophy. Whereof he knew that there is nothing extant in Latin that is to any purpose, saving a few of Seneca's and Cicero's doings.[6] His patrimony that he was born unto he left to his brethren (for he is a Portugal born), and for the desire that he had to see and know the far countries of the world, he joined himself in company with Amerigo Vespucci,[7] and in the three last voyages of those four that be now in print and abroad in every man's hands, he continued still in his company, saving that in the last voyage he came not home again with him. For he made such means and shift, what by entreatance and what by importune suit, that he got license of Master Amerigo (though it were sore against his will) to be one of the twenty-four

Raphael Hythloday.

---

*Outward appearance; perhaps, face.

which in the end of the last voyage were left in the country of Gulike.[8] He was, therefore, left behind for his mind's sake, as one that took more thought and care for traveling than dying, having customably in his mouth these sayings: 'He that hath no grave is covered with the sky,' and, 'the way to heaven out of all places is of like length and distance.'[9] Which fantasy of his (if God had not been his better friend) he had surely bought full dear. But after the departing of Master Vespucci, when he had traveled through and about many countries with five of his companions, Gulikians, at the last by marvelous chance he arrived in Taprobane,[10] from whence he went to Calicut, where he chanced to find certain of his country ships, wherein he returned again into his country, nothing less than looked for."

All this, when Peter had told me, I thanked him for his gentle kindness, that he had vouchsafed to bring me to the speech of that man, whose communication he thought should be to me pleasant and acceptable. And therewith I turned me to Raphael. And when we had hailed each other and had spoken these common words that be customably spoken at the first meeting and acquaintance of strangers, we went thence to my house, and there in my garden, upon a bench covered with green torves,* we sat down talking together.

There he told us how that after the departing of Vespucci, he and his fellows that tarried behind in Gulike began by little and little, through fair and gentle speech, to win the love and favor of the people of that country, insomuch that within short space they did dwell amongst them not only harmless, but also occupying with them very familiarly.† He told us also that they were in high reputation and favor with a certain great man (whose name and country is now quite out of my remembrance) which of his mere‡ liberality did bear the costs and charges of him and his five companions, and besides that,

---

*Turfs of grass.
†Having dealings with them on friendly terms.
‡Pure, absolute.

gave them a trusty guide to conduct them in their journey (which by water was in boats, and by land in wagons) and to bring them to other princes with very friendly commendations.

Thus after many days' journeys, he said, they found towns and cities and weal publics,* full of people, governed by good and wholesome laws. For under the line equinoctial,† and on both sides of the same as far as the sun doth extend his course, lieth (quoth he) great and wide deserts and wildernesses, parched, burned, and dried up with continual and intolerable heat. All things be hideous, terrible, loathsome, and unpleasant to behold; all things out of fashion and comeliness‡ inhabited with wild beasts and serpents, or at the leastwhile, with people that be no less savage, wild, and noisome than the very beasts themselves be. But a little farther beyond that all things begin by little and little to wax pleasant: the air soft, temperate, and gentle; the ground covered with green grass; less wildness in the beasts. At the last shall you come again to people, cities, and towns wherein is continual intercourse and occupying of merchandise and chaffer,§ not only among themselves and with their borderers, but also with merchants of far countries, both by land and water. "There I had occasion," said he, "to go to many countries on every side, for there was no ship ready to any voyage or journey, but I and my fellows were into it very gladly received." The ships that they found first were made plain, flat, and broad in the bottom, trow-wise.‖ The sails were made of great rushes, or of wickers, and in some places of leather. Afterward they found ships with ridged keels and sails of canvas, yea, and shortly after, having all things like ours, the shipmen also very expert and cunning, both in the sea and in the weather. But he said

Ships of strange fashions.

---

*Commonwealths (Latin: *respublicae*).
†Equator.
‡Shapeless and unattractive.
§Trade.
‖Barge-like.

The lodestone. that he found great favor and friendship among them for teaching them the feat* and the use of the lodestone,† which to them before that time was unknown, and therefore, they were wont to be very timorous and fearful upon the sea, nor to venture upon it but only in the summer time. But now they have such a confidence in that stone that they fear not stormy winter, in so doing farther from care than danger; insomuch that it is greatly to be doubted,‡ lest that thing, through their own foolish hardiness,§ shall turn them to evil and harm, which at the first was supposed should be to them good and commodious.‖

But what he told us that he saw in every country where he came, it were very long to declare; neither it is my purpose at this time to make rehearsal thereof. But peradventure in another place I will speak of it, chiefly such things as shall be profitable to be known, as in special be those decrees and ordinances that he marked to be well and wittily provided and enacted among such peoples as do live together in a civil policy# and good order. For of such things did we basely inquire and demand of him, and he likewise very willingly told us of the same. But as for monsters, because they be no news, of them we were nothing inquisitive, for nothing is more easy to be found than be barking Scyllas, ravening Celaenos, and Laestrygons, devourers of people, and such, like great and incredible monsters.[11] But to find citizens ruled by good and wholesome laws, that is an exceeding rare and hard thing. But as he marked many fond and foolish laws in those new found lands, so he rehearsed divers acts and constitutions whereby these our cities, nations, countries, and kingdoms may take example to amend their faults, enormities, and errors, whereof in another place, as I said, I will entreat.

---

*Working.
†Magnetic compass.
‡Feared.
§Boldness.
‖Advantageous.
#State.

Now at this time I am determined to rehearse only that he told us of the manners, customs, laws, and ordinances of the Utopians. But first I will repeat our former communication, by the occasion and, as I might say, the drift whereof he was brought into the mention of that weal public.[12]

For when Raphael had very prudently touched divers things that be amiss, some here and some there, yea, very many on both parts, and again had spoken of such wise laws and prudent decrees as be established and used, both here among us and also there among them, as a man so perfect and expert in the laws and customs of every several country, as though into what place soever he came guest-wise, there he had led all his life. Then Peter, much marveling at the man: "Surely Master Raphael," quoth he, "I wonder greatly why you get you not into some king's court? For I am sure there is no prince living that would not be very glad of you, as a man not only able highly to delight him with your profound learning, and this your knowledge of countries and peoples, but also meet to instruct him with examples, and help him with counsel. And thus doing, you shall bring yourself in a very good case,* and also be of ability to help all your friends and kins-folk."

"As concerning my friends and kinsfolk," quoth he, "I pass not† greatly for them. For I think I have sufficiently done my part towards them already. For these things that other men do not depart from until they be old and sick, yea, which they be then very loath to leave when they can no longer keep, those very same things did I, being not only lusty‡ and in good health but also in the flower of my youth, divide among my friends and kinsfolk. Which I think with this my liberality ought to hold them contented, and not to require nor to look that besides this I should for their sakes give myself in bondage unto kings."

---

*Situation.
†I am not concerned.
‡Vigorous.

"Nay, God forbid that," quoth Peter. "It is not my mind that you should be in bondage to kings, but as a retainer to them at your pleasure.[13] Which surely I think is the nighest* way that you can devise how to bestow your time fruitfully, not only for the private commodity† of your friends and for the general profit of all sorts of people, but also for the advancement of yourself to a much wealthier state and condition than you be now in."

"To a wealthier condition," quoth Raphael, "by that means that my mind standeth clean against? Now I live at liberty after my own mind and pleasure, which I think very few of these great states‡ and peers of realms can say. Yea, and there be enough of them that sue for great men's friendships and therefore think it no great hurt, if they have not me, nor three or four such other as I am."

"Well, I perceive plainly, friend Raphael," quoth I, "that you be desirous neither of riches nor of power. And truly, I have in no less reverence and estimation a man of your mind than any of them all that be so high in power and authority. But you shall do as it becometh you, yea, and according to this wisdom, to this high and free courage§ of yours, if you can find in your heart so to appoint and dispose yourself that you may apply your wit and diligence to the profit of the weal public, though it be somewhat to your own pain and hindrance. And this shall you never so well do, nor with so great profit perform, as if you be of some great prince's council and put into his head (as I doubt not but you will) honest opinions and virtuous persuasions. For from the prince, as from a perpetual wellspring, cometh among the people the flood of all that is good or evil. But in you is so perfect learning that without any experience, and again so great experience that without any learning, you may well be any king's counselor."

---

*Nearest.
†Advantage.
‡Statesmen, high officials.
§Spirit, mind.

"You be twice deceived, Master More," quoth he, "first in me, and again in the thing itself, for neither is in me the ability that you force upon me, and if it were never so much, yet in disquieting mine own quietness I should nothing further the weal public. For first of all, the most part of all princes have more delight in warlike matters and feats of chivalry (the knowledge whereof I neither have nor desire) than in the good feats of peace, and employ much more study how by right or by wrong to enlarge their dominions than how well and peaceably to rule and govern that they have already. Moreover, they that be counselors to kings, every one of them either is of himself so wise indeed that he needeth not, or else he thinketh himself so wise that he will not allow another man's counsel, saving that they do shamefully and flatteringly give assent to the fond and foolish sayings of certain great men, whose favors, because they be in high authority with their prince, by assentation* and flattery they labor to obtain. And, verily, it is naturally given to all men to esteem their own inventions best. So both the raven and the ape think their own young ones fairest. Then if a man in such a company, where some disdain and have despite at† other men's inventions,‡ and some count their own best—if among such men," I say, "a man should bring forth anything that he hath read done in times past, or that he hath seen done in other places—there the hearers fare as though the whole existimation§ of their wisdom were in jeopardy to be overthrown, and that ever after they should be counted for very dizzards,‖ unless they could in other men's inventions pick out matter to reprehend and find fault at.

"If all other poor helps fail, then this is their extreme refuge. 'These things,' say they, 'pleased our forefathers and ancestors; would God we could be so wise as they were.' And as though *Triptakers.#*

---

*Servile assent.
†Scorn.
‡Arguments, ideas.
§Estimation.
‖Fools.
#Fault finders.

they had wittily concluded the matter, and with this answer stopped every man's mouth, they sit down again. As who should say, it were a very dangerous matter if a man in any point should be found wiser than his forefathers were. And yet be we content to suffer the best and wittiest* of their decrees to lie unexecuted. But if in anything a better order might have been taken than by them was, there we take fast hold, finding therein many faults. Many times have I chanced upon such proud, lewd, overthwart† and wayward judgments, yea, and once in England."

Partial judgments.

"I pray you, sir," quoth I, "have you been in our country?"

"Yea, forsooth," quoth he, "and there I tarried for the space of four or five months together, not long after the insurrection that the western Englishmen made against their king, which by their own miserable and pitiful slaughter was suppressed and ended.[14] In the mean season I was much bound and beholden to the right reverend father John Morton,[15] Archbishop and Cardinal of Canterbury, and at that time also Lord Chancellor of England, a man, Master Peter (for Master More knoweth already that I will say), not more honorable for his authority than for his prudence and virtue. He was of a mean stature, and though stricken in age, yet bore he his body upright. In his face did shine such an amiable reverence,‡ as was pleasant to behold, gentle in communication, yet earnest and sage. He had great delight many times with rough speech to his suitors, to prove, but without harm, what prompt wit and what bold spirit were in every man. In the which, as in a virtue much agreeing with his nature, so that therewith were not joined impudency, he took great delectation. And the same person, as apt and meet to have an administration in the weal public, he did lovingly embrace. In his speech he was fine, eloquent, and pithy; in the law he had profound knowledge; in wit he was incomparable, and in memory wonderful excellent. These qualities, which in him were by nature singular, he by learning and use had made perfect. The king put much trust in his counsel; the weal public

Cardinal Morton.

---

*Most intelligent.
†Vulgar, obstructive.
‡A quality inspiring lovable reverence.

also in a manner leaned unto him when I was there. For even in the chief of his youth he was taken from school into the court, and there passed all his time in much trouble and business, being continually tumbled and tossed in the waves of divers misfortunes and adversities. And so by many and great dangers he learned the experience of the world, which so being learned cannot be easily forgotten.

"It chanced on a certain day, when I sat at his table, there was also a certain layman cunning in* the laws of your realm, who, I cannot tell whereof, taking occasion, began diligently and earnestly to praise that strait and rigorous justice, which at that time was there executed upon felons, who, as he said, were for the most part twenty hanged together upon one gallows. And, seeing so few escaped punishment, he said he could not choose but greatly wonder and marvel, how and by what evil luck it should so come to pass that thieves, nevertheless, were in every place so rife and so rank. 'Nay sir,' quoth I (for I durst boldly speak my mind before the cardinal), 'marvel nothing hereat, for this punishment of thieves passes the limits of justice and is also very hurtful to the weal public, for it is too extreme and cruel a punishment for theft, and yet not sufficient to refrain and withhold men from theft. For simple theft is not so great an offense that it ought to be punished with death, neither there is any punishment so horrible that it can keep them from stealing which have no other craft whereby to get their living. Therefore, in this point not you only, but also the most part of the world, be like evil schoolmasters which be readier to beat than to teach their scholars. For great and horrible punishments be appointed for thieves, whereas much rather provision should have been made that there were some means whereby they might get their living, so that no man should be driven to this extreme necessity, first to steal, and then to die.' 'Yes,' quoth he, 'this matter is well enough provided for already. There be handicrafts, there is husbandry to get their living by, if they would not willing be naught.'†

Of laws not made according to equity.

By what means there might be fewer thieves and robbers.

---

*Knowledgeable of.
†Willingly be wicked.

"'Nay,'" quoth I, 'you shall not escape so. For, first of all, I will speak nothing of them that come home out of the wars maimed and lame, as not long ago out of Blackheath field, and a little before that out of the wars in France.[16] Such, I say, as put their lives in jeopardy for the weal public's or the king's sake, and by reason of weakness and lameness be not able to occupy their old crafts, and be too aged to learn new: of them I will speak nothing, forasmuch as wars have their ordinary recourse. But let us consider those things that chance daily before our eyes. First, there is a great number of gentlemen which cannot be content to live idle themselves, like dors,* of that which other have labored for, their tenants, I mean, whom they poll† and shave to the quick by raising their rents (for this only point of frugality do they use, men else through their lavish and prodigal spending able to bring themselves to very beggary). These gentlemen, I say, do not only live in idleness themselves, but also carry about with them at their tails a great flock or train of idle and loitering servingmen, which never learned any craft whereby to get their livings. These men, as soon as their master is dead, or be sick themselves, be incontinent‡ thrust out of doors. For gentlemen had rather keep idle persons than sick men, and many times the dead man's heir is not able to maintain so great a house and keep so many servingmen as his father did. Then in the mean season§ they that be thus destitute of service either starve for hunger or manfully play the thieves. For what would you have them to do? When they have wandered abroad so long, until they have worn threadbare their apparel and also appaired‖ their health, then gentlemen, because of their pale and sickly faces and patched coats, will not take them into service. And husbandmen# dare not set them a work, knowing well

Idleness, the mother of thieves.

Landlords by the way checked for rent-raising.

Of idle servingmen come thieves.

---

*Drones—that is, lazy idlers.
†Clip (hair).
‡Straightway.
§Meanwhile.
‖Impaired.
#Farmers.

enough that he is nothing meet* to do true and faithful service to a poor man with a spade and a mattock for small
wages and hard fare, which, being daintily and tenderly pam-
pered up in idleness and pleasure, was wont with a sword and
a buckler by his side to jet† through the street with a bragging
look and to think himself too good to be any man's mate."

"'Nay, by Saint Mary, sir,' quoth the lawyer, 'not so. For this
kind of men must we make most of. For in them, as men of
stouter stomachs,‡ bolder spirits, and manlier courages than
handicraftsmen and ploughmen be, doth consist the whole
power, strength, and puissance§ of our army when we must
fight in battle.' 'Forsooth, sir, as well you might say,' quoth I,
"that for war's sake you must cherish thieves, for surely you
shall never lack thieves while you have them. No, nor thieves
be not the most false and faint-hearted soldiers, nor soldiers be
not the cowardliest thieves: so well these two crafts agree together. But this fault, though it be much used among you, yet
is it not peculiar to you only, but common also almost to all
nations.

Between soldiers and thieves small diversity.

"'Yet France, besides this, is troubled and infected with a
much sorer plague. The whole realm is filled and besieged
with hired soldiers in peacetime (if that be peace) which be
brought in under the same color and pretence that hath persuaded you to keep these idle servingmen. For these wisefools[17] and very arch-dolts thought the wealth of the whole
country herein to consist, if there were ever in a readiness a
strong and a sure garrison, specially of old practiced soldiers, for they put no trust at all in men unexercised. And
therefore, they must be forced to seek for war to the end they
may ever have practiced soldiers and cunning manslayers,
lest that (as it is prettily said of Sallust) their hands and their
minds, through idleness or lack of exercise, should wax
dull.[18]

---

*Fit.
†Strut.
‡High spirits, courage.
§Power.

What inconveniences cometh by continual garrisons of soldiers.

"'But how pernicious and pestilent a thing it is to maintain such beasts, the Frenchmen by their own harms have learned, and the examples of the Romans, Carthaginians, Syrians, and many other countries do manifestly declare.[19] For not only the empire, but also the fields and cities of these by divers occasions have been overrun and destroyed of their own armies beforehand had in a readiness.* Now how unnecessary a thing this is, hereby it may appear: that the French soldiers, which from their youth have been practiced and inured in feats of arms, do not crack nor advance themselves† to have very often got the upper hand and mastery of your new-made and unpracticed soldiers. But in this point I will not use many words, lest perchance I may seem to flatter you. No, nor those same handicraftmen of yours in cities, nor yet the rude and uplandish‡ ploughmen of the country, are not supposed to be greatly afraid of your gentlemen's idle servingmen, unless it be such as be not of body or stature correspondent to their strength and courage, or else whose bold stomachs be discouraged through poverty. Thus you may see that it is not to be feared lest they should be effeminated, if they were brought up in good crafts and laborsome works whereby to get their livings, whose stout and sturdy bodies (for gentlemen vouchsafe to corrupt and spill§ none but picked and chosen men) now either by reason of rest and idleness be brought to weakness, or else by too easy and womanly exercises to be made feeble and unable to endure hardness. Truly, howsoever the case standeth, this methinketh is nothing available‖ to the weal public, for war sake, which you never have, but when you will yourselves to keep and maintain an innumerable flock of that sort of men that be so troublesome and

---

*That is, by their own standing armies.
†Boast.
‡Rustic.
§Spoil—that is, ruin.
‖Beneficial.

noyous* in peace, whereof you ought to have a thousand times more regard than of war.

"'But yet this is not only the necessary cause of stealing. There is another, which, as I suppose, is proper and peculiar to you Englishmen alone.' 'What is that?' quoth the Cardinal. 'Forsooth my lord,' quoth I, 'your sheep, that were wont to be so meek and tame and so small eaters, now, as I hear say, be become so great devourers and so wild that they eat up and swallow down the very men themselves. They consume, destroy, and devour whole fields, houses, and cities. For look, in what parts of the realm doth grow the finest and therefore dearest wool, there noblemen and gentlemen, yea, and certain abbots, holy men no doubt, not contenting themselves with the yearly revenues and profits that were wont to grow to their forefathers and predecessors of their lands, nor being content that they live in rest and pleasure, nothing profiting, yea much annoying the weal public, leave no ground for tillage.[20] They enclose all into pastures; they throw down houses; they pluck down towns, and leave nothing standing but only the church to be made a sheephouse. And as though you lost no small quantity of ground by forests, chases, lands,† and parks, those good holy men turn all dwelling places and all glebe land‡ into desolation and wilderness.

English sheep, devourers of men.

"'Therefore, that one covetous and insatiable cormorant[21] and very plague of his native country may compass about and enclose many thousand acres of ground together within one pale§ or hedge, the husbandmen be thrust out of their own, or else either by covin‖ and fraud or by violent oppression, they be put besides it, or by wrongs and injuries they be so wearied that they be compelled to sell all. By one means, therefore, or by other, either by hook or crook, they

Sheepmasters, decayers of husbandry.

---

*Noxious, troublesome.
†Clearings.
‡Land for cultivation assigned a clergyman as part of his benefice.
§Fence.
‖Conspiracy.

must needs depart away, poor, silly, wretched souls, men, women, husbands, wives, fatherless children, widows, woeful mothers with their young babes, and their whole household small in substance and much in number, as husbandry requireth many hands. Away they trudge, I say, out of their known and accustomed houses, finding no place to rest in. All their household stuff, which is very little worth, though it might well abide the sale—yet, being suddenly thrust out,

The decay of husbandry causeth beggary, which is the mother of vagabonds and thieves.

they be constrained to sell it for a thing of naught. And when they have wandered abroad till that be spent, what can they then else do but steal, and then justly, pardy,* be hanged, or else go about a-begging? And yet then also they be cast in prison as vagabonds, because they go about and work not, whom no man will set a-work, though they never so willingly proffer themselves thereto. For one shepherd or herdsman is enough to eat up that ground with cattle,† to the occupying whereof about husbandry many hands were requisite. And this is also the cause why victuals be now in

The cause of dearth of victuals.

many places dearer. Yea, besides this the price of wool is so risen that poor folks, which were wont to work it and make cloth thereof, be now able to buy none at all. And by this means very many be forced to forsake work and to give themselves to idleness. For after that so much ground was

What inconvenience cometh of dearth of wool.

enclosed for pasture, an infinite multitude of sheep died of the rot, such vengeance God took of their inordinate and insatiable covetousness, sending among the sheep that pestiferous murrain‡ which much more justly should have fallen on the sheepmasters' own heads. And though the number of sheep increase never so fast, yet the price falleth not one

The cause of dearth of wool.

mite, because there be so few sellers. For they be almost all coming into a few rich men's hands, whom no need forceth to sell before they lust,§ and they lust not before they may sell as dear as they lust.[22]

---

*By God.
†Livestock.
‡Disease, such as anthrax, afflicting domesticated animals.
§Desire.

"'Now the same cause bringeth in like dearth of the other kinds of cattle, yea, and that so much the more because that, after farms plucked down and husbandry decayed, there is no man that passeth for the breeding of young store.* For these rich men bring not up the young ones of great cattle as they do lambs. But first they buy them abroad very cheap, and afterward, when they be fatted in their pastures, they sell them again exceedingly dear, and therefore, as I suppose, the whole incommodity hereof is not yet felt, for that they make dearth only in those places where they sell. But when they shall fetch them away from thence whereby they be bred faster than they can be brought up, then shall there also be felt great dearth, store beginning there to fail where the ware is bought.

Dearth of cattle with the cause thereof.

"'Thus the unreasonable covetousness of a few hath turned that thing to the utter undoing of your island, in the which thing the chief felicity of your realm did consist. For this great dearth of victuals causeth men to keep as little houses and as small hospitality as they possibly may, and to put away their servants. Whither, I pray you, but a-begging, or else (which these gentle bloods and stout stomachs will sooner set their minds unto) a-stealing? Now, to amend the matter,† to this wretched beggary and miserable poverty is joined great wantonness, importunate superfluity, and excessive riot.‡ For not only gentlemen's servants, but also handicraftmen, yea, and almost the ploughmen of the country, with all other sorts of people, use much strange and proud newfangledness in their apparel and too much prodigal riot and sumptuous fare at their table. Now bawds, queans,§ whores, harlots, strumpets, brothelhouses, stews,‖ and yet another stews, wine taverns, alehouses, and tippling houses, with so many naughty, lewd, and unlawful games, as dice, cards, tables,# tennis, bowls,

Dearth of victuals is the decay of housekeeping, whereof ensueth beggary and theft.

Excess in apparel and diet, a maintainer of beggary and theft.

Bawds, whores, wine taverns, alehouses, and unlawful games be very mothers of thieves.

---

*Cares about the breeding of young stock.
†To make it even better.
‡Extravagant expenditure, importunate superfluity, and dissipation.
§Prostitutes.
‖Bathhouses, which were identified with brothels; a red-light district.
#Backgammon.

quoits—do not all these send the haunters of them straight a-stealing when their money is gone? Cast out these pernicious abominations. Make a law that they, which plucked down farms and towns of husbandry, shall re-edify them, or else yield and uprender* the possession thereof to such as will go to the cost of building them anew. Suffer not these rich men to buy up all, to engross and forestall,† and with their monopoly to keep the market alone as please them. Let not so many be brought up in idleness; let husbandry and tillage be restored; let clothworking be renewed that there may be honest labors for this idle sort to pass their time in profitably, which hitherto either poverty hath caused to be thieves, or else now be either vagabonds or idle servingmen, and shortly will be thieves.

Rich men, engrossers, and forestallers.

"'Doubtless, unless you find a remedy for these enormities, you shall in vain advance yourselves of executing justice upon felons, for this justice is more beautiful in appearance and more flourishing to the show than either just or profitable. For by suffering your youth wantonly and viciously‡ to be brought up and to be infected, even from their tender age, by little and little with vice, then, a§ God's name, to be punished when they commit the same faults after being come to man's state which from their youth they were ever like to do—in this point, I pray you, what other thing do you than make thieves and then punish them?'

The corrupt education of youth, a mother of thievery.

"Now, as I was thus speaking, the lawyer began to make himself ready to answer and was determined with himself to use the common fashion and trade of disputers, which be more diligent in rehearsing than answering, as thinking the memory worthy of the chief praise." 'Indeed, sir,' quoth he, 'you have said well, being but a stranger, and one that might rather hear something of these matters than have any exact or perfect knowledge of the same, as I will incontinent by open proof

---

*That is, render up.
†Buy up wholesale and secure in advance (to drive up the price).
‡Luxuriously and dissolutely.
§In.

make manifest and plain. For first I will rehearse in order all that you have said; then I will declare wherein you be deceived through lack of knowledge in all our fashions, manners, and customs; and last of all I will answer your arguments and confute them every one. First, therefore, I will begin where I promised. Four things you seemed to me—'

"'Hold your peace,' quoth the Cardinal, 'for it appeareth *He is worthily* that you will make no short answer which make such a be- *put to flight* ginning. Wherefore, at this time you shall not take the pains *that is too full* to make your answer, but keep it to your next meeting, which *of words.* I would be right glad that it might be even tomorrow next, unless either you or Master Raphael have any earnest let.* But now, Master Raphael, I would very gladly hear of you why you think theft not worthy to be punished with death, or what other punishment you can devise more expedient to the weal public, for I am sure you are not of that mind, that you would have theft escape unpunished. For if now the extreme punishment of death cannot cause them to leave stealing, then, if ruffians and robbers should be sure of their lives, what violence, what fear were able to hold their hands from robbing, which would take the mitigation of the punishment as a very provocation to the mischief?'

"'Surely, my lord,' quoth I, 'I think it not right nor justice *The theft* that the loss of money should cause the loss of man's life. For *ought not to* mine opinion is that all the goods in the world are not able to *be punished* countervail man's life. But if they would thus say that the *by death.* breaking of justice and the transgression of the laws is recompensed with this punishment and not the loss of the money, then why may not this extreme and rigorous justice well be called plain injury? For so cruel governance, so strait rules *Strait laws* and unmerciful laws be not allowable, that if a small offense *not allowed.* be committed, by and by the sword should be drawn.[23] Nor so stoical ordinances are to be borne withal, as to count all offenses of such equality that the killing of a man or the taking of his money from him were both a matter, and the one no

---

*Impediment.

more heinous offense than the other, between the which two, if we have any respect to equity, no similitude or equality consisteth. God commandeth us that we shall not kill. And be we then so hasty to kill a man for taking a little money? And if any man would understand killing by this commandment of God to be forbidden after no larger wise than man's constitutions define killing to be lawful, then why may it not likewise by man's constitutions be determined after what sort whoredom, fornication, and perjury may be lawful?[24] For, whereas by the permission of God no man hath power to kill neither himself nor yet any other man, then, if a law, made by the consent of men concerning slaughter of men, ought to be of such strength, force, and virtue, that they which, contrary to the commandment of God, have killed those whom this constitution of man commanded to be killed, be clean quit and exempt out of the bonds and danger of God's commandment, shall it not then by this reason follow that the power of God's commandment shall extend no further than man's law doth define and permit? And so shall it come to pass that in like manner man's constitutions in all things shall determine how far the observation of all God's commandments shall extend. To be short, Moses' law, though it were ungentle and sharp, as a law that was given to bondmen, yea, and them very obstinate, stubborn, and stiff-necked, yet it punished theft by the purse and not with death.[25] And let us not think that God, in the new law of clemency and mercy, under the which He ruleth us with fatherly gentleness as His dear children, hath given us greater scope and license to the execution of cruelty one upon another.

"'Now ye have heard the reasons whereby I am persuaded that this punishment is unlawful. Furthermore, I think there is nobody that knoweth not how unreasonable, yea, how pernicious a thing it is to the weal public that a thief and a homicide or murderer should suffer equal and like punishment. For the thief, seeing that man that is condemned for theft in no less jeopardy, nor judged to no less punishment, than him that is convict of manslaughter, through this cogitation only he is strongly and forcibly provoked and in a manner constrained to

That man's law ought not to be prejudicial to God's law.

Theft in the old law not punished by death.

What inconvenience ensueth of punishing theft with death.

Punishing of theft by death causeth the thief to be a murderer.

kill him whom else he would have but robbed. For the murder being once done, he is in less fear and in more hope that the deed shall not be betrayed or known, seeing the party is now dead and rid out of the way which only might have uttered and disclosed it. But if he chance to be taken and descried,* yet he is in no more danger and jeopardy than if he had committed but single felony. Therefore, whiles we go about with such cruelty to make thieves afraid, we provoke them to kill good men."

"'Now, as touching this question: what punishment were more commodious and better? That truly in my judgment is easier to be found than what punishment might be worse. For why should we doubt that to be a good and a profitable way for the punishment of offenders which we know did in times past so long please the Romans, men in the administration of a weal public most expert, politic, and cunning? Such as among them were convict of great and heinous trespasses, them they condemned into stone quarries, and into mines to dig metal, there to be kept in chains all the days of their life. But as concerning this matter, I allow the ordinance of no nation so well as that which I saw while I traveled abroad about the world, used in Persia among the people that commonly be called the Polylerites,[26] whose land is both large and ample and also well and wittily governed, and the people in all conditions free and ruled by their own laws, saving that they pay a yearly tribute to the great king of Persia. But because they be far from the sea, compassed and enclosed almost round about with high mountains, and do content themselves with the fruits of their own land, which is of itself very fertile and fruitful, for this cause neither they go to other countries, nor other come to them. And according to the old custom of the land, they desire not to enlarge the bounds of their dominions; and those that they have by reason of the high hills be easily defended; and the tribute which they pay to their chief lord and king sets them quit and free from warfare. Thus their life is commodious rather than gallant,† and may better be

Marginal notes:

What lawful punishment may be devised for theft.

How the Romans punished theft.

A worthy and commendable punishment of thieves in the weal public of the Polylerites in Persia.

---

*Denounced publicly.
†Comfortable rather than grand.

called happy or wealthy than notable or famous. For they be not known as much as by name, I suppose, saving only to their next neighbors and borders. They that in the land be attainted* and convict of felony make restitution of that which

*A privy nip†
for them that
do otherwise.*

they stole to the right owner and not (as they do in other lands) to the king, whom they think to have no more right to the thief-stolen thing than the thief himself hath. But if the thing be lost or made away, then the value of it is paid of the goods of such offenders, which else remaineth all whole to their wives and children. And they themselves be condemned to be common laborers, and unless the theft be very heinous, they be

neither locked in prison nor fettered in gyves,‡ but be untied and go at large, laboring in the common works. They that refuse labor, or go slowly and slackly to their work, be not only tied in chains, but also pricked forward with stripes.§ But being diligent about their work, they live without check or rebuke. Every night they be called in by name and be locked in their chambers. Beside their daily labor, their life is nothing hard or incommodious. Their fare is indifferent good, borne at the charges of the weal public, because they be common servants to the commonwealth. But their charges in all places of the land is not borne alike, for in some parts that which is bestowed upon them is gathered of alms. And though that way be uncertain, yet the people be so full of mercy and pity that none is found more profitable or plentiful. In some places certain lands be appointed hereunto, of the revenues whereof they be maintained. And in some places every man giveth a certain tribute for the same use and purpose. Again in

some parts of the land these servingmen (for so be these damned persons called) do no common work, but as every private man needeth laborers, so he cometh into the marketplace and there hireth some of them for meat and drink and a certain limited wages by the day, somewhat cheaper than he

---

*Accused.
†Private rebuke.
‡Shackles.
§Lashes.

should hire a free man. It is also lawful for them to chastise
the sloth of these servingmen with stripes. By this means they
never lack work, and besides the gaining of their meat and
drink, every one of them bringeth daily something into the
common treasury. All and every one of them be appareled in
one color. Their heads be not polled or shaven, but rounded a
little above the ears, and the tip of the one ear is cut off. Every
one of them may take meat and drink of their friends, and
also a coat of their own color, but to receive money is death,
as well to the giver as to the receiver. And no less jeopardy it is
for a free man to receive money of a servingman for any manner of cause, and likewise for servingmen to touch weapons.
The servingmen of every several shire be distinct and known
from other by their several and distinct badges, which to cast
away is death, as it is also to be seen out of the precinct of
their own shire, or to talk with a servingman of another shire.
And it is no less danger to them for to intend to run away than
to do it in deed. Yea, and to conceal such an enterprise, in a
servingman it is death, in a free man servitude. Of the contrary part, to him that openeth and uttereth such counsels be
decreed large gifts: to a free man a great sum of money, to a
serving-man freedom, and to them both forgiveness and pardon of that they were of counsel in that pretence. So that it
can never be so good for them to go forward in their evil purpose as by repentance to turn back.

An evil intent esteemed as the deed.

"'This is the law and order in this behalf, as I have showed
you. Wherein what humanity is used, how far it is from cruelty, and how commodious it is, you do plainly perceive.
Forasmuch as the end of their wrath and punishment inten-
deth nothing else but the destruction of vices and saving of
men, with so using and ordering them that they cannot
choose but be good, and what harm soever they did before, in
the residue of their life to make amends for the same. Moreover, it is so little feared that they should turn again to their
vicious conditions, that wayfaring* men will for their safeguard

The right end and intent of punishment.

---

*Traveling.

choose them to their guides before any other, in every shire changing and taking new, for if they would commit robbery, they have nothing about them meet for that purpose. They may touch no weapons. Money found about them should betray the robbery. They should be no sooner taken with the manner, but forthwith they should be punished. Neither they can have any hope at all to escape away by fleeing, for how should a man that in no part of his apparel is like other men fly privily* and unknown, unless he would run away naked? Howbeit, so also flying he should be descried by the rounding of his head and his earmark. But it is a thing to be doubted that they will lay their heads together and conspire against the weal public. No, no, I warrant you. For the servingmen of one shire alone could never hope to bring to pass such an enterprise without soliciting, enticing, and alluring the servingmen of many other shires to take their parts, which thing is to them so impossible that they may not as much as speak or talk together, or salute one another. No, it is not to be thought that they would make their own countrymen and companions of their counsel† in such a matter, which they know well should be jeopardy to the concealer thereof and great commodity and goodness to the opener and detector of the same. Whereas, on the other part, there is none of them all hopeless or in despair to recover again his former state of freedom, by humble obedience, by patient suffering, and by giving good tokens and likelihood of himself that he will ever after that live like a true and an honest man. For every year divers of them be returned to their freedom through the commendation of their patience.'

"When I had thus spoken, saying, moreover, that I could see no cause why this order might not be had in England with much more profit than the justice which the lawyer so highly praised: 'Nay,' quoth the lawyer, 'this could never be so

---

*Secretly.
†Privy to their plans.

established in England, but that it must needs bring the weal public into great jeopardy and hazard.' And as he was thus saying, he shook his head and made a wry mouth, and so he held his peace. And all that were there present with one assent agreed to his saying.

"'Well,' quoth the cardinal, 'yet it were hard to judge without a proof whether this order would do well here or no. But when the sentence of death is given, if then the king should command execution to be deferred and spared, and would prove* this order and fashion, taking away the privileges of all sanctuaries,²⁷ if then the proof should declare the thing to be good and profitable, then it were well done that it were established, else the condemned and reprieved persons may as well and as justly be put to death after this proof as when they were first cast. Neither any jeopardy can in the mean space grow hereof. Yea, and methinketh that these vagabonds may very well be ordered after the same fashion, against whom we have hitherto made so many laws and so little prevailed.' *Vagabonds.*

"When the cardinal had thus said, then every man gave great praise to my sayings, which a little before they had disallowed. But most of all was esteemed that which was spoken of vagabonds, because it was the cardinal's own addition. I cannot tell whether it were best to rehearse the communication that followed, for it was not very sad.† But yet you shall hear it, for there was no evil in it, and partly it pertained to the matter beforesaid. *The wavering judgments of flatterers.*

"There chanced to stand by a certain jesting parasite, or scoffer, which would seem to resemble and counterfeit the fool. But he did in such wise counterfeit that he was almost the very same indeed that he labored to represent: he so studied with words and sayings brought forth so out of time and place to make sport and move laughter that he himself was oftener laughed at than his jests were. Yet the foolish fellow

---

*Try out.
†Serious.

brought out now and then such indifferent and reasonable stuff, that he made the proverb true which saith: he that shooteth oft at the last shall hit the mark.[28] So that when one of the company said that through my communication a good order was found for thieves, and that the cardinal also had well provided for vagabonds, so that only remained some good provision to be made for them that through sickness and age were fallen into poverty and were become so impotent and unwieldy that they were not able to work for their living: 'Tush,' quoth he, 'let me alone with them; you shall see me do well enough with them. For I had rather than any good* that this kind of people were driven somewhere out of my sight, they have so sore troubled me many times and oft, when they have with their lamentable tears begged money of me, and yet they could never to my mind so tune their song that thereby they ever got of me one farthing. For evermore the one of these two chanced: either that I would not, or else that I could not, because I had it not. Therefore, now they be waxed wise, for when they see me go by, because they will not leese† their labor, they let me pass and say not one word to me. So they look for nothing of me, no, in good sooth no more than if I were a priest or a monk. But I will make a law that all these beggars shall be distributed and bestowed into houses of religion. The men shall be made lay brethren, as they call them, and the women nuns.' Hereat the cardinal smiled and allowed it in jest, yea, and all the residue in good earnest.

"But a certain friar, graduate in divinity,‡ took such pleasure and delight in this jest of priests and monks that he also, being else a man of grizzly§ and stern gravity, began merrily and wantonly to jest and taunt. 'Nay,' quoth he, 'you shall not so be rid and dispatched of beggars unless you make some provision also for us friars.' 'Why,' quoth the jester, 'that is done already,

Sick, aged, impotent persons and beggars.

A common proverb among beggars.

A merry talk between a friar and a fool.

---

*More than anything.

†Lose.

‡Having a university degree in theology.

§Gray.

for my lord himself set a very good order for you when he decreed that vagabonds should be kept strait and set to work, for you be the greatest and veriest vagabonds that be.'" This jest also, when they saw the cardinal not disprove it, every man took it gladly, saving only the friar, for he (and that no marvel), being thus touched on the quick and hit on the gall,* so fret, so fumed and chafed at it, and was in such a rage that he could not refrain himself from chiding, scolding, railing, and reviling. He called the fellow ribald, villain, javel,† backbiter, slanderer, and the child of perdition, citing therewith terrible threatenings out of Holy Scripture. Then the jesting scoffer began to play the scoffer indeed, and verily, he was good at it, for he could play a part in that play, no man better. 'Patient yourself, good master friar,' quoth he, 'and be not angry, for Scripture saith: *In your patience you shall save your souls.*'[29] Then the friar (for I will rehearse his own very words): 'No, gallows wretch, I am not angry,' quoth he, 'or at the leastwise I do not sin, for the psalmist saith: *Be you angry, and sin not.*' Then the cardinal spake gently to the friar, and desired him to quiet himself. 'No, my lord,' quoth he, "I speak not but of a good zeal as I ought, for holy men had a good zeal. Wherefore it is said: *The zeal of thy house hath eaten me.* And it is sung in the church: *The scorners of Elisha, whiles he went up into the house of God, felt the zeal of the bald,* as peradventure this scorning villain ribald shall feel.' 'You do it,' quoth the cardinal, 'perchance of a good mind and affection, but methinketh you should do, I cannot tell whether more holily, certes‡ more wisely, if you would not set your wit to a fool's wit, and with a fool take in hand a foolish contention.' 'No forsooth, my lord,' quoth he, 'I should not do more wisely. For Solomon the wise saith: *Answer a fool according to his folly*, like as I do now, and do show him the pit that he shall fall into, if he take not heed. For if many scorners of Elisha, which was but one bald man, felt the zeal of the bald, how much more shall one scorner of

Talk qualified according to the person that speaketh.

---

*Touched on a sore point.
†Worthless fellow.
‡Certainly.

many friars feel, among whom be many bald men? And we have also the pope's bulls, whereby all that mock and scorn us be excommunicate, suspended, and accursed.' The cardinal, seeing that none end would be made, sent away the jester by a privy beck,* and turned the communication to another matter. Shortly after, when he was risen from the table, he went to hear his suitors, and so dismissed us.

"Look, Master More, with how long and tedious a tale I have kept you, which surely I would have been ashamed to have done, but that you so earnestly desired me and did after such a sort give ear unto it, as though you would not that any parcel of that communication should be left out. Which, though I have done somewhat briefly, yet could I not choose but rehearse it for the judgment of them which, when they had improved† and disallowed my sayings, yet incontinent, hearing the cardinal allow them, did themselves also approve the same: so impudently flattering him that they were nothing ashamed to admit, yea, almost in good earnest, his jester's foolish inventions, because that he himself by smiling at them did seem not to disprove them. So that hereby you may right well perceive how little the courtiers would regard and esteem me and my sayings."

"I ensure you, Master Raphael," quoth I, "I took great delectation in hearing you; all things that you said were spoken so wittily and so pleasantly. And methought myself to be in the meantime not only at home in my country, but also through the pleasant remembrance of the cardinal, in whose house I was brought up of a child, to wax a child again. And, friend Raphael, though I did bear very great love towards you before, yet seeing you do so earnestly favor this man, you will not believe how much my love towards you is now increased. But yet, all this notwithstanding, I can by no means change my mind, but that I must needs believe that you, if you be disposed and can find in your heart to follow‡ some prince's

---

*Signal.
†Disapproved of.
‡Join.

court, shall with your good counsels greatly help and further
the commonwealth, wherefore there is nothing more apper-
taining to your duty, that is to say, to the duty of a good man.
For whereas your Plato judgeth that weal publics shall by this
means attain perfect felicity, either if philosophers be kings,
or else if kings give themselves to the study of philosophy,
how far, I pray you, shall commonwealths then be from this
felicity, if philosophers will [not] vouchsafe to instruct kings
with their good counsel?"[30]

"They be not so unkind," quoth he, "but they would gladly
do it, yea, many have done it already in books that they have
put forth, if kings and princes would be willing and ready to
follow good counsel. But Plato doubtless did well foresee, unless kings themselves would apply their minds to the study of
philosophy, that else they would never thoroughly allow the
counsel of philosophers, being themselves before even from
their tender age infected and corrupt with perverse and evil
opinions, which thing Plato himself proved true in King
Dionysius. If I should propose to any king wholesome decrees, doing my endeavor to pluck out of his mind the pernicious original causes of vice and naughtiness, think you not
that I should forthwith either be driven away or else made a
laughingstock?

"Well, suppose I were with the French king, and there sitting in his council, whiles in that most secret consultation the
king himself there being present in his own person, they beat
their brains and search the very bottoms of their wits to discuss by what craft and means the king may still keep Milan *The*
and draw to him again fugitive Naples and then how to con- *Frenchmen*
quer the Venetians, and how to bring under his jurisdiction all *privily*
counseled
Italy; then how to win the dominion of Flanders, Brabant, *from the*
and of all Burgundy, with divers other lands whose kingdoms *desire of Italy.*
he hath long ago in mind and purpose invaded.[31] Here whiles
one counseleth to conclude a league of peace with the Venetians, so long to endure as shall be thought meet and expedient for their purpose, and to make them also of their counsel,
yea, and besides that to give them part of the prey, which afterward, when they have brought their purpose about after

*Lance knights.**

their own minds, they may require and claim again; another thinketh best to hire the Germans; another would have the favor of the Switzers won with money; another's advice is to appease the puissant power of the Emperor's majesty with gold, as with a most pleasant and acceptable sacrifice; whiles another giveth counsel to make peace with the King of Aragon and to restore unto him his own kingdom of Navarre as a full assurance of peace. Another cometh in with his five eggs[32] and adviseth to hook in the King of Castile with some hope of affinity or alliance, and to bring to their part certain peers of his court for great pensions. Whiles they all stay at the chiefest doubt of all, what to do in the meantime with England, and yet agree all in this, to make peace with the Englishmen, and with most sure and strong bands to bind that weak and feeble friendship, so that they must be called friends, and had in suspicion as enemies. And that, therefore, the Scots must be had in a readiness, as it were in a standing, ready at all occasions, in aunters† the Englishmen should stir never so little, incontinent to set upon them. And, moreover, privily and secretly (for openly it may not be done by the truce that is taken), privily, therefore, I say, to make much of some peer of England that is banished his country, which must claim title to the crown of the realm and affirm himself just inheritance thereof, that by this subtle means they may hold to them the king, in whom else they have but small trust and affiance. Here, I say, where so great and high matters be in consultation, where so many noble and wise men counsel their king only to war, here if I, silly‡ man, should rise up and will them to turn over the leaf and learn a new lesson, saying that my counsel is not to meddle with Italy but to tarry still at home, and that the kingdom of France alone is almost greater than that it may well be governed of one man, so that the king should not need to study how to get more; and then should

---

*German and Swiss pikemen were called *Landsknechte*—hence, "lance knights."

†Case.

‡Simple.

propose unto them the decrees of the people that be called the Achorians,[33] which be situate over against the island of Utopia on the southeast side.

"These Achorians once made war in their king's quarrel for to get him another kingdom, which he laid claim unto and advanced himself right inheritor to the crown thereof by the title of an old alliance. At the last when they had gotten it, and saw that they had even as much vexation and trouble in keeping it as they had in getting it, and that either their new-conquered subjects by sundry occasions were making daily insurrections to rebel against them, or else that other countries were continually with divers inroads and foragings invading them, so that they were ever fighting either for them or against them, and never could break up their camps. Seeing themselves in the mean season pilled* and impoverished, their money carried out of the realm, their own men killed to maintain the glory of another nation, when they had no war, peace nothing better than war, by reason that their people in war had so inured themselves to corrupt and wicked manners that they had taken a delight and pleasure in robbing and stealing, that through manslaughter they had gathered† boldness to mischief, that their laws were had in contempt and nothing set by or regarded, that their king, being troubled with the charge and governance of two kingdoms, could not, nor was not able, perfectly to discharge his office towards them both, seeing again that all these evils and troubles were endless—at the last laid their heads together and like faithful and loving subjects gave to their king free choice and liberty to keep still the one of these two kingdoms whether he would, alleging that he was not able to keep both, and that they were more than might well be governed of half a king, forasmuch as no man would be content to take him for his muleteer that keepeth another man's mules besides his. So, this good prince was constrained to be content with his old kingdom and to

A notable example, and worthy to be followed.

---

*Plundered.
†United.

give over the new to one of his friends, who shortly after was violently driven out.

"Furthermore, if I should declare unto them that all this busy preparance to war, whereby so many nations for his sake should be brought into a troublesome hurly-burly, when all his coffers were emptied, his treasures wasted and his people destroyed, should at the length through some mischance be in vain and to none effect; and that therefore it were best for him to content himself with his own kingdom of France, as his forefathers and predecessors did before him, to make much of it, to enrich it, and to make it as flourishing as he could, to endeavor himself to love his subjects and again to be beloved of them, willingly to live with them, peaceably to govern them, and with other kingdoms not to meddle, seeing that which he hath already is even enough for him, yea, and more than he can well turn him to—this mine advice, Master More, how think you it would be heard and taken?"

"So God help me, not very thankfully," quoth I.

"Well, let us proceed then," quoth he. "Suppose that some king and his council were together whetting their wits and devising what subtle craft they might invent to enrich the king with great treasures of money.[34] First one counseleth to raise and enhance the valuation of money when the king must pay any, and again to call down the value of coin to less than it is worth when he must receive or gather any. For thus great sums shall be paid with a little money, and where little is due, much shall be received. Another counseleth to feign war that when, under this color and pretence the king hath gathered great abundance of money, he may, when it shall please him, make peace with great solemnity and holy ceremonies to blind the eyes of the poor commonalty, as taking pity and compassion, forsooth, upon man's blood, like a loving and a merciful prince. Another putteth the king in remembrance of certain old and motheaten laws, that of long time have not been in execution, which, because no man can remember that they were made, every man hath transgressed. The fines of these laws he counseleth the king to require, for there is no way so profitable, nor more honorable, as the which hath a show and

Enhancing and imbasing of coins.

Counterfeit wars.

The renewing of old laws.

color of justice. Another adviseth him to forbid many things *Restraints.*
under great penalties and fines, especially such things as is for
the people's profit not [to] be used, and afterward to dispense
for money with them which by this prohibition sustain loss
and damage, for by this means the favor of the people is won,
and profit riseth two ways. First by taking forfeits of them
whom covetousness of gains hath brought in danger of this *Selling of*
statute, and also by selling privileges and licenses, which the *licenses.*
better that the prince is, forsooth, the dearer he selleth them,
as one that is loath to grant to any private person anything
that is against the profit of his people, and, therefore, may sell
none but at an exceeding dear price. Another giveth the king
counsel to endanger* unto his grace the judges of the realm,
that he may have them ever on his side, and that they may in
every matter dispute and reason for the king's right. Yea, and
further to call them into his palace and to require them there
to argue and discuss his matters in his own presence. So there
shall be no matter of his so openly wrong and unjust, wherein
one or other of them, either because he will have something to
allege and object, or that he is ashamed to say that which is
said already, or else to pick a thank† with his prince, will not
find some hole open to set a snare in, wherewith to take the
contrary part in a trip.‡ Thus, whiles the judges cannot agree
among themselves, reasoning and arguing of that which is
plain enough and bringing the manifest truth in doubt, in the
mean season the king may take a fit occasion to understand
the law as shall most make for his advantage, whereunto all
other, for shame or for fear, will agree. Then the judges may be
bold to pronounce on the king's side, for he that giveth sentence for the king cannot be without a good excuse. For it shall
be sufficient for him to have equity on his part, or the bare
words of the law, or a writhen§ and wrested understanding of
the same, or else (with which good and just judges is of greater

---

*To subject to absolute control.
†Curry favor.
‡Blunder.
§Twisted.

force than all laws be), the king's indisputable prerogative. To
conclude, all the counselors agree and consent together with
the rich Crassus, that no abundance of gold can be sufficient
for a prince, which must keep and maintain an army.[35] Furthermore, that a king, though he would, can do nothing unjustly, for all that all men have, yea, also the men themselves,
be all his, and that every man hath so much of his own as the
king's gentleness hath not taken from him. And that it shall
be most for the king's advantage that his subjects have very little or nothing in their possession, as whose safeguard doth
herein consist that his people do not wax wanton and wealthy
through riches and liberty, because where these things be,
there men be not wont patiently to obey hard, unjust, and unlawful commandments; whereas, on the other part, need and
poverty doth hold down and keep under stout courages, and
maketh them patient perforce, taking from them bold and rebelling stomachs.

"Here again, if I should rise up and boldly affirm that all
these counsels be to the king dishonor and reproach, whose
honor and safety is more and rather supported and upholden
by the wealth and riches of his people than by his own treasures, and if I should declare that the commonality chooseth
their king for their own sake and not for his sake, to the intent
that through his labor and study they might all live wealthily,
safe from wrongs and injuries, and that therefore the king
ought to take more care for the wealth of his people than for
his own wealth, even as the office and duty of a shepherd is,
in that he is a shepherd, to feed his sheep rather than himself.
For as touching this, that they think the defense and maintenance of peace to consist in the poverty of the people, the
thing itself showeth that they be far out of the way. For where
shall a man find more wrangling, quarreling, brawling and
chiding than among beggars, who be more desirous of new
mutations and alterations than they that be not content with
the present state of their life? Or, finally, who be bolder stom-
ached to bring all in a hurly-burly (thereby trusting to get
some windfall) than they that have now nothing to lose? And
if any king were so smally regarded and so lightly esteemed,

The saying of rich Crassus.

Poverty, the mother of debate and decay of realms.

yea, so behated of his subjects that other ways he could not keep them in awe, but only by open wrongs, by polling and shaving, and by bringing them to beggary, surely it were better for him to forsake his kingdom than to hold it by this means, whereby, though the name of the king be kept, yet the majesty is lost, for it is against the dignity of a king to have rule over beggars, but rather over rich and wealthy men.

"Of this mind was the hardy and courageous Fabricius, *A worthy* when he said that he had rather be a ruler of rich men than be *saying of* rich himself.[36] And, verily, one man to live in pleasure and *Fabricius.* wealth, whiles all other weep and smart for it, that is the part not of a king, but of a jailor. To be short, as he is a foolish physician that cannot cure his patient's disease unless he cast him in another sickness, so he that cannot amend the lives of his subjects but by taking from them the wealth and commodity of life, he must needs grant that he knoweth not the feat how to govern men. But let him rather amend his own life, renounce unhonest pleasures, and forsake pride, for these be the chief vices that cause him to run in the contempt or hatred of his people. Let him live of his own, hurting no man. Let him do cost* not above his power. Let him restrain wickedness. Let him prevent vices and take away the occasions of offenses by well ordering his subjects and not suffering wickedness to increase, afterwards to be punished. Let him not be too hasty in calling again laws which a custom hath abrogated, especially such as have been long forgotten and never lacked nor needed. And let him never, under the cloak and pretence of transgression, take such fines and forfeits as no judge will suffer a private person to take, as unjust and full of guile.

"Here if I should bring forth before them the law of the *A strange* Macarians,[37] which be not far distant from Utopia, whose *and notable* king, the day of his coronation, is bound by a solemn oath *law of the* that he shall never at anytime have in his treasure above a *Macarians.* thousand pounds of gold or silver. They say a very good king,

---

*Have expenses.

which took more care for the wealth and commodity of his country than for the enriching of himself, made this law to be a stop and a bar to kings from heaping and hoarding up so much money as might impoverish their people. For he foresaw that this sum of treasure would suffice to support the king in battle against his own people, if they should chance to rebel, and also to maintain his wars against the invasions of his foreign enemies. Again, he perceived the same stock of money to be too little and unsufficient to encourage and enable him wrongfully to take away other men's goods, which was the chief cause why the law was made. Another cause was this: he thought that by this provision his people should not lack money, wherewith to maintain their daily occupying and chaffer.* And seeing the king could not choose but lay out and bestow all that came in above the prescript† sum of his stock, he thought he would seek no occasions to do his subjects injury. Such a king shall be feared of evil men and loved of good men. These and such other informations, if I should use among men wholly inclined and given to the contrary part, how deaf hearers think you should I have?"

"Deaf hearers doubtless," quoth I, "and in good faith no marvel. And to be plain with you, truly I cannot allow that such communication shall be used, or such counsel given, as you be sure shall never be regarded nor received. For how can so strange informations be profitable, or how can they be beaten into their heads, whose minds be already prevented‡ with clean contrary persuasions? This school philosophy[38] is not unpleasant among friends in familiar communication, but in the councils of kings where great matters be debated and reasoned with great authority, these things have no place."

School philosophy in the consultations of princes hath no place.

"That is it which I meant," quoth he, "when I said philosophy had no place among kings."

"Indeed," quoth I, "this school philosophy hath not, which thinketh all things meet for every place. But there is another

---

*Trading and doing business.
†Prescribed.
‡Preoccupied.

philosophy more civil, which knoweth, as ye would say, her own stage, and thereafter ordering and behaving herself in the play that she hath in hand, playeth her part accordingly with comeliness, uttering nothing out of due order and fashion. And this is the philosophy that you must use.[39] Or else, whiles *A fine and fit* a comedy of Plautus is playing and the vile bondmen scoffing *similitude.* and trifling among themselves, if you should suddenly come upon the stage in a philosopher's apparel and rehearse out of *Octavia* the place wherein Seneca disputeth with Nero, had it not been better for you to have played the dumb person, than *A dumb place.* by rehearsing that which served neither for the time nor place to have made such a tragical comedy or gallimaufry?* For by bringing in other stuff that nothing appertaineth to the present matter, you must needs mar and pervert the play that is in hand, though the stuff that you bring be much better. What part soever you have taken upon you, play that as well as you can and make the best of it, and do not, therefore, disturb and bring out of order the whole matter because that another, which is merrier and better, cometh to your remembrance. So the case standeth in a commonwealth, and so it is in the consultations of kings and princes. If evil opinions and naughty persuasions† cannot be utterly and quite plucked out of their hearts, if you cannot, even as you would, remedy vices which use and custom hath confirmed, yet for this cause you must not leave and forsake the commonwealth; you must not forsake the ship in a tempest because you cannot rule and keep down the winds. No, nor you must not labor to drive into their heads new and strange informations, which you know well shall be nothing regarded with them that be of clean contrary minds. But you must with a crafty wile and a subtle train study and endeavor yourself, as much as in you lieth, to handle the matter wittily and handsomely‡ for the purpose, and that which you cannot turn to good, so to order it that it be not very bad. For it is not possible for all things to be well,

---

*Hodgepodge.
†Wicked convictions.
‡Deftly.

unless all men were good, which I think will not be yet these good many years."

"By this means," quoth he, "nothing else will be brought to pass, but whiles that I go about to remedy the madness of others, I should be even as mad as they. For if I would speak such things that be true, I must needs speak such things, but as for to speak false things, whether that be a philosopher's part or no I cannot tell; truly it is not my part. Howbeit, this communication of mine, though peradventure it may seem unpleasant to them, yet can I not see why it should seem strange or foolishly newfangled. If so be that I should speak those things that Plato feigneth* in his weal public or that the Utopians do in theirs, these things though they were (as they be indeed) better, yet they might seem spoken out of place. Forasmuch as here amongst us every man hath his possessions several to himself, and there all things be common.

The Utopian weal public.

"But what was in my communication contained that might not and ought not in any place to be spoken—saving that to them which have thoroughly decreed and determined with themselves to run headlongs the contrary way, it cannot be acceptable and pleasant, because it calleth them back and showeth them the jeopardies? Verily, if all things that evil and vicious manners have caused to seem inconvenient and naughty should be refused as things unmeet and reproachful, then we must among Christian people wink at the most part of all those things which Christ taught us, and so straitly forbade them to be winked at, that those things also which He whispered in the ears of his disciples He commanded to be proclaimed in open houses. And yet the most part of them is more dissident† from the manners of the world nowadays than my communication was. But preachers, sly and wily men, following your counsel (as I suppose) because they saw men evil willing‡ to frame their manners to Christ's rule, they have wrested and wried§ his

---

*Feigns—that is, imagines.
†At variance.
‡Scarcely willing.
§Twisted.

doctrine, and like a rule of lead* have applied it to men's manners, that by some means at the least way, they might agree together. Whereby I cannot see what good they have done, but that men may more sickerly† be evil. And I truly should prevail even as little in kings' councils. For either I must say otherways than they say, and then I were as good to say nothing, or else I must say the same that they say and (as Mitio saith in Terence) help to further their madness.[40] For that crafty wile and subtle train of yours, I cannot perceive to what purpose it serveth, wherewith you would have me to study and endeavor myself, if all things cannot be made good, yet to handle them wittily and handsomely for the purpose that as far forth as is possible they may not be very evil, for there is no place to dissemble in nor to wink in. Naughty counsels must be openly allowed and very pestilent decrees must be approved. He shall be counted worse than a spy, yea, almost as evil as a traitor, that with a faint heart doth praise evil and noisome decrees.

"Moreover, a man can have no occasion to do good, chancing into the company of them which will sooner pervert a good man than be made good themselves, through whose evil company he shall be marred, or else, if he remain good and innocent, yet the wickedness and folly of others shall be imputed to him and laid in his neck. So that it is impossible with that crafty wile and subtle train to turn anything to better. Wherefore Plato by a goodly similitude declareth why wise men refrain to meddle in the commonwealth, for when they see the people swarm into the streets and daily wet to the skin with rain, and yet cannot persuade them to go out of the rain and to take their houses—knowing well that if they should go out to them, they should nothing prevail nor win ought by it, but with them be wet also in the rain—they do keep themselves within their houses, being content that they be safe themselves, seeing they cannot remedy the folly of the people.[41] Howbeit, doubtless, Master More (to speak truly as my mind

---

*A malleable ruler made of lead (used by the ancient Greeks).
†Securely.

giveth me), where possessions be private, where money beareth all the stroke,* it is hard and almost impossible that there the weal public may justly be governed and prosperously flourish. Unless you think thus: that justice is there executed where all things come into the hands of evil men; or that prosperity there flourisheth where all is divided among a few, which few nevertheless do not lead their lives very wealthily,† and the residue live miserably, wretchedly, and beggarly.

"Wherefore, when I consider with myself and weigh in my mind the wise and godly ordinances of the Utopians, among whom with very few laws all things be so well and wealthily ordered that virtue is had in price and estimation, and yet, all things being there common, every man hath abundance of everything. Again, on the other part, when I compare with them so many nations ever making new laws, yet none of them all well and sufficiently furnished with laws, where every man calleth that he hath gotten his own proper and private goods, where so many new laws daily made be not sufficient for every man to enjoy, defend, and know from another man's that which he calleth his own (which thing the infinite controversies in the law, daily rising, never to be ended, plainly declare to be true)—these things, I say, when I consider with myself, I hold well with Plato and do nothing marvel that he would make no laws for them that refused those laws whereby all men should have and enjoy equal portions of wealths and commodities. For the wise man did easily foresee this to be the one and only way to the wealth of a commonalty, if equality of all things should be brought in and established, which I think is not possible to be observed where every man's goods be proper and peculiar to himself. For where every man under certain titles and pretences draweth and plucketh to himself as much as he can, so that a few divide among themselves all the whole riches, be there never so much abundance and

Plato willed all things in a common-wealth to be common.

---

*Has all the influence.
†In a comfortable and/or healthy manner.

store, there to the residue is left lack and poverty. And for the most part it chanceth that this latter sort is more worthy to enjoy that state of wealth than the other be, because the rich men be covetous, crafty, and unprofitable.* On the other part, the poor be lowly, simple, and by their daily labor more profitable to the commonwealth than to themselves.

"Thus I do fully persuade myself that no equal and just distribution of things can be made, nor that perfect wealth shall ever be among men, unless this propriety† be exiled and banished. But so long as it shall continue, so long shall remain among the most and best part of men the heavy and inevitable burden of poverty and wretchedness, which, as I grant that it may be somewhat eased, so I utterly deny that it can wholly be taken away. For if there were a statute made that no man should possess above a certain measure of ground, and that no man should have in his stock above a prescript and appointed sum of money; if it were by certain laws decreed that neither the king should be of too great power, neither the people too haut‡ and wealthy, and that offices should not be obtained by inordinate suit§ or by bribes and gifts—that they should neither be bought nor sold, nor that it should be needful for the officers to be at any cost or charge in their offices (for so occasion is given to them by fraud and ravin‖ to gather up their money again, and by reason of gifts and bribes the offices be given to rich men, which should rather have been executed of wise men)—by such laws, I say, like as sick bodies that be desperate and past cure be wont with continual good cherishing to be kept and botched# up for a time, so these evils also might be lightened and mitigated. But that they may be perfectly cured and brought to a good and upright state, it is not to be hoped for whiles every man is master of his own to himself.

---

*Not beneficial (to the community).
†Private ownership of things (Latin: *proprietas*).
‡High, lofty.
§Excessive petitioning.
‖Robbery.
#Patched.

Yea, and whiles you go about to do your cure of one part, you shall make bigger the sore of another part, so the help of one causeth another's harm, forasmuch as nothing can be given to any one unless it be taken from another."

"But I am of a contrary opinion," quoth I, "for methinketh that men shall never there live wealthily where all things be common.[42] For how can there be abundance of goods, or of anything, where every man withdraweth his hand from labor? Whom the regard of his own gains driveth not to work, but the hope that he hath in other men's travails maketh him slothful. Then, when they be pricked with poverty, and yet no man can by any law or right defend that for his own which he hath gotten with the labor of his own hands, shall not there of necessity be continual sedition and bloodshed? Especially the authority and reverence of magistrates being taken away, which, what place it may have with such men among whom is no difference, I cannot devise."*

"I marvel not," quoth he, "that you be of this opinion. For you conceive in your mind either none at all, or else a very false image and similitude of this thing. But if you had been with me in Utopia and had presently seen their fashions and laws, as I did, which lived there five years and more, and would never have come thence but only to make that new land known here, then doubtless you would grant that you never saw people well ordered, but only there."

"Surely," quoth Master Peter, "it shall be hard for you to make me believe that there is better order in that new land than is here in these countries that we know. For good wits be as well here as there. And I think our commonwealth be ancienter than theirs, wherein long use and experience hath found out many things commodious for man's life. Besides that, many things here among us have been found by chance, which no wit could ever have devised."

"As touching the ancientness," quoth he, "of commonwealths, then you might better judge if you had read the histo-

---

*Guess.

ries and chronicles of that land, which, if we may believe, cities were there before men were here. Now what thing soever hitherto by wit hath been devised or found by chance, that might be as well there as here. But I think, verily, though it were so that we did pass them in wit, yet in study, in travail, and in laborsome endeavor they far pass us. For (as their chronicles testify) before our arrival there they never heard anything of us, whom they call the ultra-equinoctials, saving that once about 1,200 years ago a certain ship was lost by the Isle of Utopia, which was driven thither by tempest. Certain Romans and Egyptians were cast on land, which after that never went thence. Mark now what profit they took of this one occasion through diligence and earnest travail. There was no craft nor science within the empire of Rome, whereof any profit could rise, but they either learned it of these strangers, or else of them taking occasion to search for it, found it out. So great profit was it to them that ever any went thither from hence. But if any like chance before this hath brought any man from thence hither, that is as quite out of remembrance, as this also perchance in time to come shall be forgotten, that ever I was there. And like as they quickly, almost at the first meeting, made their own whatsoever is among us wealthily devised, so I suppose it would be long before we would receive anything that among them is better instituted than among us. And this, I suppose, is the chief cause why their commonwealths be wiselier governed and do flourish in more wealth than ours, though we neither in wit nor riches be their inferiors."

"Therefore, gentle Master Raphael," quoth I, "I pray you and beseech you describe unto us the island. And study not to be short, but declare largely in order their grounds, their rivers, their cities, their people, their manners, their ordinances, their laws, and to be short, all things that you shall think us desirous to know. And you shall think us desirous to know whatsoever we know not yet."

"There is nothing," quoth he, "that I will do gladlier, for all these things I have fresh in mind. But the matter requireth leisure."

"Let us go in, therefore," quoth I, "to dinner; afterward we will bestow the time at our pleasure."

"Content," quoth he, "be it."

So we went in and dined. When dinner was done, we came into the same place again and sat us down upon the same bench, commanding our servants that no man should trouble us. Then I and Master Peter Giles desired Master Raphael to perform his promise. He, therefore, seeing us desirous and willing to harken to him, when he had sit still and paused a little while, musing and bethinking himself, thus he began to speak.

THE END OF THE FIRST BOOK.

THE SECOND BOOK OF UTOPIA.

THE SECOND BOOK
OF THE

Communication of
Raphael Hythloday concerning the best
state of a commonwealth,
containing the description of Utopia, with a large
declaration of the politic government and of
all the good laws and orders of the same island.

THE ISLAND OF UTOPIA containeth in breadth in the middle *The site and* part of it (for there it is broadest) two hundred miles, which *fashion of the* breadth continueth through the most part of the land, saving *new island* that by little and little it cometh in and waxeth narrower to- *Utopia.* wards both the ends, which, fetching about a circuit or com- pass of five hundred miles, do fashion the whole island like to the new moon. Between these two corners the sea runneth in, dividing them asunder by the distance of eleven miles or thereabouts, and there surmounteth into* a large and wide sea, which, by reason that the land on every side compasseth it about and sheltereth it from the winds, is not rough, nor mounteth not with great waves, but almost floweth quietly, not much unlike a great standing pool, and maketh well-nigh all the space within the belly† of the land in manner of a haven, and to the great commodity of the inhabitants re- ceiveth in ships towards every part of the land. The forefronts or frontiers of the two corners, what with fords and shelves‡ and what with rocks be very jeopardous and dangerous. In the middle distance between them both standeth up above the water a great rock, which, therefore, is nothing perilous

---

*Spreads out over.
†That is, center (the Latin *alvus* means "belly" or "womb").
‡Shallows and reefs.

61

*A place
naturally
fenced
needeth but
one garrison.*

because it is in sight. Upon the top of this rock is a fair and a strong tower builded, which they hold with a garrison of men. Other rocks there be lying hid under the water, which, therefore, be dangerous. The channels be known only to themselves, and, therefore, it seldom chanceth that any stranger, unless he be guided by an Utopian, can come into this haven, insomuch that they themselves could scarcely enter without jeopardy, but that their way is directed and ruled by certain landmarks standing on the shore. By turning, translating,* and removing these marks into other places, they may destroy their enemies' navies, be they never so many. The outside or utter† circuit of the land is also full of havens, but the landing is so surely fenced, what by nature and what by workmanship of man's hand, that a few defenders may drive back many armies.

*A politic
device in
changing of
landmarks.*

*The island of
Utopia so
named of
King Utopus.*

Howbeit, as they say and as the fashion of the place itself doth partly show, it was not ever compassed about with the sea. But King Utopus,[1] whose name as conqueror the island beareth (for before his time it was called Abraxa[2])—which also brought the rude and wild people to that excellent perfection in all good fashions, humanity, and civil gentleness, wherein they now go beyond all the people of the world—even at his first arriving and entering upon the land, forthwith obtaining the victory, caused fifteen miles space of uplandish‡ ground, where the sea had no passage, to be cut and digged up, and so brought the sea round about the land. He set to this work not only the inhabitants of the island (because they should not think it done in contumely§ and despite) but also all his own soldiers. Thus the work, being divided into so great a number of workmen, was with exceeding marvelous speed dispatched, insomuch that the borderers, which at the first began to mock and to jest at this vain

*Many hands
make light
work.*

---

*Transporting.
†Farthest.
‡Inland, hilly.
§Scorn.

enterprise, then turned their derision to marvel at the success, and to fear.

There is in the island fifty-four large and fair cities, or shire towns, agreeing all together in one tongue, in like manners, institutions, and laws.[3] They be all set and situate alike, and in all points fashioned alike, as far forth as the place or plot suffereth. Of these cities they that be nighest together be twenty-four miles asunder. Again, there is none of them distant from the next above one day's journey afoot.

There come yearly to Amaurote out of every city three old men wise and well-experienced, there to entreat and debate of the common matters of the land. For this city (because it standeth just in the midst of the island and is, therefore, most meet for the ambassadors of all parts of the realm) is taken for the chief and head city. The precincts and bounds of the shires be so commodiously appointed out and set forth for the cities that none of them all hath of any side less than twenty miles of ground, and of some side also much more, as of that part where the cities be of farther distance asunder. None of the cities desire to enlarge the bounds and limits of their shire, for they count themselves rather the good husbands than the owners of their lands.

They have in the country in all parts of the shire houses or farms builded, well appointed, and furnished with all sorts of instruments and tools belonging to husbandry.* These houses be inhabited of the citizens, which come thither to dwell by course.† No household or farm in the country hath fewer than forty persons, men and women, besides two bondmen, which be all under the rule and order of the good man and the good wife of the house, being both very sage, discreet, and ancient persons. And every thirty farms or families have one head ruler, which is called a phylarch, being as it were a head bailiff.[4] Out of every one of these families or farms cometh every year into the city twenty persons which have continued two years before in the country. In their place so many fresh

Margin notes:
Cities in Utopia.

Similitude causeth concord.

A mean distance between city and city.

The distribution of lands.

But this nowadays is the ground of all mischief.

Husbandry and tillage chiefly and principally regarded and advanced.

---

*Farming.
†In turn.

be sent thither out of the city, who, of them that have been there a year already and be therefore expert and cunning* in husbandry, shall be instructed and taught. And they the next year shall teach other. This order is used for fear that either scarceness of victuals or some other like incommodity should chance, through lack of knowledge, if they should be altogether new and fresh and unexpert in husbandry. This manner and fashion of yearly changing and renewing the occupiers of husbandry, though it be solemn and customably used to the intent that no man shall be constrained against his will to continue long in that hard and sharp kind of life, yet many of them have such a pleasure and delight in husbandry that they obtain a longer space of years.

The duties of men of husbandry.

These husbandmen plow and till the ground, and breed up cattle, and provide and make ready wood, which they carry to the city either by land or by water, as they may most conveniently. They bring up a great multitude of pullen,† and that by a marvelous policy,‡ for the hens do not sit upon the eggs, but by keeping them in a certain equal heat, they bring life into them and hatch them. The chickens, as soon as they

A strange fashion of hatching and bringing up pullen.

be come out of the shell, follow men and women instead of the hens. They bring up very few horses, nor none but very fierce§ ones and that for none other use or purpose but only to exercise their youth in riding and feats of arms. For oxen be put to all the labor of plowing and drawing, which they grant

The use of horses.

to be not so good as horses at a sudden brunt and (as we say) at a dead lift,‖ but yet they hold opinion that oxen will abide and suffer much more labor, pain, and hardness than horses

The use of oxen.

will. And they think that oxen be not in danger and subject unto so many diseases, and that they be kept and maintained with much less cost and charge, and finally that they be good for meat, when they be past labor.

---

*Knowledgeable.
†Poultry.
‡System.
§High-spirited.
‖Quick spurt . . . pulling dead weight.

They sow corn* only for bread. For their drink is either *Bread and* wine made of grapes, or else of apples or pears, or else it is *drink.* clear water, and many times mead† made of honey or licorice sod‡ in water, for thereof they have great store. And though they know certainly (for they know it perfectly indeed) how much victuals the city with the whole country or shire round about it doth spend, yet they sow much more corn and breed *A great* up much more cattle than serveth for their own use, parting *discretion in* the overplus among their borderers. Whatsoever necessary *sowing of* things be lacking in the country, all such stuff they fetch out *corn.* of the city, where without any exchange they easily obtain it of the magistrates of the city, for every month many of them go into the city on the holy day. When their harvest day draweth near and is at hand, then the phylarchs, which be the head officers and bailiffs of husbandry, send word to the magistrates *Mutual help* of the city what number of harvest men is needful to be sent *quickly* to them out of the city. The which company of harvest men, *dispatcheth.* being ready at the day appointed, almost in one fair day dispatcheth all the harvest work.

Of the Cities and Namely of Amaurote.

As for their cities, whoso knoweth one of them, knoweth them all: they be all so like one to another as far forth as the nature of the place permitteth. I will describe, therefore, to you one or other of them, for it skilleth not§ greatly which, but which rather than Amaurote? Of them all this is the worthiest and of most dignity, for the residue knowledge‖ it for the head city, because there is the council house. Nor to me any of them all is better beloved, as wherein I lived five whole years together.[5]

The city of Amaurote standeth upon the side of a low hill in fashion almost four-square. For the breadth of it beginneth a

---

*Any cereal grain.
†A fermented drink (typically made of honey).
‡Boiled.
§It does not matter.
‖Acknowledge.

The description of Amaurote, the chief city of Utopia.

The description of the river Anyder.

The very like in England in the river Thames.

Herein also doth London agree with Amaurote.

The use of fresh water.

little beneath the top of the hill and still continueth by the space of two miles, until it come to the river of Anyder.* The length of it, which lieth by the river's side, is somewhat more. The river of Anyder riseth four and twenty miles above Amaurote out of a little spring, but being increased by other small rivers and brooks that run into it, and among other two somewhat big ones, before the city it is half a mile broad, and farther broader, and forty miles beyond the city it falleth into the ocean sea. By all that space that lieth between the sea and the city, and certain miles also above the city, the water ebbeth and floweth six hours together with a swift tide. When the sea floweth in, for the length of thirty miles it filleth all the Anyder with salt water and driveth back the fresh water of the river, and somewhat farther it changeth the sweetness of the fresh water with saltness. But a little beyond that, the river waxeth sweet and runneth forby† the city fresh and pleasant, and when the sea ebbeth and goeth back again, the fresh water followeth it almost even to the very fall into the sea.

There goeth a bridge over the river made not of piles or of timber, but of stonework with gorgeous and substantial arches, at that part of the city that is farthest from the sea, to the intent that ships may pass along forby all the side of the city without let.‡ They have also another river, which indeed is not very great, but it runneth gently and pleasantly, for it riseth even out of the same hill that the city standeth upon and runneth down a slope through the midst of the city into Anyder.[6] And because it riseth a little without the city, the Amaurotians have enclosed the head spring of it with strong fences and bulwarks and so have joined it to the city. This is done to the intent that the water should not be stopped nor turned away or poisoned if their enemies should chance to come upon them. From thence the water is derived and conveyed down in canals of brick divers ways into the lower parts of the city. Where that cannot be done, by reason that the

---

*Waterless (from Greek).
†Alongside.
‡Hindrance.

place will not suffer it, there they gather the rain water in great cisterns, which doth them as good service.

The city is compassed about with a high and thick stone wall full of turrets and bulwarks. A dry ditch, but deep and broad and overgrown with bushes, briers, and thorns, goeth about three sides or quarters of the city. To the fourth side the river itself serveth for a ditch. The streets be appointed and set forth very commodious and handsome, both for carriage and also against the winds. The houses be of fair and gorgeous building, and on the street side they stand joined together in a long row through the whole street without any partition or separation. The streets be twenty feet broad. On the back side of the houses, through the whole length of the street, lie large gardens enclosed round about with the back part of the streets. Every house hath two doors, one into the street and a postern door on the back side into the garden. These doors be made with two leaves, never locked nor bolted, so easy to be opened that they will follow the least drawing of a finger and shut again alone. Whoso will, may go in, for there is nothing within the houses that is private, or any man's own. And every tenth year they change their houses by lot.

The defense of town walls.

Streets. Buildings and houses.

To every dwelling house a garden plot adjoining.

This gear smelleth of Plato, his community.[7]

They set great store by their gardens. In them they have vineyards, all manner of fruit, herbs, and flowers, so pleasant, so well furnished, and so finely kept, that I never saw thing more fruitful nor better trimmed in any place. Their study and diligence herein cometh not only of pleasure, but also of a certain strife and contention that is between street and street concerning the trimming, husbanding, and furnishing of their gardens, every man for his own part. And, verily, you shall not lightly find in all the city anything that is more commodious, either for the profit of the citizens or for pleasure. And, therefore, it may seem that the first founder of the city minded nothing so much as these gardens. For they say that King Utopus himself even at the first beginning appointed and drew forth the platform* of the city into this fashion and

The commodity of gardens is commended also of Vergil.[8]

---

*Ground plan.

figure that it hath now, but the gallant garnishing and the beautiful setting forth of it, whereunto he saw that one man's age would not suffice, that he left to his posterity. For their chronicles, which they keep written with all diligent circumspection, containing the history of 1,760 years, even from the first conquest of the island, record and witness that the houses in the beginning were very low and like homely cottages or poor shepherd houses, made at all adventures* of every rude piece of timber that came first to hand, with mud walls and ridged roofs thatched over with straw. But now the houses be curiously† built after a gorgeous and gallant sort, with three stories one over another. The outsides of the walls be made either of hard flint or of plaster, or else of brick, and the inner sides be well strengthened with timber work. The roofs be plain and flat, covered with a certain kind of plaster that is of no cost, and yet so tempered that no fire can hurt or perish‡ it, and withstandeth the violence of the weather better

Glazed or canvassed windows.

than any lead. They keep the wind out of their windows with glass, for it is there much used, and some here also with fine linen cloth dipped in oil or amber, and that for two commodities, for by this means more light cometh in, and the wind is better kept out.

Of the Magistrates.

A Tranibore in the Utopians' tongue signifieth a head or chief peer. A marvelous strange fashion in choosing magistrates.

EVERY thirty families or farms choose them yearly an officer, which in their old language is called the syphogrant, and by a newer name, the phylarch. Every ten syphogrants with all their thirty families be under an officer which was called the tranibore, now the chief phylarch.[9] Moreover, as concerning the election of the prince,§ all the syphogrants, which be in number two hundred, first be sworn to choose him whom they think most meet and expedient. Then by a secret election they name prince one of those four whom the people before

---

*Haphazardly.
†Skillfully, artfully.
‡Destroy.
§Leader (Latin: *princeps*).

named unto them, for out of the four quarters of the city there be four chosen, out of every quarter one, to stand for the election, which be put up to the council. The prince's office continueth all his lifetime, unless he be deposed or put down for suspicion of tyranny. They choose the tranibores yearly, but lightly they change them not. All the other officers be but for one year. The tranibores every third day, and sometimes if need be oftener, come into the council house with the prince. Their counsel is concerning the commonwealth. If there be any controversies among the commoners, which be very few, they dispatch and end them by and by.* They take every two syphogrants to them in council, and every day a new couple.[10] And it is provided that nothing touching the commonwealth shall be confirmed and ratified, unless it have been reasoned of and debated three days in the council before it be decreed. It is death to have any consultation for the commonwealth out of the council or the place of the common election. This statute, they say, was made to the intent that the prince and tranibores might not easily conspire together to oppress the people by tyranny and to change the state of the weal public. Therefore, matters of great weight and importance be brought to the election house of the syphogrants, which open the matter to their families. And afterward, when they have consulted among themselves, they show their device† to the council. Sometimes the matter is brought before the council of the whole island. Furthermore, this custom also the council useth: to dispute or reason of no matter the same day that it is first proposed or put forth, but to defer it to the next sitting of the council. Because that no man, when he hath rashly there spoken that cometh to his tongue's end, shall then afterward rather study for reasons wherewith to defend and maintain his first foolish sentence‡ than for the commodity of the commonwealth, as one rather willing the harm or hindrance of the weal public than any loss or diminution of his own

Marginal notes: *Tyranny in a well-ordered weal public utterly to be abhorred.* / *Suits and controversies between party and party forthwith to be ended which nowadays of a set purpose be unreasonably delayed.* / *Against hasty or rash decrees or statutes.* / *A custom worthy to be used these days in our councils and parliaments.*

*Right away.
†What they have devised.
‡Opinion, idea.

existimation,* and as one that would be ashamed (which is a
very foolish shame) to be counted anything at the first over-
seen† in the matter, who at the first ought to have spoken
rather wisely than hastily or rashly.

Of Sciences,‡ Crafts, and Occupations.

*Husbandry or
tillage
practiced of
all estates,
which
nowadays is
reject unto a
few of the
basest sort.*

HUSBANDRY is a science common to them all in general, both
men and women, wherein they be all expert and cunning. In
this they be all instructed even from their youth, partly in their
schools with traditions and precepts, and partly in the country nigh the city, brought up as it were in playing, not only beholding the use of it, but by occasion of exercising their
bodies practicing it also.

*Sciences or
occupations
should be
learned for
necessity's
sake, and not
for the
maintenance
of riotous
excess and
wanton plea-
sure.*

*Similitude in
apparel.*

*No citizen
without a
science.*

Besides husbandry, which (as I said) is common to them
all, every one of them learneth one or other several and particular science as his own proper craft. That is most commonly either clothworking in wool or flax, or masonry, or
the smith's craft, or the carpenter's science, for there is none
other occupation that any number to speak of doth use
there. For their garments, which throughout all the island
be of one fashion (saving that there is a difference between the
man's garment and the woman's, between the married and the
unmarried), and this one continueth for evermore unchanged,
seemly and comely to the eye, no let to the moving and wield-
ing of the body, also fit both for winter and summer—as for
these garments (I say) every family maketh their own. But
of the other foresaid crafts every man learneth one, and not
only the men, but also the women. But the women, as the
weaker sort, be put to the easier crafts, as to work wool and
flax. The more laborsome sciences be committed to the men.
For the most part every man is brought up in his father's
craft, for most commonly they be naturally thereto bent and
inclined. But if a man's mind stand to any other, he is by
adoption put into a family of that occupation which he doth

*Estimation.
†Mistaken.
‡Arts, branches of knowledge.

most fantasy,* whom not only his father but also the magistrates do diligently look to, that he be put to a discreet and an
honest householder. Yea, and if any person, when he hath
learned one craft, be desirous to learn also another, he is likewise suffered† and permitted. When he hath learned both, he
occupieth‡ whether he will, unless the city have more need of
the one than of the other.

*To what
occupation
everyone is
naturally
inclined, that
let him learn.*

The chief and almost the only office of the syphogrants is
to see and take heed that no man sit idle, but that every one
apply his own craft with earnest diligence. And yet for all
that, not to be wearied from early in the morning to late in
the evening with continual work like laboring and toiling
beasts. For this is worse than the miserable and wretched
condition of bondmen, which nevertheless is almost everywhere the life of workmen and artificers, saving in Utopia.
For they, dividing the day and the night into twenty-four
just§ hours, appoint and assign only six of these hours to
work: three [before noon], upon the which they go straight
to dinner; and after dinner, when they have rested two hours,
then they work three hours, and upon that they go to supper.
About eight of the clock in the evening (counting one of the
clock at the first hour after noon) they go to bed; eight hours
they give to sleep. All the void‖ time that is between the hours
of work, sleep, and meat# that they be suffered to bestow,
every man as he liketh best himself, not to the intent that
they should misspend this time in riot or slothfulness, but,
being then licensed from the labor of their own occupations,
to bestow the time well and thriftly upon some other science,
as shall please them. For it is a solemn custom there to have
lectures daily early in the morning, where to be present they
only be constrained that be namely chosen and appointed

*Idle persons to
be driven out
of the weal
public.*

*A moderation
in the labor
and toll of
artificers.*

*The study of
good
literature.*

---

*Fancy, take a liking to.
†Allowed.
‡Practices his occupation.
§Equal.
‖Unfilled.
#Food.

to* learning. Howbeit, a great multitude of every sort of people, both men and women, go to hear lectures, some one and some another as every man's nature is inclined. Yet, this notwithstanding, if any man had rather bestow this time upon his own occupation (as it chanceth in many whose minds rise not in the contemplation of any science liberal†), he is not letted nor prohibited, but is also praised and commended as profitable to the commonwealth.

Playing after supper.

After supper they bestow one hour in play: in summer in their gardens, in winter in their common halls where they dine and sup. There they exercise themselves in music, or else in honest and wholesome communication. Diceplay and such other foolish and pernicious games they know not, but they use two games not much unlike the chess. The one is the battle of numbers, wherein one number stealeth away another. The other is wherein vices fight with virtues, as it were in battle array or a set field, in the which game is very properly showed both the strife and discord that vices have among themselves, and again their unity and concord against virtues; and also what vices be repugnant to what virtues; with what power and strength they assail them openly; by what wiles and subtlety they assault them secretly; with what help and aid the virtues resist and overcome the puissance‡ of the vices; by what craft they frustrate their purposes; and finally by what sleight or means the one getteth the victory.

But nowadays dice-play is the pastime of princes.

Plays or games also profitable.

But here lest you be deceived, one thing you must look more narrowly upon. For seeing they bestow but six hours in work, perchance you may think that the lack of some necessary things hereof may ensue. But this is nothing so. For that small time is not only enough but also too much for the store and abundance of all things that be requisite either for the necessity or commodity of life. The which thing you also shall perceive, if you weigh and consider with yourselves how great

---

*Ordained for.
†One of the liberal arts.
‡Power.

a part of the people in other countries liveth idle. First, almost all women, which be the half of the whole number, or, else if the women be somewhere occupied, there most commonly in their stead the men be idle.[11] Besides this, how great and how idle a company is there of priests and religious men, as they call them? Put thereto all rich men, especially all landed men, which commonly be called gentlemen and noblemen. Take into this number also their servants: I mean all that flock of stout, bragging rush-bucklers.* Join to them also sturdy and valiant beggars, cloaking their idle life under the color of some disease or sickness, and truly you shall find them much fewer than you thought, by whose labor all these things are wrought that in men's affairs are now daily used and frequented.

Now consider with yourself, of these few that do work, how few be occupied in necessary works. For where money beareth all the swing,† there many vain and superfluous occupations must needs be used to serve only for riotous superfluity and unhonest pleasure. For the same multitude that now is occupied in work, if they were divided into so few occupations as the necessary use of nature requireth, in so great plenty of things as then of necessity would ensue, doubtless the prices would be too little for the artificers to maintain their livings. But if all these that be now busied about unprofitable occupations, with all the whole flock of them that live idly and slothfully, which consume and waste every one of them more of these things that come by other men's labor than two of the workmen themselves do—if all these (I say) were set to profitable occupations, you easily perceive how little time would be enough, yea, and too much to store us with all things that may be requisite either for necessity or for commodity, yea, or for pleasure, so that the same pleasure be true and natural.

And this in Utopia the thing itself maketh manifest and plain, for there in all the city, with the whole country or shire adjoining to it, scarcely five hundred persons of all the whole

The kinds and sorts of idle people: women.

Priests and religious men; rich men and landed men.

Servingmen.

Sturdy and valiant beggars.

Wonderful wittily spoken.

---

*Swaggering bullies.
†Sway.

number of men and women that be neither too old nor too weak to work, be licensed and discharged from labor. Among

Not as much as the magistrates live idly.

them be the syphogrants, who, though they be by the laws exempt and privileged from labor, yet they exempt not themselves, to the intent that they may the rather by their example provoke others to work. The same vacation from labor do they also enjoy to whom the people, persuaded by the commendation of the priests and secret election of the syphogrants, have given a perpetual license from labor to learning. But if any one of them prove not according to the expectation and hope of him conceived, he is forthwith plucked back to the company of artificers. And, contrariwise, often it chanceth that a handicraftsman doth so earnestly bestow his vacant and spare hours in learning, and through diligence so profiteth therein that he is taken from his handy

Only learned men called to offices.

occupation and promoted to the company of the learned. Out of this order of the learned be chosen ambassadors, priests, tranibores, and finally the prince himself, whom they in their old tongue call Barzanes, and by a newer name, Adamus.* The residue of the people being neither idle nor yet occupied about unprofitable exercises, it may be easily judged in how few hours how much good work by them may be done and dispatched towards those things that I have spoken of.

This commodity they have also above other, that in the

How to avoid excessive cost in building.

most part of necessary occupations they need not so much work as other nations do. For first of all the building or repairing of houses asketh everywhere so many men's continual labor, because that the unthrifty heir suffereth the houses that his father builded in continuance of time to fall in decay. So that which he might have upholden with little cost, his successor is constrained to build it again anew to his great charge. Yea, many times also the house that stood one man in† much money, another is of so nice and so delicate a mind that he

---

*"Son of Zeus" . . . "Peopleless."
†Cost one man.

setteth nothing by* it. And it being neglected, and therefore shortly falling into ruin, he buildeth up another in another place with no less cost and charge. But among the Utopians, where all things be set in good order and the commonwealth in a good stay,† it very seldom chanceth that they choose a new plot to build an house upon. And they do not only find speedy and quick remedies for present faults, but also prevent them that be like to fall. And by this means their houses continue and last very long with little labor and small reparations, insomuch that this kind of workmen sometimes have almost nothing to do, but that they be commanded to hew timber at home and to square and trim up stones, to the intent that, if any work chance, it may the speedilier rise.

Now, sir, in their apparel, mark, I pray you, how few workmen they need. First of all, whilst they be at work, they be covered homely‡ with leather or skins that will last seven years. When they go forth abroad, they cast upon them a cloak, which hideth the other homely apparel. These cloaks throughout the whole island be all of one color, and that is the natural color of the wool. They, therefore, do not only spend much less woolen cloth than is spent in other countries, but also the same standeth them in much less cost. But linen cloth is made with less labor and is, therefore, had more in use. But in linen cloth only whiteness, in woolen only cleanliness is regarded. As for the smallness or fineness of the thread, that is nothing passed§ for. And this is the cause wherefore in other places four or five cloth gowns of divers colors and as many silk coats are not enough for one man. Yea, and if he be of the delicate and nice sort, ten be too few, whereas there one garment will serve a man most commonly two years. For why should he desire more? Seeing if he had them, he should not be the better hapt,‖ or covered from cold, neither in his apparel any whit the comelier.

How to lessen the charge in apparel.

---

*Thinks nothing of.
†Support.
‡Plainly.
§Cared.
‖Wrapped up.

Wherefore, seeing they be all exercised in profitable occupations and that few artificers in the same crafts be sufficient, this is the cause that, plenty of all things being among them, they do sometimes bring forth an innumerable company of people to amend the highways if any be broken. Many times also, when they have no such work to be occupied about, an open proclamation is made that they shall bestow fewer hours in work. For the magistrates do not exercise their citizens against their wills in unneedful labors. For why in the institution of that weal public this end is only and chiefly pretended* and minded, that what time may possibly be spared from the necessary occupations and affairs of the commonwealth, all that the citizens should withdraw from the bodily service to the free liberty of the mind and garnishing of the same, for herein they suppose the felicity of this life to consist.

Of Their Living and Mutual Conversation† Together.

But now will I declare how the citizens use themselves one towards another; what familiar occupying and entertainment‡ there is among the people; and what fashion they use in the distribution of every thing.

First, the city consisteth of families; the families most commonly be made of kindreds. For the women, when they be married at a lawful age, they go into their husbands' houses. But the male children, with all the whole male offspring, continue still in their own family and be governed of the eldest and ancientest father, unless he dote for age, for then the next to him in age is placed in his room.§

The number of citizens.

But to the intent the prescript‖ number of the citizens should neither decrease nor above measure increase, it is ordained that no family (which in every city be six thousand in the whole, besides them of the country) shall at once have

---

*Intended.
†Social intercourse.
‡Social relations.
§Office, position.
‖Prescribed.

fewer children of the age of fourteen years or thereabout than ten or more than sixteen, for of children under this age no number can be prescribed or appointed. This measure or number is easily observed and kept by putting them that in fuller families be above the number into families of smaller increase. But if chance be that in the whole city the store increase above the just number, therewith they fill up the lack of other cities. But if so be that the multitude throughout the whole island pass and exceed the due number, then they choose out of every city certain citizens and build up a town under their own laws in the next land where the inhabitants have much waste* and unoccupied ground, receiving also of the same country people to them, if they will join and dwell with them. They thus joining and dwelling together do easily agree in one fashion of living, and that to the great wealth of both the peoples. For they so bring the matter about by their laws that the ground, which before was neither good nor profitable for the one nor for the other, is now sufficient and fruitful enough for them both. But if the inhabitants of that land will not dwell with them to be ordered by their laws, then they drive them out of those bounds which they have limited and appointed out for themselves. And if they resist and rebel, then they make war against them, for they count this the most just cause of war, when any people holdeth a piece of ground void and vacant to no good nor profitable use, keeping others from the use and possession of it, which notwithstanding by the law of nature ought thereof to be nourished and relieved. If any chance do so much diminish the number of any of their cities that it cannot be filled up again without the diminishing of the just number of the other cities (which they say chanced but twice since the beginning of the land through a great pestilent plague), then they fulfill and make up the number with citizens fetched out of their own foreign towns, for they had rather suffer their foreign towns to decay and perish than any city of their own island to be diminished.

---

*Uncultivated.

But now again to the conversation of the citizens among themselves. The eldest (as I said) ruleth the family. The wives be ministers* to their husbands, the children to their parents, and, to be short, the younger to their elders. Every city is divided into four equal parts or quarters. In the midst of every quarter there is a marketplace of all manner of things. Thither the works of every family be brought into certain houses, and every kind of thing is laid up several in barns or storehouses. From hence the father of every family or every householder fetcheth whatsoever he and his have need of and carrieth it away with him without money, without exchange,† without gage, pawn, or pledge. For why should any thing be denied unto him, seeing there is abundance of all things and that it is not to be feared lest any man will ask more than he needeth? For why should it be thought that that man would ask more than enough, which is sure never to lack? Certainly in all kinds of living creatures either fear of lack doth cause covetousness and ravin,‡ or in man only pride, which counteth it a glorious thing to pass and excel other in the superfluous and vain ostentation of things. The which kind of vice among the Utopians can have no place.

Next to the marketplaces that I spake of stand meat markets, whither be brought not only all sorts of herbs and the fruits of trees, with bread, but also fish and all manner of four-footed beasts and wild fowl that be man's meat. But first the filthiness and ordure thereof is clean washed away in the running river without the city, in places appointed meet for the same purpose. From thence the beasts be brought in, killed, and clean washed by the hands of their bondmen, for they permit not their free citizens to accustom themselves to the killing of beasts, through the use whereof they think clemency, the gentlest affection of our nature, by little and lit-

So might we well be discharged and eased of the idle company of servingmen.

The cause of covetousness and extortion.

Of the slaughter of beasts we have learned manslaughter.

---

*Attendants.
†Act of reciprocal giving.
‡Voracity, gluttony.

tle to decay and perish. Neither they suffer any thing that is *Filth and* filthy, loathsome, or uncleanly to be brought into the city, lest *ordure bring* the air, by the stench thereof infected and corrupt, should *the infection of pestilence* cause pestilent diseases. *into cities.*

Moreover, every street hath certain great large halls set in equal distance one from another, every one known by a several* name. In these halls dwell the syphogrants, and to every one of the same halls be appointed thirty families, on either side fifteen. The stewards of every hall at a certain hour come into the meat markets, where they receive meat according to the number of their halls.

But first and chiefly of all, respect is had to the sick, that be *Care,* cured† in the hospitals. For in the circuit of the city, a little *diligence, and* without the walls, they have four hospitals, so big, so wide, so *attendance* ample, and so large, that they may seem four little towns, *about the sick.* which were devised of that bigness partly to the intent the sick, be they never so many in number, should not lie too throng‡ or strait, and therefore uneasily and incommodiously, and partly that they which were taken and holden with contagious diseases, such as be wont by infection to creep from one to another, might be laid apart far from the company of the residue. These hospitals be so well appointed, and with all things necessary to health so furnished, and moreover, so diligent attendance through the continual presence of cunning physicians is given, that, though no man be sent thither against his will, yet notwithstanding there is no sick person in all the city that had not rather lie there than at home in his own house.

When the steward of the sick hath received such meats as the physicians have prescribed, then the best is equally divided among the halls according to the company of every one, saving that there is had a respect to the prince, the bishop,§ the tranibores, and to ambassadors and all strangers, if there

---

*Its own particular.
†Cared for.
‡Crowded together.
§Head of the priests (Latin: *pontifex*).

be any, which be very few and seldom. But they also, when they be there, have certain several houses appointed and prepared for them.

To these halls at the set hours of dinner and supper cometh all the whole syphogranty or ward, warned by the noise of a brazen trumpet, except such as be sick in the hospitals, or else in their own houses. Howbeit no man is prohibited or forbid, after the halls be served, to fetch home meat out of the market to his own house, for they know that no man will do it without a cause reasonable. For though no man be prohibited to dine at home, yet no man doth it willingly, because it is counted a point of small honesty.* And also it were a folly to take the pain to dress† a bad dinner at home, when they may be welcome to good and fine fare so nigh handy at the hall.

Every man is at his liberty so that nothing is done by compulsion.

In this hall all vile service, all slavery and drudgery, with all laborsome toil and base business, is done by bondmen. But the women of every family, by course, have the office and charge of cookery for seething‡ and dressing the meat and ordering all things thereto belonging. They sit at three tables or more, according to the number of their company. The men sit upon the bench next the wall and the women against them on the other side of the table, that if any sudden evil should chance to them, as many times happeneth to women, they may rise without trouble or disturbance of anybody and go thence to the nursery.

Women both dress and serve the meat.

Nurses.

The nurses sit several alone with their young sucklings in a certain parlor appointed and deputed to the same purpose, never without fire and clean water, nor yet without cradles, that when they will, they may lay down the young infants and at their pleasure take them out of their swathing§ clothes and hold them to the fire and refresh them with play. Every mother is nurse to her own child, unless either death or sickness

---

*Little honor or decency.
†Prepare.
‡Boiling, stewing.
§Swaddling.

be the let.* When that chanceth, the wives of the syphogrants quickly provide a nurse, and that is not hard to be done, for they that can do it proffer themselves to no service so gladly as to that, because that there this kind of pity is much praised, and the child that is nourished ever after taketh his nurse for his own natural mother. Also among the nurses sit all the children that be under the age of five years. All the other children of both kinds, as well boys as girls, that be under the age of marriage do either serve at the tables or else, if they be too young thereto, yet they stand by with marvelous† silence. That which is given to them from the table they eat, and other several dinnertime they have none.

Nothing sooner provoketh men to well doing than praise and commendation.

The education of young children.

The syphogrant and his wife sit in the midst of the high table, forasmuch as that is counted the honorablest place, and because from thence all the whole company is in their sight, for that table standeth overthwart the over‡ end of the hall. To them are joined two of the ancientest and eldest, for at every table they sit four at a mess. But if there be a church standing in that syphogranty or ward, then the priest and his wife sitteth with the syphogrant, as chief in the company. On both sides of them sit young men, and next unto them again old men. And thus throughout all the house equal of age be set together, and yet be mixed and matched with unequal ages. This, they say, was ordained to the intent that the sage gravity and reverence of the elders should keep the youngers from wanton license of words and behavior, forasmuch as nothing can be so secretly spoken or done at the table, but either they that sit on the one side or on the other must needs perceive it. The dishes be not set down in order from the first place, but all the old men (whose places be marked with some special token to be known) are first served of their meat, and then the residue equally. The old men divide their dainties§ as they think best to the younger on each side of them. Thus the

The young mixed with their elders.

Old men regarded and reverenced.

---

*Prevent her.
†Worthy of marvel.
‡Across the upper.
§Delicacies.

elders be not defrauded of their due honor, and nevertheless, equal commodity cometh to every one.

This nowadays is observed in our universities.

They begin every dinner and supper of reading something that pertaineth to good manners and virtue, but it is short, because no man shall be grieved therewith. Hereof the elders take occasion of honest communication, but neither sad nor unpleasant. Howbeit, they do not spend all the whole dinner-time themselves with long and tedious talks, but they gladly hear also the young men, yea, and purposely provoke them to talk, to the intent that they may have a proof of every man's wit and towardness or disposition to virtue, which commonly in the liberty of feasting doth show and utter itself. Their din-

Talk at the table.

This is repugnant to the opinion of our physicians.

ners be very short, but their suppers be somewhat longer, because that after dinner followeth labor, after supper sleep and natural rest, which they think to be of more strength and efficacy to wholesome and healthful digestion. No supper is passed without music, nor their banquets lack no conceits nor junkets.* They burn sweet gums and spices or perfumes and pleasant smells, and sprinkle about sweet ointments and waters; yea, they leave nothing undone that maketh for the cheering of the company, for they be much inclined to this opinion: to think no kind of pleasure forbidden whereof cometh no harm. Thus, therefore, and after this sort they live together in the city, but in the country they that dwell alone far from any neighbors do dine and sup at home in their own houses, for no family there lacketh any kind of victuals, as from whom cometh all that the citizens eat and live by.

Music at the table.

Pleasure without harm not discommendable.

Of Their Journeying or Traveling Abroad, with Divers Other Matters Cunningly Reasoned and Wittily Discussed.

BUT if any be desirous to visit either their friends dwelling in another city or to see the place itself, they easily obtain license of their syphogrants and tranibores, unless there be some profitable let.† No man goeth out alone, but a company is sent

---

*Desserts . . . trifles (such as apples) . . . sweet dishes.
†Useful reason against it.

forth together with their prince's letters, which do testify that they have license to go that journey and prescribeth also the day of their return. They have a wagon given them with a common bondman which driveth the oxen and taketh charge of them. But unless they have women in their company, they send home the wagon again, as an impediment and a let. And though they carry nothing forth with them, yet in all their journey they lack nothing, for wheresoever they come, they be at home. If they tarry in a place longer than one day, then there every one of them falleth to his own occupation and be very gently* entertained of the workmen and companies of the same crafts. If any man, of his own head and without leave, walk out of his precinct and bounds,† taken without the prince's letters, he is brought again for a fugitive or a runaway with great shame and rebuke, and is sharply punished. If he be taken in that fault again, he is punished with bondage.

If any be desirous to walk abroad into the fields or into the country that belongeth to the same city that he dwelleth in, obtaining the goodwill of his father and the consent of his wife, he is not prohibited. But into what part of the country soever he cometh he hath no meat given him until he have wrought out his forenoon's task, or dispatched so much work as there is wont to be wrought before supper. Observing this law and condition, he may go whither he will within the bounds of his own city, for he shall be no less profitable to the city than if he were within it.

Now you see how little liberty they have to loiter; how they can have no cloak or pretense‡ to idleness. There be neither wine taverns, nor alehouses, nor stews nor any occasion for vice or wickedness, no lurking corners, no places of wicked councils or unlawful assemblies. But they be in the present sight and under the eyes of every man, so that of necessity they must either apply§ their accustomed labors, or else recreate themselves with honest and laudable pastimes.

O holy commonwealth, and of Christians to be followed.

---

*In a gentlemanly manner.
†Home territory.
‡Covering excuse or pretext.
§Ply.

Equality is the cause that every man hath enough.

This fashion and trade of life being used among the people, it cannot be chosen but they must of necessity have store and plenty of all things. And seeing they be all thereof partners equally, therefore, can no man there be poor or needy. In the council of Amaurote, whither, as I said, every city sendeth three men apiece yearly, as soon as it is perfectly known of what things there is in every place plenty, and again what things be scant in any place, incontinent* the lack of the one is performed† and filled up with the abundance of the other. And this they do freely without any benefit,‡ taking nothing again of them to whom the things are given, but those cities that have given of their store to any other city that lacketh, requiring nothing again of the same city, do take such things as they lack of another city, to the which they gave nothing. So the whole island is as it were one family or household.

A commonwealth is nothing else but a great household.

But when they have made sufficient provision or store for themselves (which they think not done until they have provided for two years following, because of the uncertainty of the next year's proof§) then of those things whereof they have abundance they carry forth into other countries great plenty, as grain, honey, wool, flax, wood, madder,‖ purple dye, fells,# wax, tallow, leather, and living beasts. And the seventh part of all these things they give frankly and freely to the poor of that country. The residue they sell at a reasonable and mean** price. By this trade of traffic or merchandise they bring into their own country not only great plenty of gold and silver, but also all such things as they lack at home, which is almost nothing but iron. And by reason they have long used this trade, now they have more abundance of these things than any man will believe.

The traffic and merchandise of the Utopians.

---

*Straightway.
†Made up.
‡Compensation.
§Results—that is, harvest.
‖Reddish vegetable dye.
#Animal skins stripped of hair.
**Middling.

Now therefore, they care not whether they sell for ready money, or else upon trust to be paid at a day and to have the most part in debts. But in so doing they never follow the credence of private men, but the assurance or warrantise* of the whole city by instruments and writings made in that behalf accordingly. When the day of payment is come and expired, the city gathereth up the debt of the private debtors and putteth it into the common box, and so long hath the use and profit of it until the Utopians, their creditors, demand it. The most part of it they never ask, for that thing which is to them no profit, to take it from other, to whom it is profitable, they think it no right nor conscience. But if the case so stand that they must lend part of that money to another people, then they require their debt, or when they have war. For the which purpose only they keep at home all the treasure which they have, to be helped and succored by it either in extreme jeopardies or in sudden dangers, but especially and chiefly to hire therewith, and that for unreasonable great wages, strange soldiers.† For they had rather put strangers in jeopardy than their own countrymen, knowing that for money enough their enemies themselves many times may be bought or sold, or else through treason be set together by the ears among themselves. For this cause they keep an inestimable treasure, but yet not as a treasure, but so they have it and use it as in good faith I am ashamed to show, fearing that my words shall not be believed. And this I have more cause to fear, for that I know how difficultly and hardly I myself would have believed another man telling the same, if I had not presently seen it with mine own eyes. For it must needs be that how far a thing is dissonant and disagreeing from the guise and trade‡ of the hearers, so far shall it be out of their belief. Howbeit, a wise and indifferent§ esteemer of things will not greatly marvel perchance, seeing all their other laws and customs do so much differ

In all things and above all things to the continuity they have an eye.

By what policy money may be in less estimation.

It is better either with money or by policy to avoid war than with much loss of man's blood to fight.

A fine wit.

---

*Guarantee.
†Foreign soldiers—that is, mercenaries.
‡Course of life.
§Impartial.

from ours, if the use also of gold and silver among them be applied rather to their own fashions than to ours. I mean in that they occupy* not money themselves, but keep it for that chance, which as it may happen, so it may be that it shall never come to pass.

In the meantime gold and silver, whereof money is made, they do so use, as none of them doth more esteem it than the very nature of the thing deserveth. And then, who doth not plainly see how far it is under iron, as without the which men can no better live than without fire and water? Whereas to gold and silver nature hath given no use that we may not well lack, if that the folly of men had not set it in higher estimation for the rareness sake. But of the contrary part, nature, as a most tender and loving mother, hath placed the best and most necessary things open abroad, as the air, the water, and the earth itself, and hath removed and hid farthest from us vain and unprofitable things. Therefore if these metals among them should be fast† locked up in some tower, it might be suspected that the prince and the council (as the people is ever foolishly imagining) intended by some subtlety to deceive the commons and to take some profit of it to themselves. Furthermore, if they should make thereof plate and such other finely and cunningly wrought stuff, if at any time they should have occasion to break it and melt it again, therewith to pay their soldiers' wages, they see and perceive very well that men would be loath to part from those things that they once began to have pleasure and delight in.

To remedy all this they have found out a means, which, as it is agreeable to all their other laws and customs, so it is from ours, where gold is so much set by and so diligently kept, very far discrepant and repugnant,‡ and therefore uncredible—but only to them that be wise. For whereas they eat and drink in earthen and glass vessels, which indeed be curiously and properly made and yet be of very small value, of gold and

Gold worse than iron as touching the necessary use thereof.

O wonderful contumely of gold.

---

*Use.
†Securely.
‡Dissimilar and divergent.

silver they make commonly chamber pots and other vessels that serve for most vile uses, not only in their common halls but in every man's private house. Furthermore of the same metals they make great chains, fetters, and gyves, wherein they tie their bondmen. Finally, whosoever for any offense be infamed,* by their ears hang rings of gold, upon their fingers they wear rings of gold, and about their necks chains of gold, and in conclusion their heads be tied about with gold. Thus by all means possible they procure to have gold and silver among them in reproach and infamy. And these metals, which other nations do as grievously and sorrowfully forgo as in a manner their own lives, if they should altogether at once be taken from the Utopians, no man there would think that he had lost the worth of one farthing.

Gold, the reproachful badge of infamed persons.

They gather also pearls by the sea-side, and diamonds and carbuncles† upon certain rocks and yet they seek not for them, but by chance finding them, they cut and polish them, and therewith they deck their young infants. Which, like as in the first years of their childhood they make much and be fond and proud of such ornaments, so when they be a little more grown in years and discretion, perceiving that none but children do wear such toys and trifles, they lay them away even of their own shamefastness, without any bidding of their parents, even as our children, when they wax big, do cast away nuts, brooches, and puppets.[12]

Gems and precious stones, toys for young children to play withal.

Therefore, these laws and customs, which be so far different from all other nations, how divers fantasies also and minds they do cause, did I never so plainly perceive as in the ambassadors of the Anemolians.‡ These ambassadors came to Amaurote whiles I was there, and because they came to entreat of great and weighty matters, those three citizens apiece out of every city were come thither before them. But all the ambassadors of the next countries, which had been there before and knew the fashions and manners of the Utopians,

A very pleasant tale.

---

*Made infamous.
†Precious red stones.
‡Windy (or Boastful) Ones.

among whom they perceived no honor given to sumptuous apparel, silks to be contemned, gold also to be infamed and reproachful,* were wont to come thither in very homely and simple array. But the Anemolians, because they dwell far thence and had very little acquaintance with them, hearing that they were all apparelled alike, and that very rudely and homely, thinking them not to have the things which they did not wear, being therefore more proud than wise, determined in the gorgeousness of their apparel to represent very gods and with the bright shining and glistering of their gay clothing to dazzle the eyes of the silly† poor Utopians. So there came in three ambassadors with a hundred servants all appareled in changeable‡ colors, the most of them in silks; the ambassadors themselves (for at home in their own country they were noblemen) in cloth of gold, with great chains of gold, with gold hanging at their ears, with gold rings upon their fingers, with brooches and aglets§ of gold upon their caps which glistered full of pearls and precious stones—to be short, trimmed and adorned with all those things which among the Utopians were either the punishment of bondmen, or the reproach of infamed persons, or else trifles for young children to play withal.

Therefore, it would have done a man good at his heart to have seen how proudly they displayed their peacock's feathers, how much they made of their painted sheaths,‖ and how loftily they set forth and advanced themselves, when they compared their gallant apparel with the poor raiment of the Utopians, for all the people were swarmed forth into the streets. And, on the other side, it was no less pleasure to consider how much they were deceived and how far they missed of their purpose, being contrariwise taken than they thought they should have been. For to the eyes of all the Utopians,

---

*Deserving reproach.
†Simple.
‡Varying.
§Points at the tips of ribbons.
‖External finery.

except very few which had been in other countries for some reasonable cause, all that gorgeousness of apparel seemed shameful and reproachful, insomuch that they most reverently saluted the vilest and most abject of them for lords, passing over the ambassadors themselves without any honor, judging them by their wearing of gold chains to be bondmen. Yea, you should have seen children also, that had cast away their pearls and precious stones, when they saw the like sticking upon the ambassadors' caps, dig and push their mothers under the sides, saying thus to them: "Look, mother, how great a lubber* doth yet wear pearls and precious stones, as though he were a little child still." But the mother, yea, and that also in good earnest: "Peace, son," saith she, "I think he be some of the ambassadors' fools." Some found fault at their golden chains as to no use nor purpose, being so small and weak that a bondman might easily break them, and again so wide and large that when it pleased him, he might cast them off and run away at liberty whither he would. *O witty head.*

But when the ambassadors had been there a day or two and saw so great abundance of gold so lightly esteemed, yea, in no less reproach than it was with them in honor, and besides that more gold in the chains and gyves of one fugitive bondman than all the costly ornaments of them three was worth, they began to abate their courage† and for very shame laid away all that gorgeous array, whereof they were so proud. And especially when they had talked familiarly with the Utopians and had learned all their fashions and opinions. For they marvel that any men be so foolish as to have delight and pleasure in the doubtful glistering‡ of a little trifling stone, which may behold any of the stars or else the sun itself. Or that any man is so mad as to count himself the nobler for the smaller or finer thread of wool, which selfsame wool (be it now in never so fine a spun thread) a sheep did once wear, and yet was she all that time no other thing than a sheep. They marvel also that *Doubtful he calleth it, either in consideration and respect of counterfeit stones, or else he calleth doubtful very little worth.*

---

*Lout.
†Haughtiness.
‡Glistening.

gold, which of the own nature is a thing so unprofitable, is now among all people in so high estimation that man himself, by whom, yea, and for the use of whom it is so much set by, is in much less estimation than the gold itself. Insomuch that a

A true saying and a witty.

lumpish, blockheaded churl,* and which hath no more wit than an ass, yea, and as full of naughtiness† as of folly, shall have nevertheless many wise and good men in subjection and bondage only for this, because he hath a great heap of gold. Which, if it should be taken from him by any fortune, or by some subtle wile and cautel‡ of the law (which no less than fortune doth both raise up the low and pluck down the high) and be given to the most vile slave and abject drivel§ of all his household, then shortly after he shall go into the service of his servant as an augmentation or overplus beside his money. But

How much more wit is in the heads of the Utopians than of the common sort of Christians.

they much more marvel at and detest the madness of them which to those rich men, in whose debt and danger they be not, do give almost divine honors for none other consideration but because they be rich, and yet knowing them to be such niggish penny-fathers‖ that they be sure as long as they live not the worth of one farthing of that heap of gold shall come to them.

These and such like opinions have they conceived partly by education, being brought up in that commonwealth whose laws and customs be far different from these kinds of folly, and partly by good literature and learning. For though there be not many in every city which be exempt and discharged of all other labors and appointed only to learning—that is to say, such in whom even from their very childhood they have perceived a singular towardness, a fine wit, and a mind apt to good learning—yet all in their childhood be instructed in learning. And the better part of the people, both men and

---

*Bumpkin; lower-class person.
†Wickedness.
‡Quibble, trick.
§Drudge, menial laborer.
‖Stingy misers.

women, throughout all their whole life do bestow in learning those spare hours which we said they have vacant from bodily labors. They be taught learning in their own native tongue, for it is both copious in words and also pleasant to the ear, and for the utterance of a man's mind very perfect and sure. The most part of all that side of the world useth the same language, saving that among the Utopians it is finest and purest, and according to the diversity of the countries it is diversely altered.

The studies and literature among the Utopians.

Of all these philosophers whose names be here famous in this part of the world to us known, before our coming thither, not as much as the fame of any of them was come among them. And yet in music, logic, arithmetic, and geometry they have found out in a manner all that our ancient philosophers have taught. But as they in all things be almost equal to our old ancient clerks,* so our new logicians in subtle inventions have far passed and gone beyond them. For they have not devised one of all those rules of restrictions, amplifications, and suppositions, very wittily invented in the small logicals, which here our children in every place do learn.[13] Furthermore they were never yet able to find out the second intentions, insomuch that none of them all could ever see man himself in common, as they call him, though he be (as you know) bigger than ever was any giant, yea, and pointed to of us even with our finger.

Music, logic, arithmetic, geometry.

In this place seemeth to be a nipping taunt.†

But they be in the course of the stars and the movings of the heavenly spheres very expert and cunning. They have also wittily excogitated‡ and devised instruments of divers fashions wherein is exactly comprehended and contained the movings and situations of the sun, the moon, and of all the other stars which appear in their horizon. But as for the amities and dissensions§ of the planets and all that deceitful divination by the stars, they never as much as dreamed thereof. Rains, winds, and other courses of tempests they know before

Astronomy.

Yet among Christians this gear‖ is highly esteemed these days.

---

*Learned men.
†Biting sarcasm.
‡Thought up.
§Affinities and oppositions (terms from astrology).
‖Rubbish.

Natural philosophy is a knowledge most uncertain.

Moral philosophy.

The order of good things.

The ends of good things.

The Utopians hold opinion that felicity consisteth in honest pleasure.

The principles of philosophy grounded upon religion.

The theology of the Utopians.

The immortality of the soul, whereof these days certain Christians be in doubt.

by certain tokens, which they have learned by long use and observation. But of the causes of all these things and of the ebbing, flowing, and saltiness of the sea, and finally of the original beginning and nature of heaven and of the world, they hold partly the same opinions that our old philosophers hold, and partly, as our philosophers vary among themselves, so they also, whiles they bring new reasons of things, do disagree from all them, and yet among themselves in all points they do not accord.

In that part of philosophy which entreateth of manners and virtue, their reasons and opinions agree with ours. They dispute of the good qualities of the soul, of the body, and of fortune, and whether the name of goodness may be applied to all these or only to the endowments and gifts of the soul. They reason of virtue and pleasure, but the chief and principal question is in what thing, be it one or more, the felicity of man consisteth. But in this point they seem almost too much given and inclined to the opinion of them which defend pleasure, wherein they determine either all or the chiefest part of man's felicity to rest.[14] And (which is more to be marveled at) the defense of this so dainty and delicate an opinion they fetch even from their grave, sharp, bitter,* and rigorous religion. For they never dispute of felicity or blessedness, but they join unto the reasons of philosophy certain principles taken out of religion, without the which to the investigation of true felicity they think reason of itself weak and imperfect. Those principles be these and such like: that the soul is immortal and by the bountiful goodness of God ordained to felicity, that to our virtues and good deeds rewards be appointed after this life and to our evil deeds punishments. Though these be pertaining to religion, yet they think it meet that they should be believed and granted by proofs of reason. But if these principles were condemned and disannulled,† then without any delay they pronounce no man to be so foolish which would not do all his diligence and endeavor to obtain pleasure by

---

*Severe.
†Canceled.

right or wrong, only avoiding this inconvenience, that the less pleasure should not be a let or hindrance to the bigger, or that he labored not for that pleasure, which would bring after it displeasure, grief, and sorrow. For they judge it extreme madness to follow sharp and painful virtue, and not only to banish the pleasure of life, but also willingly to suffer grief without any hope of profit thereof ensuing. For what profit can there be if a man, when he hath passed over all his life unpleasantly, that is to say miserably, shall have no reward after his death?

As every plea-sure ought not to be embraced, so grief is not to be pursued but for virtue's sake.

But now, sir, they think not felicity to rest in all pleasure, but only in that pleasure that is good and honest, and that hereto, as to perfect blessedness, our nature is allured and drawn even of virtue, whereto only they that be of the contrary opinion do attribute felicity.[15] For they define virtue to be life ordered according to nature, and that we be hereunto ordained of God, and that he doth follow the course of nature which, in desiring and refusing things, is ruled by reason. Furthermore, that reason doth chiefly and principally kindle in men the love and veneration of the divine majesty, of whose goodness it is that we be, and that we be in possibility to attain felicity. And that, secondarily, it both stirreth and provoketh us to lead our life out of* care in joy and mirth, and also moveth us to help and further all other in respect of the society of nature† to obtain and enjoy the same. For there was never man so earnest and painful‡ a follower of virtue and hater of pleasure that would so enjoin you labors, watchings§ and fastings, but he would also exhort you to ease, lighten, and relieve, to your power, the lack and misery of others, praising the same as a deed of humanity and pity. Then if it be a point of humanity for man to bring health and comfort to man, and especially (which is a virtue most peculiarly belonging to man) to mitigate and assuage the grief of others,

In this definition they agree with the Stoics.
The work and effect of reason in man.

---

*Free from.
†Natural connectedness.
‡That is, taking pains.
§Vigils.
‖Hasten (in acquiring pain and suffering).

and by taking from them the sorrow and heaviness of life, to restore them to joy, that is to say, to pleasure, why may it not then be said that nature doth provoke every man to do the same to himself?

But nowadays some there be that willingly procure unto themselves painful griefs, as though therein rested some high point of religion, whereas rather the religiously disposed person, if they happen to hie either by chance or else by natural necessity, ought patiently to receive and suffer them.

For a joyful life, that is to say a pleasant life, is either evil— and if it be so, then thou shouldest not only help no man thereto, but rather, as much as in thee lieth, withdraw all men from it, as noisome and hurtful—or else, if thou not only mayst but also of duty art bound to procure it to others, why not chiefly to thyself, to whom thou art bound to show as much favor and gentleness as to other? For when nature biddeth thee to be good and gentle to other, she commandeth thee not to be cruel and ungentle to thyself. Therefore, even very nature (say they) prescribeth to us a joyful life, that is to say, pleasure as the end of all our operations, and they define virtue to be life ordered according to the prescript of nature. But in that that nature doth allure and provoke men one to help another to live merrily (which surely she doth not without a good cause, for no man is so far above the lot of man's state or condition that nature doth cark* and care for him only, which equally favoreth all that be comprehended under the communion of one shape, form, and fashion), verily, she commandeth thee to use diligent circumspection that thou do not so seek for thine own commodities that thou procure others' incommodities.

Bargains and laws.

Wherefore, their opinion is that not only covenants and bargains made among private men ought to be well and faithfully fulfilled, observed, and kept, but also common laws, which either a good prince hath justly published, or else the people, neither oppressed with tyranny, neither deceived by fraud and guile, hath by their common consent constituted and ratified concerning the partition of the commodities of life, that is to say, the matter of pleasure. These laws not offended, it is wisdom that thou look to thine own wealth,† and to do the same for the commonwealth is no less than thy duty,

---

*Feel anxious about.
†Well-being.

if thou bearest any reverent love or any natural zeal and affection to thy native country. But to go about to let another man of* his pleasure, whiles thou procurest thine own, that is open wrong. Contrariwise to withdraw something from thyself to give to other, that is a point of humanity and gentleness, which never taketh away so much commodity as it bringeth again. For it is recompensed with the return of benefits, and the conscience of the good deed, with the remembrance of the thankful love and benevolence of them to whom thou hast done it, doth bring more pleasure to thy mind than that which thou hast withholden from thyself could have brought to thy body. Finally (which to a godly disposed and a religious mind is easy to be persuaded), God recompenseth the gift of a short and small pleasure with great and everlasting joy. Therefore, the matter diligently weighed and considered, thus they think that all our actions, and in them the virtues themselves, be referred at the last to pleasure as their end and felicity. *The mutual recourse of kindness.*

Pleasure they call every motion and state of the body or mind wherein man hath naturally delectation. Appetite they join to nature, and that not without a good cause, for like as not only the senses, but also right reason, coveteth whatsoever is naturally pleasant, so that it may be gotten without wrong or injury, not letting or debarring a greater pleasure, nor causing painful labor, even so those things that men by vain imagination do feign against nature to be pleasant (as though it lay in their power to change the things, as they do the names of things), all such pleasures they believe to be of so small help and furtherance to felicity that they count them a great let and hindrance.[16] Because that in whom they have once taken place, all his mind they possess with a false opinion of pleasure, so that there is no place left for true and natural delectations. For there be many things which of their own nature contain no pleasantness—yea, the most part of them much grief and sorrow—and yet, through the perverse and malicious *The definition of pleasure.* *False and counterfeit pleasures.*

---

*Keep . . . from.

flickering enticements of lewd and unhonest* desires, be taken not only for special and sovereign pleasures, but also be counted among the chief causes of life. In this counterfeit kind of pleasure they put them that I spake of before, which, the better gowns they have on, the better men they think themselves. In the which thing they do twice err, for they be no less deceived in that they think their gown the better, than they be in that they think themselves the better. For if you consider the profitable use of the garment, why should wool of a finer spun thread be thought better than the wool of a coarse spun thread? Yet they, as though the one did pass† the other by nature and not by their mistaking, advance themselves and think the price of their own persons thereby greatly increased. And, therefore, the honor, which in a coarse gown they durst not have looked for, they require, as it were of duty, for their finer gown's sake. And if they be passed by without reverence, they take it displeasantly and disdainfully.

And again, is it not like madness to take a pride in vain and unprofitable honors? For what natural or true pleasure dost thou take of another man's bare head or bowed knees? Will this ease the pain of thy knees or remedy the frenzy of thy head? In this image of counterfeit pleasure they be of a marvelous madness which, for the opinion of nobility, rejoice much in their own conceit, because it was their fortune to come of such ancestors whose stock of long time had been counted rich (for now nobility is nothing else), especially rich in lands. And though their ancestors left them not one foot of land, or else they themselves have pissed it against the walls, yet they think themselves not the less noble therefore of one hair.‡

In this number also they count them that take pleasure and delight (as I said) in gems and precious stones and think themselves almost gods if they chance to get an excellent one, especially of that kind which in that time of their own countrymen

Marginal notes:

The error of them that esteem themselves the more for apparel's sake.

Foolish honors.

Vain nobility.

Pleasure in precious stones most foolish.

---

*Unchaste and indecent.
†Surpass.
‡Not a whit.

is had in highest estimation. For one kind of stone keepeth not his price still in all countries and at all times. Nor they buy them not but taken out of the gold and bare;* no, nor so neither, until they have made the seller to swear that he will warrant and assure it to be a true stone and no counterfeit gem. Such care they take lest a counterfeit stone should deceive their eyes instead of a right stone. But why shouldst thou not take even as much pleasure in beholding a counterfeit stone, which thine eye cannot discern from a right stone? They should both be of like value to thee, even as to the blind man. What shall I say of them that keep superfluous riches, to take delectation only in the beholding and not in the use or occupying thereof? Do they take true pleasure, or else be they deceived with false pleasure? Or of them that be in a contrary vice, hiding the gold which they shall never occupy nor peradventure never see more? And whiles they take care lest they shall lose it, do lose it indeed. For what is it else when they hide it in the ground, taking it both from their own use and perchance from all other men's also? And yet thou, when thou hast hid thy treasure, as one out of all care, hopest for joy. The which treasure, if it should chance to be stolen, and thou ignorant of the theft shouldst die ten years after, all that ten years' space that thou livedst after thy money was stolen, what matter was it to thee whether it had been taken away or else safe as thou leftest it? Truly both ways like profit came to thee.

The opinion and fancy of people doth augment and diminish the price and estimation of precious stones.

Beholders of treasure, not occupying the same.

Hiders of treasure.

A pretty fiction and a witty.

To these so foolish pleasures they join dicers, whose madness they know by hearsay and not by use; hunters also, and hawkers.† For what pleasure is there (say they) in casting the dice upon a table, which thou hast done so often that if there were any pleasure in it, yet the oft use might make thee weary thereof? Or what delight can there be, and not rather displeasure, in hearing the barking and howling of dogs? Or what greater pleasure is there to be felt when a dog followeth an hare, than when a dog followeth a dog? For one thing is done in both, that is to say, running, if thou hast pleasure therein.

Dice-play.

Hunting and hawking.

---

*Out of their settings.
†Men practicing falconry.

But if the hope of slaughter and the expectation of tearing in pieces the beast doth please thee, thou shouldst rather be moved with pity to see a silly, innocent hare murdered of a dog, the weak of the stronger, the fearful of the fierce, the innocent of the cruel and unmerciful. Therefore, all this exercise of hunting, as a thing unworthy to be used of free men, the Utopians have rejected* to their butchers, to the which craft (as we said before) they appoint their bondmen. For they count hunting the lowest, the vilest, and most abject part of butchery, and the other parts of it more profitable and more honest, as bringing much more commodity, in that they kill beasts only for necessity, whereas the hunter seeketh nothing but pleasure of the silly and woeful† beast's slaughter and murder. The which pleasure in beholding death they think doth rise in the very beasts, either of a cruel affection of mind, or else to be changed in continuance of time into cruelty by long use of so cruel a pleasure. These, therefore, and all such like, which be innumerable, though the common sort of people doth take them for pleasures, yet they, seeing there is no natural pleasantness in them, do plainly determine them to have no affinity with true and right pleasure. For as touching that they do commonly move the sense with delectation (which seemeth to be a work of pleasure) this doth nothing diminish their opinion. For not the nature of the thing, but their perverse and lewd custom is the cause hereof, which causeth them to accept bitter or sour things for sweet things even as women with child, in their vitiate and corrupt taste, think pitch and tallow sweeter than any honey. Howbeit, no man's judgment, depraved and corrupt either by sickness or by custom, can change the nature of pleasure, more than it can do the nature of other things.

They make divers kinds of pleasures, for some they attribute to the soul and some to the body. To the soul they give intelligence and that delectation that cometh of the contemplation of truth. Hereunto is joined the pleasant

Margin note: Hunting, the basest part of butchery among the Utopians, and yet this is now the exercise of most noblemen.

Margin note: The kinds of true pleasures.

---

*Cast off.
†Simple and sorry.

remembrance of the good life past. The pleasure of the body *The pleasures* they divide into two parts. The first is when delectation is *of the body.* sensibly felt and perceived, which many times chanceth by the renewing and refreshing of those parts which our natural heat drieth up. This cometh by meat and drink. And sometimes whiles those things be expulsed and voided, whereof is in the body overgreat abundance. This pleasure is felt when we do our natural easement, or when we be doing the act of generation, or when the itching of any part is eased with rubbing or scratching. Sometimes pleasure riseth exhibiting to any member nothing that it desireth, nor taking from it any pain that it feeleth, which nevertheless tickleth and moveth our senses with a certain secret efficacy, but with a manifest motion turneth them to it, as is that which cometh of music.

The second part of bodily pleasure, they say, is that which *Bodily health.* consisteth and resteth in the quiet and upright state of the body, and that, truly, is every man's own proper health, intermingled and disturbed with no grief. For this, if it be not letted nor assaulted with no grief, is delectable of itself, though it be moved with no external or outward pleasure, for though it be not so plain and manifest to the sense as the greedy lust* of eating and drinking, yet nevertheless many take it for the chiefest pleasure. All the Utopians grant it to be a right sovereign pleasure and, as you would say, the foundation and ground of all pleasures, as which even alone is able to make the state and condition of life delectable and pleasant, and it being once taken away, there is no place left for any pleasure. For to be without grief, not having health, that they call insensibility and not pleasure.

The Utopians have long ago rejected and condemned the opinion of them which said that steadfast and quiet health (for this question also hath been diligently debated among them) ought not, therefore, to be counted a pleasure, because they say it cannot be presently and sensibly perceived and felt

---

*Desire.

by some outward motion.* But of the contrary part now they agree almost all in this, that health is a most sovereign pleasure. For seeing that in sickness (say they) is grief, which is a mortal enemy to pleasure, even as sickness is to health, why should not then pleasure be in the quietness of health? For they say it maketh nothing to this matter whether you say that sickness is a grief or that in sickness is grief, for all cometh to one purpose. For whether health be a pleasure itself, or a necessary cause of pleasure as fire is of heat, truly, both ways it followeth that they cannot be without pleasure that be in perfect health. Furthermore, whiles we eat (say they) then health, which began to be appaired,† fighteth by the help of food against hunger. In the which fight, whiles health by little and little getteth the upper hand, that same proceeding and (as ye would say) that onwardness to the wont strength ministereth‡ that pleasure whereby we be so refreshed. Health, therefore, which in the conflict is joyful, shall it not be merry when it hath gotten the victory? But as soon as it hath recovered the pristinate§ strength, which thing only in all the fight it coveted, shall it incontinent be astonied?‖ Nor shall it not know nor embrace thy own wealth and goodness? For that it is said health cannot be felt, this, they think, is nothing true. For what man waking, say they, feeleth not himself in health, but he that is not? Is there any man so possessed with stonish# insensibility or with lethargy, that is to say, the sleeping sickness, that he will not grant health to be acceptable to him and delectable? But what other thing is delectation than that which by another name is called pleasure?

Delectation.

The pleasures of the mind.

They embrace chiefly the pleasures of the mind. For them they count the chiefest and most principal of all. The chief part of them they think doth come of the exercise of virtue

---

*Response to something external.
†Impaired.
‡Advancement to our usual strength imparts.
§Original.
‖Amazed; literally, turned to stone.
#Stone-like.

and conscience of good life. Of these pleasures that the body ministereth, they give the preeminence to health. For the delight of eating and drinking, and whatsoever hath any like pleasantness, they determine to be pleasures much to be desired, but no other ways than for health's sake. For such things of their own proper nature be not so pleasant, but in that they resist sickness privily stealing on. Therefore, like as it is a wise man's part rather to avoid sickness than to wish for medicines, and rather to drive away and put to flight careful* griefs than to call for comfort, so it is much better not to need this kind of pleasure than thereby to be eased of the contrary grief. The which kind of pleasure if any man take for his felicity, that man must needs grant that then he shall be in most felicity, if he live that life which is led in continual hunger, thirst, itching, eating, drinking, scratching, and rubbing. The which life how not only foul and unhonest, but also how miserable and wretched it is, who perceiveth not? These doubtless be the basest pleasures of all, as impure and unperfect, for they never come but accompanied with their contrary griefs. As with the pleasure of eating is joined hunger, and that after no very equal sort. For of these two the grief is both the more vehement, and also of longer continuance, for it beginneth before the pleasure and endeth not until the pleasure die with it. Wherefore, such pleasures they think not greatly to be set by but in that they be necessary. Howbeit, they have delight also in these, and thankful knowledge† the tender love of mother nature, which with most pleasant delectation allureth her children to that, to the necessary use whereof they must from time to time continually be forced and driven. For how wretched and miserable should our life be, if these daily griefs of hunger and thirst could not be driven away but with bitter potions and sour medicines, as the other diseases be wherewith we be seldomer troubled? But beauty, strength, nimbleness, these as peculiar and pleasant gifts of nature they make

---

*Full of cares.
†Acknowledge.

The gifts of nature.

much of. But those pleasures that be received by the ears, the eyes, and the nose, which nature willeth to be proper and peculiar to man (for no other living creature doth behold the fairness and the beauty of the world, or is moved with any respect of savors,* but only for the diversity of meats, neither perceiveth the concordant and discordant distances of sounds and tunes), these pleasures, I say, they accept and allow as certain pleasant rejoicings of life. But in all things this cautel† they use, that a less pleasure hinder not a bigger, and that the pleasure be no cause of displeasure, which they think to follow of necessity if the pleasure be unhonest. But yet to despise the comeliness of beauty, to waste the bodily strength, to turn nimbleness into sluggishness, to consume and make feeble the body with fasting, to do injury to health, and to reject the pleasant motions of nature (unless a man neglect these commodities whiles he doth with a fervent zeal procure the wealth of others or the common profit, for the which pleasure foreborn‡ he is in hope of a greater pleasure at God's hand) else for a vain shadow of virtue, for the wealth and profit of no man, to punish himself, or to the intent he may be able courageously to suffer adversity, which perchance shall never come to him—this to do they think a point of extreme madness and a token of a man cruelly minded towards himself and unkind towards nature, as one so disdaining to be in her danger that he renounceth and refuseth all her benefits.

Mark this well.

This is their sentence and opinion of virtue and pleasure, and they believe that by man's reason none can be found truer than this, unless any godlier be inspired into man from heaven. Wherein whether they believe well or no, neither the time doth suffer us to discuss, neither it is now necessary, for we have taken upon us to show and declare their lores§ and ordinances, and not to defend them.

But this thing I believe verily: howsoever these decrees be,

---

*Tastes, aromas.
†Strategy.
‡Shunned.
§Precepts.

that there is in no place of the world neither a more excellent people neither a more flourishing commonwealth. They be light and quick of body, full of activity and nimbleness, and of more strength than a man would judge them by their stature, which for all that is not too low. And though their soil be not very fruitful, nor their air very wholesome, yet against the air they so defend them with temperate diet, and so order and husband their ground with diligent travail,* that in no country is greater increase and plenty of corn and cattle, nor men's bodies of longer life and subject or apt to fewer diseases. There, therefore, a man may see well and diligently exploited† and furnished not only those things which husbandmen do commonly in other countries, as by craft and cunning to remedy the barrenness of the ground, but also a whole wood by the hands of the people plucked up by the roots in one place and set again in another place. Wherein was had regard and consideration, not of plenty, but of commodious carriage,‡ that wood and timber might be nigher to the sea, or the rivers, or the cities, for it is less labor and business to carry grain far by land, than wood.

The wealth and description of the Utopians.

The people be gentle, merry, quick, and fine-witted, delighting in quietness and, when need requireth, able to abide and suffer much bodily labor. Else they be not greatly desirous and fond of it, but in the exercise and study of the mind they be never weary. When they had heard me speak of the Greek literature or learning (for in Latin there was nothing that I thought they would greatly allow, besides historians and poets), they made wonderful earnest and importunate suit unto me that I would teach and instruct them in that tongue and learning. I began, therefore, to read unto them, at the first truly more because I would not seem to refuse the labor than that I hoped that they would anything profit therein. But when I had gone forward a little, I perceived incontinent by their diligence that my labor should not be bestowed in vain.

The utility of the Greek tongue.

---

*Labor.
†Worked.
‡Ease of transport.

A wonderful aptness to learning in the Utopians.

But now most blockheaded asses are set to learning, and most pregnant wits corrupt with pleasures.

For they began so easily to fashion their letters, so plainly to pronounce the words, so quickly to learn by heart, and so surely to rehearse the same, that I marveled at it, saving that the most part of them were fine and chosen wits and of ripe age, picked out of the company of the learned men, which not only of their own free and voluntary will, but also by the commandment of the council undertook to learn this language. Therefore, in less than three years' space there was nothing in the Greek tongue that they lacked. They were able to read good authors without any stay, if the book were not false.* This kind of learning, as I suppose, they took so much the sooner because it is somewhat alliant† to them. For I think that this nation took their beginning of the Greeks because their speech, which in all other points is not much unlike the Persian tongue, keepeth divers signs and tokens of the Greek language in the names of their cities and of their magistrates.

They have of me (for when I was determined to enter into my fourth voyage, I cast into the ship in the stead of merchandise a pretty fardel‡ of books, because I intended to come again rather never than shortly), they have, I say, of me the most part of Plato's works, more of Aristotle's, also Theophrastus of plants, but in divers places (which I am sorry for) unperfect.[17] For whilst we were a-shipboard, a marmoset chanced upon the book as it was negligently laid by, which wantonly playing therewith plucked out certain leaves and tore them in pieces. Of them that have written the grammar, they have only Lascaris, for Theodorus I carried not with me, nor never a dictionary but Hesychius, and Dioscorides.[18] They set great store by Plutarch's books, and they be delighted with Lucian's merry conceits and jests.[19] Of the poets they have Aristophanes, Homer, Euripides, and Sophocles in Aldus' small print. Of the historians they have Thucydides, Herodotus, and Herodian. Also my companion Tricius Apinatus carried with him physic books, certain small works of Hippocrates

---

*Containing printer's errors.
†Akin.
‡Bundle.

and Galen's *Microtechne*,[20] the which book they have in great *Physic highly regarded.* estimation. For though there is almost no nation under heaven that hath less need of physic than they, yet this notwithstanding, physic is nowhere in greater honor, because they count the knowledge of it among the goodliest and most profitable parts of philosophy. For whiles they by the help of this philosophy search out the secret mysteries of nature, they think themselves to receive thereby not only wonderful great pleasure, but also to obtain great thanks and favor of the author and maker thereof, whom they think, according to the fashion of other artificers, to have set forth the marvelous and *The contemplation of nature.* gorgeous frame of the world for man with great affection attentively to behold, whom only he hath made of wit and capacity to consider and understand the excellence of so great a work. And, therefore, he beareth (say they) more goodwill and love to the curious and diligent beholder and viewer of his work and marveler at the same, than he doth to him which, like a very brute beast without wit and reason, or as one without sense or moving, hath no regard to so great and so wonderful a spectacle.

The wits, therefore, of the Utopians, inured and exercised in learning, be marvelous quick in the invention of feats helping anything to the advantage and wealth of life. Howbeit, two feats they may thank us for: that is, the science of imprinting and the craft of making paper. And yet not only us but chiefly and principally themselves. For when we showed to them Aldus's print in books of paper and told them of the stuff whereof paper is made and of the feat of graving* letters, speaking somewhat more than we could plainly declare (for there was none of us that knew perfectly either the one or the other), they forthwith very wittily conjectured the thing. And whereas before they wrote only in skins, in barks of trees, and in reeds, now they have attempted to make paper and to imprint letters. And though at the first it proved not all of the best, yet by often assaying the same they shortly got the feat of

---

*Engraving—that is, printing.

both, and have so brought the matter about, that if they had copies of Greek authors, they could lack no books. But now they have no more than I rehearsed before, saving that by printing of books they have multiplied and increased the same into many thousands of copies.

Whosoever cometh thither to see the land, being excellent in any gift of wit, or through much and long journeying well experienced and seen in the knowledge of many countries (for the which cause we were very welcome to them), him they receive and entertain wondrous gently and lovingly, for they have delight to hear what is done in every land, howbeit very few merchantmen come thither. For what should they bring thither, unless it were iron, or else gold and silver, which they had rather carry home again? Also such things as are to be carried out of their land, they think it more wisdom to carry that gear forth themselves than that other should come thither to fetch it, to the intent they may the better know the outlands on every side of them and keep in ure* the feat and knowledge of sailing.

Of Bondmen, Sick Persons, Wedlock, and Divers Other Matters.

THEY neither make bondmen of prisoners taken in battle, unless it be in battle that they fought themselves, nor of bondmen's children, nor (to be short) of any such as they can get out of foreign countries, though he were there a bondman, but either such as among themselves for heinous offenses be punished with bondage, or else such as in the cities of other lands for great trespasses be condemned to death. And of this sort of bondmen they have most store. For many of them they bring home, sometimes paying very little for them, yea, most commonly getting them for gramercy.† These sorts of bondmen they keep not only in continual work and labor, but also in bands.‡ But their own men they handle hardest, whom they judge more desperate and to have deserved greater punishment,

A marvelous equity of this nation.

---

*Use.
†A thank-you (French: *grand merci*).
‡Shackles.

because they, being so godly brought up to virtue in so excellent a commonwealth, could not for all that be refrained from misdoing. Another kind of bondmen they have, when a vile drudge,* being a poor laborer in another country, doth choose of his own free will to be a bondman among them. These they entreat and order honestly and entertain almost as gently as their own free citizens, saving that they put them to a little more labor, as thereto accustomed. If any such be disposed to depart thence (which seldom is seen), they neither hold him against his will, neither send him away with empty hands.

The sick (as I said) they see to with great affection and let nothing at all pass concerning either physic or good diet whereby they may be restored again to their health. Such as be sick of incurable diseases they comfort with sitting by them, with talking with them, and, to be short, with all manner of helps that may be. But if the disease be not only incurable but also full of continual pain and anguish, then the priests and the magistrates exhort the man, seeing he is not able to do any duty of life, and by overliving his own death, is noisome and irksome to others and grievous to himself, that he will determine with himself no longer to cherish that pestilent and painful disease, and seeing his life is to him but a torment, that he will not be unwilling to die, but rather take a good hope to him and either dispatch himself out of that painful life, as out of a prison or a rack of torment, or else suffer himself willingly to be rid out of it by others. And in so doing they tell him he shall do wisely, seeing by his death he shall lose no commodity, but end his pain. And because in that act he shall follow the counsel of the priests, that is to say, of the interpreters of God's will and pleasure, they show him that he shall do like a godly and a virtuous man. They that be thus persuaded finish their lives willingly, either with hunger, or else die in their sleep without any feeling of death. But they cause none such to die against his will, nor they use no less diligence and attendance about him, believing this to be an honorable death.

Of them that be sick.

Voluntary death.

---

*Menial laborer.

Else he that killeth himself before that the priests and the council have allowed the cause of his death, him as unworthy either to be buried or with fire to be consumed, they cast unburied into some stinking marsh.

Of wedlock. The woman is not married before she be eighteen years old. The man is four years older before he marry. If either the man or the woman be proved to have actually offended before their marriage with another, the party that so hath trespassed is sharply punished, and both the offenders be forbidden ever after in all their life to marry, unless the fault be forgiven by the prince's pardon. But both the good man and the good wife of the house where the offense was committed, as being slack and negligent in looking to their charge, be in danger of great reproach and infamy. That offense is so sharply punished because they perceive that unless they be diligently kept from the liberty of this vice, few will join together in the love of marriage, wherein all the life must be led with one, and also all the griefs and displeasures coming therewith patiently be taken and borne.

Though not very honestly, yet not unwisely. Furthermore, in choosing wives and husbands they observe earnestly and straitly a custom which seemed to us very fond and foolish. For a sad and honest matron showeth the woman, be she maid or widow, naked to the wooer. And likewise, a sage and discreet man exhibiteth the wooer naked to the woman.[21] At this custom we laughed and disallowed it as foolish. But they, on the other part, do greatly wonder at the folly of all other nations which in buying a colt, whereas a little money is in hazard, be so chary and circumspect that though he be almost all bare, yet they will not buy him unless the saddle and all the harness be taken off, lest under those coverings be hid some gall or sore. And yet in choosing a wife, which shall be either pleasure or displeasure to them all their life after, they be so reckless that all the residue of the woman's body being covered with clothes, they esteem her scarcely by one handbreadth (for they can see no more but her face), and so to join her to them not without great jeopardy of evil agreeing together, if anything in her body afterward should chance to offend and mislike them. For all men be not so wise as to have respect to the virtuous conditions of the party, and the endowments of the body cause the virtues of the mind more to be esteemed and regarded, yea, even in the marriages of wise men. Verily, so foul deformity may be hid under those coverings that it may quite alienate and take away the man's mind from his wife, when it shall not be lawful for their bodies to be separate again. If such deformity happen by any chance after the marriage is consummate and finished, well, there is no remedy but patience. Every man must take his fortune well a worth.* But it were well done that a law were made whereby all such deceits might be eschewed and avoided beforehand.

And this were they constrained more earnestly to look upon, because they only of the nations in that part of the world be content every man with one wife apiece. And matrimony is there never broken, but by death, except adultery break the bond or else the intolerable wayward manners of either party. For if either of them find themselves for any such cause grieved, they may by the license of the council change and take another, but the other party liveth ever after in in- *Divorcement.* famy and out of wedlock. Howbeit, the husband to put away his wife for no other fault but for that some mishap is fallen to her body, this by no means they will suffer. For they judge it a great point of cruelty that anybody in their most need of help and comfort should be cast off and forsaken, and that old age, which both bringeth sickness with it and is a sickness itself, should unkindly and unfaithfully be dealt withal. But now and then it chanceth, whereas the man and the woman cannot well agree between themselves, both of them finding other with whom they hope to live more quietly and merrily, that they by the full consent of them both, be divorced asunder and married again to others. But that not without the authority of the council, which agreeth to no divorces before they and their wives have diligently tried and examined the matter. Yea, and then also they be loath to consent to it, because they

---

*As chance provides.

know this to be the next way to break love between man and wife, to be in easy hope of a new marriage.

Breakers of wedlock be punished with most grievous bondage. And if both the offenders were married, then the parties which in that behalf have suffered wrong, being divorced from the avoutrers,* be married together, if they will, or else to whom they lust. But if either of them both do still continue in love toward so unkind a bedfellow, the use of wedlock† is not to them forbidden, if the party faultless be disposed to follow in toiling and drudgery the person which for that offense is condemned to bondage. And very oft it chanceth that the repentance of the one and the earnest diligence of the other doth so move the prince with pity and compassion that he restoreth the bond person from servitude to liberty and freedom again. But if the same party be taken eftsoons‡ in that fault, there is no other way but death.

The discerning§ of punishment put to the discretion of the magistrates.

To other trespasses no prescript punishment is appointed by any law, but according to the heinousness of the offense, or contrary, so the punishment is moderated by the discretion of the council. The husbands chastise their wives, and the parents their children, unless they have done any so horrible an offense that the open punishment thereof maketh much for the advancement of honest manners. But most commonly the most heinous faults be punished with the incommodity of bondage, for that they suppose to be to the offenders no less grief, and to the commonwealth more profit, than if they should hastily put them to death and so make them quite out of the way. For there cometh more profit of their labor than of their death, and by their example they fear‖ other the longer from like offenses. But if they, being thus used, do rebel and kick again, then, forsooth, they be slain as desperate and wild beasts, whom neither prison nor chain could restrain and

---

*Adulterers.
†Continuation in a wedded state.
‡Again.
§Determining.
‖Scare away.

keep under. But they which take their bondage patiently be not left all hopeless. For after they have been broken and tamed with long miseries, if then they show such repentance as thereby it may be perceived that they be sorrier for their offenses than for their punishment, sometimes by the prince's prerogative, and sometimes by the voice and consent of the people, their bondage either is mitigated or else clean released and forgiven. He that moveth to avoutry* is in no less danger and jeopardy than if he had committed avoutry indeed. For in all offenses they count the intent and pretensed purpose as evil as the act or deed itself, thinking that no let ought to excuse him that did his best to have no let. *Motion to avoutry punished.*

They have singular delight and pleasure in fools. And as it is a great reproach to do any of them hurt or injury, so they prohibit not to take pleasure of foolishness, for that, they think, doth much good to the fools. And if any man be so sad and stern that he cannot laugh neither at their words nor at their deeds, none of them be committed to his tuition,† for fear lest he would not treat them gently and favorably enough, to whom they should bring no delectation (for other goodness in them is none), much less any profit should they yield him. To mock a man for his deformity or for that he lacketh any part or limb of his body is counted great dishonesty and reproach, not to him that is mocked, but to him that mocketh, which unwisely doth upbraid any man of that as a vice that was not in his power to eschew. *Pleasure of fools.*

Also, as they count and reckon very little wit to be in him that regardeth not natural beauty and comeliness, so to help the same with paintings‡ is taken for a vain and a wanton pride, not without great infamy. For they know, even by very experience, that no comeliness of beauty doth so highly commend and advance the wives in the conceit§ of their husbands as honest conditions and lowliness.‖ For as love is oftentimes *Counterfeit beauty.*

---

*Adultery.
†Custody, care.
‡Cosmetics.
§Opinion.
‖Humility.

won with beauty, so it is not kept, preserved, and continued but by virtue and obedience.

They do not only fear their people from doing evil by punishments, but also allure them to virtue with rewards of honor. Therefore, they set up in the marketplace the images of notable men and of such as have been great and bountiful benefactors to the commonwealth for the perpetual memory of their good acts, and also that the glory and renown of the ancestors may fire and provoke their posterity to virtue. He

that inordinately and ambitiously desireth promotions is left all hopeless for ever attaining any promotion as long as he liveth.

They live together lovingly, for no magistrate is either haughty or fearful.* Fathers they be called, and like fathers they use themselves. The citizens (as it is their duty) willingly

exhibit unto them due honor without any compulsion. Nor the prince himself is not known from the other by princely apparel or a robe of state, nor by a crown or diadem royal, or cap of maintenance,[22] but by a little sheaf of corn carried before him. And so a taper of wax is borne before the bishop, whereby only he is known.

They have but few laws, for to people so instruct and institute† very few do suffice. Yea, this thing they chiefly reprove among other nations, that innumerable books of laws and expositions upon the same be not sufficient. But they think it against all right and justice that men should be bound to those laws which either be in number more than be able to be read, or else blinder and darker than that any man can well understand

them. Furthermore, they utterly exclude and banish all attorneys, proctors, and sergeants-at-the-law,[23] which craftily handle matters and subtly dispute of the laws. For they think it most meet that every man should plead his own matter, and tell the same tale before the judge that he would tell to his man of law.‡

---

*Supercilious or frightening.
†Educated.
‡Lawyer.

So shall there be less circumstance of words, and the truth shall
sooner come to light, whiles the judge with a discreet judgment doth weigh the words of him whom no lawyer hath instruct with deceit, and whiles he helpeth and beareth out
simple wits against the false and malicious circumventions of
crafty children. This is hard to be observed in other countries,
in so infinite a number of blind and intricate laws. But in
Utopia every man is a cunning lawyer, for (as I said) they have
very few laws, and the plainer and grosser* that any interpretation is, that they allow as most just. For all laws (say they) be
made and published only to the intent that by them every
man should be put in remembrance of his duty. But the crafty
and subtle interpretation of them (forasmuch as few can attain thereto) can put very few in that remembrance, whereas
the simple, the plain, and gross meaning of the laws is open to
every man.

The intent of laws.

Else as touching the vulgar sort of the people, which be
both most in number and have most need to know their duties, were it not as good for them that no law were made at all,
as when it is made, to bring so blind an interpretation upon it
that without great wit and long arguing no man can discuss
it? To the finding out whereof neither the gross judgment of
the people can attain, neither the whole life of them that be
occupied in working for their livings can suffice thereto.

These virtues of the Utopians have caused their next
neighbors and borderers, which live free and under no subjection (for the Utopians long ago have delivered many of
them from tyranny), to take magistrates of them, some for a
year and some for five years' space, which, when the time of
their office is expired, they bring home again with honor and
praise, and take new again with them into their country.
These nations have undoubtedly very well and wholesomely
provided for their commonwealths. For seeing that both the
making and marring of the weal public doth depend and
hang upon the manners of the rulers and magistrates, what

---

*More obvious, commoner.

officers could they more wisely have chosen, than those which cannot be led from honesty by bribes (for to them that shortly after shall depart thence into their own country, money should be unprofitable), nor yet be moved either with favor or malice towards any man, as being strangers and unacquainted with the people? The which two vices of affection* and avarice, where they take place in judgments, incontinent they break justice, the strongest and surest bond of a commonwealth. These peoples which fetch their officers and rulers from them, the Utopians call their fellows, and other to whom they have been beneficial, they call their friends.

Of leagues.   As touching leagues,† which in other places between country and country be so oft concluded, broken, and renewed, they never make none with any nation. For to what purpose serve leagues, say they, as though nature had not set sufficient love between man and man? And who so regardeth not nature, think you that he will pass‡ for words? They be brought into this opinion chiefly because that in those parts of the world leagues between princes be wont to be kept and observed very slenderly.§ For here in Europa, and especially in these parts where the faith and religion of Christ reigneth, the majesty of leagues is everywhere esteemed holy and inviolable, partly through the justice and goodness of princes, and partly at the reverence and motion of the head bishops,[24] which, like as they make no promise themselves, but they do very religiously perform the same, so they exhort all princes in any wise to abide by their promises, and them that refuse or deny so to do by their pontifical power and authority they compel thereto. And surely they think well that it might seem a very reproachful thing, if in the leagues of them which by a peculiar name be called faithful, faith should have no place.

---

*Prejudice.
†Military, political, or commercial treaties.
‡Care.
§To a slight degree.

But in that newfound part of the world, which is scarcely so far from us beyond the line equinoctial as our life and manners be dissident from theirs, no trust nor confidence is in leagues. But the more and holier ceremonies the league is knit up with, the sooner it is broken by some cavillation* found in the words, which many times of purpose be so craftily put in and placed that the bands† can never be so sure nor so strong but they will find some hole open to creep out at, and to break both league and truth. The which crafty dealing, yea, the which fraud and deceit, if they should know it to be practiced among private men in their bargains and contracts, they would incontinent cry out at it with an open mouth and a sour countenance as an offense most detestable and worthy to be punished with a shameful death—yea, even very they that advance themselves‡ authors of like counsel given to princes. Wherefore it may well be thought either that all justice is but a base and a low virtue, and which avaleth§ itself far under the high dignity of kings, or at the leastwise that there be two justices: the one meet for the inferior sort of the people, going afoot and creeping low by the ground, and bound down on every side with many bands because it shall not run at rovers;‖ the other a princely virtue, which like as it is of much higher majesty than the other poor justice, so also it is of much more liberty as to the which nothing is unlawful that it lusteth after. These manners of princes, as I said, which be there so evil keepers of leagues, cause the Utopians, as I suppose, to make no leagues at all, which perchance would change their mind if they lived here. Howbeit, they think that though leagues be never so faithfully observed and kept, yet the custom of making leagues was very evil begun. For this causeth men (as though nations which be separate asunder by the space of a little hill or a river were coupled together by no

---

*Quibble.
†Bonds.
‡Put themselves forward as.
§Lowers.
‖At random.

society or bond of nature) to think themselves born adversaries and enemies one to another, and that it were lawful for the one to seek the death and destruction of the other, if leagues were not. Yea, and that after the leagues be accorded, friendship doth not grow and increase, but the license of robbing and stealing doth still remain, as farforth as, for lack of foresight and advisement in writing the words of the league, any sentence or clause to the contrary is not therein sufficiently comprehended.* But they be of a contrary opinion, that is: that no man ought to be counted an enemy which hath done no injury; and that the fellowship of nature is a strong league; and that men be better and more surely knit together by love and benevolence than by covenants of leagues, by hearty affection of mind than by words.

Of Warfare.

WAR or battle, as a thing very beastly and yet to no kind of beasts in so much use as to man,† they do detest and abhor. And contrary to the custom almost of all other nations, they count nothing so much against glory as glory gotten in war. And therefore, though they do daily practice and exercise themselves in the discipline of war, and not only the men but also the women, upon certain appointed days, lest they should be to seek‡ in the feat of arms if need should require, yet they never go to battle but either in the defense of their own country, or to drive out of their friends' land the enemies that have invaded it, or by their power to deliver from the yoke and bondage of tyranny some people that be therewith oppressed, which thing they do of mere§ pity and compassion. Howbeit, they send help to their friends, not ever in their defense, but sometimes also to requite and revenge injuries before to them done. But this they do not unless their counsel and advice in the matter be asked whiles it is yet new

---

*Included (in the treaty).
†That is, it is to man.
‡Lacking.
§Pure.

and fresh. For if they find the cause probable, and if the contrary part* will not restore again such things as be of them justly demanded, then they be the chief authors and makers of the war, which they do not only as oft as by inroads and invasions of soldiers, preys and booties be driven away, but then also much more mortally when their friends' merchants in any land, either under the pretense of unjust laws or else by the wresting and wrong understanding of good laws, do sustain an unjust accusation under the color of justice.[25]

Neither the battle which the Utopians fought for the Nephelogetes against the Alaopolitanes[†] a little before our time was made for any other cause but that the Nephelogete merchantmen, as the Utopians thought, suffered wrong of the Alaopolitanes, under the pretense of right. But whether it were right or wrong, it was with so cruel and mortal war revenged, the countries round about joining their help and power to the puissance and malice of both parties, that most flourishing and wealthy peoples, being some of them shrewdly shaken and some of them sharply beaten, the mischiefs were not finished nor ended until the Alaopolitanes at the last were yielded up as bondmen into the jurisdiction of the Nephelogetes, for the Utopians fought not this war for themselves. And yet the Nephelogetes before the war, when the Alaopolitanes flourished in wealth, were nothing to be compared with them.

So eagerly the Utopians prosecute the injuries done to their friends, yea, in money matters, and not their own likewise. For if they by covin[‡] or guile be wiped beside[§] their goods, so that no violence be done to their bodies, they wreak their anger by abstaining from occupying[||] with that nation, until they have made satisfaction. Not for because they set less store by their own citizens than by their friends, but that they take

---

*Opponents.
[†]"Cloud-dwellers" . . . "Citizens of a Land Without Citizens."
[‡]Collusion.
[§]Cheated out of.
[||]Trading.

the loss of their friends' money more heavily than the loss of their own, because that their friends' merchantmen, forasmuch as that they lose is their own private goods, sustain great damage by the loss. But their own citizens lose nothing but of the common goods, and of that which was at home plentiful and almost superfluous, else had it not been sent forth. Therefore, no man feeleth the loss, and for this cause they think it too cruel an act to revenge that loss with the death of many, the incommodity of the which loss no man feeleth neither in his life nor yet in his living. But if it chance that any of their men in any other country be maimed or killed, whether it be done by a common or a private counsel, knowing and trying out the truth of the matter by their ambassadors, unless the offenders be rendered unto them in recompense of the injury, they will not be appeased, but incontinent they proclaim war against them. The offenders yielded; they punish either with death or with bondage.

Victory dear bought.   They be not only sorry, but also ashamed to achieve the victory with bloodshed, counting it great folly to buy precious wares too dear. They rejoice and avaunt themselves,* if they vanquish and oppress their enemies by craft and deceit. And for that act they make a general triumph, and as if the matter were manfully handled, they set up a pillar of stone in the place where they so vanquished their enemies, in token of the victory. For then they glory, then they boast and crack† that they have played the men indeed, when they have so overcome as no other living creature but only man could, that is to say, by the might and puissance of wit. For with bodily strength (say they) bears, lions, boars, wolves, dogs, and other wild beasts do fight. And as the most part of them do pass us in strength and fierce courage, so in wit and reason we be much stronger than they all.

Their chief and principal purpose in war is to obtain that thing, which if they had before obtained, they would not have

---

*Boast.
†Brag.

moved battle. But if that be not possible, they take so cruel vengeance of them which be in the fault, that ever after they be afraid to do the like. This is their chief and principal intent, which they immediately and first of all prosecute and set forward, but yet so, that they be more circumspect in avoiding and eschewing jeopardies than they be desirous of praise and renown. Therefore, immediately after that war is once solemnly denounced,* they procure many proclamations signed with their own common seal to be set up privily at one time in their enemy's land in places most frequented. In these proclamations they promise great rewards to him that will kill their enemy's prince, and somewhat less gifts, but them very great also, for every head of them whose names be in the said proclamations contained. They be those whom they count their chief adversaries next unto the prince. Whatsoever is prescribed unto him that killeth any of the proclaimed persons, that is doubled to him that bringeth any of the same to them alive, yea, and to the proclaimed persons themselves, if they will change their minds and come into them, taking their parts, they proffer the same great rewards with pardon and surety of their lives.

Therefore, it quickly cometh to pass that their enemies have all other men in suspicion, and be unfaithful and mistrusting among themselves one to another, living in great fear and in no less jeopardy. For it is well known that divers times the most part of them (and especially the prince himself) hath been betrayed of them in whom they put their most hope and trust, so that there is no manner of act nor deed that gifts and rewards do not enforce men unto. And in rewards they keep no measure, but remembering and considering into how great hazard and jeopardy they call them, endeavor themselves to recompense the greatness of the danger with like great benefits. And, therefore, they promise not only wonderful great abundance of gold, but also lands of great revenues lying in most safe places among their friends.

---

*Announced.

And their promises they perform faithfully without any fraud or covin.

This custom of buying and selling adversaries among other people is disallowed as a cruel act of a base and a cowardish mind. But they in this behalf think themselves much praiseworthy, as who like wise men by this means dispatch great wars without any battle and skirmish. Yea, they count it also a deed of pity and mercy, because that by the death of a few offenders the lives of a great number of innocents, as well of their own men as also of their enemies, be ransomed and saved, which in fighting should have been slain. For they do no less pity the base and common sort of their enemy's people than they do their own, knowing that they be driven and enforced to war against their wills by the furious madness of their princes and heads. If by none of these means the matter go forward as they would have it, then they procure occasions of debate and dissension to be spread among their enemies, as by bringing the prince's brother or some of the noblemen in hope to obtain the kingdom. If this way prevail not, then they raise up the people that be next neighbors and borderers to their enemies, and them they set in their necks under the color of some old title of right, such as kings do never lack. To them they promise their help and aid in their war, and as for money, they give them abundance. But of their own citizens they send to them few or none, whom they make so much of and love so entirely that they would not be willing to change any of them for their adversary's prince.

But their gold and silver, because they keep it all for this only purpose, they lay it out frankly and freely, as who should live even as wealthily if they had bestowed it every penny. Yea, and besides their riches, which they keep at home, they have also an infinite treasure abroad, by reason that (as I said before) many nations be in their debt. Therefore, they hire soldiers out of all countries and send them to battle, but chiefly of the Zapoletes.[26] This people is five hundred miles from Utopia eastward. They be hideous, savage, and fierce, dwelling in wild woods and high mountains, where they were bred and brought up. They be of an hard nature, able to abide and

sustain heat, cold, and labor, abhorring from* all delicate
dainties, occupying no husbandry nor tillage of the ground,
homely and rude both in building of their houses and in their
apparel, given unto no goodness, but only to the breeding and
bringing up of cattle. The most part of their living is by hunting and stealing. They be born only to war, which they diligently and earnestly seek for, and when they have gotten it,
they be wondrous glad thereof. They go forth of their country in great companies together, and whosoever lacketh soldiers, there they proffer their service for small wages. This is
only the craft they have to get their living by. They maintain
their life by seeking their death. For them whom with they be
in wages, they fight hardily, fiercely, and faithfully, but they
bind themselves for no certain time. But upon this condition
they enter into bonds, that the next day they will take part
with the other side for greater wages, and the next day after
that they will be ready to come back again for a little more
money. There be few wars thereaway wherein is not a great
number of them in both parties. Therefore, it daily chanceth
that nigh kinsfolk which were hired together on one part and
there very friendly and familiarly used themselves one with
another, shortly after, being separate in contrary parts, run
one against another enviously and fiercely, and forgetting
both kindred and friendship, thrust their swords one in another, and that for none other cause, but that they be hired of
contrary princes for a little money. Which they do so highly
regard and esteem, that they will easily be provoked to change
parts for a halfpenny more wages by the day. So quickly they
have taken a smack in covetousness,† which for all that is to
them no profit, for that they get by fighting, immediately they
spend unthriftily and wretchedly in riot.

This people fighteth for the Utopians against all nations,
because they give them greater wages than any other nation
will. For the Utopians, like as they seek good men to use well,
so they seek these evil and vicious men to abuse, whom, when

---

*Being disgusted by.
†Acquired a taste for greed.

need requireth, with promises of great rewards they put forth
into great jeopardies, from whence the most part of them never
cometh again to ask their rewards. But to them that remain
alive they pay that which they promised faithfully, that they
may be the more willing to put themselves in like danger another time. Nor the Utopians pass not how many of them they
bring to destruction, for they believe that they should do a very
good deed for all mankind, if they could rid out of the world all
that foul stinking den of that most wicked and cursed people.

Next unto these they use the soldiers of them for whom
they fight; and then the help of their other friends, and last of
all, they join to their own citizens, among whom they give to
one of tried virtue and prowess the rule, governance, and con-
duction* of the whole army. Under him they appoint two
other, which, whiles he is safe, be both private and out of office. But if he be taken or slain, the one of the other two suc-
ceedeth him, as it were by inheritance. And if the second
miscarry, then the third taketh his room, lest that (as the
chance of battle is uncertain and doubtful) the jeopardy or
death of the captain should bring the whole army in hazard.

They choose soldiers out of every city those which put
forth themselves willingly, for they thrust no man forth into
war against his will, because they believe if any man be fearful and faint-hearted of nature, he will not only do no manful and hardy act himself, but also be occasion of cowardness
to his fellows. But if any battle be made against their own
country, then they put these cowards (so that they be strong-
bodied) in ships among other bold-hearted men or else they
dispose them upon the walls from whence they may not fly.
Thus, what for shame that their enemies be at hand, and what
for because they be without hope of running away, they forget all fear. And many times extreme necessity turneth cowardness into prowess and manliness.

But as none of them is thrust forth of his country into war
against his will, so women that be willing to accompany their

---

*Leading.

husbands in times of war be not prohibited or letted. Yea, they provoke and exhort them to it with praises. And in set field* the wives do stand every one by their own husband's side. Also every man is compassed next about with his own children, kinsfolks, and alliance,† that they, whom nature chiefly moveth to mutual succor, thus standing together, may help one another. It is a great reproach and dishonesty for the husband to come home without his wife, or the wife without her husband, or the son without his father. And therefore, if the other part stick so hard by it that the battle come to their hands, it is fought with great slaughter and bloodshed, even to the utter destruction of both parts. For as they make all the means and shifts that may be to keep themselves from the necessity of fighting, or that they may dispatch the battle by their hired soldiers, so when there is no remedy but that they must needs fight themselves, they do as courageously fall to it, as before, whiles they might, they did wisely avoid and refuse it. Nor they be not most fierce at the first brunt,‡ but in continuance by little and little their fierce courage increaseth with so stubborn and obstinate minds that they will rather die than give back an inch. For that surety of living, which every man hath at home, being joined with no careful anxiety or remembrance how their posterity shall live after them (for this pensiveness oftentimes breaketh and abateth courageous stomachs) maketh them stout and hardy and disdainful to be conquered. Moreover, their knowledge in chivalry§ and feats of arms putteth them in a good hope. Finally, the wholesome and virtuous opinions wherein they were brought up even from their childhood, partly through learning and partly through the good ordinances and laws of their weal public, augment and increase their manful courage. By reason whereof they neither set so little store by their lives that they will rashly and unadvisedly cast them away, nor they be not so

---

*Battle array.
†Relations.
‡Assault.
§Military skill.

far in lewd and fond love therewith that they will shamefully covet to keep them when honesty biddeth leave them.

The captain is chiefly to be pursued to the intent the battle may the sooner be ended.

When the battle is hottest and in all places most fierce and fervent, a band of chosen and picked young men, which be sworn to live and die together, take upon them to destroy their adversary's captain, whom they invade,* now with privy wiles, now by open strength. At him they strike both near and far off. He is assailed with a long and a continual assault, fresh men still coming in the wearied men's places. And seldom it chanceth (unless he save himself by flying) that he is not either slain or else taken prisoner and yielded to his enemies alive.

If they win the field, they persecute† not their enemies with the violent rage of slaughter, for they had rather take them alive than kill them. Neither they do so follow the chase and pursuit of their enemies, but they leave behind them one part of their host in battle array under their standards. Insomuch that if all their whole army be discomfitted‡ and overcome, saving the rearward,§ and that they therewith achieve the victory, then they had rather let all their enemies escape, than to follow them out of array.‖ For they remember it hath chanced unto themselves more than once: the whole power and strength of their host being vanquished and put to flight, whiles their enemies rejoicing in the victory have persecuted them, flying some one way and some another, a small company of their men lying in an ambush, there ready at all occasions, have suddenly risen upon them thus dispersed and scattered out of array, and through presumption of safety unadvisedly pursuing the chase, and have incontinent changed the fortune of the whole battle, and spite of their teeth# wresting out of their hands the sure and undoubted

---

*Attack.
†Pursue.
‡Defeated.
§Rear guard.
‖Formation.
#Despite their fierce resistance.

victory, being a little before conquered, have for their part conquered the conquerors.

It is hard to say whether they be craftier in laying an ambush, or wittier in avoiding the same. You would think they intend to fly when they mean nothing less. And, contrariwise, when they go about that purpose, you would believe it were the least part of their thought. For if they perceive themselves either overmatched in number or closed in too narrow a place, then they remove their camp either in the night season with silence, or by some policy they deceive their enemies, or in the daytime they retire back so softly that it is no less jeopardy to meddle with them when they give back than when they press on. They fence and fortify their camp surely* with a deep and a broad trench. The earth thereof is cast inward. Nor they do not set drudges and slaves a-work about it, it is done by the hands of the soldiers themselves. All the whole army worketh upon it, except them that keep watch and ward in harness† before the trench for sudden adventures.‡ Therefore, by the labor of so many a large trench closing in a great compass of ground is made in less time than any man would believe.

Their armor or harness which they wear is sure and strong *Their armor.* to receive strokes and handsome§ for all movings and gestures of the body, insomuch that it is not unwieldy to swim in for in the discipline of their warfare, among other feats, they learn to swim in harness. Their weapons be arrows aloof,‖ which they shoot both strongly and surely, not only footmen but also horsemen. At hand strokes they use not swords but poleaxes, which be mortal as well in sharpness as in weight, both for foins# and downstrokes. Engines for war they devise and invent wondrous wittily, which when they be made, they

---

*Securely.
†Armed.
‡Surprise attacks.
§Easy to manipulate.
‖From afar.
#Thrusts.

keep very secret lest, if they should be known before need require, they should be but laughed at and serve to no purpose. But in making them, hereunto they have chief respect that they be both easy to be carried and handsome to be moved and turned about.

Truce taken with their enemies for a short time they do so firmly and faithfully keep that they will not break it, no, not though they be thereunto provoked. They do not waste nor destroy their enemies' land with foragings,* nor they burn not up their corn. Yea, they save it as much as may be from being overrun and trodden down either with men or horses, thinking that it groweth for their own use and profit. They hurt no man that is unharmed, unless he be an espial.† All cities that be yielded unto them they defend, and such as they win by force of assault they neither despoil nor sack, but them that withstood and dissuaded the yielding up of the same they put to death. The other soldiers they punish with bondage. All the weak multitude they leave untouched. If they know that any citizens counseled to yield and render up the city, to them they give part of the condemned men's goods. The residue they distribute and give freely among them whose help they had in the same war, for none of themselves taketh any portion of the prey.

But when the battle is finished and ended, they put their friends to never a penny cost of all the charges that they were at, but lay it upon their necks that be conquered. Them they burden with the whole charge of their expenses, which they demand of them partly in money to be kept for like use of battle, and partly in lands of great revenues to be paid unto them yearly forever. Such revenues they have now in many countries, which by little and little rising of divers and sundry causes be increased above seven hundred thousand ducats by the year.[27] Thither they send forth some of their citizens as lieutenants‡ to live there sumptuously like men of honor and

---

*Plundering.
†Spy.
‡Representatives.

renown. And yet, this notwithstanding, much money is saved, which cometh to the common treasury, unless it so chance that they had rather trust the country with the money, which many times they do so long until they have need to occupy it. And it seldom happeneth that they demand all. Of these lands they assign part unto them which, at their request and exhortation, put themselves in such jeopardies as I spoke of before. If any prince stir up war against them, intending to invade their land, they meet him incontinent out of their own borders with great power and strength, for they never lightly make war in their own country, nor they be never brought into so extreme necessity as to take help out of foreign lands into their own island.

Of the Religions in Utopia.

THERE be divers kinds of religion not only in sundry parts of the island, but also in divers places of every city. Some worship for god the sun; some, the moon; some, some other of the planets. There be that give worship to a man that was once of excellent virtue or of famous glory, not only as god, but also as the chiefest and highest god. But the most and the wisest part (rejecting all these) believe that there is a certain godly power, unknown, everlasting, incomprehensible, inexplicable, far above the capacity and reach of man's wit, dispersed throughout all the world, not in bigness but in virtue and power. Him they call the father of all. To him alone they attribute the beginnings, the increasings, the proceedings, the changes, and the ends of all things. Neither they give any divine honors to any other than to him.

Yea, all the other also, though they be in divers opinions, yet in this point they agree all together with the wisest sort, in believing that there is one chief and principal god, the maker and ruler of the whole world, whom they all commonly in their country language call Mythra.[28] But in this they disagree, that among some he is counted one, and among some another. For every one of them, whatsoever that is which he taketh for the chief god, thinketh it to be the very same nature, to whose only divine might and majesty the sum and sovereignty of all things by the consent of all people is attributed and given. Howbeit, they all begin by little and little to forsake and fall from this variety of superstitions, and to agree together in that religion which seemeth by reason to pass and excel the residue. And it is not to be doubted, but all the others would long ago have been abolished, but that whatsoever unprosperous thing happened to any of them as he was minded to change his religion, the fearfulness of people did take it not as a thing coming by chance, but as sent from god out of heaven—as though the god whose honor he was forsaking would revenge that wicked purpose against him.

But after they heard us speak of the name of Christ, of his doctrine, laws, miracles, and of the no less wonderful constancy of so many martyrs, whose blood willingly shed brought a great number of nations throughout all parts of the world into their sect, you will not believe with how glad minds they agreed unto the same, whether it were by the secret inspiration of God, or else for that they thought it nighest unto that opinion which among them is counted the chiefest. Howbeit, I think this was no small help and furtherance in the matter, that they heard us say that Christ instituted among His* all things common, and that the same community doth yet remain amongst the rightest Christian companies. Verily, howsoever it came to pass, many of them consented together in our religion and were washed in the holy water of baptism.

Religious houses.

But because among us four (for no more of us was left alive, two of our company being dead) there was no priest—which I am right sorry for—they, being entered† and instructed in all other points of our religion, lack only those sacraments which here none but priests do minister.[29] Howbeit, they understand and perceive them and be very desirous of the same. Yea, they reason and dispute the matter earnestly among themselves whether without the sending of a Christian

---

*That is, His followers.
†Initiated.

bishop, one chosen out of their own people may receive the order of priesthood. And, truly, they were minded to choose one. But at my departure from them they had chosen none.

They also which do not agree to Christ's religion fear* no man from it, nor speak against any man that hath received it, saving that one of our company in my presence was sharply punished. He, as soon as he was baptized, began against our wills, with more earnest affection than wisdom, to reason of Christ's religion, and began to wax so hot in his matter that he did not only prefer our religion before all other, but also did utterly despise and condemn all other, calling them profane and the followers of them wicked and devilish and the children of everlasting damnation. When he had thus long reasoned the matter, they laid hold on him, accused him, and condemned him into exile, not as a despiser of religion, but as a seditious person and a raiser-up of dissension among the people. For this is one of the ancientest laws among them: that no man shall be blamed for reasoning in the maintenance of his own religion.[30]

For King Utopus, even at the first beginning, hearing that the inhabitants of the land were before his coming thither at continual dissension and strife among themselves for their religions—perceiving also that this common dissension (whiles every several sect took several parts† in fighting for their country) was the only occasion of his conquest over them all—as soon as he had gotten the victory, first of all, he made a decree that it should be lawful for every man to favor and follow what religion he would, and that he might do the best he could to bring others to his opinion, so that he did it peaceably, gently, quietly, and soberly, without hasty and contentious rebuking and inveighing against others. If he could not by fair and gentle speech induce them unto his opinion, yet he should use no kind of violence, and refrain from displeasant and seditious words. To him that would vehemently

---

*Frighten.
†Sides.

Seditious reasoners punished.

and fervently in this cause strive and contend was decreed banishment or bondage.

This law did King Utopus make not only for the maintenance of peace, which he saw through continual contention and mortal hatred utterly extinguished, but also because he thought this decree should make for the furtherance of religion. Whereof he durst define and determine nothing unadvisedly, as doubting whether God, desiring manifold and divers sorts of honor, would inspire sundry men with sundry kinds of religion. And this surely he thought a very unmeet* and foolish thing, and a point of arrogant presumption, to compel all other by violence and threatenings to agree to the same that thou believest to be true. Furthermore, though there be one religion which alone is true, and all other vain and superstitious, yet did he well foresee (so that the matter were handled with reason and sober modesty) that the truth of the† own power would at the last issue out and come to light. But if contention and debate in that behalf should continually be used, as the worst men be most obstinate and stubborn and in their evil opinion most constant, he perceived that then the best and holiest religion would be trodden underfoot and destroyed by most vain superstitions, even as good corn is by thorns and weeds overgrown and choked. Therefore, all this matter he left undiscussed and gave to every man free liberty and choice to believe what he would, saving that he earnestly and straightly charged them that no man should conceive so vile and base an opinion of the dignity of man's nature as to think that the souls do die and perish with the body, or that the world runneth at all adventures‡ governed by no divine providence.

No vile opinion to be conceived of man's worthy nature.

And, therefore, they believe that after this life vices be extremely punished and virtues bountifully rewarded. Him that is of a contrary opinion they count not in the number of men, as one that hath avaled the high nature of his soul to the

---

*Inappropriate.
†Its.
‡By chance.

vileness of brute beasts' bodies, much less in the number of
their citizens, whose laws and ordinances, if it were not for
fear, he would nothing at all esteem. For you may be sure that
he will study either with craft privily to mock or else violently
to break the common laws of his country, in whom remaineth
no further fear than of the laws, nor no further hope than of
the body. Wherefore, he that is thus minded is deprived of all
honors, excluded from all offices, and reject from all common
administrations in the public weal. And thus he is of all sorts
despised, as of an unprofitable and of a base and vile nature.
Howbeit, they put him to no punishment, because they be
persuaded that it is in no man's power to believe what he list.
No, nor they constrain him not with threatenings to dissemble his mind and show countenance contrary to his thought.
For deceit and falsehood and all manners of lies, as next unto
fraud, they do marvelously detest and abhor. But they suffer
him not to dispute in his opinion, and that only among the
common people. For else apart among the priests and men of
gravity they do not only suffer, but also exhort him to dispute
and argue, hoping that at the last that madness will give place
to reason.

    There be also others, and of them no small number, which
be not forbidden to speak their minds, as grounding their
opinion upon some reason, being in their living neither evil
nor vicious. Their heresy is much contrary to the other, for
they believe that the souls of brute beasts be immortal and
everlasting, but nothing to be compared with ours in dignity,
neither ordained nor predestinate to like felicity.[31] For all they
believe certainly and surely that man's bliss shall be so great
that they do mourn and lament every man's sickness but no
man's death, unless it be one whom they see depart from his
life carefully* and against his will. For this they take for a very
evil token, as though the soul, being in despair and vexed in
conscience through some privy and secret forefeeling of the
punishment now at hand, were afraid to depart. And they

Irregious people secluded from all honors.

A very strange saying.

Deceit and falsehood detested.

A marvelous strange opinion touching the souls of brute beasts.

To die unwillingly, an evil token.

---

*Full of cares.

Utopia

think he shall not be welcome to God, which, when he is called, runneth not to him gladly, but is drawn by force and sore against his will. They, therefore, that see this kind of death do abhor it, and them that so die they bury with sorrow and silence. And when they have prayed God to be merciful to the soul and mercifully to pardon the infirmities thereof, they cover the dead corpse with earth.

A willing and merry death, not to be lamented.   Contrariwise, all that depart merrily and full of good hope, for them no man mourneth, but followeth the hearse with joyful singing, commending the souls to God with great affection. And at the last, not with mourning sorrow but with a great reverence, they burn the bodies. And in the same place they set up a pillar of stone with the dead man's titles therein graved. When they be come home, they rehearse his virtuous manners and his good deeds, but no part of his life is so oft or gladly talked of as his merry death. They think that this remembrance of the virtue and goodness of the dead doth vehemently provoke and enforce the living to virtue, and that nothing can be more pleasant and acceptable to the dead, whom they suppose to be present among them, when they talk of them, though to the dull and feeble eyesight of mortal men they be invisible. For it were an inconvenient* thing that the blessed should not be at liberty to go whither they would. And it were a point of great unkindness in them to have utterly cast away the desire of visiting and seeing their friends, to whom they were in their lifetime joined by mutual love and amity, which in good men after their death they count to be rather increased than diminished. They believe, therefore, that the dead be presently conversant among the quick,† as beholders and witnesses of all their words and deeds. Therefore, they go more courageously to their business as having a trust and affiance‡ in such overseers. And this same belief of the present conversation of their forefathers and ancestors among them feareth them from all secret dishonesty.

---

*Unfitting.
†Engaged in familiar intercourse with the living.
‡Trust.

They utterly despise and mock soothsayings and divinations of things to come by the flight or voices of birds, and all other divinations of vain superstition, which in other countries be in great observation. But they highly esteem and worship miracles that come by no help of nature, as works and witnesses of the present power of God. And such, they say, do chance there very often. And sometimes in great and doubtful matters, by common intercession and prayers, they procure and obtain them with a sure hope and confidence and a steadfast belief. *Soothsayers not regarded nor credited.* *Miracles.*

They think that the contemplation of nature, and the praise thereof coming, is to God a very acceptable honor. Yet there be many so earnestly bent and affectioned to religion that they pass nothing for learning, nor give their minds to any knowledge of things. But idleness they utterly forsake and eschew, thinking felicity after this life to be gotten and obtained by busy labors and good exercises. Some, therefore, of them attend upon the sick, some amend highways, cleanse ditches, repair bridges, dig turfs, gravel, and stones, fell and cleave wood, bring wood, corn, and other things into the cities in carts, and serve not only in common works, but also in private labors as servants, yea, more than bondmen. For whatsoever unpleasant, hard, and vile work is anywhere, from the which labor loathsomeness and desperation doth fray* other, all that they take upon them willingly and gladly, procuring quiet and rest to other, remaining in continual work and labor themselves, not embraiding† others therewith. They neither reprove other men's lives nor glory in their own. These men, the more serviceable they behave themselves, the more they be honored of all men. *The life contemplative.* *The life active.*

Yet they be divided into two sects. The one is of them that live single and chaste, abstaining not only from the company of women, but also from eating of flesh, and some of them from all manner of beasts, which, utterly rejecting the pleasures of this present life as hurtful, be all wholly set upon the desire

---

*Frighten.
†Upbraiding.

of the life to come by watching and sweating,* hoping shortly to obtain it, being in the mean season merry and lusty. The other sect is no less desirous of labor, but they embrace matrimony, not despising the solace thereof, thinking that they cannot be discharged of their bounden duties towards nature without labor and toil, nor towards their native country without procreation of children. They abstain from no pleasure that doth nothing hinder them from labor. They love the flesh of four-footed beasts, because they believe that by that meat they be made hardier and stronger to work. The Utopians count this sect the wiser, but the other the holier, which, in *It is not all* that they prefer single life before matrimony, and that sharp *one to be wise* life before an easier life, if herein they grounded upon reason *and good.* they would mock them, but now, forasmuch as they say they be led to it by religion, they honor and worship them.[32] And these be they whom in their language by a peculiar name they call Buthrescas,† the which word by interpretation signifieth to us men of religion or religious men.

Priests. They have priests of exceeding holiness and, therefore very few, for there be but thirteen in every city, according to the number of their churches, saving when they go forth to battle, for then seven of them go forth with the army, in whose steads so many new be made at home. But the other, at their return home again, re-enter every one into his own place. They that be above the number, until such time as they succeed into the places of the other at their dying, be in the mean season continually in company with the bishop, for he is the chief head of them all. They be chosen of the people, as the other magistrates be, by secret voices‡ for the avoiding of strife. After their election they be consecrate of their own company. They be overseers of all divine matters, orderers of religions, and, as it were, judges and masters of manners. And it is a great dishonesty and shame to be rebuked or spoken to by any of them for dissolute and incontinent living.

---

*Keeping vigils and laboring.
†"Very Religious."
‡Votes.

But as it is their office to give good exhortations and counsel, so is it the duty of the prince and the other magistrates to correct and punish offenders, saving that the priests, whom they find exceeding vicious livers, them they excommunicate from having any interest in divine matters. And there is almost no punishment among them more feared, for they run in very great infamy and be inwardly tormented with a secret fear of religion, and shall not long escape free with their bodies, for unless they by quick repentance approve* the amendment of their lives to the priests, they be taken and punished of the council as wicked and irreligious.

Excommunication.

Both childhood and youth is instructed and taught of them. Nor they be not more diligent to instruct them in learning than in virtue and good manners, for they use with very great endeavor and diligence to put into the heads of their children, whiles they be yet tender and pliant, good opinions and profitable for the conservation of their weal public, which, when they be once rooted in children, do remain with them all their life after and be wonders profitable for the defense and maintenance of the state of the commonwealth, which never decayeth but through vices rising of evil opinions.

The priests, unless they be women—for that kind is not excluded from priesthood, howbeit few be chosen, and none but widows and old women—the men priests, I say, take to their wives the chiefest women in all their country, for to no office among the Utopians is more honor and preeminence given. Insomuch that if they commit any offense, they be under no common judgment, but be left only to God and themselves, for they think it not lawful to touch him with man's hand, be he never so vicious, which after so singular a sort was dedicate and consecrate to God as a holy offering. This manner may they easily observe, because they have so few priests and do choose them with such circumspection. For it scarcely ever chanceth that the most virtuous among virtuous, which in

Women priests.

The majesty and preeminence of priests.

---

*Give proof of.

respect only of his virtue is advanced to so high a dignity, can fall to vice and wickedness. And if it should chance indeed (as man's nature is mutable and frail), yet by reason they be so few and promoted to no might nor power, but only to honor, it were not to be feared that any great damage by them should happen and ensue to the commonwealth. They have so rare and few priests lest, if the honor were communicated to many, the dignity of the order, which among them now is so highly esteemed, should run in contempt, especially because they think it hard to find many so good as to be meet for that dignity, to the execution and discharge whereof it is not sufficient to be endued with mean* virtues.

Furthermore, these priests be not more esteemed of their own countrymen than they be of foreign and strange countries, which thing may hereby plainly appear, and I think also that this is the cause of it. For whiles the armies be fighting together in open field, they a little beside, not far off, kneel upon their knees in their hallowed vestments, holding up their hands to heaven, praying first of all for peace, next for victory of their own part, but to neither part a bloody victory. If their host get the upper hand, they run into the main battle and restrain their own men from slaying and cruelly pursuing their vanquished enemies, which enemies, if they do but see them and speak to them, it is enough for the safeguard of their lives. And the touching of their clothes defendeth and saveth all their goods from ravin† and spoil. This thing hath advanced them to so great worship and true majesty among all nations, that many times they have as well preserved their own citizens from the cruel force of their enemies as they have their enemies from the furious rage of their own men. For it is well known that when their own army hath reculed‡ and in despair turned back and run away, their enemies fiercely pursuing with slaughter and spoil, then the priests, coming between, have stayed the murder and parted both the hosts, so that peace

*Inferior.
†Plunder.
‡Retreated.

hath been made and concluded between both parts upon equal and indifferent conditions. For there was never any nation so fierce, so cruel and rude,* but they had them in such reverence that they counted their bodies hallowed and sanctified, and therefore not to be violently and unreverently touched.

They keep holy the first and the last day of every month and year, dividing the year into months, which they measure by the course of the moon, as they do the year by the course of the sun. The first days they call in their language Cynemernes and the last Trapemernes, the which words may be interpreted, primifest and finifest, or else in our speech, first feast and last feast.[33]

The observation of holy days among the Utopians.

Their churches be very gorgeous and not only of fine and curious workmanship, but also (which in the fewness of them was necessary) very wide and large and able to receive a great company of people. But they be all somewhat dark. Howbeit, that was not done through ignorance in building but, as they say, by the counsel of the priests because they thought that overmuch light doth disperse men's cogitations, whereas in dim and doubtful light they be gathered together and more earnestly fixed upon religion and devotion, which because it is not there of one sort among all men—and yet all the kinds and fashions of it, though they be sundry and manifold, agree together in the honor of the divine nature, as going divers ways to one end—therefore, nothing is seen nor heard in the churches but that seemeth to agree indifferently with them all. If there be a distinct kind of sacrifice† peculiar to any several‡ sect, that they execute at home in their own houses. The common sacrifices be so ordered that they be no derogation nor prejudice to any of the private sacrifices and religions. Therefore, no image of any god is seen in the church, to the intent it may be free for every man to conceive God by their religion after what likeness and similitude they will. They call

Their churches.

Churches of dim light and a reason why.

---

*Uncivilized.
†Sacred rite.
‡Separate.

upon no peculiar name of God, but only Mythra, in the which word they all agree together in one nature of the divine majesty whatsoever it be. No prayers be used but such as every man may boldly pronounce without the offending of any sect.

They come, therefore, to the church the last day of every month and year, in the evening yet fasting, there to give thanks to God for that they have prosperously passed over the year or month, whereof that holy day is the last day. The next day they come to the church early in the morning, to pray to God that they may have good fortune and success all the new year or month which they do begin of that same holy day. But in the holy days that be the last days of the months and years, *The confession* before they come to the church, the wives fall down pros- *of the* trate before their husbands' feet at home, and the children *Utopians.* before the feet of their parents, confessing and acknowledging themselves offenders either by some actual deed or by omission of their duty, and desire pardon for their offense. Thus if any cloud of privy displeasure was risen at home, by this satisfaction it is overblown, that they may be present at the sacrifices with pure and charitable minds, for they be afraid to come there with troubled consciences. Therefore, if they know themselves to bear any hatred or grudge towards any man, they presume not to come to the sacrifices before they have reconciled themselves and purged their consciences, for fear of great vengeance and punishment for their offense.

An order or When they come thither, the men go into the right side of *places in the* the church and the women into the left side. There they place *church.* themselves in such order that all they which be of the male kind in every household sit before the goodman* of the house, and they of the female kind before the goodwife.† Thus it is foreseen that all their gestures and behaviors be marked and observed abroad‡ of them by whose authority and discipline

---

*Master.
†Mistress.
‡In public (outside the house).

they be governed at home. This also they diligently see unto, that the younger evermore be coupled with his elder, lest, children being joined together, they should pass over that time in childish wantonness,* wherein they ought principally to conceive a religious and devout fear towards God, which is the chief and almost the only incitation to virtue.

They kill no living beast in sacrifice, nor they think not that the merciful clemency of God hath delight in blood and slaughter, which hath given life to beasts to the intent they should live. They burn frankincense and other sweet savors, and light also a great number of wax candles and tapers, not *Ceremonies.* supposing this gear to be anything available to† the divine nature, as neither the prayers of men. But this unhurtful and harmless kind of worship pleased them, and by these sweet savors and lights and other such ceremonies, men feel themselves secretly lifted up and encouraged to devotion with more willing and fervent hearts.

The people weareth in the church white apparel. The priest is clothed in changeable colors, which in workmanship be excellent, but in stuff not very precious, for their vestments be neither embroidered with gold, nor set with precious stones, but they be wrought so finely and cunningly with divers feathers of fowls, that the estimation‡ of no costly stuff is able to countervail§ the price of the work. Furthermore, in these birds' feathers and in the due order of them, which is observed in their setting, they say, is contained certain divine mysteries, the interpretation whereof known, which is diligently taught by the priests, they be put in remembrance of the bountiful benefits of God toward them, and of the love and honor which of their behalf is due to God, and also of their duties one toward another.

When the priest first cometh out of the vestry thus appareled, they fall down incontinent every one reverently to the

---

*Naughtiness.
†Needed by, effectual with.
‡Value.
§Equal.

ground, with so still silence on every part that the very fashion of the thing striketh into them a certain fear of God, as though he were there personally present. When they have lain a little space on the ground, the priest giveth them a sign

Their church music. for to rise. Then they sing praises unto God, which they intermix with instruments of music, for the most part of other fashions than these that we use in this part of the world. And like as some of ours be much sweeter than theirs, so some of theirs do far pass ours. But in one thing doubtless they go exceeding far beyond us, for all their music, both that they play upon instruments and that they sing with man's voice, doth so resemble and express natural affections, the sound and tune is so applied and made agreeable to the thing, that whether it be a prayer or else a ditty of gladness, of patience, of trouble, of mourning, or of anger, the fashion of the melody doth so represent the meaning of the thing that it doth wonderfully move, stir, pierce, and inflame the hearers' minds.

Prayers. At the last the people and the priest together rehearse solemn prayers in words, expressly pronounced,* so made that every man may privately apply to himself that which is commonly spoken of all. In these prayers every man recogniseth and acknowledgeth God to be his maker, his governor, and the principal cause of all other goodness, thanking him for so many benefits received at his hand, but namely† that through the favor of God he hath chanced into that public weal which is most happy and wealthy, and hath chosen that religion which he hopeth to be most true. In the which thing if he do anything err, or if there be any other better than either of them is, being more acceptable to God, he desireth Him that He will of His goodness let him have knowledge thereof, as one that is ready to follow what way soever He will lead him. But if this form and fashion of a commonwealth be best and his own religion most true and perfect, then he

---

*In prescribed terms.
†Especially.

desireth God to give him a constant steadfastness in the same and to bring all other people to the same order of living and to the same opinion of God, unless there be anything that in this diversity of religions doth delight His unsearchable pleasure. To be short, he prayeth Him that after his death he may come to Him, but how soon or late, that he dare not assign or determine. Howbeit, if it might stand with His majesty's pleasure, he would be much gladder to die a painful death and so to go to God, than by long living in worldly prosperity to be away from Him. When this prayer is said, they fall down to the ground again, and a little after they rise up and go to dinner. And the residue of the day they pass over in plays and exercise of chivalry.*

Now I have declared and described unto you as truly as I could the form and order of that commonwealth, which verily in my judgment is not only the best, but also that which alone of good right may claim and take upon it the name of a commonwealth or public weal. For in other places they speak still of the commonwealth, but every man procureth his own private gain. Here, where nothing is private, the common affairs be earnestly looked upon. And, truly, on both parts they have good cause so to do as they do, for in other countries who knoweth not that he shall starve for hunger, unless he make some several provision for himself, though the commonwealth flourish never so much in riches? And therefore he is compelled even of very necessity to have regard to himself rather than to the people, that is to say, to others. Contrariwise, there, where all things be common to every man, it is not to be doubted that any man shall lack anything necessary for his private uses, so that the common storehouses and barns be sufficiently stored, for there nothing is distributed after a niggish† sort, neither there is any poor man or beggar, and though no man have anything, yet every man is rich. For what can be more rich than to live joyfully and merrily,

---

*Pastimes and military exercises.
†Niggardly.

without all grief and pensiveness,* not caring for his own living, nor vexed or troubled with his wife's importunate complaints, nor dreading poverty to his son, nor sorrowing for his daughter's dowry? Yea, they take no care at all for the living and wealth of themselves and all theirs: of their wives, their children, their nephews, their children's children, and all the succession that ever shall follow in their posterity. And yet, besides this, there is no less provision for them that were once laborers and be now weak and impotent, than for them that do now labor and take pain.

Here now would I see if any man dare be so bold as to compare with this equity the justice of other nations, among whom I forsake God if I can find any sign or token of equity and justice. For what justice is this, that a rich goldsmith, or an usurer, or, to be short, any of them which either do nothing at all, or else that which they do is such that it is not very necessary to the commonwealth, should have a pleasant and a wealthy living either by idleness or by unnecessary business, when in the meantime poor laborers, carters,† ironsmiths, carpenters, and plowmen, by so great and continual toil as drawing and bearing beasts be scant‡ able to sustain, and again so necessary toil that without it no commonwealth were able to continue and endure one year, should yet get so hard and poor a living, and live so wretched and miserable a life, that the state and condition of the laboring beasts may seem much better and wealthier? For they be not put to so continual labor, nor their living is not much worse, yea, to them much pleasanter, taking no thought in the mean season for the time to come. But these silly poor wretches be presently tormented with barren and unfruitful labor, and the remembrance of their poor, indigent, and beggarly old age killeth them up.[34] For their daily wages is so little that it will not suffice for the same day, much less it yieldeth any overplus that may daily be laid up for the relief of old age.

---

*Anxious or melancholy thought.
†Peasants, farmers.
‡Scarcely.

Is not this an unjust and an unkind public weal, which giveth great fees and rewards to gentlemen, as they call them, and to goldsmiths, and to such other, which be either idle persons or else only flatterers and devisers of vain pleasures, and of the contrary part maketh no gentle provision for poor plowmen, colliers, laborers, carters, ironsmiths, and carpenters, without whom no commonwealth can continue? But after it hath abused the labors of their lusty and flowering age, at the last, when they be oppressed with old age and sickness, being needy, poor, and indigent of all things, then, forgetting their so many painful watchings, not remembering their so many and so great benefits, recompenseth and acquitteth them most unkindly with miserable death. And yet besides this, the rich men not only by private fraud, but also by common laws do every day pluck and snatch away from the poor some part of their daily living, so whereas it seemed before unjust to recompense with unkindness their pains that have been beneficial to the public weal, now they have to this their wrong and unjust dealing (which is yet a much worse point) given the name of justice, yea, and that by force of a law.

Therefore, when I consider and weigh in my mind all these commonwealths which nowadays anywhere do flourish, so God help me, I can perceive nothing but a certain conspiracy of rich men procuring their own commodities under the name and title of the commonwealth. They invent and devise all means and crafts, first how to keep safely, without fear of losing, that which they have unjustly gathered together, and next how to hire and abuse the work and labor of the poor for as little money as may be. These devices when the rich men have decreed to be kept and observed under color of the commonalty,* that is to say, also of the poor people, then they be made laws. But these most wicked and vicious men, when they have by their insatiable covetousness divided among themselves all those things which would have sufficed all men, yet how far be they from the wealth and felicity of the

---

*Pretext of (serving) the people.

Utopian commonwealth? Out of the which, in that all the desire of money with the use thereof is utterly secluded* and banished, how great a heap of cares is cut away! How great an occasion of wickedness and mischief is plucked up by the roots! For who knoweth not that fraud, theft, ravin, brawling, quarreling, brabbling,† strife, chiding, contention, murder, treason, poisoning, which by daily punishments are rather revenged than refrained, do die when money dieth? And also that fear, grief, care, labors, and watchings do perish even the very same moment that money perisheth? Yea, poverty itself, which only seemed to lack money, if money were gone, it also would decrease and vanish away.

And that you may perceive this more plainly, consider with yourselves some barren and unfruitful year, wherein many thousands of people have starved for hunger. I dare be bold to say that in the end of that penury so much corn or grain might have been found in the rich men's barns, if they had been searched, as, being divided among them whom famine and pestilence then consumed, no man at all should have felt that plague and penury. So easily might men get their living, if that same worthy princess, Lady Money, did not alone stop up the way between us and our living, which, in God's name, was very excellently devised and invented, that by her the way thereto should be opened. I am sure the rich men perceive this, nor they be not ignorant how much better it were to lack no necessary thing than to abound with overmuch superfluity, to be rid out of innumerable cares and troubles than to be besieged and encumbered with great riches.

And I doubt not that either the respect of every man's private commodity or else the authority of our savior Christ (which for His great wisdom could not but know what were best, and for His inestimable goodness could not but counsel to that which He knew to be best) would have brought all the world long ago into the laws of this weal public, if it were not that one only beast, the princess and mother of all mischief,

---

*Cut off.
†Wrangling.

Pride, doth withstand and let it. She measureth not wealth and prosperity by her own commodities, but by the misery and incommodities of others; she would not by her good will be made a goddess, if there were no wretches left over whom she might, like a scornful lady, rule and triumph, over whose miseries her felicities might shine, whose poverty she might vex, torment, and increase by gorgeously setting forth her riches. This hell-hound creepeth into men's hearts and plucketh them back from entering the right path of life and is so deeply rooted in men's breasts that she cannot be plucked out.

This form and fashion of a weal public, which I would gladly wish unto all nations, I am glad yet that it hath chanced to the Utopians, which have followed those institutions of life, whereby they have laid such foundations of their commonwealth as shall continue and last not only wealthily, but also, as far as man's wit may judge and conjecture, shall endure for ever. For, seeing the chief causes of ambition and sedition with other vices be plucked up by the roots and abandoned at home, there can be no jeopardy of domestical dissension, which alone hath cast under foot and brought to naught the well-fortified and strongly defensed wealth and riches of many cities. But forasmuch as perfect concord remaineth and wholesome laws be executed at home, the envy* of all foreign princes be not able to shake or move the empire, though they have many times long ago gone about to do it, being evermore driven back.

Thus when Raphael had made an end of his tale, though many things came to my mind which in the manners and laws of that people seemed to be instituted and founded of no good reason, not only in the fashion of their chivalry, and in their sacrifices and religions, and in other of their laws, but also, yea, and chiefly in that which is the principal foundation of all their ordinances, that is to say, in the community of their life and living, without any occupying† of money, by the

---

*Enmity.
†Making use.

which thing only all nobility, magnificence, worship, honor, and majesty, the true ornaments and honors, as the common opinion is, of a commonwealth, utterly be overthrown and destroyed—yet, because I knew that he was weary of talking and was not sure whether he could abide that anything should be said against his mind* (especially remembering that he had reprehended this fault in other, which be afraid lest they should seem not to be wise enough unless they could find some fault in other men's inventions), therefore, I, praising both their institutions and his communication, took him by the hand and led him in to supper, saying that we would choose another time to weigh and examine the same matters and to talk with him more at large therein. Which would God it might once come to pass! In the meantime, as I cannot agree and consent to all things that be said, being else without doubt a man singularly well learned and also in all worldly matters exactly and profoundly experienced, so must I needs confess and grant that many things be in the Utopian weal public, which in our cities I may rather wish for than hope.

Thus endeth the afternoon's talk of Raphael Hythloday concerning the laws and institutions of the island of Utopia.

---

*Opinion.

LETTER OF
PETER GILES TO BUSLYDE

To the Right Honorable Hieronymus Buslyde,[1]
Provost of Arienn and Counselor to the
Catholic King Charles, Peter Giles, Citizen of
Antwerp, wisheth health and felicity.

THOMAS MORE, THE SINGULAR ornament of this our age, as
you yourself, right honorable Buslyde, can witness, to whom
he is perfectly well known, sent unto me this other day the *Island of Utopia*, to very few as yet known, but most worthy.
Which, as far excelling Plato's *Commonwealth*,* all people
should be willing to know, especially of a man most eloquent
so finely set forth, so cunningly painted out, and so evidently
subject to the eye, that as oft as I read it, methinketh that I see
somewhat more than when I heard Raphael Hythloday himself (for I was present at that talk as well as Master More) uttering and pronouncing his own words. Yea, though the same
man, according to his pure eloquence, did so open and declare the matter that he might plainly enough appear to report not things which he had learned of others only by
hearsay, but which he had with his own eyes presently seen
and thoroughly viewed, and wherein he had no small time
been conversant and abiding: a man truly, in mine opinion,
as touching the knowledge of regions, peoples, and worldly
experience, much passing,† yea, even the very famous and
renowned traveler Ulysses; and indeed, such a one as for the
space of these eight hundred years past I think nature into
the world brought not forth his like, in comparison of whom
Vespucci may be thought to have seen nothing. Moreover,

---

*That is, the *Republic*.
†Surpassing.

whereas we be wont more effectually and pithily to declare and express things that we have seen than which we have but only heard, there was besides that in this man a certain peculiar grace and singular dexterity to describe and set forth a matter withal.

Yet the selfsame things as oft as I behold and consider them drawn and painted out with Master More's pencil, I am therewith so moved, so delighted, so inflamed, and so rapt, that sometime methink I am presently conversant, even in the island of Utopia. And I promise you, I can scant believe that Raphael himself, by all that five years' space that he was in Utopia abiding, saw there so much as here in Master More's description is to be seen and perceived. Which description with so many wonders and miraculous things is replenished* that I stand in great doubt whereat first and chiefly to muse or marvel, whether at the excellence of his perfect and sure memory, which could wellnigh† word by word rehearse so many things once only heard, or else at his singular prudence, who so well and wittily marked and bare away all the original causes and fountains (to the vulgar people commonly most unknown) whereof both issueth and springeth the mortal confusion and utter decay of a commonwealth, and also the advancement and wealthy‡ state of the same may rise and grow; or else at the efficacy and pith of his words, which in so fine a Latin style, with such force of eloquence hath couched together and comprised so many and divers matters, especially being a man continually encumbered with so many busy and troublesome cares, both public and private, as he is. Howbeit, all these things cause you little to marvel (right honorable Buslyde) for that you are familiarly and thoroughly acquainted with the notable, yea almost divine, wit of the man.

But now to proceed to other matters, I surely know noth-

---

*Filled.
†Almost.
‡Flourishing.

ing needful or requisite to be adjoined unto his writings, only a meter* of four verses written in the Utopian tongue, which after Master More's departure Hythloday by chance showed me, that have I cause to be added thereto, with the alphabet of the same nation,[2] and have also garnished the margin of the book with certain notes. For, as touching the situation of the island, that is to say, in what part of the world Utopia standeth, the ignorance and lack whereof not a little troubleth and grieveth Master More, indeed Raphael left not that unspoken of. Howbeit, with very few words he lightly touched it, incidentally by the way passing it over, as meaning of likelihood to keep and reserve that to another place. And the same, I wot† not how, by a certain evil and unlucky chance escaped us both. For when Raphael was speaking thereof, one of Master More's servants came to him and whispered in his ear. Wherefore I being then of purpose more earnestly addict‡ to hear, one of the company, by reason of cold taken, I think, a-shipboard, coughed out so loud that he took from my hearing certain of his words. But I will never stint§ nor rest until I have got the full and exact knowledge hereof, insomuch that I will be able perfectly to instruct you, not only in the longitude or true meridian of the island, but also in the just latitude thereof, that is to say, in the sublevation‖ or height of the pole in that region, if our friend Hythloday be in safety and alive. For we hear very uncertain news of him. Some report that he died in his journey homeward. Some again affirm that he returned into his country, but partly for that he could not away# with the fashions of his country folk,** and partly for that his mind and affection was altogether set and fixed upon Utopia, they say that he hath taken his voyage thitherward again.

---

*Metrical composition—that is, poem.
†Know.
‡Inclined.
§Cease.
‖Elevation.
#Go along.
**Customs of his people.

Now as touching this, that the name of this island is nowhere found among the old and ancient cosmographers, this doubt Hythloday himself very well dissolved. For why, it is possible enough (quoth he) that the name which it had in old time was afterward changed, or else that they never had knowledge of this island, forasmuch as now in our time divers lands be found, which to the old geographers were unknown. Howbeit, what needeth it in this behalf to fortify the matter with arguments, seeing Master More is author hereof sufficient? But whereas he doubteth* of the edition or imprinting of the book, indeed herein I both commend and also knowledge† the man's modesty. Howbeit, unto me it seemeth a work most unworthy to be long suppressed, and most worthy to go abroad into the hands of men, yea, and under the title of your name to be published to the world, either because the singular endowments and qualities of Master More be to no man better known than to you, or else because no man is more fit and meet than you with good counsels to further and advance the commonwealth, wherein you have many years already continued and travailed with great glory and commendation both of wisdom and knowledge, and also of integrity and uprightness. Thus, O liberal supporter of good learning and flower of this our time, I bid you most heartily well to fare.

At Antwerp 1516, the first day of November.

---

*Fears.
†Acknowledge.

POEMS ON *UTOPIA*

A meter of four verses in the Utopian tongue, briefly touching
as well the strange beginning, as also the happy and wealthy
continuance, of the same commonwealth.[1]

> *Utopos ha Boccas peula chama polta chamaan.*
> *Bargol he maglomi Baccan soma gymnosophaon,*
> *Agrama gymonsophon labarem bacha bodamilomin.*
> *Volvala barchin heman la lavolvala dramme pagloni.*

Which verses the translator, according to his simple knowledge and
mean understanding in the Utopian ßtongue hath thus rudely
Englished.

> My king and conqueror, Utopus by name,[2]
> A prince of much renown and immortal fame,
> Hath made me an isle that erst* no island was,
> Full fraught with worldly wealth, with pleasure and solace.
> I one of all other without philosophy
> Have shaped for man a philosophical city.
> As mine I am nothing dangerous† to impart,
> So better to receive I am with all my heart.

A Short Meter of Utopia, Written by Anemolius,[3] Poet Laureate
and Nephew to Hythloday by His Sister

> Me Utopie cleped Antiquity,‡
> Void of haunt and herborough.§
> Now am I like to Plato's city,
> Whose fame flieth the wide world through.

---

*Formerly.
†Am not reluctant, make no difficulty.
‡Called Antiquity.
§Empty of people and buildings—that is, "no place."

Yes, like, or rather more likely,
Plato's plat* to excel and pass.†
For what Plato's pen hath platted briefly
In naked words, as in a glass,‡
The same have I performed fully,
The laws, with men and treasure fitly.
Wherefore, not Utopie, but rather rightly
My name is Eutopie, a place of felicity.[4]

Gerard Noviomage: Of Utopia[5]

Doth pleasure please? Then place thee here, and well thee rest.
Most pleasant pleasures thou shalt find here.
Doth profit ease? Then here arrive, this isle is best,
For passing§ profits do here appear.
Doth both thee tempt, and wouldst thou grip both gain and pleasure?
This isle is fraught with both bounteously.
To still thy greedy intent, reap here incomparable treasure,
Both mind and tongue to garnish richly.
The hid wells and fountains both of vice and virtue
Thou hast them here subject unto thine eye.
Be thankful now, and thanks where thanks be due,
Give to Thomas More, London's immortal glory.

Cornelius Graphey: To the Reader[6]

Wilt thou know what wonders strange be in the land that late was found?
Wilt thou learn thy life to lead by divers ways that godly be?
Wilt thou of virtue and vice understand the very ground?

---

*Model.
†Surpass.
‡Mirror.
§Surpassing.

Wilt thou see this wretched world, how full it is of vanity?
Then read and mark and bear in mind, for thy behoof, as thou may'st best,
All things that in this present work that worthy clerk Sir Thomas More,
With wit divine full learnedly, unto the world hath plain expressed,
In whom London well glory may, for wisdom and for godly lore.

The Printer to the Reader

The Utopian alphabet, good reader, which in the above written epistle is promised, hereunto I have not now adjoined, because I have not as yet the true characters or forms of the Utopian letters. And no marvel, seeing it is a tongue to us much stranger than the Indian, the Persian, the Syrian, the Arabic, the Egyptian, the Macedonian, the Sclavonian,* the Cyprian, the Scythian, etc. Which tongues, though they be nothing so strange among us as the Utopian is, yet their characters we have not. But I trust, God willing, at the next impression hereof to perform that which now I cannot, that is to say, to exhibit perfectly unto thee the Utopian alphabet. In the meantime, accept my good will. And so fare well.

Imprinted at London in Paul's Churchyard,

at the sign of the Lamb,

by Abraham Vele

MDLVI

---

*Slavic.

Appendix: Dedicatory Epistle by the Translator of the *Utopia*

To the Right Honorable, and his very singular good master, Master William Cecil, Esquire,[1] one of the two principal secretaries to the King his most excellent Majesty, Ralph Robinson wisheth continuance of health, with daily increase of virtue and honor.

UPON A TIME, WHEN tidings came to the city of Corinth that King Philip, father to Alexander surnamed the Great, was coming thitherward with an army royal to lay siege to the city, the Corinthians, being forthwith stricken with great fear, began busily and earnestly to look about them and to fall to work of all hands, some to scour and trim up harness, some to carry stones, some to amend and build higher the walls, some to rampire* and fortify the bulwarks and fortresses, some one thing and some another for the defending and strengthening of the city. The which busy labor and toil of theirs when Diogenes the philosopher saw, having no profitable business whereupon to set himself on work (neither any man required his labor and help as expedient for the commonwealth in that necessity) immediately girded about him his philosophical cloak and began to roll and tumble up and down hither and thither upon the hillside that lieth adjoining to the city, his great barrel or tun, wherein he dwelled, for other dwelling-place would he have none. This seeing one of his friends, and not a little musing thereat, came to him. "And I pray thee, Diogenes," quoth he "why dost thou thus, or what meanest thou hereby?" "Forsooth, I am tumbling my tub so," quoth he,

---

*Build ramparts.

"because it were no reason that I only should be idle where so many be working."[2]

In semblable* manner, right honorable sir, though I be, as I am indeed, of much less ability than Diogenes was to do anything that shall or may be for the advancement and commodity of the public wealth† of my native country, yet I, seeing every sort and kind of people in their vocation and degree busily occupied about the commonwealth's affairs, and especially learned men daily putting forth in writing new inventions and devices to the furtherance of the same, thought it my bounden duty to God and to my country so to tumble my tub; I mean, so to occupy and exercise meself in bestowing such spare hours as I, being at the beck and commandment of others, could conveniently win to meself, that though no commodity of that my labor and travail to the public weal‡ should arise, yet it might by this appear that mine endeavor and goodwill hereunto was not lacking.

To the accomplishment, therefore, and fulfilling of this my mind and purpose, I took upon me to turn and translate out of Latin into our English tongue the fruitful and profitable book which Sir Thomas More, knight, compiled and made of the new isle Utopia, containing and setting forth the best state and form of a public weal, a work (as it appeareth) written almost forty years ago by the said Sir Thomas More, the author thereof. The which man, forasmuch as he was a man of late time, yea, almost of these our days, and for the excellent qualities wherewith the great goodness of God had plentifully endowed him, and for the high place and room§ whereunto his prince had most graciously called him, notably well known, not only among us his countrymen, but also in foreign countries and nations—therefore I have not much to speak of him. This only I say: that it is much to be lamented of all, and not only of us Englishmen, that a man of so incomparable wit, of so profound knowledge, of so absolute‖ learning, and of so fine eloquence, was yet nevertheless

---

*Similar.
†Well-being.
‡Commonwealth (Latin: *respublica*).
§Office.
‖Complete, perfect.

so much blinded, rather with obstinacy than with ignorance, that he could not or rather would not see the shining light of God's holy truth in certain principal points of Christian religion, but did rather choose to persevere and continue in his willful and stubborn obstinacy even to the very death. This I say is a thing much to be lamented.

But letting this matter pass, I return again to *Utopia*, which (as I said before) is a work not only for the matter that it containeth fruitful and profitable, but also for the writer's eloquent Latin style, pleasant and delectable.* Which he that readeth in Latin, as the author himself wrote it, perfectly understanding the same, doubtless he shall take great pleasure and delight both in the sweet eloquence of the writer and also in the witty invention and fine conveyance,† or disposition, of the matter, but most of all in the good and wholesome lessons, which be there in great plenty and abundance.

But now I fear greatly that in this my simple translation, through my rudeness and ignorance in our English tongue, all the grace and pleasure of the eloquence wherewith the matter in Latin is finely set forth may seem to be utterly excluded and lost, and therefore the fruitfulness of the matter itself much peradventure diminished and appaired.‡ For who knoweth not, which knoweth anything, that an eloquent style setteth forth and highly commendeth a mean matter, whereas on the other side rude and unlearned speech defaceth and disgraceth a very good matter? According as I heard once a wise man say: A good tale evil§ told were better untold, and an evil tale well told needeth none other solicitor.

This thing I, well pondering and weighing with myself, and also knowing and knowledging‖ the barbarous rudeness of my translation, was fully determined never to have put it forth in print, had it not been for certain friends of mine, and especially one, whom above all other I regarded, a man of sage and discreet wit and in worldly matters by long use well experienced, whose name is George

---

*Delightful.
†Arrangement.
‡Impaired.
§Ill.
‖Acknowledging.

Tadlowe,[3] an honest citizen of London and in the same city well accepted and of good reputation, at whose request and instance I first took upon my weak and feeble shoulders the heavy and weighty burden of this great enterprise. This man with divers others, but this man chiefly (for he was able to do more with me than many others), after that I had once rudely brought the work to an end, ceased not by all means possible continually to assault me, until he had at the last, what by the force of his pithy arguments and strong reasons and what by his authority, so persuaded me that he caused me to agree and consent to the imprinting hereof. He, therefore, as the chief persuader, must take upon him the danger which upon this bold and rash enterprise shall ensue. I, as I suppose, am herein clearly acquit and discharged of all blame.

Yet, honorable sir, for the better avoiding of envious and malicious tongues, I (knowing you to be a man not only profoundly learned and well affected towards all such as either can or will take pains in the well bestowing of that poor talent which God hath endued them with, but also for your godly disposition and virtuous qualities not unworthily now placed in authority and called to honor) am the bolder humbly to offer and dedicate unto your good mastership this my simple work. Partly that under the safe conduct of your protection it may the better be defended from the obloquy of them which can say well by nothing that pleaseth not their fond* and corrupt judgments, though it be else both fruitful and godly, and partly that by the means of this homely present I may the better renew and revive (which of late, as you know, I have already begun to do) that old acquaintance that was between you and me in the time of our childhood, being then schoolfellows together.[4] Not doubting that you for your native goodness and gentleness† will accept in good part this poor gift as an argument or token that mine old goodwill and hearty affection towards you is not, by reason of long tract of time and separation of our bodies, anything at all quailed‡ and diminished, but rather (I assure you) much augmented and increased.

---

*Foolish.
†Nobility.
‡Withered.

This, verily, is the chief cause that hath encouraged me to be so bold with your mastership. Else truly this my poor present is of such simple and mean sort that it is neither able to recompense the least portion of your great gentleness to me, of my part undeserved, both in the time of our old acquaintance and also now lately again bountifully showed, neither yet fit and meet for the very baseness of it to be offered to one so worthy as you be. But Almighty God (who therefore ever be thanked) hath advanced you to such fortune and dignity that you be of ability to accept thankfully as well a man's goodwill as his gift. The same God grant you and all yours long and joyfully to continue in all godliness and prosperity.

THE LIFE OF SIR THOMAS MORE
BY WILLIAM ROPER

FORASMUCH AS SIR THOMAS More, Knight, sometime Lord Chancellor of England, a man of singular virtue and of a clear unspotted conscience, as witnesseth Erasmus,[1] more pure and white than the whitest snow, and of such an angelical wit, as England, he saith, never had the like before, nor never shall again, universally as well in the laws of our realm, a study in effect able to occupy the whole life of a man, as in all other sciences* right well studied, was in his days accounted a man worthy famous memory; I, William Roper, though most unworthy, his son-in-law by marriage of his eldest daughter,[2] knowing—at this day—no one man that of him and his doings understood so much as myself, for that I was continually resident in his house by the space of sixteen years and more, thought it therefore my part to set forth such matters touching his life as I could at present call to remembrance. Among which very many notable things not meet† to have been forgotten, through negligence and long continuance of time, are slipped out of my mind. Yet to the intent the same shall not all utterly perish, I have at the desire of divers worshipful friends of mine, though very far from the grace and worthiness of them, nevertheless as far forth as my mean wit, memory, and learning would serve me, declared so much thereof as in my poor judgment seemed worthy to be remembered.

This Sir Thomas More, after he had been brought up in the Latin tongue at Saint Anthony's[3] in London, was by his father's procurement received into the house of the right reverend, wise, and learned prelate Cardinal Morton,[4] where, though he was young of years, yet would he at Christmastide suddenly sometimes step in among the players, and never studying for the matter, make a part

---

*Fields of knowledge.
†Fit.

of his own there presently among them, which made the lookers-on more sport than all the players beside. In whose wit and toward-ness* the cardinal much delighting would often say of him unto the nobles that divers times dined with him: "This child here waiting at the table, whosoever shall live to see it, will prove a marvelous man."

Whereupon for his better furtherance in learning he placed him at Oxford, where when he was both in the Greek and Latin tongue sufficiently instructed, he was then for the study of the law of the realm put to an Inn of Chancery called New Inn, where for his time he very well prospered, and from thence was committed to Lin-coln's Inn, with very small allowance, continuing there his study until he was made and accounted a worthy utter barrister.[5] After this, to his great commendation, he read for a good space a public lecture of Saint Augustine *De Civitate Dei*[6] in the church of Saint Lawrence in the Old Jewry, whereunto there resorted Doctor Gro-cyn, an excellent, cunning† man, and all the chief learned of the city of London. Then was he made Reader‡ of Furnival's Inn, so remain-ing by the space of three years and more.

After which time he gave himself to devotion and prayer in the Charterhouse of London,[7] religiously living there without vow about four years, until he resorted to the house of one Master Colt, a gentleman of Essex that had oft invited him thither, having three daughters whose honest conversation§ and virtuous education pro-voked him there especially to set his affection. And albeit his mind most served him to the second daughter, for that he thought her the fairest and best favored, yet when he considered that it would be both great grief and some shame also to the eldest to see her younger sister in marriage preferred before her, he then of a certain pity framed his fancy towards her, and soon after married her,[8] never-theless not discontinuing his study of the law at Lincoln's Inn, but applying still the same until he was called to the Bench, and had

---

*Aptitude.
†Knowledgeable, learned.
‡Lecturer (on law).
§Behavior.

read* there twice, which is as often as ordinarily any judge of the law doth read. Before which time he had placed himself and his wife at Bucklersbury in London, where he had by her three daughters and one son, in virtue and learning brought up from their youth, whom he would often exhort to take virtue and learning for their meat, and play but for their sauce.

Who [More], ere ever he had been reader in Court,† was in the latter time of King Henry the Seventh made a burgess of the Parliament, wherein there were by the king demanded (as I have heard it reported) about three-fifteenths for the marriage of his eldest daughter,[9] that then should be the Scottish queen, at the last debating whereof he [More] made such arguments and reasons thereagainst that the king's demands were thereby overthrown. So that one of the king's privy chamber, named Master Tyler, being present thereat, brought word to the king out of Parliament House that a beardless boy had disappointed all his purpose. Whereupon the king, conceiving great indignation towards him, could not be satisfied until he had some way revenged it. And forasmuch as he nothing having, nothing could lose, His Grace devised a causeless quarrel against his father, keeping him in the Tower until he had paid him an hundred pounds fine. Shortly hereupon it fortuned‡ that this Sir Thomas More, coming in a suit to Doctor Fox, Bishop of Winchester, one of the king's Privy Council, the bishop called him aside, and pretending great favor towards him, promised him that if he would be ruled by him, he would not fail into the king's favor again to restore him, meaning, as it was after conjectured, to cause him thereby to confess his offense against the king, whereby His Highness might with the better color§ have occasion to revenge his displeasure against him. But when he came from the bishop, he fell in communication with one Master Whitford, his familiar friend, then chaplain to the bishop and later a Father of Sion,[10] and showed him what the bishop had said unto him, desiring to have his advice therein, who for the Passion of God prayed him in no

---

*Given a series of lectures.
†That is, an Inn of Court.
‡Chanced.
§Appearance, pretense.

wise to follow his [the bishop's] counsel, "for my Lord my Master," quoth he, "to serve the king's turn will not stick* to agree to his own father's death." So Sir Thomas More returned to the bishop no more. And had not the king soon after died,[11] he was determined to have gone over the sea, thinking that being in the king's indignation he could not live in England without great danger.

After this he [More] was made one of the Under Sheriffs of London,[12] by which office and his learning together, as I have heard him say, he gained without grief not so little as four hundred pounds by the year, since there was at that time in none of the prince's courts of the laws of the realm any matter of importance in controversy wherein he was not with the one party of counsel.[13] Of whom, for his learning, wisdom, knowledge, and experience, men had such estimation, that before he came to the service of King Henry the Eighth, at the suit and instance of the English merchants, he was, by the king's consent, made twice ambassador in certain causes between them and the merchants of the Steelyard,[14] whose wise and discreet dealing therein, to his high commendation, coming to the king's understanding, provoking His Highness to cause Cardinal Wolsey, then Lord Chancellor, to procure him to his service. And albeit the cardinal, according to the king's request, earnestly travailed† with him therefore—many other his persuasions alleging unto him how dear his service must needs be unto His Majesty, which could not with his honor, with less than he should yearly lose thereby to recompense him—yet he, loath to change his estate,‡ made such means to the king by the cardinal to the contrary that His Grace for that time was well satisfied.[15]

Now happened there after this a great ship of his that then was pope[16] to arrive at Southampton, which the king claiming for a forfeiture, the pope's ambassador by suit unto His Grace [Wolsey] obtained that he might for his master the pope have counsel learned in the laws of this realm, and the matter in his [Wolsey's] own presence, being himself a singular civilian,§ in some public place to be

---

*Hesitate.
†Labored.
‡Social and economic position.
§Person distinguished in civil law.

openly heard and discussed. At which time there could none of our law be found so meet* to be of counsel with this ambassador as Sir Thomas More, who could report to the ambassador in Latin all the reasons and arguments by the learned counsel on both sides alleged. Upon this, the counselors of either part, in presence of the Lord Chancellor and the other judges in the Star Chamber[17] had audience accordingly. Where Sir Thomas More not only declared to the ambassador the whole effect of all their opinions, but also in defense on the pope's side argued so learnedly himself that both was the foresaid forfeiture to the pope restored and himself among all the hearers for his upright and commendable demeanor therein so greatly renowned, that for no entreaty would the king from thenceforth be induced any longer to forbear† his service. At whose first entry thereunto he made him Master of the Requests, having then no better room‡ void, and within a month after, knight and one of his Privy Council.[18]

And so from time to time was he by the prince advanced, continuing in his singular favor and trusty service twenty years and above, a good part whereof used the king upon holidays, when he had done his own devotions, to send for him [More] into his traverse,§ and there sometime in matters of astronomy, geometry, divinity, and such other faculties,‖ and sometime in his worldly affairs, to sit and confer with him, and other whiles would he in the night have him up into the leads,# there to consider with him the diversities, courses, motions, and operations of the stars and planets. And because he was of a pleasant disposition, it pleased the king and queen after the council had supped, at the time of their supper for their pleasure commonly to call for him to be merry with them. When he perceived so much in his talk to delight that he could not once in a month get leave to go home to his wife and children, whose company he most desired, and to be absent from the court two days

---

*Suitable.

†Spare.

‡Office.

§A room set off by a traverse or screen.

‖Disciplines, subjects.

#Roof (made of lead).

together, but that he should be thither sent for again, he, much misliking this restraint of liberty, began thereupon somewhat to dissemble his nature, and so little by little from his former mirth to
disuse* himself, that he was of them from thenceforth at such seasons no more so ordinarily sent for. Then died one Master Weston,
Treasurer of the Exchequer, whose office after his death the king, of his
own offer, without any asking, freely gave unto Sir Thomas More.[19]

In the fourteenth year of His Grace's reign was there a Parliament
holden,[20] whereof Sir Thomas More was chosen Speaker, who being
very loath to take that room upon him, made an oration, not now
extant, to the King's Highness for his discharge† thereof. Whereunto,
when the king would not consent, he spake unto His Grace in form
following:

> Sith‡ I perceive, most redoubted§ sovereign, that it standeth not with
> your highness' pleasure to reform‖ this election and cause it to be
> changed, but have, by the mouth of the Reverend Father in God, the
> Legate, your highness' chancellor, thereunto given your most royal
> assent, and have of your benignity determined, far above that I may
> bear, to enable me, and for this office to repute me meet,# rather than
> ye should seem to impute unto your Commons that they had un-
> meetly chosen, I am therefore, and always shall be, ready obediently
> to conform myself to the accomplishment of your high command-
> ment. In my most humble wise beseeching your most noble Majesty
> that I may, with Your Grace's favor, before I farther enter thereunto,
> make mine humble intercession unto your highness for two lowly
> petitions, the one privately concerning myself, the other the whole
> assembly of your Common House.
>
> And for myself, gracious sovereign, that if it mishap me** in any-
> thing hereafter, that is in the behalf of your Commons in your high

---

*Disengage.
†Relief (from his duty to be Speaker).
‡Since.
§Feared.
‖Revoke.
#Fit.
**It is my misfortune.

presence to be declared, to mistake my message, and for lack of good utterance by my misrehearsal* to pervert or impair their prudent instructions, it may then like your most noble Majesty, of your abundant grace, with the eye of your accustomed pity, to pardon my simpleness, giving me leave again to repair to the Common House, and there to confer with them, and to take their substantial advice what thing and in what wise I shall on their behalf utter and speak before your Noble Grace, to the intent their prudent devices and affairs be not by my simpleness and folly hindered or impaired. Which thing, if it should so mishap, as it were well likely to mishap in me, if your gracious benignity relieved not my oversight, it could not fail to be during my life a perpetual grudge† and heaviness to my heart. The help and remedy whereof, in manner aforesaid remembered, is, most gracious sovereign, my first lowly suit and humble petition unto your most noble grace.

Mine other humble request, most excellent prince, is this. Forasmuch as there be of your Commons, here by your commandment assembled for your Parliament, a great number which are after the accustomed manner appointed in the Common House to treat and advise of the common affairs among themselves apart; and albeit, most dear liege-lord, that according to your prudent advice, by your honorable writs everywhere declared, there hath been as due diligence used in sending up to your highness' Court of Parliament the most discreet persons out of every quarter that men could esteem meet thereunto—whereby it is not to be doubted but that there is a very substantial assembly of right wise and politic‡ persons—yet, most victorious prince, sith among so many wise men, neither is every man wise alike, nor among so many men, like well-witted, every man like well-spoken. And it often happeneth that likewise as much as folly is uttered with painted, polished speeches, so many boisterous and rude in language see deep indeed and give right substantial counsel; and since also in matters of great importance the mind is often so occupied in the matter that a man rather studieth what to say than how, by reason whereof the wisest man and best spoken in

---

*Misrepresentation.
†Uneasiness.
‡Politically astute.

a whole country fortuneth among,* while his mind is fervent in the matter, somewhat to speak in such wise as he would afterward wish to have been uttered otherwise, and yet no worse will had, when he spake it, than he hath when he would so gladly change it—therefore, most gracious sovereign, considering that in all your high Courts of Parliament is nothing entreated† but matters of weight and importance concerning your realm and your own royal estate, it could not fail to let‡ and put to silence from the giving of their advice and counsel many of your discreet Commons to the general hindrance of the common affairs, except that every of your Commons were utterly discharged§ of all doubt and fear how anything that it should happen them to speak, should happen of your Highness to be taken. And in this point, though your well-known benignity putteth every man in right good hope, such is the reverend dread that the timorous hearts of your natural subjects conceive toward your high Majesty, our most redoubted king and undoubted sovereign, that they cannot in this point find themselves satisfied except your gracious bounty herein declared put away the scruple of their timorous minds, and animate and encourage them out of doubt.

It may therefore like your most abundant grace, our most benign and gracious king, to give to all your Commons here assembled your most gracious license and pardon freely, without doubt‖ of your dreadful displeasure, every man to discharge his conscience, and boldly in everything incident among us to declare his advice. And whatsoever happeneth any man to say, it may like your Majesty, of your inestimable goodness, to take all in good part, interpreting every man's words, how uncunningly# soever they be couched, to proceed yet of a good zeal towards the profit of your realm and honor of your royal person, the most prosperous estate and preservation whereof, most excellent sovereign, is the thing which we all,

---

*Sometimes.
†Considered.
‡Hinder.
§Relieved.
‖Fear.
#Unskillfully, unknowledgeably.

your most humble and loving subjects, according to the most bounden duty of our natural allegiance, most highly desire and pray for.

At this Parliament Cardinal Wolsey found himself much grieved with the burgesses thereof, for that nothing was so soon done or spoken therein, but that it was immediately blown abroad in every alehouse. It fortuned at that Parliament a very great subsidy* to be demanded, which the cardinal, fearing it would not pass the Common House, determined for the furtherance thereof to be there present himself. Before whose coming, after long debating there whether it were better but with a few of his lords (as the most opinion of the House was) or with his whole train royally to receive him there amongst them, "Masters," quoth Sir Thomas More, "forasmuch as my Lord Cardinal lately, you wot† well, laid to our charge the lightness‡ of our tongues for things uttered out of this house, it shall not in my mind be amiss with all his pomp to receive him, with his maces, his pillars, his pole-axes, his crosses, his hat, and Great Seal, too—to the intent, if he find the like fault with us hereafter, we may be the bolder from ourselves to lay the blame upon those that His Grace bringeth hither with him." Whereunto the House wholly agreeing, he was received accordingly.

Where, after he [Wolsey] had in a solemn oration by many reasons proved how necessary it was the demand there moved to be granted, and further showed that less would not serve to maintain the prince's purpose, he—seeing the company sitting still silent and thereunto answering nothing, and contrary to his expectation showing in themselves towards his requests no towardness of inclination§— said unto them: "Masters, ye have many wise and learned men among you, and sith I am from the king's own person sent hither unto you for the preservation of yourselves and all the realm, I think it meet you give me some reasonable answer." Whereat, every man holding his peace, then began he to speak to one Master Marney, who making him no answer neither, he severally asked the same

---

question of divers others accounted the wisest of the company. To whom, when none of them all would give so much as one word, being before agreed, as the custom was, by their speaker to make answer: "Masters," quoth the cardinal, "unless it be the manner of your house, as of likelihood it is, in such causes to utter your minds by the mouth of your speaker, whom ye have chosen for trusty and wise, as indeed he is, here is without doubt a marvelous obstinate silence." And thereupon he required answer of Master Speaker, who first reverently upon his knees excusing the silence of the House, abashed at the presence of so noble a personage able to amaze* the wisest and best learned in a realm, and after by many probable arguments proving that for them to make answer was it neither expedient nor agreeable with the ancient liberty of the House, in conclusion, for himself showed that though they had all with their voices trusted him, yet except every one of them could put into his own head all their several wits, he alone in so weighty a matter was unmeet to make His Grace an answer.

Whereupon the cardinal, displeased with Sir Thomas More that had not in this Parliament in all things satisfied his desire, suddenly arose and departed. And after the Parliament ended, in his gallery at Whitehall in Westminster[21] uttered unto him all his griefs, saying, "Would to God you had been at Rome, Master More, when I made you Speaker." "Your Grace not offended, so would I, too, my Lord," quoth he, and to wind such quarrels out of the cardinal's head, he began to talk of that gallery and said, "I like this gallery of yours, my Lord, much better than your gallery at Hampton Court." Wherewith so wisely brake he off the cardinal's displeasant talk that the cardinal at that present, as it seemed, wist† not what more to say to him.

But for revengement of his [Wolsey's] displeasure counseled the king to send him [More] ambassador into Spain, commending to His Highness his wisdom, learning, and meetness for that voyage, and the difficulty of the cause considered, none was there, he said, so well able to serve His Grace therein. Which, when the king had broken to Sir Thomas More, and that he had declared unto His

---

*Confound.
†Knew.

Grace how unfit a journey it was for him, the nature of the country and disposition of his complexion* so disagreeing together that he should never be likely to do His Grace acceptable service there, knowing right well that if His Grace sent him thither, he should send him to his grave; but showing himself nevertheless ready, according to his duty, all were it with the loss of his life, to fulfill His Grace's pleasure in that behalf. The king, allowing well† of his answer, said unto him, "It is not our meaning, Master More, to do you hurt, but to do you good would we be glad. We will therefore for this purpose devise some other, and employ your service otherwise." And such entire favor did the king bear him that he made him Chancellor of the Duchy of Lancaster upon the death of Sir Richard Wingfield, who had the office before.[22]

And for the pleasure he [Henry] took in his [More's] company would His Grace suddenly sometimes come home to his house at Chelsea to be merry with him, whither on a time, unlooked for, he came to dinner, and after dinner in a fair garden of his walked with him by the space of an hour, holding his arm about his neck. As soon as His Grace was gone, I, rejoicing thereat, told Sir Thomas More how happy he was, whom the king had so familiarly entertained, as I never had seen him do to any other except Cardinal Wolsey, whom I saw His Grace once walk with arm in arm. "I thank our Lord, son," quoth he, "I find His Grace my very good lord indeed, and I believe he doth as singularly favor me as any subject within this realm. Howbeit, son Roper, I may tell thee, I have no cause to be proud thereof, for if my head could win him a castle in France (for then there was war between us), it should not fail to go."[23]

This Sir Thomas More, among all his other virtues, was of such meekness that if it fortuned him with any learned men resorting to him from Oxford, Cambridge, or elsewhere, as there did divers, some for the desire of his acquaintance, some for the famous report of his wisdom and learning, and some for suits of‡ the universities, to have entered into argument, wherein few were comparable to him, and so far to have discoursed with them therein that he might perceive they could not, without some inconvenience, hold out

---

*Constitution.
†Accepting as satisfactory.
‡Petitions to.

much further disputation with him, then, lest he should discomfort them—as he that sought not his own glory, but rather would seem conquered than to discourage students in their studies, ever showing himself more desirous to learn than to teach—would he by some witty device courteously break off into some other matter and give over.

Of whom for his wisdom and learning had the king such an opinion that at such time as he [More] attended upon His Highness, taking his progress* either to Oxford or Cambridge, where he [Henry] was received with very eloquent orations, His Grace would always assign him, as one that was prompt and ready therein, *ex tempore* to make answer thereunto. Whose manner was, whensoever he had occasion either here or beyond the sea to be in any university, not only to be present at the readings and disputations there commonly used, but also learnedly to dispute among them himself. Who, being Chancellor of the Duchy, was made ambassador twice,[24] joined in commission with Cardinal Wolsey, once to the emperor Charles into Flanders, the other time to the French king into France.

Not long after this, the Water Bailiff of London,[25] sometime his [More's] servant, hearing, where he had been at dinner, certain merchants liberally† to rail against his old master, waxed so discontented therewith that he hastily came to him and told him what he had heard. "And were I, sir," quoth he, "in such favor and authority with my prince as you are, such men surely should not be suffered so villainously and falsely to misreport and slander me. Wherefore I would wish you to call them before you and, to their shame, for their lewd‡ malice to punish them." Who, smiling upon him, said, "Why, Master Water Bailiff, would you have me punish them by whom I receive more benefit than by you all that be my friends? Let them, a God's name, speak as lewdly as they list§ of me and shoot never so many arrows at me. As long as they do not hit me, what am I the worse? But if they should once hit me, then would it indeed not a little trouble me. Howbeit, I trust, by God's help, there shall none of

---

*Formal state journey.
†Freely, unrestrainedly.
‡(Socially) base.
§Desire.

them all once be able to touch me. I have more cause, I assure thee, Master Water Bailiff, to pity them than to be angry with them." Such fruitful communication had he oftentimes with his familiar friends.

So on a time, walking with me along the Thames-side at Chelsea,[26] in talking of other things, he said to me, "Now would to our Lord, son Roper, upon condition that three things were well established in Christendom, I were put in a sack and here presently cast into the Thames." "What great things be those, sir," quoth I, "that should move you so to wish?" "Wouldest thou know what they be, son Roper?" quoth he. "Yea, marry,* with a good will, sir, if it please you," quoth I. "In faith, son, they be these," quoth he. "The first is that whereas the most part of Christian princes be at mortal war, they were all at an universal peace. The second, that where the Church of Christ is at present sore afflicted with many errors and heresies, it were well settled in a perfect uniformity of religion. The third, that where the king's matter of his marriage is now come into question, it were to the glory of God and quietness of all parts brought to a good conclusion." Whereby, as I could gather, he judged that otherwise it would be a disturbance to a great part of Christendom. Thus did it by his doings throughout the whole course of his life appear that all his travail and pains, without respect of earthly commodities† either to himself or any of his, were only upon the service of God, the prince, and the realm wholly bestowed and employed. Whom I heard in his later time to say that he never asked the king himself the value of one penny.

As Sir Thomas More's custom was daily, if he were at home, besides his private prayers, with his children to say the seven psalms, litany, and suffrages following,[27] so was his guise nightly, before he went to bed, with his wife, children, and household to go to his chapel and there upon his knees ordinarily to say certain psalms and collects‡ with them. And because he was desirous for godly purposes sometime to be solitary and sequester himself from worldly company, a good distance from his mansion house he builded a place, called the New Building, wherein was a chapel, a library, and a

---

*An oath: by the Virgin Mary.
†Benefits.
‡Short prayers.

gallery, in which as his use was upon other days to occupy himself in prayer and study together, so on the Friday there usually continued he from morning to evening, spending his time only in devout prayers and spiritual exercises. And to provoke* his wife and children to the desire of heavenly things, he would sometimes use these words unto them: "It is now no mastery† for you children to go to heaven, for everybody giveth you good counsel, everybody giveth you good example; you see virtue rewarded and vice punished; so that you are carried up to heaven even by the chins. But if you live in the time that no man will give you good counsel, nor no man will give you good example, when you shall see virtue punished and vice rewarded, if you will then stand fast and firmly stick to God, upon pain of my life, though you be but half good, God will allow you for the whole good."

If his wife or any of his children had been diseased or troubled, he would say to them: "We may not look at our pleasure to go to heaven in feather beds; it is not the way. For our Lord Himself went thither with great pain and by many tribulations, which was the path wherein he walked thither. For the servant may not look to be in better case than his master." And as he would in this sort persuade them to take their troubles patiently, so would he in like sort teach them to withstand the devil and his temptations valiantly, saying: "Whosoever will mark the devil and his temptations shall find him therein much like to an ape. For, like as an ape, not well looked unto, will be busy and bold to do shrewd turns,‡ and contrariwise, being spied, will suddenly leap back and adventure no farther, so the devil, finding a man idle, slothful, and without resistance ready to receive his temptations, waxeth so hardy§ that he will not fail still to continue with him until to his purpose he have thoroughly brought him. But on the other side, if he see a man persevere with diligence to prevent and withstand his temptations, he waxeth so weary that in conclusion he utterly forsaketh him. For as the devil of disposition is a spirit of so high a pride that he cannot abide to be mocked, so is he

---

*Encourage.
†Achievement.
‡Mischievous tricks.
§Bold.

of nature so envious that he feareth any more to assault him, lest that he should thereby not only catch a foul fall himself, but also minister to the man more matter of merit." Thus delighted he evermore not only in virtuous exercises to be occupied himself, but also to exhort his wife, children, and household to embrace and follow the same.

To whom for his notable virtue and godliness, God showed, as it seemed, a manifest, miraculous token of his special favor towards him, at such time as my wife, as many others that year were, was sick of the sweating sickness.[28] Who, lying in so great an extremity of that disease as by no invention or devices that physicians in such case commonly use—of whom she had divers, both expert,* wise, and well learned, then continually attendant upon her—she could be kept from sleep, so that both physicians and all other there despaired of her recovery and gave her over. Her father, as he that most entirely tendered† her, being in no small heaviness for her, by prayer at God's hand sought to get her remedy. Whereupon, going up after his usual manner into his foresaid New Building, there in his chapel, upon his knees, with tears most devoutly besought almighty God that it would like His goodness, unto whom nothing was impossible, if it were His blessed will, at his mediation to vouchsafe graciously to hear his petition. Where incontinent‡ came into his mind that a clyster§ should be the only way to help her. Which, when he had told the physicians, they by and by‖ confessed that if there were any hope of health, that it was the very best help indeed, much marveling of themselves that they had not before remembered it. Then was it immediately ministered unto her sleeping, which she could by no means have been brought unto waking, and albeit she was thereby thoroughly awaked, God's marks,# evident, undoubted token of death, plainly appeared upon her, yet she, contrary to all their expectation, was (as it was thought) by her father's fervent prayer

---

*Experienced.
†Loved.
‡Straightway.
§Enema.
‖Immediately.
#Signs of death in any disease, especially plague.

miraculously recovered and at length again to perfect health restored. Whom, if it had pleased God at that time to have taken to His mercy, her father said he would never have meddled with worldly matters after.

Now while Sir Thomas More was Chancellor of the Duchy, the See of Rome chanced to be void, which was the cause of much trouble. For Cardinal Wolsey, a man very ambitious, and desirous (as good hope and likelihood he had) to aspire unto that dignity, perceiving himself of his expectation disappointed by means of the Emperor Charles so highly commending one Cardinal Adrian,[29] sometime his schoolmaster, to the cardinals of Rome in the time of their election for his virtue and worthiness, that thereupon he was chosen pope. Who from Spain, where he was then resident, coming on foot to Rome, before his entry into that city did put off his hosen and shoes, barefooted and barelegged passing through the streets towards his palace with such humbleness that all the people had him in great reverence. Cardinal Wolsey, I say, waxed so wood* therewith that he studied to invent all ways of revengement of his grief against the emperor, which, as it was the beginning of a lamentable tragedy, so some part of it as not impertinent to my present purpose I reckoned requisite here to put in remembrance.

This cardinal, therefore—not ignorant of the king's unconstant and mutable disposition, soon inclined to withdraw his devotion from his own most noble and virtuous wife Queen Catherine, aunt to the emperor,[30] upon every light† occasion; and upon other,‡ to her in nobility, wisdom, virtue, favor, and beauty far incomparable, to fix his affection—meaning to make his [Henry's] so light§ disposition an instrument to bring about his [Wolsey's] ungodly intent, devised to allure the king (then already, contrary to his [Wolsey's] mind, nothing less looking for, falling in love with the Lady Anne Boleyn) to cast fantasy‖ to one of the French king's sisters.[31] Which thing, because of the enmity and war was at that time between the

---

*Became so enraged.
†Trivial.
‡Another.
§Wanton.
‖Fall in love with.

French king and the emperor (whom for the cause afore remembered he [Wolsey] mortally maligned), he was desirous to procure. And for the better achieving thereof requested Longland, Bishop of Lincoln and ghostly father* to the king,[32] to put a scruple into the king's head that it was not lawful for him to marry his brother's wife. Which the king, not sorry to hear of, opened it first to Sir Thomas More, whose counsel he required therein, showing him certain places of scripture that somewhat seemed to serve his appetite.† Which when he had perused and thereupon, as one that never had professed the study of divinity, himself excused to be unmeet many ways to meddle with such matters, the king, not satisfied with this answer, so sore still pressed upon him therefore, that in conclusion he condescended to His Grace his motion.‡ And further, forasmuch as the case was of such importance as needed great advisement and deliberation, he besought His Grace of sufficient respite advisedly to consider of it. Wherewith the king, well contented, said unto him that Tunstall and Clerk,[33] bishops of Durham and Bath, with other of his Privy Council should be dealers therein.

So, Sir Thomas More, departing, conferred§ those places of scripture with the exposition of divers of the old holy doctors, and at his coming to the court, in talking with His Grace of the aforesaid matter, he said: "To be plain with Your Grace, neither my Lord of Durham nor my Lord of Bath, though I know them both to be wise, virtuous, learned, and honorable prelates, nor myself with the rest of your council—being all Your Grace's own servants, for your manifold benefits daily bestowed on us, so most bounden unto you—be in my judgment meet counselors for Your Grace herein. But if Your Grace mind to understand the truth, such counselors may you have devised, as neither for respect of their own worldly commodity, nor for fear of your princely authority, will be inclined to deceive you." To whom he named Saint Jerome, Saint Augustine, and divers other holy doctors, both Greek and Latin, and moreover showed him what authority he had gathered out of them. Which,

---

*Confessor.
†Desire.
‡Assented to His Grace's proposal.
§Compared.

although the king did not very well like of (as disagreeable to His Grace's desire), yet were they by Sir Thomas More—who, in all his communication with the king in that matter, had always most discreetly behaved himself—so wisely tempered that he both presently took them in good part and oftentimes had thereof conference with him again.

After this there were certain questions among his council proponed,* whether the king needed in this case to have any scruple at all, and if he had, what way were best to be taken to deliver him of it. The most part of whom were of the opinion that there was good cause, and that, for discharging of it, suit were meet to be made to the See of Rome, where the king hoped by liberality† to obtain his purpose. Wherein, as after it appeared, he was far deceived. Then was there for the trial and examination of this matrimony procured from Rome a commission, in which Cardinal Campeggio and Cardinal Wolsey were joined commissioners, who, for the determination thereof, sat at the Blackfriars in London.[34] Where a libel‡ was put in for the annulling of the said matrimony, alleging the marriage between the king and the queen to be unlawful. And for proof of the marriage to be lawful was there brought in a dispensation, in which, after divers disputations thereupon holden, there appeared an imperfection, which by an instrument or brief,§ upon search found in the Treasury of Spain and sent to the commissioners into England, was supplied. And so should judgment have been given by the pope accordingly, had not the king, upon intelligence thereof, before the same judgment, appealed to the next general council. After whose appellation‖ the cardinal upon that matter sat no longer.[35]

It fortuned before the matter of the said matrimony brought in question when I, in talk with Sir Thomas More, of a certain joy commended unto him the happy estate of this realm that had so catholic a prince that no heretic durst show his face, so virtuous and learned a clergy, so grave and sound a nobility, so loving and obedient subjects

---

*Proposed.
†Either by a generous interpretation or by gift giving—that is, bribes.
‡Plea.
§Formal legal document or short papal letter.
‖Appeal.

all in one faith agreeing together: "Troth,* it is indeed, son Roper," quoth he, and in commending all degrees and estates of the same went far beyond me. "And yet, son Roper, I pray God," said he, "that some of us, as high as we seem to sit upon the mountains treading heretics under our feet like ants, live not the day that we gladly would wish to be at league and composition with them to let them have their churches quietly to themselves, so that they would be content to let us have ours quietly to ourselves." After that I had told him many considerations why he had no cause so to say: "Well," said he, "I pray God, son Roper, some of us live not till that day," showing me no reason why he should put any doubt therein. To whom I said, "By my troth, sir, it is very desperately† spoken." That vile term, I cry God mercy, did I give him, who by these words perceiving me in a fume‡ said merrily unto me, "Well, well, son Roper, it shall not be so, it shall not be so." Whom in sixteen years and more, being in his house conversant§ with him, I could never perceive him so much as once in a fume.

But now to return again where I left. After supplying of imperfections of the dispensation set, as is before rehearsed, to the commissioners into England, the king, taking the matter for ended and then meaning no further to proceed in that matter, assigned the Bishop of Durham and Sir Thomas More to go ambassadors to Cambrai, a place neither Imperial nor French, to treat‖ a peace between the French king, the emperor, and him.[36] In the concluding whereof Sir Thomas More so worthily handled himself, procuring in our league far more benefits unto this realm than at that time by the king or his council was thought possible to be compassed,# that for his good service in that voyage the king, when he after made him Lord Chancellor, caused the Duke of Norfolk openly to declare unto the people (as you shall hear hereafter more at large) how much all England was bound unto him.

---

*(By my) troth: an affirmative oath.
†Despairingly.
‡Angry state.
§Living intimately.
‖Negotiate.
#Achieved.

Now, upon the coming home of the Bishop of Durham and Sir Thomas More from Cambrai, the king was as earnest in persuading Sir Thomas More to agree unto the matter of his marriage as before, by many and divers ways provoking* him thereunto. For the which cause, as it was thought, he the rather† soon after made him Lord Chancellor, and further declaring unto him that though at his going over the sea to Cambrai, he was in utter despair thereof, yet he had conceived since some good hope to compass it.[37] For albeit his marriage, being against the positive laws of the Church and the written laws of God, was holpen‡ by the dispensation, yet was there another thing found out of late, he said, whereby his marriage appeared to be so directly against the law of nature that it could in no wise by the Church be dispensable—as Doctor Stokesley,[38] whom he had then preferred to be Bishop of London and in that case chiefly credited, was able to instruct him—with whom he prayed him in that point to confer. But for all his [the bishop's] conference with him, he [More] saw nothing of such force as could induce him to change his opinion therein. Which notwithstanding, the bishop showed himself in his report of him to the King's Highness so good and favorable that he said he found him [More] in His Grace's cause very toward§ and desirous to find some good matter wherewith he might truly serve His Grace to his contentation.

This Bishop Stokesley—being by the cardinal not long before in the Star Chamber openly put to rebuke and awarded to the Fleet‖— not brooking his contumelious usage and thinking that forasmuch as the cardinal, for lack of such forwardness in setting forth the king's divorce as His Grace looked for, was out of His Highness's favor, he had now a good occasion offered him to revenge his quarrel against him [Wolsey], further to incense the king's displeasure towards him, busily travailed to invent some colorable# device for the king's furtherance in that behalf. Which, as before is mentioned,

---

*Urging.
†The more quickly.
‡Helped.
§Favorably disposed.
‖Sentenced to Fleet Prison.
#Labored . . . plausible.

he to His Grace revealed, hoping thereby to bring the king to the better liking of himself, and the more misliking of the cardinal. Whom His Highness therefore was soon after of his office* displaced and to Sir Thomas More, the rather to move him to incline to his side, the same in his stead committed.[39]

Who between the Dukes of Norfolk and Suffolk being brought through Westminster Hall to his place in the Chancery, the Duke of Norfolk, in audience of all the people there assembled, showed that he was from the king himself straitly charged, by special commission, there openly in the presence of all to make declaration how much all England was beholden to Sir Thomas More for his good service, and how worthy he was to have the highest room in the realm, and how dearly His Grace loved and trusted him, for which, said the duke, he had great cause to rejoice. Whereunto Sir Thomas More, among many other his humble and wise sayings not now in my memory, answered: that although he had good cause to take comfort of His Highness's singular favor towards him—that he had far above his deserts so highly commended him, to whom therefore he acknowledged himself most deeply bounden—yet, nevertheless, he must for his own part needs confess that in all things by His Grace alleged, he had done no more than was his duty. And further disabled himself as unmeet for that room, wherein, considering how wise and honorable a prelate had lately before taken so great a fall, he had, he said, thereof no cause to rejoice. And as they on the king's behalf charged him uprightly to minister indifferent† justice to the people without corruption or affection,‡ so did he likewise charge them again that if they saw him at any time in anything digress from any part of his duty in that honorable office, even as they would discharge their own duty and fidelity to God and the king, so should they not fail to disclose it to His Grace, who otherwise might have just occasion to lay his fault wholly to their charge.

While he was Lord Chancellor, being at leisure, as seldom he was, one of his sons-in-law[40] on a time said merrily unto him: "When Cardinal Wolsey was Lord Chancellor, not only divers of his privy

---

*That is, Wolsey's office.
†Impartial.
‡Bias.

chamber, but such also as were his doorkeepers got great gain." And since he had married one of his daughters and gave still* attendance upon him, he thought he might of reason look for some, where† he indeed, because he was so ready himself to hear every man, poor and rich, and kept no doors shut from them, could find none, which was to him a great discouragement. And whereas else, some for friendship, some for kindred, and some for profit would gladly have had his furtherance in bringing them to his presence, if he should now take anything of them, he knew, he said, he should do them great wrong, for that they might do as much for themselves as he could do for them. Which condition, although he thought in Sir Thomas More very commendable, yet to him, said he, being his son, he found it nothing profitable.[41] When he had told him this tale: "You say well, son," quoth he, "I do not mislike that you are of conscience so scrupulous, but many other ways be there, son, that I may do both yourself good and pleasure your friend also. For sometime may I by my word stand your friend in stead, and sometime may I by my letter help him; or if he have a cause depending‡ before me, at your request I may hear him before another; or if his cause be not all the best, yet may I move the parties to fall to some reasonable end by arbitrement.§ Howbeit, this one thing, son, I assure thee on my faith, that if the parties will at my hands call for justice, then all were it my father stood on the one side and the devil on the other, his cause being good, the devil should have right." So offered he his son, as he thought, he said, as much favor as with reason he could require.

And that he would for no respect digress from justice well appeared by a plain example of another of his sons-in-law called Master Heron.[42] For when he, having a matter before him in the Chancery, and presuming too much of his favor, would by him in no wise be persuaded to agree to any indifferent order, then made he in conclusion a flat decree against him.

This Lord Chancellor used commonly every afternoon to sit in his open hall, to the intent that if any persons had any suit unto him,

---

*Assiduous.
†Whereas.
‡Pending.
§Arbitration.

they might the more boldly come to his presence and there open complaints before him. Whose manner was also to read every bill* himself ere he would award any subpoena, which, bearing matter sufficient worthy a subpoena, would he set his hand unto, or else cancel it.

Whensoever he passed through Westminster Hall to his place in the Chancery by the court of the King's Bench, if his father, one of the judges thereof, had been set ere he came, he would go into the same court, and there reverently kneeling down in the sight of them all duly ask his father's blessing. And if it fortuned that his father and he at readings in Lincoln's Inn met together, as they sometime did, notwithstanding his high office, he would offer in argument the preeminence to his father, though he [More's father] for his office's sake would refuse to take it. And for the better declaration of his natural affection towards his father, he not only while he lay on his deathbed, according to his duty, oft-times with comfortable words most kindly came to visit him, but also at his departure out of this world, with tears taking him about the neck, most lovingly kissed and embraced him, commending him into the merciful hands of almighty God, and so departed from him.[43]

And as few injunctions[44] as he granted while he was Lord Chancellor, yet were they by some of the judges of the law misliked, which I, understanding, declared the same to Sir Thomas More, who answered me that they should have little cause to find fault with him therefore. And thereupon caused he one Master Crooke, chief of the six clerks, to make a docket containing the whole number and causes of all such injunctions as either in his time had already passed or at that present time depended in any of the king's courts at Westminster before him. Which done he invited all the judges to dinner with him in the council chamber at Westminster, where after dinner, when he had broken with them what complaints he had heard of his injunctions, and moreover showed them both the number and causes of every one of them in order so plainly that, upon full debating of those matters, they were all enforced to confess that they in like case could have done no otherwise themselves. Then offered he this unto them: that if the justices of every court—unto whom

---

*Written statement of a case.

the reformation of the rigor of the law, by reason of their office, most especially appertained—would upon reasonable considerations by their own discretion, as they were (as he thought) in conscience bound, mitigate and reform the rigor of the law themselves, there should from thenceforth by him no more injunctions be granted. Whereunto, when they refused to condescend,* then said he unto them: "Forasmuch as yourselves, my Lords, drive me to that necessity for awarding out injunctions to relieve the people's injury, you cannot hereafter any more justly blame me." After that he said secretly unto me: "I perceive, son, why they like not so to do, for they see that by the verdict of the jury they may cast off all quarrels from themselves upon them, which they account their chief defense. And therefore am I compelled to abide the adventure† of all such reports."

And as little leisure as he had to be occupied in the study of Holy Scripture and controversies upon religion and such other virtuous exercises, being in manner continually busied about the affairs of the king and the realm, yet such watch‡ and pain in setting forth of divers profitable works in defense of the true Catholic religion against heresies, secretly sown abroad in the realm, assuredly sustained§ he, that the bishops, to whose pastoral cure the reformation thereof principally appertained, thinking themselves by his travail—wherein, by their own confession, with him they were not able to make comparison—of their duties in that behalf discharged, and considering that for all his prince's favor he was no rich man nor in yearly revenues advanced as his worthiness deserved, therefore, at a convocation among themselves and other of the clergy, they agreed together and concluded upon a sum of four or five thousand pounds at the least, to my remembrance, for his pains to recompense him.

Whereupon Tunstall, Bishop of Durham, Clerk, Bishop of Bath, and as far as I can call to mind, Vaysey, Bishop of Exeter[45] repaired unto him, declaring how thankfully for his travails, to their discharge in God's cause bestowed, they reckoned themselves bound to

---

*Assent.
†Chance, risk.
‡Vigilance.
§Maintained with assurance.

consider him. And that albeit they could not, according to his deserts so worthily as they gladly would, requite him therefore, but must reserve that only to the goodness of God, yet for a small part of recompense—in respect of his estate, so unequal to his worthiness—in the name of their whole convocation they presented unto him that sum, which they desired him to take in good part.* Who, forsaking† it, said that like as it were no small comfort unto him that so wise and learned men so well accepted his simple doings, for which he never intended to receive reward but at the hands of God only, to whom alone was the thank thereof chiefly to be ascribed, so gave he most humble thanks to their honors all for their so bountiful and friendly consideration.

When they—for all their importune pressing upon him that few would have went‡ he could have refused it—could by no means make him to take it, then besought they him to be content yet that they might bestow it upon his wife and children. "Not so, my Lords," quoth he, "I had liefer see it all cast into the Thames than I or any of mine should have thereof the worth of one penny. For though your offer, my Lords, be indeed very friendly and honorable, yet set I so much by my pleasure and so little by my profit that I would not, in good faith, for so much, and much more too, have lost the rest of so many a night's sleep as was spent upon the same. And yet wish would I, for all that, upon condition that all heresies were suppressed, that all my books were burned and my labor utterly lost." Thus departing were they fain to restore to every man his own again.

This Lord Chancellor, albeit he was to God and the world well known of notable virtue, though not so of every man considered, yet for the avoiding of singularity would he appear no otherwise than other men in his apparel and other behavior. And albeit he appeared honorable outwardly like one of his calling, yet inwardly he, no such vanities esteeming, secretly next his body wore a shirt of hair, which my sister More,[46] a young gentlewoman, in the summer as he sat at supper singly§ in his doublet and hose, wearing thereupon a plain

---

*Without offense.
†Refusing.
‡Believed.
§Simply.

shirt without ruff or collar, chancing to espy, began to laugh at it. My wife, not ignorant of his manner, perceiving the same, privily told him of it, and he, being sorry that she saw it, presently amended it. He used also sometimes to punish his body with whips, the cords knotted, which was known only to my wife, his eldest daughter, whom for her secrecy above all other he specially trusted, causing her as need required to wash the same shirt of hair.

Now shortly upon his entry into the high office of the chancellorship, the king eftsoons* again moved him to weigh and consider his great matter. Who, falling down upon his knees, humbly besought His Highness to stand his gracious sovereign, as he ever since his entry into his gracious service had found him, saying there was nothing in the world had been so grievous unto his heart as to remember he was not able—as he willingly would with the loss of one of his limbs—for that matter anything to find whereby he could, with his conscience safely, serve His Grace's contentation, as he that always bore in mind the most godly words that His Highness spake unto him at his first coming into his noble service, the most virtuous lesson that prince ever taught his servant, willing him first to look unto God, and after God to him. As in good faith, he said, he did, or else might His Grace well account him his most unworthy servant. To this the king answered that if he could not with his conscience serve him, he was content to accept his service otherwise. And using the advice of other his learned council, whose consciences could well enough agree thereto, he would nevertheless continue his gracious favor towards him and never with that matter molest his conscience after.

But Sir Thomas More in process of time, seeing the king fully determined to proceed forth in the marriage of Queen Anne, and when he with the bishops and nobles of the higher house of Parliament were, for the furtherance of that marriage, commanded by the king to go down to the Common House to show unto them both what the universities, as well of other parts beyond the seas as at Oxford and Cambridge, had done in that behalf, and their seals also testifying the same—all which matters, at the king's request, not

---

*Soon.

showing of what mind himself was therein, he opened to the lower house of the Parliament. Nevertheless, doubting* lest further attempts should after follow, which, contrary to his conscience, by reason of his office he was likely to be put unto, he made suit unto the Duke of Norfolk, his singular† dear friend, to be a mean‡ to the king that he might, with His Grace's favor, be discharged of that chargeable room of the chancellorship, wherein for certain infirmities of his body he pretended himself unable any longer to serve.

This duke, coming on a time to Chelsea to dine with him, fortuned to find him at the church, singing in the choir with a surplice on his back. To whom after service, as they went home together arm-in-arm, the duke said: "God body,§ God body, my Lord Chancellor, a parish clerk, a parish clerk. You dishonor the king and his office." "Nay," quoth Sir Thomas More, smiling upon the duke, "Your Grace may not think that the king, your master and mine, will with me, for serving of God his master, be offended, or thereby count his office dishonored."

When the duke, being thereunto solicited, by importunate suit had at length of the king obtained for Sir Thomas More a clear discharge of his office, then at a time convenient, by His Highness's appointment, repaired he to His Grace, to yield up unto him the Great Seal.[47] Which, as His Grace, with thanks and praise for his worthy service in that office, courteously at his hands received, so pleased it His Highness further to say unto him that, for the good service he before had done him, in any suit which he should have after unto him that either should concern his honor (for that word it liked‖ His Highness to use unto him), or that should appertain unto his profit, he should find His Highness a good and gracious lord unto him.

After he had thus given over his chancellorship,[48] and placed all his gentlemen and yeomen with bishops and noblemen, and his eight watermen with the Lord Audley, that after in the same office succeeded him, to whom also he gave his great barge, then, calling us

---

*Fearing.
†Special.
‡Intercessor, means.
§An oath: "By God's Body."
‖Pleased.

that were his children unto him and asking our advice how we might now in this decay of his ability*—by the surrender of his office so impaired that he could not, as he was wont and gladly would, bear out the whole charge of them all himself—from henceforth be able to live and continue together, as he wished we should. When he saw us all silent and in that case not ready to show our opinions unto him—"Then will I," said he, "show my poor mind unto you. I have been brought up at Oxford, at an Inn of Chancery, at Lincoln's Inn, and in the king's court, and so forth from the lowest degree to the highest, and yet have I in yearly revenues at this present left me little above an hundred pounds by the year. So that now must we hereafter, if we like† to live together, be contented to become contributaries together. But, by my counsel, it shall not be best for us to fall to the lowest fare first. We will not, therefore, descend to Oxford fare, nor to the fare of New Inn, but we will begin with Lincoln's Inn diet, where many right worshipful and of good years do live full well. Which, if we find not ourselves the first year able to maintain, then will we the next year go one step down to New Inn fare, wherewith many an honest man is well contented. If that exceed our ability, too, then will we the next year after descend to Oxford fare, where many grave, learned, and ancient fathers be continually conversant.‡ Which, if our power stretch not to maintain neither, then may we yet with bags and wallets go a-begging together, and hoping that for pity some good folk will give us their charity, at every man's door to sing *Salve Regina*,[49] and so still keep company and be merry together."

And whereas you have heard before he was by the king from a very worshipful living taken into His Grace's service, with whom all the great and weighty causes that concerned His Highness or the realm, he consumed and spent with painful cares and travails and troubles as well beyond the seas as within the realm—in effect the whole substance of his life—yet with all the gain he got thereby, being never no wasteful spender thereof, was he not able,

---

*Estate.
†Wish.
‡Familiar.

after the resignation of his office of the Lord Chancellor, for the maintenance of himself and such as necessarily belonged unto him, sufficiently to find meat, drink, fuel, apparel, and such other necessary charges. All the land that ever he purchased, which also he purchased before he was Lord Chancellor, was not, I am well assured, above the value of twenty marks by the year, and after his debts paid, he had not, I know, his chain[50] excepted, in gold and silver left him the worth of one hundred pounds. And whereas upon the holidays during high chancellorship one of his gentlemen, when service at the church was done, ordinarily used to come to my Lady his wife's pew himself and say unto her, "Madam, my Lord [More] is gone," the next holiday after the surrender of his office and departure of his gentlemen he came unto my Lady his wife's pew himself, and making a low curtsy, said unto her, "Madam, my Lord is gone."

In the time somewhat before his trouble, he would talk with his wife and children of the joys of heaven and the pains of hell, of the lives of holy martyrs, and of their grievous martyrdoms, of their marvelous patience, and of their passions and deaths that they suffered rather than they would offend God. And what an happy and a blessed thing it was, for the love of God, to suffer loss of goods, imprisonment, loss of lands, and life also. He would further say unto them that, upon his faith, if he might perceive his wife and children would encourage him to die in a good cause, it should so comfort him that, for very joy thereof, it would make him merrily to run to death. He showed unto them afore what trouble might after fall unto him. Wherewith and the like virtuous talk he had so long before his trouble encouraged them that when he after fell into the trouble indeed, his trouble to him was a great deal the less, *quia spicula previsa minus laedunt.*[51]

Now upon this resignment of his office came Sir Thomas Cromwell,[52] then in the king's high favor, to Chelsea to him on a message from the king. Wherein when they had thoroughly communed together, "Master Cromwell," quoth he, "you are now entered into the service of a most noble, wise, and liberal prince. If you will follow my poor advice, you shall, in your counsel-giving unto His Grace, ever tell him what he ought to do, but never tell him what he is able to do. So shall you show yourself a true faithful servant, and a right worthy counselor. For if the lion knew his own strength, hard were it for any man to rule him."

Shortly thereupon was there a commission directed to Cranmer,[53] then Archbishop of Canterbury, to determine the matter of the matrimony between the king and Queen Catherine at Saint Albans, where according to the king's mind it was thoroughly determined. Who, pretending he had no justice at the pope's hands, from thenceforth sequestered himself from the See of Rome, and so married the Lady Anne Boleyn.[54] Which Sir Thomas More, understanding, said unto me: "God give grace, son, that these matters within a while be not confirmed with oaths." I, at that time seeing no likelihood thereof, yet fearing lest for his forespeaking it would the sooner come to pass, waxed therefore for his so saying much offended with him.

It fortuned not long before the coming of Queen Anne through the streets of London from the Tower to Westminster to her coronation that he received a letter from the Bishops of Durham, Bath, and Winchester, requesting him both to keep them company from the Tower to the coronation, and also to take twenty pounds that by the bearer thereof they had sent him to buy him a gown with. Which he thankfully receiving, and at home still tarrying, at their next meeting said merrily unto them: "My Lords, in the letters which you lately sent me, you required two things of me, the one whereof, sith I was so well contented to grant you, the other therefore I thought I might be the bolder to deny you. And like as the one—because I took you for no beggars and myself I knew to be no rich man— I thought I might the rather fulfill, so the other did put me in remembrance of an emperor that had ordained a law that whosoever committed a certain offense, which I now remember not, except it were a virgin, should suffer the pains of death.[55] Such a reverence had he to virginity. Now so it happened that the first committer of that offense was indeed a virgin, whereof the emperor hearing was in no small perplexity, as he that by some example fain would have had the law to have been put in execution. Whereupon, when his council had sat long solemnly debating this case, suddenly arose there up one of his council, a good plain man among them, and said: 'Why make you so much ado, my Lords, about so small a matter? Let her first be deflowered and then after may she be devoured.' And so, though Your Lordships have in the matter of the matrimony kept yourselves pure virgins, yet take good heed, my Lords, that you may keep your virginity still. For some there be that—by procuring Your Lordships first at the coronation to be present, and next to preach for the setting forth of it, and finally to write books to all the world in defense thereof—are desirous to deflower you, and when they have deflowered you, then will they not fail soon after to devour you. Now, my Lords," quoth he, "it lieth not in my power but that they may devour me. But God, being my good Lord, I will provide they shall never deflower me."

In continuance, when the king saw that he could by no manner of benefits win him to his side, then, lo, went he about by terrors and threats to drive him thereunto. The beginning of which trouble grew by occasion of a certain nun dwelling in Canterbury, for her virtue and holiness among the people not a little esteemed.[56] Unto whom, for that cause, many religious persons, doctors of divinity and divers other of good worship of the laity used to resort. Who, affirming that she had revelations from God to give the king warning of his wicked life and of the abuse of the sword and authority committed unto him by God, and understanding my Lord of Rochester, Bishop Fisher,[57] to be a man of notable virtuous living and learning, repaired to Rochester, and there disclosed to him all her revelations, desiring his advice and counsel therein. Which the bishop perceiving might well stand with the laws of God and his holy Church, advised her (as she before had warning and intended) to go to the king herself and to let him understand the whole circumstance thereof. Whereupon she went unto the king and told him all her revelations, and so returned home again. And in short space after, she, making a voyage to the nuns of Sion by the means of one Master Reynolds, a father of the same house, there fortuned—concerning such secrets as had been revealed unto her, some part whereof seemed to touch the matter of the king's supremacy and marriage, which shortly thereupon followed—to enter into talk with Sir Thomas More.[58] Who, notwithstanding he might well at that time without danger of any law—though after, as himself had prognosticated before, those matters were established by statues and confirmed by oaths—freely and safely have talked with her therein, nevertheless, in all the communication between them, as in process* it appeared, had always so discreetly demeaned† himself that he deserved not to be blamed, but contrariwise to be commended and praised.

And had he not been one that in all his great offices and doings for the king and realm so many years together had from all corruption of wrong-doing or bribes-taking kept himself so clear that no man was able therewith once to blemish him or make any just quarrel against him, it would without doubt, in this troublesome time of the king's indignation towards him, have been deeply laid to his charge and of the King's Highness most favorably accepted, as in the case of one Parnell that most manifestly appeared. Against whom, because Sir Thomas More while he was Lord Chancellor, at the suit of one Vaughan, his‡ adversary, had made a decree.[59] This Parnell to the King's Highness most grievously complained that Sir Thomas More, for making the decree, had of the same Vaughan, unable for the gout to travel abroad himself, by the hands of his wife taken a fair great gilt cup for a bribe. Who thereupon, by the king's appointment, being called before the whole Council, where that matter was heinously laid to his charge, forthwith confessed that, forasmuch as that cup was long after the foresaid decree brought unto him for a New Year's gift, he, upon her importunate pressing upon him, therefore of courtesy refused not to receive it. Then the Lord of Wiltshire[60]—for hatred of his religion preferrer§ of this suit—with much rejoicing said unto the lords: "Lo, my Lords, lo, did I not tell you that you should find this matter true?" Whereupon Sir Thomas More desired their worships that as they courteously heard him tell the one part of his tale, so they would vouchsafe of their honors indifferently to hear the other. After which obtained, he further declared unto them that, albeit he had indeed with much work received that cup, yet immediately thereupon he caused his butler to fill it with wine, and of that cup drank to her, and that when he had so done and she had pledged him, then as freely as her husband had given it to him, even so freely gave the same unto her again to give

---

*Process of time.
†Conducted.
‡That is, Parnell's.
§Promoter.

unto her husband for his New Year's gift. Which at his instant* request, though much against her will, at length yet she was fain to receive, as herself and certain other there presently deposed before them. Thus was the great mountain turned scant† to a little molehill.

So I remember that another time, upon a New Year's Day, there came unto him one Mistress Crocker, a rich widow, for whom with no small pains he had made a decree in the Chancery against the Lord of Arundel, to present him with a pair of gloves and forty pounds in angels‡ in them for a New Year's gift. Of whom he, thankfully receiving the gloves, but refusing the money, said unto her, "Mistress, since it were against good manners to forsake a gentlewoman's New Year's gift, I am content to receive your gloves, but as for your money I utterly refuse." So, much against her mind, enforced he her to take her gold again. And one Master Gresham, likewise, having at the same time a cause depending§ in the Chancery before him, sent him for a New Year's gift a fair gilted cup, the fashion whereof he, very well liking, caused one of his own (though not in his fantasy of so good a fashion, yet better in value) to be brought to him out of his chamber, which he willed the messenger in recompense to deliver to his master. And under other condition would he in no wise receive it. Many things more of like effect, for the declaration of his innocency and clearness from all corruption or evil affection,‖ could I here rehearse besides, which for tediousness omitting, I refer to the readers by these few fore-remembered examples with their own judgments wisely to weigh and consider the same.

At this Parliament was there put into the Lords' House a bill to attaint# the nun and divers other religious persons of high treason, and the Bishop of Rochester, Sir Thomas More, and certain others of misprision of treason,** the king presupposing of likelihood this bill would be to Sir Thomas More so troublous and terrible that that

---

*Urgent.
†Diminished.
‡Gold coin worth between 6 and 10 shillings.
§Pending.
‖Partiality.
#Accuse.
**Concealment of treasonable information.

would force him to relent and condescend to his request, wherein His Grace was much deceived. To which bill Sir Thomas More was a suitor, personally to be received in his own defense to make answer, but the king, not liking that, assigned the Bishop of Canterbury, the Lord Chancellor, the Duke of Norfolk, and Master Cromwell, at a day and place appointed, to call Sir Thomas More before them. At which time I, thinking I had good opportunity, earnestly advised him to labor unto those lords for the help of his discharge out of that Parliament Bill, who answered me, he would.

And at his coming before them, according to their appointment, they entertained him very friendly, willing him to sit down with them, which in no wise he would. Then began the Lord Chancellor to declare unto him how many ways the king had showed his love and favor towards him, how fain he would have had him continue in his office, how glad he would have been to have heaped more benefits upon him, and finally how he could ask no worldly honor or profit at His Highness's hands that were likely to be denied him—hoping by the declaration of the king's kindness and favor towards him to provoke him to recompense His Grace with the like again, and unto those things that the Parliament, the bishops, and universities had already passed to add his consent.

To this Sir Thomas More mildly made answer, saying: "No man living is there, my Lords, that would with better will do the thing that should be acceptable to the King's Highness than I, which must needs confess his manifold goodness and bountiful benefits most benignly bestowed on me. Howbeit, I verily hoped that I should never have heard of this matter more, considering that I have from time to time, always from the beginning, so plainly and truly declared my mind unto His Grace, which His Highness to me ever seemed like a most gracious prince very well to accept, never minding, as he said, to molest me more therewith. Since which time any further thing that was able to move me to any change could I never find, and if I could, there is none in all the world that could have been gladder of it than I."

Many things were there of like sort uttered on both sides. But in the end, when they saw they could by no manner of persuasions remove him from his former determinations, then began they more terribly to touch him, telling him that the King's Highness had given them in commandment, if they could by no gentleness win him, in his name with his great ingratitude to charge him: that never was there servant to his sovereign so villainous, no subject to his prince so traitorous as he. For he, by his subtle, sinister sleights most unnaturally procuring and provoking him to set forth a book of *The Assertion of Seven Sacraments*—and maintenance of the pope's authority—had caused him, to his dishonor throughout all Christendom, to put a sword in the pope's hands to fight against himself.[61]

When they had thus laid forth all the terrors they could imagine against him: "My Lords," quoth he, "these terrors be arguments for children and not for me. But to answer that wherewith you do chiefly burden me, I believe the King's Highness of his honor will never lay that to my charge. For none is there that can in that point say in my excuse more to me than His Highness himself, who right well knoweth that I was never procurer or counselor of His Majesty thereunto; but after it was finished, by His Grace's appointment and consent of the makers of the same, only a sorter-out and placer of the principal matters therein contained. Wherein when I found the pope's authority highly advanced and with strong arguments mightily defended, I said unto His Grace: 'I must put Your Highness in remembrance of one thing and that is this: the pope, as Your Grace knoweth, is a prince as you are, and in league with all other Christian princes. It may hereafter so fall out that Your Grace and he may vary upon some points of the league, whereupon may grow some breach of amity and war between you both. I think it best, therefore, that that place be amended and his authority more slenderly touched.' 'Nay,' quoth His Grace, 'that it shall not. We are so much bounden unto the See of Rome that we cannot do too much honor unto it.' Then did I put him further in remembrance of the Statute of Praemunire,[62] whereby a good part of the pope's pastoral cure here was pared away. To that answered His Highness: 'Whatsoever impediment be to the contrary, we will set forth that authority to the uttermost, for we received from that See our Crown Imperial'— which till His Grace with his own mouth told it me, I never heard of before. So that I trust when His Grace shall be once truly informed of this and call to his gracious remembrance my doings in that behalf, His Highness will never speak of it more, but clear me thoroughly therein himself." And thus displeasantly departed they.

Then took Sir Thomas More his boat towards his house at Chelsea, wherein by the way he was very merry, and for that was I nothing sorry, hoping that he had got himself discharged out of the Parliament bill. When he was landed and come home, then walked we twain alone into his garden together, where I, desirous to know how he had sped, said: "I trust, sir, all is well, because you are so merry." "It is so, indeed, son Roper, I thank God," quoth he. "Are you then put out of the Parliament bill?" said I. "By my troth, son Roper," quoth he, "I never remembered it." "Never remembered it, sir!" said I, "a case that toucheth yourself so near, and us all for your sake. I am sorry to hear it. For I verily trusted, when I saw you so merry, that all had been well." Then said he: "Wilt thou know, son Roper, why I was so merry?" "That would I gladly, sir," quoth I. "In good faith, I rejoiced, son," quoth he, "that I had given the devil a foul fall, and that with those lords I had gone so far as, without great shame, I could never go back again." At which words waxed I very sad, for though himself liked it well, yet liked it me but a little.

Now upon the report made by the Lord Chancellor and the other lords to the king of all their whole discourse had with Sir Thomas More, the king was so highly offended with him that he plainly told them he was fully determined that the aforesaid Parliament bill should undoubtedly proceed forth against him. To whom the Lord Chancellor and the rest of the lords said that they perceived the lords of the Upper House so precisely bent to hear him, in his own defense, make answer for himself, that if he were not put out of the bill, it would without fail be utterly an overthrow of all. But, for all this, needs would the king have his own will therein, or else he said that at the passing thereof, he would be personally present himself.

Then the Lord Audley and the rest, seeing him so vehemently set thereupon, on their knees most humbly besought His Grace to forbear the same, considering that if he should, in his own presence, receive an overthrow, it would not only encourage his subjects ever after to contemn* him, but also throughout all Christendom redound to his dishonor forever, adding thereunto that they mistrusted not in time to find some meeter matter to serve his turn

---

*Despise.

better. For in this case of the nun he was accounted, they said, so innocent and clear that for his dealing therein men reckoned him wor-
thier of praise than reproof. Whereupon at length, through their
earnest persuasion, he was content to condescend to their petition.

And on the morrow after, Master Cromwell meeting me in the
Parliament House, willed me to tell my father that he was put out of
the Parliament bill. But because I had appointed to dine that day in
London, sent the message by my servant to my wife at Chelsea,
whereof, when she informed her father, "In faith, Meg," quoth he,
"quod defertur non aufertur."[63] After this, as the Duke of Norfolk and
Sir Thomas More chanced to fall in familiar talk together, the duke
said unto him: "By the Mass, Master More, it is perilous striving with
princes, and therefore I would wish you somewhat to incline to the
king's pleasure. For, by God body, Master More, *indignatio principis
mors est.*"[64] "Is that all, my Lord?" quoth he. "Then in good faith is
there no more difference between Your Grace and me, but that I
shall die today and you tomorrow?"

So fell it out within a month or thereabouts after the making of
the Statue for the Oath of the Supremacy and matrimony, that all the
priests of London and Westminster, and no temporal* men but he,
were sent to appear at Lambeth before the Bishop of Canterbury,
the Lord Chancellor, and Secretary Cromwell, commissioners appointed there to tender the oath unto them. Then Sir Thomas More,
as his accustomed manner was always, ere he entered into any matter of importance—as when he was first chosen of the king's Privy
Council, when he was sent ambassador, appointed Speaker of the
Parliament, made Lord Chancellor, or when he took any weighty
matter upon him—to go to the church and to be confessed, to hear
Mass, and be housled,† so did he likewise in the morning early the
selfsame day that he was summoned to appear before the lords at
Lambeth.

And whereas he evermore used before at his departure from his
house and children, whom he tenderly loved, to have them bring
him to his boat, and there to kiss them all and bid them farewell,

---

*Secular.
†Received the Eucharist.

then would he suffer none of them forth of the gate to follow him, but pulled the wicket after him and shut them all from him. And with an heavy heart, as by his countenance it appeared, with me and our four servants there took his boat towards Lambeth. Wherein sitting still sadly awhile, at the last he rounded* me in the ear and said: "Son Roper, I thank our Lord, the field is won." What he meant thereby, I then wist not. Yet loath to seem ignorant, I answered: "Sir, I am thereof very glad." But as I conjectured afterwards, it was for that the love he had to God wrought in him so effectually that it conquered all his carnal affections utterly.

Now at his coming to Lambeth, how wisely he behaved himself before the commissioners, at the ministration of the oath unto him, may be found in certain letters of his sent to my wife remaining in a great book of his works.[65] Where by the space of four days he was betaken to the custody of the Abbot of Westminster, during which time the king consulted with his council what order were meet to be taken with him. And albeit in the beginning they were resolved that with an oath not to be acknown whether he had to the Supremacy been sworn, or what he thought thereof, he should be discharged, yet did Queen Anne by her importunate clamor so sore exasperate the king against him that, contrary to his former resolution, he caused the said Oath of Supremacy to be ministered unto him.[66] Who, albeit he made a discreet, qualified answer, nevertheless was forthwith committed to the Tower, who, as he was going thitherward, wearing as he commonly did a chain of gold about his neck, Sir Richard Cromwell[67] that had the charge of his conveyance thither advised him to send home his chain to his wife, or some of his children. "Nay, sir," quoth he, "that will I not. For if I were taken in the field by my enemies, I would they should somewhat fare the better by me."

At whose landing Master Lieutenant at the Tower gate was ready to receive him, where the porter demanded of him his upper garment. "Master Porter," quoth he, "here it is," and took off his cap and delivered him, saying: "I am very sorry it is no better for you." "No, Sir," quoth the porter, "I must have your gown." And so was he by

---

*Whispered.

Master Lieutenant conveyed to his lodging, where he called unto him one John a Wood, his own servant, there appointed to attend upon him (who could neither write nor read), and swore him before the Lieutenant that if he should hear or see him at any time speak or write any manner of thing against the king, the council, or the state of the realm, he should open it to the Lieutenant, that the Lieutenant might incontinent reveal it to the council.

Now when he had remained in the Tower a little more than a month, my wife, longing to see her father, by her earnest suit at length got leave to go to him. At whose coming, after the Seven Psalms and Litany said—which, whensoever she came to him, ere he fell in talk of any worldly matters, he used accustomably* to say with her—among the other communication he said unto her: "I believe, Meg, that they that have put me here ween† they have done me a high displeasure. But I assure thee, on my faith, my own good daughter, if it had not been for my wife and you that be my children, whom I account the chief part of my charge, I would not have failed, long ere this, to have closed myself in as strait a room—and straiter, too. But since I am come hither without mine own desert, I trust that God of His goodness will discharge me of my care, and with His gracious help supply my lack among you. I find no cause, I thank God, Meg, to reckon myself in worse case here than in my own house. For methinketh God maketh me a wanton,‡ and setteth me on His lap and dandleth me." Thus by his gracious demeanor in tribulations appeared it that all the troubles that ever chanced unto him, by his patient sufferance thereof, were to him no painful punishments, but of his patience profitable exercises.

And at another time, when he at first questioned with my wife a while of the order of his wife and children and state of his house in his absence, he asked her how Queen Anne did. "In faith, father," quoth she, "never better." "Never better, Meg!" quoth he. "Alas, Meg, alas! It pitieth me to remember into what misery, poor soul, she shall shortly come."[68] After this, Master Lieutenant, coming into his chamber to visit him, rehearsed the benefits and friendships that he

---

*Customarily.
†Believe.
‡Spoils me (like a child).

had many times received at his hands, and how much bounden he
was, therefore, friendly to entertain him and make him good cheer.
Which, since—the case standing as it did—he could not do without
the king's indignation, he trusted, he said, he would accept his good
will and such poor cheer as he had. "Master Lieutenant," quoth he
again, "I verily believe, as you may, so are you my good friend indeed
and would, as you say, with your best cheer entertain me, for the
which I most heartily thank you. And assure yourself, Master Lieutenant," quoth he, "I do not mislike my cheer, but whensoever I so
do, then thrust me out of your doors."

Whereas the oath confirming the supremacy and matrimony was
by the first statute in few words comprised, the Lord Chancellor and
Master Secretary did of their own heads add more words unto it, to
make it appear to the king's ears more pleasant and plausible. And
that oath, so amplified, caused they to be ministered to Sir Thomas
More and to all other throughout the realm. Which Sir Thomas perceiving, said unto my wife: "I may tell thee, Meg, they that have committed me hither for refusing of this oath not agreeable with the
statute, are not by their own law able to justify my imprisonment.
And surely, daughter, it is great pity that a Christian prince should,
by a flexible Council ready to follow his affections, and by a weak
clergy lacking grace constantly to stand to their learning, with flattery
to be so shamefully abused." But at length the Lord Chancellor and
Master Secretary, espying their oversight in that behalf, were fain afterwards to find the means that another statute should be made for
the confirmation of the oath so amplified with their additions.[69]

After Sir Thomas More had given over his office and all other
worldly doings therewith, to the intent he might from thenceforth
the more quietly settle himself to the service of God, then made he
a conveyance* for the disposition of all his lands, reserving for himself an estate thereof only for term of his life; and after his decease
assuring some part of the same to his wife, some to his son's wife for
a jointure,† in consideration that she was an inheritress in possession of more than an hundred pounds land by the year, and some to
me and my wife in recompense of our marriage money, with divers

---

*Transference of property.
†Holding of property for life.

remainders over. All which conveyance and assurance was perfectly finished long before that matter, whereupon he was attainted, was made an offense, and yet after by statute clearly avoided.* And so were all his lands, that he had to his wife and children by the said conveyance in such sort assured, contrary to the order of law, taken away from them and brought into the king's hands, saving that portion that he had appointed to my wife and me. Which, although he had in the foresaid conveyance reserved, as he did the rest, for term of life to himself, nevertheless, upon further consideration, two days after by another conveyance he gave that same immediately to my wife and me in possession. And so because the statute had undone only the first conveyance, giving no more to the king but so much as passed by that, the second conveyance—whereby it was given unto my wife and me—being dated two days after, was without the compass of the statute, and so was our portion to us by that means clearly reserved.[70]

As Sir Thomas More in the Tower chanced on a time, looking out of his window, to behold one Master Reynolds, a religious, learned, and virtuous father of Sion, and three monks of the Charterhouse, for the matters of the marriage and the supremacy going out of the Tower to execution, he, as one longing in that journey to have accompanied them, said unto my wife, then standing there beside him: "Lo, dost thou not see, Meg, that these blessed fathers be now as cheerfully going to their deaths as bridegrooms to their marriages? Wherefore thereby mayest thou see, mine own good daughter, what a great difference there is between such as have in effect spent all their days in a strait, hard, penitential, and painful life religiously, and such as have in the world, like worldly wretches, as thy poor father hath done, consumed all the time in pleasure and ease licentiously. For God, considering their long-continued life in most sore and grievous penance, will not longer suffer them to remain here in this vale of misery and iniquity, but speedily hence taketh them to the fruition of his everlasting deity, whereas thy silly† father, Meg, that, like a most wicked caitiff,‡ hath passed forth the whole course

*Made void.
†Simple, foolish.
‡Wretch.

of his miserable life most sinfully, God, thinking him not worthy so soon to come to that eternal felicity, leaveth him here yet still in the world, further to be plunged and turmoiled with misery."

Within a while after, Master Secretary, coming to him into the Tower from the king, pretended much friendship towards him, and for his comfort told him that the King's Highness was his good and gracious lord and minded* not, with any matter wherein he [More] should have any cause of scruple, from henceforth to trouble his conscience. As soon as Master Secretary was gone, to express what comfort he conceived of his words, he wrote with a coal—for ink then had he none—these verses following:

> Aye, flattering Fortune, look thou never so fair,
> Nor never so pleasantly begin to smile,
> As though thou wouldst my ruin all repair,
> During my life thou shalt not me beguile.
> Trust I shall God, to enter in a while
> His haven of Heaven, sure and uniform:
> Ever after the calm, look I for no storm.

When Sir Thomas More had continued a good while in the Tower, my Lady his wife obtained license to see him, who, at her first coming, like a simple woman and somewhat worldly, too, with this manner of salutations bluntly saluted him: "What the good year,† Master More," quoth she, "I marvel that you, that have been always hitherto taken for so wise a man, will not so play the fool to lie here in this close, filthy prison and be content thus to be shut up among mice and rats, when you might be abroad at your liberty and with the favor and good will both of the king and his council, if you would but do as all the bishops and best learned of this realm have done. And seeing you have at Chelsea a right fair house, your library, your books, your gallery, your garden, your orchard, and all other necessaries so handsome about you, where you might, in the company of

---

*Intended.

†An imprecation: "What the devil!"

me your wife, your children, and household, be merry, I muse what a God's name you mean here still thus fondly* to tarry."

After he had a while quietly heard her, with a cheerful countenance he said unto her: "I pray thee, good Mistress Alice, tell me one thing." "What is that?" quoth she. "Is not this house," quoth he, "as nigh heaven as mine own?" To whom she, after her accustomed homely fashion, not liking such talk, answered, "Tilly-vally, tilly-vally."† "How say you, Mistress Alice," quoth he, "is it not so?" "*Bone deus, bone deus*, man, will this gear never be left?"‡ quoth she. "Well then, Mistress Alice, if it be so," quoth he, "it is very well. For I see no great cause why I should much joy either of my gay house or of anything belonging thereunto, when, if I should but seven years lie buried under the ground, and then arise and come thither again, I should not fail to find some therein that would bid me get me out of the doors and tell me it were none of mine. What cause have I then to like such an house as would so soon forget his master?" So her persuasions moved him but a little.

Not long after came there to him the Lord Chancellor, the Dukes of Norfolk and Suffolk, with Master Secretary, and certain others of the Privy Council—at two separate times—by all policies possible procuring him either precisely§ to confess the supremacy or precisely to deny it. Whereunto, as appeareth by his examination in the said great book, they could never bring him.

Shortly hereupon, Master Rich—afterwards Lord Rich, then newly made the King's Solicitor—Sir Robert Southwell, and one Master Palmer, servant to the Secretary, were sent to Sir Thomas More into the Tower to fetch away his books from him. And while Sir Richard Southwell and Master Palmer were busy in the trussing-up of his books, Master Rich, pretending friendly talk with him, among other things, of a set course as it seemed, said thus unto him: "Forasmuch as it is well known, Master More, that you are a man both wise and well learned, as well in the laws of the realm as otherwise,

---

*Foolishly.
†A colloquialism expressing impatience: Fiddlesticks!
‡Good lord, good lord, man, will you never stop this nonsense?
§Stratagems . . . inducing . . . specifically.

I pray you therefore, sir, let me be so bold as of good will to put unto you this case. Admit there were, sir," quoth he, "an Act of Parliament that all the realm should take me for the king, would not you, Master More, take me for the king?" "Yes, sir," quoth Sir Thomas More, "that would I." "I put the case further," quoth Master Rich, "that there were an Act of Parliament that all the realm should take me for pope. Would not you, then, Master More, take me for pope?" "For answer," quoth Sir Thomas More, "to your first case: the Parliament may well, Master Rich, meddle with the state of temporal princes. But to make answer to your second case, I will put you this case: suppose the Parliament would make a law that God should not be God. Would you, then, Master Rich, say that God were not God?" "No, sir," quoth he, "that would I not, since no Parliament may make any such law." "No more," said Sir Thomas More, as Master Rich reported of him, "could the Parliament make the king supreme head of the Church." Upon whose only report* was Sir Thomas More indicted of treason upon the statute in which it was made treason to deny the king to be supreme head of the Church, into which indictment were put these words: "maliciously, traitorously, and diabolically."

When Sir Thomas More was brought from the Tower to Westminster Hall to answer the indictment, and at the King's Bench bar before the judges thereupon arraigned, he openly told them that he would upon that indictment have abidden in law,† but that he thereby should have been driven to confess of himself the matter indeed, that was the denial of the king's supremacy, which he protested was untrue. Wherefore he thereto pleaded not guilty, and so reserved unto himself advantage to be taken of the body of the matter, after verdict, to avoid that indictment. And, moreover, added that if those only odious terms—"maliciously, traitorously, and diabolically"— were put out of the indictment, he saw therein nothing justly to charge him.[71]

And for proof to the jury that Sir Thomas More was guilty of this treason, Master Rich was called by them to give evidence unto them upon his oath, as he did. Against whom Sir Thomas More began in

---

*Report alone.
*Abided by the law.

this wise to say: "If I were a man, my Lords, that did not regard an oath, I need not, as it is well known, in this place at this time nor in this case to stand here as an accused person. And if this oath of yours, Master Rich, be true, then pray I that I never see God in the face, which I would not say, were it otherwise, to win the whole world." Then recited he to the court the discourse of all their communication in the Tower according to the truth, and said: "In faith, Master Rich, I am sorrier for your perjury than for my own peril. And you shall understand that neither I, nor no man else to my knowledge, ever took you to be a man of such credit as in any matter of importance I or any other would at any time vouchsafe to communicate with you. And I, as you well know, of no small while have been acquainted with you and your conversation,* who have known you from your youth hitherto. For we long dwelled both in one parish together, where, as yourself can tell (I am sorry you compel me so to say), you were esteemed very light of your tongue, a great dicer, and of no commendable fame. And so in your house at the Temple,† where hath been your chief bringing up, were you likewise accounted.

"Can it therefore seem likely unto your honorable Lordships, that I would, in so weighty a cause, so unadvisedly overshoot myself as to trust Master Rich—a man of me always reputed for one of so little truth, as Your Lordships have heard—so far above my sovereign lord the king or any of his noble counselors, that I would unto him utter the secrets of my conscience touching the king's supremacy, the special point and only mark at my hands so long sought for? A thing which I never did, nor never would, after the statute thereof made, reveal either to the King's Highness himself or to any of his honorable counselors, as it is not unknown unto your house, at sundry times sent from His Grace's own person unto the Tower to me for none other purpose. Can this in your judgments, my Lords, seem likely to be true?

"And yet if I had so done indeed, my Lords, as Master Rich hath sworn, seeing it was spoken but in familiar secret talk, nothing affirming and only in putting of cases without other displeasant

---

*Behavior.
†That is, the Middle Temple, one of the Inns of Court.

circumstances, it cannot justly be taken to be spoken 'maliciously.' And where there is no malice, there can be no offense. And over* this I can never think, my Lords, that so many worthy bishops, so many honorable personages, and so many other worshipful, virtuous, wise, and well-learned men, as at the making of that law were in the Parliament assembled, ever meant to have any man punished by death in whom there could be found no malice—taking *'malitia'* for *'malevolentia.'* For if *'malitia'* be generally taken for 'sin,' no man is there then that can thereof excuse himself: *Quia si dixerimus quod peccatum non habemus, nosmet ipsos seducimus, et veritas in nobis non est.*[72] And only this word 'maliciously' is in the statute material,[†] as this term 'forcible' is in the statute of forcible entries, by which statute if a man enter peacefully, and put not his adversary out forcibly, it is no offense, but if he puts him out forcibly, then by that statue it is an offense. And so shall he be punished by this term forcibly.

"Besides this, the manifold goodness of the King's Highness himself, that hath been so many ways my singular good lord and gracious sovereign, that hath so dearly loved and trusted me, even at my very first coming into his noble service with the dignity of his honorable Privy Council, vouchsafing to admit me, and to offices of great credit and worship most liberally advanced me, and finally with that weighty room of His Grace's high chancellorship (the like whereof he never did to temporal man before)[73] next to his own royal person the highest officer in this noble realm, so far above my merits or qualities able and meet therefore, of his incomparable benignity honored and exalted me, by the space of twenty years and more showing his continual favor towards me; and, until, at mine own poor suit, it pleased His Highness, giving me license with His Majesty's favor, to bestow the residue of my life for the provision of my soul in the service of God—of his special goodness thereof to discharge and unburden me—most benignly heaped honors continually more and more upon me. All this His Highness's goodness, I say, so long thus bountifully extended towards me, were in my

---

*Besides.
†Relevant.

mind, my Lords, matter sufficient to convince* this slanderous sur-
mise by this man so wrongfully imagined against me."

Master Rich, seeing himself so disproved and his credit so foully
defaced, caused Sir Richard Southwell and Master Palmer, that at the
time of their communication were in the chamber,† to be sworn
what words had passed between them. Whereupon Master Palmer,
upon his deposition, said that he was so busy about the trussing-up
of Sir Thomas More's books in a sack that he took no heed to their
talk. Sir Richard Southwell likewise, upon his deposition, said that
because he was appointed only to look to the conveyance of his
books, he gave no ear unto them. After this were there many other
reasons, not now in my remembrance, by Sir Thomas More in his
own defense alleged, to the discredit of Master Rich's foresaid evidence and proof of the clearness of his own conscience. All of which
notwithstanding the jury found him guilty.

And incontinent upon the verdict, the Lord Chancellor, for that
matter chief commissioner, beginning to proceed in judgment
against him, Sir Thomas More said to him: "My Lord, when I was to-
wards‡ the law, the manner in such case was to ask the prisoner before judgment, why judgment should not be given against him?"
Whereupon the Lord Chancellor, staying his judgment, wherein he
had partly proceeded, demanded of him what he was able to say to
the contrary. Who then in this sort mildly made answer: "Forasmuch as, my Lord," quoth he, "this indictment is grounded upon an
Act of Parliament directly oppugnant to the laws of God and His
Holy Church, the supreme government of which, or of any part
whereof, may no temporal prince presume by any law to take upon
him, as rightfully belonging to the See of Rome—a spiritual preeminence by the mouth of Our Savior himself, personally present
upon the earth, to Saint Peter and his successors, bishops of the
same See, by special prerogative granted—it is therefore in law,
amongst Christian men, insufficient to charge any Christian."

And for proof thereof like as—amongst divers other reasons and
authorities—he declared that this realm, being but one member and

---

*Refute.
†That is, More's room in the Tower.
‡Engaged in practicing.

small part of the Church, might not make a particular law disagreeable with the general law of Christ's Universal Catholic Church, no more than the City of London, being but one poor member in respect of the whole realm, might make a law against an Act of Parliament to bind the whole realm. So further showed he that it was contrary both to the laws and statues of our own land yet unrepealed, as they might evidently perceive in *Magna Carta: Quod ecclesia anglicana libera sit, et habeat omnia jura sua integra, et libertates suas illaesas;*[74] and also contrary to that sacred oath which the King's Highness himself and every other Christian prince always with great solemnity received at their coronations. Alleging, moreover, that no more might this realm of England refuse obedience to the See of Rome than might the child refuse obedience to his natural father. For as Saint Paul said of the Corinthians, "I have regenerated you my children in Christ,"[75] so might Saint Gregory, pope of Rome, of whom by Saint Augustine, his messenger, we first received the Christian faith, of us English men truly say: "You are my children because I have given to you everlasting salvation, a far higher and better inheritance than any carnal father can leave to his child, and by generation made you, my spiritual children in Christ."

Then was it thereunto by the Lord Chancellor answered that, seeing all the bishops, universities, and best learned men of the realm had to this act agreed, it was much marveled that he alone against then all would so stiffly stick and vehemently argue there against. To that Sir Thomas More replied saying, "If the number of bishops and universities be so material, as Your Lordship seemeth to take it, then see I little cause, my Lord, why that thing in my conscience should make any change. For I nothing doubt but that, though not in this realm, yet in Christendom about, of these well-learned bishops and virtuous men that are yet alive, they be not the fewer part that be of my mind therein. But if I should speak of those which already be dead, of whom many be now saints in heaven, I am very sure it is the far greater part of them that, all the while they lived, thought in this case that way that I think now. And therefore am I not bound, my Lord, to conform my conscience to the council of one realm against the general council of Christendom."

Now when Sir Thomas More, for the avoiding of the indictment, had taken as many exceptions as he thought meet, and more reasons than I can now remember alleged, the Lord Chancellor, loath to have the burden of the judgment wholly to depend upon himself, there openly asked the advice of the Lord Fitz-James,[76] then Lord Chief Justice of the King's Bench, and joined in commission with him, whether this indictment were sufficient or not. Who, like a wise man, answered: "My Lords all, by Saint Julian"—that was ever his oath—"I must needs confess that if the Act of Parliament be not unlawful, then is not the indictment in my conscience insufficient." Whereupon the Lord Chancellor said to the rest of the lords, "Lo, my Lords, lo, you hear what my Lord Chief Justice saith," and so immediately gave he judgment against him.

After which ended, the commissioners yet further courteously offered him, if he had anything else to allege for his defense, to grant him favorable audience. Who answered: "More have I not to say, my Lords, but like as the blessed apostle Saint Paul, as we read in the Acts of the Apostles, was present and consented to the death of Saint Stephen, and kept their clothes that stoned him to death, and yet be they now both twain holy saints in heaven, and shall continue there friends forever, so I verily trust, and shall therefore right heartily pray, that though Your Lordships have now here in earth been judges to my condemnation, we may yet hereafter in heaven merrily all meet together to our everlasting salvation."

Thus much touching Sir Thomas More's arraignment, being not thereat present myself, have I by the credible report partly of Sir Anthony Saint Leger, Knight,[77] and partly of Richard Heywood and John Webb, Gentleman, with others of good credit, at the hearing thereof present themselves, as far as my poor wit and memory would serve me, here truly rehearsed unto you.

Now after this arraignment departed he from the bar to the Tower again, led by Sir William Kingston, a tall, strong, and comely knight, Constable of the Tower, and his very dear friend.[78] Who, when he had brought him from Westminster to the Old Swan towards the Tower, there with an heavy heart, the tears running down by his cheeks, bade him farewell. Sir Thomas More, seeing him so sorrowful, comforted him with as good words as he could, saying: "Good Master Kingston, trouble not yourself, but be of good cheer, for I will pray for you, and my good Lady, your wife, that we may meet in heaven together, where we shall be merry for ever and ever."

Soon after, Sir William Kingston, talking with me of Sir Thomas More, said: "In faith, Master Roper, I was ashamed of myself that at my departure from your father, I found my heart so feeble, and his so strong, that he was fain to comfort me which should rather have comforted him."

When Sir Thomas More came from Westminster to the Tower-ward* again, his daughter, my wife, desirous to see her father, whom she thought she should never see in this world after, and also to have his final blessing, gave attendance about the Tower Wharf, where she knew he should pass by, before he could enter into the Tower, there tarrying for his coming home. As soon as she saw him—after his blessings on her knees reverently received—she, hasting towards him, without consideration or care of herself, pressing in amongst the midst of the throng and the company of the guard that with halberds and bills† were round about him, hastily ran to him and there openly in the sight of them all embraced him, took him about the neck, and kissed him. Who, well liking her most natural and dear daughterly affection towards him, gave her his fatherly blessing and many godly words of comfort besides. From whom after she was departed, she, not satisfied with the former sight of him, and like one that had forgotten herself, being all ravished with the entire love of her dear father, having respect neither to herself nor to the press of the people and multitude that were about him, suddenly turned back again, ran to him as before, took him about the neck, and divers times together most lovingly kissed him—and at last, with a full heavy heart was fain to depart him. The beholding whereof was to many of them that were present thereat so lamentable that it made them for very sorrow thereof to mourn and weep.

So remained Sir Thomas More in the Tower more than seven-night after his judgment. From whence, the day before he suffered,[79] he sent his shirt of hair—not willing to have it seen—to my wife, his dearly beloved daughter, and a letter, written with a coal, contained in the foresaid book of his works, plainly expressing the fervent desire he had to suffer on the morrow, in these words following: "I cumber‡ you,

---

*Toward the Tower.
†Spear-like battle-axes and swords.
‡Trouble.

good Margaret, much, but I would be sorry if it should be any longer than tomorrow. For tomorrow is Saint Thomas's Even and the Utas of Saint Peter,[80] and therefore tomorrow long I to go to God. It were a day very meet and convenient for me, etc. I never liked your manner better than when you kissed me last. For I like when daughterly love and dear charity hath no leisure to look to worldly courtesy."

And so upon the next morning, being Tuesday, Saint Thomas's even, and the Utas of Saint Peter, in the year of our Lord 1535, according as he in his letter the day before had wished, early in the morning came to him Sir Thomas Pope, his singular friend, on message from the king and council that he should before nine of the clock the same morning suffer death, and that therefore forthwith he should prepare himself thereto.

"Master Pope," quoth he, "for your good tidings I most heartily thank you. I have been always much bounden to the King's Highness for the benefits and honors that he hath still from time to time most bountifully heaped upon me. And yet more bound am I to His Grace for putting me into this place, where I have had convenient time and space to have remembrance of my end. And so help me God, most of all, Master Pope, am I bound to His Highness that it pleaseth him so shortly to rid me out of the miseries of this wretched world. And therefore will I not fail most earnestly to pray for His Grace, both here and also in another world."

"The king's pleasure is further," quoth Master Pope, "that at your execution you shall not use many words."

"Master Pope," quoth he, "you do well that you give me warning of His Grace's pleasure, for otherwise I had purposed at that time somewhat to have spoken, but of no matter wherewith His Grace or any other should have had cause to be offended. Nevertheless, whatsoever I intended, I am ready obediently to conform myself to His Grace's commandment. And I beseech you, good Master Pope, to be a mean unto His Highness that my daughter Margaret may be present at my burial."

"The king is well content already," quoth Master Pope, "that your wife, children, and other friends shall have liberty to be present thereat."

"O, how much beholden, then," said Sir Thomas More, "am I to

His Grace that unto my poor burial vouchsafeth to have so gracious consideration."

Wherewithal Master Pope, taking his leave of him, could not refrain from weeping. Which Sir Thomas More perceiving, comforted him in this wise: "Quiet yourself, good Master Pope, and be not discomforted. For I trust that we shall, once in heaven, see each other full merrily, where we shall be sure to live and love together in joyful bliss eternally."

Upon whose departure Sir Thomas More, as one that had been invited to some solemn feast, changed himself into his best apparel. Which Master Lieutenant espying, advised him to put it off, saying that he that should have it was but a javel.* "What, Master Lieutenant," quoth he, "shall I account him a javel that shall do me this day so singular a benefit? Nay, I assure you, were it cloth-of-gold, I would account it well bestowed on him, as Saint Cyprian did, who gave his executioner thirty pieces of gold."[81] And albeit, at length, through Master Lieutenant's importunate persuasion, he altered his apparel, yet, after the example of that holy martyr, Saint Cyprian, did he of that little money that was left him send one angel of gold to his executioner.

And so was he by Master Lieutenant brought out of the Tower and from thence led towards the place of execution, where, going up the scaffold, which was so weak that it was ready to fall, he said merrily to Master Lieutenant: "I pray you, Master Lieutenant, see me safe up, and for my coming down, let me shift for myself."

Then desired he all the people thereabouts to pray for him, and to bear witness with him that he should now there suffer death in and for the faith of the Holy Catholic Church. Which done, he kneeled down, and after his prayers said, he turned to the executioner and with a cheerful countenance spake thus unto him: "Pluck up thy spirits, man, and be not afraid to do thine office. My neck is very short. Take heed therefore thou strike not awry, for saving of thine honesty."

So passed Sir Thomas More out of this world to God upon the very same day in which himself had most desired.

---

*Worthless fellow—that is, the executioner.

Soon after whose death came intelligence thereof to the Emperor Charles, whereupon he sent for Sir Thomas Elyot,[82] our English ambassador, and said unto him: "My Lord Ambassador, we understand that the king, your master, hath put his faithful servant and grave, wise counselor, Sir Thomas More, to death." Whereunto Sir Thomas Elyot answered that he understood nothing thereof. "Well," said the emperor, "it is too true. And this will we say, that if we had been master of such a servant, of whose doings ourselves have had these many years no small experience, we would rather have lost the best city of our dominions than have lost such a worthy counselor." Which matter was by the same Sir Thomas Elyot to myself, to my wife, to Master Clement and his wife, to Master John Heywood and his wife, and unto divers others of his friends accordingly reported.

Endnotes

Translator to the Gentle Reader

1. (p. 3) *at the request of a friend for his own private use:* The "friend" in question here is George Tadlowe. On him, see the Dedicatory Epistle to William Cecil printed on pages 155–159; Tadlowe is mentioned on p. 158.

2. (p. 3) *Ita vita est hominum . . . id arte ut corrigas: Adelphi* (*The Brothers*), lines 739–741: "Human life is just like playing dice. / If that which is best does not happen when you throw [the dice], / You should try to correct by art that which by chance has happened." (In modern editions of Terence the passage is slightly different.)

Letter of Thomas More to Peter Giles

1. (p. 5) *I am almost ashamed . . . within a month and a half:* Peter Giles, or Gillis (1486–1533), a prominent humanist, was the chief clerk of the court of justice in Antwerp. More probably met him in September 1515, when More went to Flanders with Cuthbert Tunstall (1474–1559) to negotiate a commercial arrangement between an English trading company, the Merchant Adventurers, and the German trading association known as the Hanseatic League. More wrote the second book of *Utopia* that fall, but added the bulk of the first book the following year and sent it to Giles only in November 1516—hence his apology for sending the book so late.

2. (p. 7) *For John Clement:* John Clement (d. 1572) studied at Saint Paul's School under the humanist John Colet, served as tutor to More's children, accompanied More on his trip to Flanders, and achieved distinction as a physician who translated Galen (1525). Clement was named personal physician to Henry VIII (1528) and was elected president of the College of Physicians (1544).

3. (p. 7) *For whereas Hythloday . . . paces in breadth:* A fictitious character, Hythloday has an "allegorical" name. His first name, Raphael, is that of one of the archangels and means "the healing of God," which fits his desire to cure the economic, social, and political maladies of Europe. His last name, Hythloday, means "speaker of trifles" or "speaker of nonsense," and it is thus consistent with the name More invents for his ideal state, "Utopia"—that is

"nowhere." Amaurote (Latin: *Amauroticum*) is More's name for the capital of Utopia; it derives from a Greek word and means something like "dark city," an appropriate term for foggy London. The river Anyder (Latin: *Anydrus*) flows through the city; the name means "waterless," which fits the Thames with its strong tides.

4. (p. 7) *For as I will take good heed that there be in my book nothing false . . . I had rather be good than wily:* More is distinguishing between inadvertently lying because one thinks something to be true when it is not ("tell a lie") and lying deliberately ("make a lie"). His conclusion to this sentence in Latin is actually that he would rather "be good than prudent" (*bonus esse quam prudens*).

5. (p. 8) *obtain this bishopric with suit:* To apply for a bishopric to the pope, a word the Protestant Robinson here translates as "high bishop," went against the traditions of the Church. More is satirizing Rowland Phillips (d. 1538?), vicar of Croyden (served 1497–1538) and royal chaplain, who was hostile to humanism and to such innovations as printing.

6. (p. 9) *out of all danger of gunshot:* In the original More uses a Greek phrase meaning "beyond the reach of missiles."

Book One of Utopia

1. (p. 15) *Charles, the right high and mighty King of Castile:* Charles (1500–1558) was the grandson of Ferdinand of Aragon and Isabella of Castile; he would be elected Holy Roman Emperor in 1519. In 1515 and 1516 he was actually the prince of Castile, which is what More has in his Latin text (*princeps*), not "king." On More's mission, see note 1 to the prefatory "Letter of Thomas More to Peter Giles," above.

2. (p. 15) *Cuthbert Tunstall:* Tunstall (1474–1559) was a humanist-educated official who became master of the rolls of the Chancery and vice-chancellor of England under Cardinal Thomas Wolsey on May 16, 1516. He later became bishop of London (1522–1530) and then bishop of Durham (1530–1552 and 1553–1559).

3. (p. 15) *the Margrave (as they call him) of Bruges . . . but the wisest and the best spoken of them was George Temsice:* A margrave was a count of a frontier area (a "march"); in More's Latin, the title is *praefectus*, which would be translated as "governor" or "mayor." George Temsice was Georges de Themsecke (d. 1536), a doctor of laws and an official in Flanders. The town of Cassel is currently part of France but then belonged to Flanders.

4. (p. 16) *Our Lady's Church:* Nôtre Dame, built between 1352 and 1516, is the cathedral of Antwerp.

5. (p. 17) *Nay (quoth he) there ye were greatly deceived: . . . the ancient and sage philosopher Plato:* Palinurus was Aeneas's helmsman who fell overboard just before Aeneas's fleet landed in Italy (see Vergil, *Aeneid* 5.833–861, 6.337–383). Ulysses, or Odysseus, who spent ten years after the fall of Troy traveling the Mediterranean before returning home to Ithaca, was celebrated for his prudence and eloquence. Plato also had a reputation for traveling (see Diogenes Laertius, *Lives of Eminent Philosophers,* 3 [Plato]: 6–8, 18–24), although Giles is more likely thinking of the mental "voyages" Plato made in his philosophy, in particular, in his imagining his ideal state in *Republic.*

6. (p. 17) *a few of Seneca's and Cicero's doings:* Seneca (c.2–65 C.E.) was a Stoic philosopher who wrote moral essays and many sets of letters; he was the tutor of the emperor Nero, who ordered his death. Cicero (106–43 B.C.E.), the great Roman orator, also wrote a series of philosophical treatises largely derived from Greek thinking.

7. (p. 17) *Amerigo Vespucci:* Vespucci (1451–1512), the Florentine explorer from whom the Americas take their name, made four voyages there between 1497 and 1502, the last two for the king of Portugal. The voyages were described in two Latin treatises published around 1504: *Quatuor Navigationes (Four Voyages)* and *Cosmographiae Introductio (Introduction to Cosmography).* He described some of the indigenous peoples of the Americas as being Epicureans and as holding all things in common—ideas that clearly affected More's conception of Utopia. On his last voyage he sailed along the coast of South America, where he left behind a garrison of twenty-four men before returning to Portugal.

8. (p. 18) *country of Gulike:* In More's Latin, Hythloday is left behind in a *castellum,* a "fort" or "castle," which is also the word Vespucci uses. There is no precedent, in other words, for Robinson's "Gulike." It may be a play on *gull,* a common Renaissance English term for "fool." Thus, *Gulike* may mean something like "the country of fools," a witty neologism that fits a text whose ideal state is called "no place." Two sentences below, Robinson has Hythloday traveling with five Gulikians, whereas More merely assigns him five "people from the fort" (*Castellani*).

9. (p. 18) *'he that hath no grave is covered with the sky,' and, 'the way to heaven out of all places is of like length and distance':* The first saying comes from Lucan, *Pharsalia* 7.819; the second, from Cicero, *Tusculan Disputations* 1.43.104.

10. (p. 18) *in Taprobane:* More has Hythloday return to Europe by way of Sri Lanka (Taprobane) and Calcutta (Calicut). Although Vespucci had been trying to reach the Indian Ocean, he had only managed to get to South America, from which he then returned.

11. (p. 20) *For nothing is more easy to be found . . . such like great and incredible monsters:* These monsters appear in Homer's *Odyssey* and Vergil's *Aeneid*. Scylla is a six-headed sea monster (*Odyssey* 12.73–100, 234–259, and *Aeneid* 3.420–432); Celaenos is a being half-bird and half-woman called a harpy (*Aeneid* 3.209–258); and the Laestrygons were a tribe of giant cannibals (*Odyssey* 10.76–132).

12. (p. 21) *that weal public:* As J. H. Hexter has argued (in *More's* Utopia; see "For Further Reading"), More's original draft of *Utopia* probably stopped at the end of the preceding paragraph, which then led directly into a description of the ideal state, the present book 2. However, as he was being enticed into royal service in 1516, More redirected his work at this point to the subject of "counsel"—that is, to the question of whether a wise man, such as Hythloday (or More) ought to serve as adviser to a monarch.

13. (p. 22) *It is not my mind that you should be in bondage to kings, but as a retainer to them at your pleasure:* At this point Robinson omits and changes much in More's text. More has Giles defend his advice by saying there is a distinction between being a slave (*servire*) and being someone's servant (*inservire*), to which Hythloday replies that the difference involves merely one syllable (in Latin).

14. (p. 24) *the insurrection that the western Englishmen made against their king, which . . . was suppressed and ended:* In 1497 more than 15,000 people in Cornwall rebelled against the heavy taxes being imposed by the crown to finance war in Scotland. More than a thousand rebels were slain at Blackheath, and their leaders were executed.

15. (p. 24) *John Morton:* Morton (1420?–1500), who supported the Lancastrians and the Tudors during the War of the Roses, became archbishop in 1486 and lord chancellor in 1487, just after Henry VII began his reign, and was made cardinal at Henry's request in 1493. More entered his household in 1490 and spent several years in service there.

16. (p. 26) *as not long ago out of Blackheath field, and a little before that out of the wars in France:* For Blackheath see note 14 above. Henry VII invaded France in 1492 and laid siege to Boulogne.

17. (p. 27) *these wisefools:* This is a literal translation of More's Latinized Greek oxymoron, derived ultimately from the late Greek writer Lucian: *morosophi* (from *moros*, "fool," and *sophos*, "wise").

18. (p. 27) *lest that (as it is prettily said of Sallust) their hands and their minds . . . should wax dull:* See Sallust, *Cataline* 16.3.

19. (p. 28) *the examples of the Romans, Carthaginians, Syrians . . . do manifestly declare:* The Roman civil wars of the first century B.C.E. were brought about by quarrels among Roman leaders who possessed standing armies. Moreover, under the empire the army frequently chose the emperor. In Carthage rulers owed their positions to the army as well. As for Syria, More may have been thinking of the Janissaries, an elite corps of the Ottoman army in the fifteenth and sixteenth centuries that was a powerful political force in its own right (Syria was part of the Ottoman Empire).

20. (p. 29) *For look . . . ground for tillage:* The last portion of Robinson's sentence is slightly confusing. He is saying that the gentlemen and abbots, not content "to live in rest and pleasure," "leave no ground for tillage," thereby not benefiting ("profiting") but indeed doing much damage to ("annoying") the commonwealth. More's protest over the enclosing of land once cultivated by peasants but now used for sheep-raising is not isolated in the period. The enclosure movement led to the destruction of villages and the dislocation of important segments of the population. Despite even acts of Parliament against it, however, it continued unabated throughout the century.

21. (p. 29) *that one covetous and insatiable cormorant:* The cormorant was proverbially greedy and is featured as such in Erasmus's *Adages*, where it appears as *Larus hians* ("Open-mouthed cormorant"); see Desiderius Erasmus, *Collected Works* 34 (*Adages II vii 1 to III iii 100*), translated by R. A. B. Mynors (Toronto: University of Toronto Press, 1992) pp. 145–146 (II.x.48). In More's Latin the word is *helluo* ("glutton" or "spendthrift").

22. (p. 30) *For they be almost all coming into a few rich men's hands . . . as dear as they lust:* In More's Latin text he goes on to say that this situation is not a monopoly, because no single individual owns the sheep. But because many do, he dubs it an oligopoly. For his thinking here on monopolistic practices, More is ultimately indebted to Aristotle, *Politics* 1.10.1259a6–36.

23. (p. 33) *For so cruel governance . . . the sword should be drawn:* At this point More's Latin text refers to *Manliana imperia* ("Manlian edicts")—that is, to the very strict laws promulgated when Lucius Manlius was Roman dictator in 363 B.C.E. More's source for this was Livy, *History of Rome* (*Ab urbe condita*) 4.29. "By and by" in this sentence means "immediately." The reference to "stoical ordinances" in the next sentence is to the stoic argument that all crimes were equal, an argument Cicero refutes in *De finibus* 4.9.21–23.

24. (p. 34) *And if any man would understand killing . . . may be lawful:* Hythlo-day's argument is: if anyone thinks that God's command against killing takes no precedence over man's laws ("constitutions") that define it as permissible, then what prevents people from passing laws that make crimes such as whoredom, fornication, and perjury also, to some degree, lawful?

25. (p. 34) *Moses' law . . . punished theft by the purse and not with death:* See the Bible, Exodus 22:1–4.

26. (p. 35) *called the Polylerites:* More has made up this word from two Greek words; it means "much nonsense."

27. (p. 39) *privileges of all sanctuaries:* More refers to the immunity from crime granted to those who took refuge within a church or monastery.

28. (p. 40) *he that shooteth oft at the last shall hit the mark:* In More's Latin, the reference is to throwing the dice and eventually coming up with a winning number.

29. (p. 41) *In your patience you shall save your souls:* See the Bible, Luke 21:19. The next three quotations come from: Psalms 4:4, Psalms 69:9, and a medieval hymn by Adam of Saint Victor, which is based on 2 Kings 2:23–24.

30. (p. 42) *For whereas your Plato judgeth . . . their good counsel:* For Plato's philosopher-king, see *Republic* 5.473c–d. Plato attempted to apply his theory to Dionysius the Younger of Syracuse and failed resoundingly, as Hythloday says in his next response to More.

31. (p. 43) *Well, suppose I were with the French king . . . whose kingdoms he hath long ago in mind and purpose invaded:* The French king in question here was Francis I (ruled 1515–1547). In this sentence, Hythloday refers initially to the series of wars fought by the French in the Italian peninsula, starting with Charles VIII (ruled 1483–1498), who invaded Italy in 1494 and took Naples in 1495, but lost it a year later. Charles's successor Louis XII (ruled 1498–1515) captured Naples in 1501 but lost it in 1503; he also took Milan, which he held until 1512, when he was driven out by the Swiss. Francis's ambition was to retake those two cities (he would be decisively defeated in the battle of Pavia in 1525 by the forces of the Emperor Charles V and made to renounce all claims to Italy). The Venetians often opposed the French and lost their holdings on the Italian mainland to a coalition including France and Spain in 1508, although the city itself maintained its independence. Finally, the French were concerned to regain Flanders, Brabant, and Burgundy, since the first two had become part of the empire when Mary of Burgundy married the emperor Maximilian in 1477, to whom the French also yielded Burgundy in 1482.

32. (p. 43) *with his five eggs:* This is probably an allusion to a proverb such as "Five eggs a penny, and four of them rotten." What seems to be implied is that the suggestion being made is superfluous and defective. This expression has no equivalent in More's Latin text.

33. (p. 45) *the people that be called the Achorians:* "Achorians" is almost a synonym for "Utopians," since the name derives from two Greek words meaning "no country."

34. (p. 46) *Suppose that some king and his council . . . great treasures of money:* The policies described here were actually used by European monarchs in the period, including English rulers such as Edward IV and Henry VII.

35. (p. 48) *maintain an army:* This saying is derived from Cicero, *De officiis* 1.8.25. Crassus, with Julius Caesar and Pompey, was a member of the First Triumvirate that controlled Rome roughly from 59 to 53 B.C.E. Crassus's death in 53 led to the outbreak of civil war between Caesar and Pompey.

36. (p. 49) *he had rather be a ruler of rich men than be rich himself:* For this saying, see Plutarch, *Sayings of Romans*, "Manius Curius," 2 (*Moralia* 194F); note that More mistakenly assigns this remark to Curius' colleague Gaius Fabricius, whose sayings immediately follow those of Curius in Plutarch's work.

37. (p. 49) *law of the Macarians:* The name Macarian comes from a Greek word meaning "blessed."

38. (p. 50) *This school philosophy:* By "school philosophy" (*philosophia scholastica*) More means a kind of abstract, academic discussion disconnected from practical experience. He may be thinking of the scholastic philosophy still taught in universities.

39. (p. 51) *And this is the philosophy that you must use:* See Cicero, *Orator* 35.123.

40. (p. 53) *(as Mitio saith in Terence) help to further their madness:* See Terence, *Adelphi (The Brothers)* 1.145–147.

41. (p. 53) *seeing they cannot remedy the folly of the people:* See Plato, *Republic* 6.496d–e.

42. (p. 56) *men shall never there live wealthily where all things be common:* More's arguments here against communism derive ultimately from Aristotle, *Politics* 2.1–4.1260b25–1262b36.

Book Two of Utopia

1. (p. 62) *But King Utopus:* Utopus is not referred to as a king in More's Latin text, either here or elsewhere, but as a *dux* ("leader").

2. (p. 62) *it was called Abraxa:* Abraxa, from the Greek *Abraxas*, was the name given to the highest of the 365 heavens posited by the ancient Gnostics (the numerological value given to all the letters in the name add up to 365).

3. (p. 63) *There is in the island fifty-four large and fair cities . . . in like manners, institutions, and laws:* If one includes London, which was counted as a county in its own right, the number of counties in England and Wales is fifty-four, thus equaling the number of cities in Utopia.

4. (p. 63) *one head ruler, which is called a phylarch, being as it were a head bailiff:* Phylarch derives from a Greek word for the head of a clan. "Bailiff" is Robinson's addition here to provide an English equivalent for the Greek name. He is not thinking of a bailiff as a public administrator or an officer of justice, but as a steward who runs a manor for its owner.

5. (p. 65) *Nor to me any of them all is better beloved, as wherein I lived five whole years together:* From the details of the description of Amaurote that follows, More wanted readers to see it as an idealized version of London.

6. (p. 66) *runneth down a slope through the midst of the city into Anyder:* The parallel in London is the Fleet River.

7. (p. 67) margin *This gear smelleth of Plato, his community:* See Plato, *Republic* 5.416d.

8. (p. 67) margin *The commodity of gardens is commended also of Vergil:* See Vergil, *Georgics* 4.116–48.

9. (p. 68) *Every thirty families or farms . . . the chief phylarch:* The meanings of *syphogrant* and *tranibore* are obscure. The first may derive from Greek roots and mean "wise old man" or "silly old man." The second may mean "master eater" or "glutton." For *Phylarch*, see note 4 above.

10. (p. 69) *They take every two syphogrants to them in council, and every day a new couple:* That is, they rotate the syphogrants a pair at a time in the council.

11. (p. 73) *The which thing you also shall perceive . . . the men be idle:* More's statement identifies work in a very limited manner here as something done in connection with an occupation, such as farming, which allows him to dismiss the domestic labor virtually all women did in the home as not being work. Moreover, although it was true that women in the gentry and above during the Renaissance did not normally have an occupation, many wives of craftsmen, tradesmen, and peasants actually did work of different sorts alongside their husbands.

12. (p. 87) *nuts, brooches, and puppets:* More's Latin reads *nucas, bullas, et pupas:* "trifles, trinkets (worn about the neck), and dolls." Robinson has

confused *nucas* ("trifles") with *nuces* ("nuts"), and supplies "brooches" for the more generic "trinkets." "Puppets" means "dolls."

13. (p. 91) *For they have not devised . . . our children in every place do learn:* The "rules" mentioned here are those of Scholastic logic, which was still being taught. The "small logicals" is the *Parva logicalia* of 1277, which was based on the *Summulae logicales*, a logic treatise by Peter of Spain, who became Pope John XXI (d. 1277). The "second intentions" mentioned in the next sentence also comes from Scholastic logic. Our "first intention" is our first perception of an entity, such as a man, whom we see as a particular human being; our "second intention" is our perception of that entity as the representation of a class or species—in this case, humanity. Hythloday (that is, More) is being ironic here with regard to the supposedly superior wisdom exemplified by Scholastic logic.

14. (p. 92) *pleasure, wherein they determine either all or the chiefest part of man's felicity to rest:* This philosophical tendency among the Utopians allied them to ancient Epicureanism, which saw happiness as the ultimate goal of human existence.

15. (p. 93) *our nature is allured and drawn even of virtue, whereto only they that be of the contrary opinion do attribute felicity:* Hythloday is referring to the Stoics, for whom living a life according to nature was identified as virtue and was thus the key to happiness.

16. (p. 95) *of so small help and furtherance to felicity that they count them a great let and hindrance:* Hythloday here claims that human beings have a natural desire for pleasures that are good, thus effectively undermining the notion that we are all corrupted because of original sin.

17. (p. 104) *Theophrastus of plants, but in divers places (which I am sorry for) unperfect:* Theophrastus (d. 287 B.C.E.), a philosopher and a pupil of Aristotle, wrote numerous works, including two books on plants. Only these books and his *Characters* survive.

18. (p. 104) *they have only Lascaris, for Theodorus I carried not with me, nor never a dictionary but Hesichius, and Dioscorides:* Constantine Lascaris (d. 1493 or 1500), a Byzantine Greek who fled to Italy at the fall of Constantinople to the Turks in 1453, wrote a four-book grammar that was published in 1476. Theodorus of Gaza (c.1400–1475), also a Byzantine exile, likewise wrote a grammar that was published in 1495. Hesychius of Alexandria (fifth century C.E.) compiled a dictionary that was published in Venice in 1514. Pedanius Dioscorides, who lived in Rome in the first century

C.E., wrote an account of plants and pharmacology, not a dictionary; it was published in Venice in 1499.

19. (p. 104) *They set great store by Plutarch's books, and they be delighted with Lucian's merry conceits and jests:* Plutarch (c.50–120 C.E.), now known primarily as the author of *Parallel Lives*, accounts of famous men from the ancient world, also produced the *Moralia*, an eclectic collection of works concerned not just with ethics, but with many other subjects. Lucian of Samosata (c.120–180) was a satirist; More and Erasmus had translated some of his dialogues from Greek into Latin around 1504. Most of the poets and historians mentioned in the next sentences are well known. The exception is the historian Herodian of Syria (c.175–250), who wrote a history of the Roman emperors who ruled between 180 and 238. "Aldus" refers to the great Venetian scholar and printer Aldus Manutius (1449–1515), whose press produced most of the first printed editions of Greek and Latin classics. His edition of Aristophanes appeared in 1498, his Sophocles in 1502, and his Homer and his Euripides in 1504.

20. (pp. 104–105) *my companion Tricius Apinatus carried with him physic books, certain small works of Hippocrates and Galen's* Microtechne: "Tricius Apinatus" is a name borrowed from Martial's *Epigrams* (14.1.7) that is based on the names of two Italian towns, Apina and Trica, which were synonymous with triviality. Hippocrates of Cos (fifth century B.C.E.) and Galen of Pergamum (second century C.E.) were the best-known writers on medicine ("physic") in the ancient world and remained authorities into the Renaissance. Galen's *Microtechne* was also known as *Ars medica*.

21. (p. 108) *For a sad and honest matron . . . naked to the woman:* This practice parallels one in Plato's *Laws* (6.771e–772a).

22. (p. 112) *cap of maintenance:* The "cap of maintenance" was a cap borne before the English king and queen in procession that signified the dignity and authority of the offices they held.

23. (p. 112) *they utterly exclude and banish all attorneys, proctors, and sergeants-at-the-law:* "Attorneys" were those delegated to handle legal business for others in court. "Proctors" were lawyers who handled cases in civil or canon law; they corresponded to solicitors, who handled cases in courts of equity or common law. "Sergeants-at-the-law" were the highest order of barristers, from among whom common law judges were chosen.

24. (p. 114) *the head bishops:* More's Latin speaks of the "supreme pontiffs"— that is, the popes—whom Robinson, a Protestant, here avoids mentioning. This passage is, of course, highly ironic.

25. (p. 117) *For if they find the cause probable . . . do sustain an unjust accusation under the color of justice:* The sense of Robinson's sentence is: the
Utopians wage war on behalf of their friends not only when enemy in-
vaders have taken away booty from their friends' lands, but also—and
more vigorously—when merchants from that land have been unjustly
oppressed.

26. (p. 120) *Therefore, they hire soldiers out of all countries and send them to battle, but chiefly of the Zapoletes:* "Zapoletes" means the "Hard Sellers"—that
is, mercenaries. More is thinking of the Swiss, who were renowned as ruth-
less mercenaries in the period. In the 1516 edition of the work, Erasmus
and Giles identified them as such in a marginal note to this passage.

27. (p. 126) *Such revenues they have now in many countries . . . above seven hundred thousand ducats by the year:* The ducat was a gold coin of the Holy
Roman Empire worth about a quarter of a pound sterling. Seven hundred
thousand ducats per year would have been a sum that exceeded the annual
income of the king of England.

28. (p. 127) *whom they all commonly in their country language call Mythra:*
Mythra, or Mithras, was the ancient Persian god of light initially worshiped by the Zoroastrians. By the first century c.e., he was worshiped
throughout the Roman Empire in a cult that shared certain features with
early Christianity, including baptism and a sacred meal. Note that the
Utopian language is said to resemble Persian.

29. (p. 128) *which here none but priests do minister:* In Catholicism, infants can
be baptized by a lay person in extreme circumstances, but all the rest of the
sacraments (communion, penance, extreme unction, confirmation, ordi-
nation, and marriage) require a priest.

30. (p. 129) *no man shall be blamed for reasoning in the maintenance of his own
religion:* Many have noted that the Utopian tolerance of religious difference is at odds with More's strenuous persecution of heretical views in his
governmental career.

31. (p. 131) *nothing to be compared with ours in dignity, neither ordained nor
predestinate to like felicity:* Some ancient followers of Pythagoras and of
Plato believed that animals had souls.

32. (p. 134) *forasmuch as they say they be led to it by religion, they honor and
worship them:* The sense of the last parts of this sentence is that the Utopians would mock this sect if its members based their preference for an ab-
stemious life on reason, but since they base it on religion, the Utopians
honor them for it.

33. (p. 137) *The first days they call . . . first feast and last feast: Cynemernes* derives from Greek and means something like "dog day"; *Trapemernes* means "turning day"—that is, the day when the month or year turns. Robinson's "primifest" and "finifest" are taken directly from More's Latin.

34. (p. 142) *the remembrance of their poor, indigent, and beggarly old age killeth them up:* That is, the thought of their unfortunate old age destroys them.

Letter of Peter Giles to Buslyde

1. (p. 147) *Hieronymus Buslyde:* Hieronymus Buslyde, or, more accurately, Jerome Busleyden (1470–1519), was the provost of Saint Peter's Church in Aire (Airenn) in Artois and a counselor of Charles V, the Holy Roman Emperor, who inherited the throne of Aragon from his grandfather Ferdinand along with the title "the Catholic." Busleyden was a patron of humanist learning and was responsible for founding the Trilingual College in Louvain, where they taught Hebrew as well as Latin and Greek. This letter was written by Giles to give a certain verisimilitude to More's work.

2. (p. 149) *four verses written in the Utopian tongue . . . the alphabet of the same nation:* The four lines in "Utopian" that follow this letter are most likely of Giles's invention. The marginal notes that appeared in the second edition of Robinson's translation were probably composed by the publisher Abraham Vele. They were intended to take the place of the marginal notes composed by Giles and Erasmus that appeared in the original Latin edition of More's work. See also page xlvii of the Introduction.

Poems on Utopia

1. (p. 151) *A meter of four verses . . . of the same commonwealth:* In the original Latin edition of this work, this poem and the ones following appeared, along with other material written by various humanists, before More's letter to Peter Giles that prefaces *Utopia*. The original printer provided an alphabet as well as the original spelling of this poem in "Utopian," which mixes Greek and Latin forms and endings. The printer of Robinson's translation says, after these poems, that he was unable to do so.

2. (p. 151) *Utopus by name:* Here, as in the text of *Utopia*, Robinson makes Utopus a king. In the Latin original of this passage, he is merely a *dux* ("leader").

3. (p. 151) *Written by Anemolius:* It is uncertain who Anemolius is. More himself may have supplied these verses for the original edition. The name means "windbag."

4. (p. 152) *a place of felicity:* "Eutopie" means "beautiful place" or "good place." "Anemolius" makes the pun in the name of the island explicit here.

5. (p. 152) *"Gerard Noviomage: Of Utopia":* Noviomage was Gerhard Gelden-hauer (1482–1542), called "Noviomagus" (after his birthplace Nijmegen). A monk who taught philosophy at Louvain, he was chaplain to the Holy Roman Emperor Charles V and secretary to Bishop Philip of Utrecht. A friend of Erasmus, he became a Protestant and was made professor of theology at Marburg. He assisted Dirk Martens, a Louvain printer, in seeing the first edition of *Utopia* through the press.

6. (p. 152) *Cornelius Graphey: To the Reader:* Cornelius Grapheus, or Cornelis de Schrijver (1482–1558), was a Latin poet who was a secretary to the city of Antwerp. He was arrested and put in prison as a Protestant in 1521 but was released the following year when he recanted. He was a friend of Giles and Erasmus.

Appendix: Dedicatory Epistle by the Translator of the Utopia

1. (p. 155) *Master William Cecil, Esquire:* William Cecil (1520–1598), baron Burghley, was born into a gentry family in Northamptonshire, studied at Saint John's College, Cambridge, and briefly at Grey's Inn in London. He was a member of Parliament in 1543, and became a member of the Privy Council during the reign of Edward VI. He discontinued his political activities after being interrogated by Mary's royal counselors in 1555 but returned to governmental service when Elizabeth came to the throne in 1558, soon becoming her most trusted counselor. He was made a baron in 1571 and appointed lord treasurer in 1572, a position he held until his death.

2. (p. 156) *Upon a time, when tidings came . . . when so many be working:* For this story about Diogenes, the Cynic philosopher, see Lucian, "How to Write History," 3.

3. (p. 158) *George Tadlowe:* Tadlowe was a member of the Company of Haberdashers in London, where he was fairly prominent, serving on the city council in the 1550s. He supported humanism and was most likely a moderate Protestant in his religion.

4. (p. 158) *being then schoolfellows together:* Robinson attended grammar schools in Stamford and Grantham with Cecil. The two men then matriculated at different universities, Robinson at Oxford and Cecil at Cambridge.

The Life of Sir Thomas More

1. (p. 163) *as witnesseth Erasmus:* In the prefatory letter to *The Praise of Folly*, Erasmus praises More for his learning and wit.

2. (p. 163) *I, William Roper, though most unworthy, his son-in-law by marriage of his eldest daughter:* Roper married Margaret, More's eldest and favorite daughter, on July 2, 1521.

3. (p. 163) *Saint Anthony's:* A free school in London associated with the Hospital of Saint Anthony, it was considered one of the best in the city.

4. (p. 163) *Cardinal Morton:* John Morton (1420?–1500), who supported the Lancastrians and the Tudors during the War of the Roses, became archbishop in 1486 and lord chancellor in 1487, just after Henry VII began his reign, and was made cardinal at Henry's request in 1493. More entered his household in 1490 and spent several years in service there.

5. (p. 164) *for the study of the law . . . continuing there his study until he was made and accounted a worthy utter barrister:* Legal training in England was not given at the universities, but at the so-called Inns of Court in London, which included Lincoln's Inn, Gray's Inn, the Inner Temple, and the Middle Temple. The Inns of Chancery, such as New Inn, provided a more rudimentary legal training that was concerned with the framing of legal documents. By More's time, the Inns of Chancery were all controlled by the Inns of Court. More began his legal training at New Inn in 1494 and was then admitted to Lincoln's Inn in February 1496. He became an "utter barrister"—that is, a full member of the profession—in 1502. Furnival's Inn, mentioned below, was one of the Inns of Chancery.

6. (p. 164) *he read . . . a public lecture of Saint Augustine* De Civitate Dei: More's giving a "public lecture" on Augustine's book, some time in 1501, involved his reading and commenting on the text. William Grocyn (1446?–1519), the vicar of Saint Lawrence from 1496 to 1517, was one of the first men to bring the New Learning (the study of classical Latin and Greek) to England after having studied with prominent Italian Humanists such as Angelo Poliziano in the late 1480s and early 1490s.

7. (p. 164) *he gave himself to devotion and prayer in the Charterhouse of London:* More was a lay brother in the Charterhouse (that is, Carthusian monastery) for about four years, probably between 1500 and 1504, participating, as much as his work and studies permitted, in the religious life of its members, but he never took holy orders himself (he was "without vow"). It was here that he acquired the austere habits of rising early, fasting, and

wearing a hair shirt in order to mortify the flesh. Roper has More becoming a barrister, then lecturing on Augustine, and then entering the monastery. The correct sequence would be that he was, most likely, in the monastery by 1500, lectured on Augustine in 1501, and became a barrister in 1502.

8. (p. 164) *soon after married her:* More married Jane Colt in 1505. When she died in 1511, he married Alice Middleton soon thereafter; she is referred to as Dame Alice in the biography. Jane bore More four children, whereas Alice bore him none, although her daughter Alice, by a former husband, became part of the family.

9. (p. 165) *there were by the king demanded . . . about three-fifteenths for the marriage of his eldest daughter:* When Henry VII wished to marry his daughter Margaret to James IV of Scotland in 1503, he asked the Parliament to levy a tax on three-fifteenths of the value of individuals' personal property.

10. (p. 165) *Master Whitford, his familiar friend, then chaplain to the bishop and later a Father of Sion:* Whiteford was a member of the Bridgettine monastery of Sion on the Thames near Isleworth between Kew and Richmond in Middlesex.

11. (p. 166) *had not the king soon after died:* Henry VII died in April 1509.

12. (p. 166) *he [More] was made one of the Under Sherriffs of London:* Serving under the high sheriff, under-sheriffs supervised prisoners, served writs, and executed death sentences.

13. (p. 166) *there was at that time in none of the prince's courts . . . any matter of importance . . . wherein he was not with the one party of counsel:* Roper is saying that More was always engaged in important cases as counsel for one side or the other.

14. (p. 166) *the merchants of the Steelyard:* These merchants were the "Merchant Adventurers," a company founded in the early fifteenth century that was a member of the Hanseatic League, a German trading association that had colonies located in cities throughout northern Europe in the fifteenth and sixteenth centuries. The Steelyard was a wharf on the Thames. In 1515 More went to Flanders on behalf of the Merchant Adventurers, visiting Brussels, Bruges, and Antwerp, and meeting Peter Giles, who appears in *Utopia*, in this last city, where the conversations of More's book take place.

15. (p. 166) *he, loath to change his estate, made such means to the king . . . that His Grace for that time was well satisfied:* Roper is saying that the Cardinal expressed satisfactorily to the King More's reluctance to enter royal service at that time.

16. (p. 166) *his that then was pope:* The pope at that time was Leo X (Giovanni de' Medici, 1475–1521; pope from 1513). His ambassador was probably Lorenzo Cardinal Campeggio (1474–1539).

17. (p. 167) *the Star Chamber:* So called because its ceiling was decorated with gilded stars, the Star Chamber was a room in Westminster Palace in which a court, consisting of the King's Council, tried primarily civil and criminal cases. It eventually became synonymous with tyranny and was abolished in 1641.

18. (p. 167) *he made him Master of the Requests . . . one of his Privy Council:* In 1517 More was appointed as a judge of the Court of Requests, which heard the complaints of the poor. He became a member of the Privy Council a little later that same year.

19. (p. 168) *whose office after his death the king . . . freely gave unto Sir Thomas More:* Roper is mistaken: More was made Under-Treasurer, and his predecessor was Sir John Cutte.

20. (p. 168) *was there a Parliament holden:* The Parliament began meeting in April 1523.

21. (p. 172) *Whitehall in Westminster:* Whitehall was the royal palace located outside of London in the suburb of Westminster. Of it only the Banqueting House, built by Inigo Jones for James I, still remains. Hampton Court, mentioned later, was also a royal palace and has survived, much of it still in the form it had in the sixteenth century.

22. (p. 173) *Sir Richard Wingfield, who had the office before:* Wingfield was sent in More's place as ambassador to Spain but died there in July 1525, after which More was given the chancellorship of the Duchy of Lancaster.

23. (p. 173) *"if my head could win him a castle in France . . . it should not fail to go":* Henry, allied with the emperor Charles V, had declared war against France in 1522.

24. (p. 174) *was made ambassador twice:* Roper gets the chronology slightly confused here. More went with Wolsey to arrange an alliance between Henry and Charles V in the summer and autumn of 1521, was made the chancellor of the Duchy of Lancaster in 1525, and went with Wolsey to France to negotiate a treaty with Francis I in July and August 1527.

25. (p. 174) *Water Bailiff of London:* The water bailiff of London was an important official charged with enforcing shipping regulations, collecting customs duties, etc.; he was one of four attendants on the lord mayor. At this time he was Sebastian Hillary. It is not known if he was ever a servant in More's household, although Hillary's wife, Margaret, certainly had been.

26. (p. 175) *along the Thames-side at Chelsea:* Chelsea, then a separate town some 10 miles upriver from London, was the site of More's estate, which he and others regarded as an ideal, bucolic retreat from the court and the city.

27. (p. 175) *the seven psalms, litany, and suffrages following:* The *seven psalms,* also called the penitential psalms, was the name given to the biblical Psalms 6, 32, 38, 51, 102, 130, and 143, which give special expression to the feeling of penitence. The *litany* was a more general prayer, whereas the *suffrages* were more specific, intercessory prayers.

28. (p. 177) *the sweating sickness:* The sweating sickness was a largely fatal febrile disease that was epidemic in England in the fifteenth and sixteenth centuries.

29. (p. 178) *the Emperor Charles so highly commending one Cardinal Adrian:* Charles V (1500–1558) was the Holy Roman Emperor from 1519 to 1556. Adrian Boeyens (1459–1523) was a Dutchman who tutored Charles. He became a cardinal in 1517 and was elected pope (as Adrian VI) on January 9, 1522; he died the following year.

30. (p. 178) *Queen Catherine, aunt to the emperor:* Catherine (1485–1536) was the youngest daughter of Ferdinand II of Aragon and Isabella I of Castile. Charles was the son of their third daughter, Juana, who inherited the throne from them in 1504, and of her husband, Philip of Habsburg, the son of the Holy Roman Emperor, Maximilian I of Habsburg.

31. (p. 178) *This cardinal . . . to one of the French king's sisters:* Roper is saying that Wolsey knew the King was ready at any moment to drop Catherine for someone greatly inferior to her, so that Wolsey attempted to achieve his "ungodly intent" (of separating the King and the Queen) by using Henry's "light disposition" to attract him to the sister of the French king; however, at that very time Henry had already taken a fancy to Anne Boleyn.

32. (p. 179) *Longland, Bishop of Lincoln and ghostly father to the king:* John Longland (1473–1547), Wolsey's friend and ally, was bishop of Lincoln from 1521 to 1547, and served as the King's confessor ("ghostly father").

33. (p. 179) *Tunstall and Clerk:* Cuthbert Tunstall (1474–1559) was bishop of London from 1522 to 1530, and was appointed bishop of Durham from 1530 to 1552 and between 1553 and 1559. John Clerk (d. 1541) was bishop of Bath from 1523 to 1541.

34. (p. 180) *Cardinal Campeggio . . . sat at the Blackfriars in London:* Lorenzo Cardinal Campeggio (1474–1539) arrived in London on October 9, 1528, as the representative of Pope Clement VII, who had succeeded Adrian VI in 1523. Blackfriars was a Dominican monastery located on the riverside

southwest of St. Paul's Cathedral. Founded in 1221, it was taken over by Henry after his break with Rome when he dissolved all the monasteries and nunneries in 1538. It was later the location of a theater that Shakespeare's company purchased in 1608.

35. (p. 180) *And so should judgment have been given by the pope. . . . the cardinal upon that matter sat no longer:* Roper's argument here is that Henry would have received a favorable decision from the pope if he had waited and not appealed the matter to Parliament (the "general council" referred to). In actuality, however, Campeggio adjourned the meeting of the Commission, and the case was recalled to Rome, where Henry and Catherine were expected to appear.

36. (p. 181) *the king . . . assigned the Bishop of Durham and Sir Thomas More . . . to treat a peace between the French king, the emperor, and him:* More and Tunstall (then bishop of London, not Durham) were sent to Cambrai in June 1529, where they were parties to the peace treaty signed on August 3 between the Emperor Charles V and the French King Francis I in which the latter confirmed Spanish hegemony in Italy. England gained thirteen years of peace with the other European powers as a result. At that time Cambrai was part of Flanders; it is now in northern France.

37. (p. 182) *some good hope to compass it:* That is, to secure More's agreement to the divorce.

38. (p. 182) *Doctor Stokesley:* John Stokesley (1475?–1539) was made bishop of London in 1530, at which time Tunstall was appointed bishop of Durham.

39. (p. 183) *Whom His Highness . . . the same in his stead committed:* More was made lord chancellor on October 26, 1529.

40. (p. 183) *one of his sons-in-law:* Roper refers to William Daunce, who married More's daughter Elizabeth in 1525.

41. (p. 184) *yet to him, said he, being his son, he found it nothing profitable:* Daunce seems to be complaining that More should reward him financially, since he has not accepted gifts from the people he put in contact with More, and since Daunce really could not do anything on their behalf because of More's commendable impartiality.

42. (p. 184) *another of his sons-in-law called Master Heron:* Giles Heron, son of Sir John Heron, Henry VIII's treasurer of the chamber, married More's youngest daughter, Cecily, in 1525. He was executed for treason in 1540 on dubious charges.

43. (p. 185) *And for the better declaration of his natural affection towards his father . . . departed from him:* More's father, John, died in the winter of 1530.

44. (p. 185) *injunctions:* The Court of Chancery could issue injunctions to stop proceedings in other courts if equity seemed to be violated.

45. (p. 186) *Vaysey, Bishop of Exeter:* John Vaysey, or Veysey (1465?–1554), was bishop of Exeter from 1519 to 1551 and in 1553 and 1554.

46. (p. 187) *my sister More:* Roper refers to his sister-in-law Anne Cresacre, the wife of More's son, John.

47. (p. 189) *the Great Seal:* The Great Seal was the emblem of the lord chancellor's office.

48. (p. 189) *After he had thus given over his chancellorship:* More resigned the chancellorship on May 16, 1532. Sir Thomas Audeley (1488–1544) succeeded him.

49. (p. 190) Salve Regina: The title of this popular medieval hymn to the Virgin translates as "Hail Queen."

50. (p. 191) *his chain:* More's gold chain was the symbol of his (former) high office.

51. (p. 191) quia specula previsa minus laedunt: The Latin translates as "because anticipated spears wound less."

52. (p. 191) *Thomas Cromwell:* Cromwell (1485?–1540), the son of a brewer and tavern owner, was ruthlessly ambitious. He rose through the ranks thanks to the falls of Wolsey and More, eventually becoming Henry's secretary and assisting him in the persecution of resistant Catholics and in the dissolving of the monasteries. He himself fell from favor and was executed in 1540.

53. (p. 192) *Cranmer:* Thomas Cranmer (1489–1556) was archbishop of Canterbury from 1533 to 1556. One of the architects of the English Reformation, he was burned at the stake after Mary's accession to the throne. The commission met at Dunstable, not Saint Albans.

54. (p. 192) *and so married the Lady Anne Boleyn:* Henry married Anne on January 25, 1533, and had her crowned queen on June 1.

55. (p. 192) *an emperor that had ordained a law that whosoever committed a certain offense, . . . except it were a virgin, should suffer the pains of death:* The emperor in question here is Tiberius Caesar, and the story concerns the daughter of his ambitious underling Sejanus. More derives it freely from Tacitus (*Annals,* 6).

56. (p. 193) *a certain nun dwelling in Canterbury . . . not a little esteemed:* Elizabeth Barton (1506?–1534), known as the "Holy Maid of Kent," was alleged to have the gift of prophecy, denounced the coming of Protestantism, and predicted that Henry would die a miserable death within a month after marrying Anne. Arrested and tortured, she confessed she was an imposter and was executed, together with a number of her adherents, at Tyburn on April 21, 1534.

57. (p. 193) *my Lord of Rochester, Bishop Fisher:* John Fisher (1469–1535) was bishop of Rochester from 1504 to his death. He refused to subscribe to Henry's oath of supremacy and was beheaded just two weeks before More.

58. (p. 193) *And in short space after . . . to enter into talk with Sir Thomas More:* Roper is saying that while Barton was at Sion House, where she went thanks to Master Reynolds, she talked with More about the King's supremacy and his marriage. Reynolds is Richard Reynolds, the spiritual father of Sion House, who also denied the supremacy and was executed on May 4, 1535.

59. (p. 194) *as in the case of one Parnell . . . the suit of one Vaughan, his adversary, had made a decree:* The case of Richard and Geoffrey Vaughan versus John Parnell was heard on January 20, 1531.

60. (p. 194) *the Lord of Wiltshire:* This was Sir Thomas Boleyn, Anne's father.

61. (p. 197) *to set forth a book of* The Assertion of Seven Sacraments . . . *to put a sword in the pope's hand to fight against himself:* In 1521 Henry published his *Assertion*, which he had written explicitly against what he regarded as Martin Luther's heresies and in defense of the papacy. For writing it he was named Defender of the Faith by the pope. More did not instigate Henry's writing of the book but did help polish it at the end.

62. (p. 197) *The Statute of Praemunire:* This law made it treason to prosecute suits in foreign courts, such as that of the Vatican, or to accept the edicts of those courts.

63. (p. 199) "quod defertur non aufertur": The Latin translates as "what is deferred is not avoided."

64. (p. 199) "indignatio principis mors est": The Latin translates as "the anger of the prince is death."

65. (p. 200) *in a great book of his works:* More's *English Works* were printed only in 1557, so Roper may be referring to an advance copy he had seen or to a manuscript version of them.

66. (p. 200) *And albeit in the beginning . . . he caused the said Oath of Supremacy to be ministered unto him:* Roper is saying that although the king and the Privy Council initially wanted to have More released if he swore an oath not to reveal to others ("not to be acknown") whether he had taken the Oath of Supremacy and what his thoughts about it might be, the Queen got the King to insist that the Oath be administered to More.

67. (p. 200) *Sir Richard Cromwell:* The son of Thomas Cromwell's sister, he assumed the surname of Cromwell when he began serving his uncle.

68. (p. 201) *"It pitieth me to remember into what misery, poor soul, she shall shortly come":* Anne Boleyn married Henry in 1533, but in 1536, the year after More's execution, she was accused of adultery, tried, and beheaded.

69. (p. 202) *But at length the Lord Chancellor and Master Secretary . . . for the confirmation of the oath so amplified with their additions:* Initially the Act of Succession, passed in March 1534, declared Henry's marriage to Catherine null and void and that with Anne to be lawful. The oath of loyalty demanded obedience to the Act and rejection of allegiance to all foreign authorities. In November the Act of Supremacy was added, reinforcing the preceding act and declaring the sovereign to be the only head of the English Church. Another act made it treason to deny this supremacy.

70. (p. 203) *And so because the statute had undone only the first conveyance . . . so was our portion to us by that means clearly reserved:* The King seized the lands that More's conveyance willed to his heirs after his death. However, since by this second conveyance he gave Roper and his wife their inheritance right away, it was not confiscated.

71. (p. 206) *When Sir Thomas More was brought from the Tower . . . he saw therein nothing justly to charge him:* More was avoiding making any pronouncement about the "body of the matter"—namely, whether the King was the head of the Church. Engaging in a legal quibble of sorts, he was pleading not guilty on the grounds that although he had refused to take the oath, technically speaking he had never denied that the King was the head of the Church.

72. (p. 208) Quia si dixerimus quod peccatum non habemus, nosmet ipsos seducimus, et veritas in nobis non est: The Latin, from the Bible (1 John 1:8), translates as "If we say that we have no sin, we deceive ourselves, and the truth is not in us." More's distinction between *malitia* and *malevolentia* here centers on the will; it is the difference between doing something with ill will or hatred and being willing to do such a thing—that is, doing it maliciously. More is insisting that if he had denied the King's supremacy, as Rich claimed, then his doing so was not malicious since he was only dealing with a hypothetical and did not have a clear intention to deny the supremacy. Thus he should not be punished by a statute that said the denial had to be spoken "maliciously."

73. (p. 208) *"His Grace's high chancellorship (the like whereof he never did to temporal man before)":* More's predecessor and successor in the office were

both churchmen. Indeed, he was the first layman appointed to that office in a hundred years.

74. (p. 210) Quod ecclesia anglicana libera sit, et habeat omnia jura sua integra, et libertates suas illaesas: The Latin translates as "That the English Church may be free and have all of its laws uncorrupted and its liberties inviolate." The Magna Carta was a charter of liberties granted initially by King John to the English people in 1215; it has served over the years as a battle cry against royal oppression and subsequently influenced the formation of English and American civil law.

75. (p. 210) "*I have regenerated you my children in Christ*": The text is from the Bible, 1 Corinthians 3:1. Roper does not cite the verse accurately. In the English Standard version it is translated: "But I, brothers, could not address you as spiritual people, but as people of the flesh, as infants in Christ."

76. (p. 211) *the Lord Fitz-James:* Sir John Fitz-James (1470?–1542?) became lord chief justice in 1526.

77. (p. 211) *Sir Anthony Saint Leger, Knight:* Saint Leger (1496?–1559) supported the supremacy and carried out Henry's policies in Ireland after being appointed lord deputy there in 1540. He continued to serve Edward VI and even became a member of the Privy Council under Mary.

78. (p. 211) *Sir William Kingston . . . his very dear friend:* Kingston (d. 1540), a distinguished soldier, was made constable of the Tower in 1524.

79. (p. 212) *suffered:* Roper's verb here implies martyrdom.

80. (p. 213) *Saint Thomas's Even and the Utas of Saint Peter:* Saint Thomas's Even and the Utas (the "octave," or eighth day after the festival) of Saint Peter is July 6. Since More was sentenced on July 1, Roper is thus wrong that More spent "more than a seven-night" in prison before his execution.

81. (p. 214) *as Saint Cyprian did, who gave his executioner thirty pieces of gold:* Saint Cyprian (200–258) was a theologian and the bishop of Carthage who led Christians in North Africa during a period of persecution by the Romans and who was executed by them on September 14, 258.

82. (p. 215) *Sir Thomas Elyot:* Elyot (c.1490–1546), an English humanist, author, administrator, and a member of the circle around Sir Thomas More, authored *The Book Named the Governour* (1531), a popular work on the education of the gentleman.

Inspired by Sir Thomas More and Utopia

Plato was the first to write about an ideal society, and Thomas More took the *Republic* (c.370s B.C.E.) as a model for his *Utopia*. More's coinage—from the Greek words *ou* ("not") and *topos* ("place"), so literally "nowhere"—has entered the English language to connote the perfect society. Some utopian works, including More's and Plato's, give an account of idealized realms; others (labeled "dystopian," in a takeoff on "utopia" that changes the first syllable to one that means "bad," "faulty," or "disordered") satirize society or warn of impending dangers. In the best utopian and dystopian writings, the descriptions of the imagined world shed new light on real-life society.

Utopian and Dystopian Writings

In the five-book series *Gargantua et Pantagruel* (*Gargantua and Pantagruel*; 1532–1564), begun not long after the publication in 1516 of *Utopia*, François Rabelais used bawdy humor, a farcical atmosphere, and outrageous anecdotes to tell the story of two giants, father and son, and along the way he commented on the political issues of his day. The kingdom ruled over by Gargantua and his son is called "Utopie" in French ("Utopia" in translation), and the people are called "Amaurots." Rabelais also describes the Abbeye of Thélème, where men and women who live together in freedom realize the full potential of their inherently good natures. In the essay "On Cannibals" (1580), Michel de Montaigne compares the social organization of a primitive South American tribe to the civilized life of Europeans; repeatedly, the latter group proves to be the more brutal. Of seventeenth-century utopian texts, the most important are Tommaso Campanella's *Civitas Solis* (*The City of the Sun*; 1623) and Francis Bacon's *New Atlantis* (1627), both influenced by More and Plato, though these two works make science (the investigation and harnessing of nature) a more important ingredient in the advancement of human society than did More. Utopian novels written in response to seventeenth-century politics include James Harrington's *The*

Commonwealth of Oceana (1656) and Henry Neville's *The Isle of Pines* (1668).

In Jonathan Swift's satire *Gulliver's Travels* (1726), sensible English surgeon Lemuel Gulliver embarks on an ocean voyage. Each of the imaginary nations he visits—including Lilliput (where the people are six inches tall), Brobdingnag (a land of giants), Laputa (a floating island that oppresses the land that lies below), and Houyhnhnmland (ruled by horses)—possesses a distinct set of quirks and presents a different set of problems. All are dystopias that allow Swift to hold up to ridicule particular ridiculous aspects of English society and human nature. Even Gulliver's favorite among the four, the nation ruled by the reasonable equine Houyhnhnms, imposes conformity upon its residents. In his philosophical works, French writer Jean-Jacques Rousseau (1712–1778) favored a return to nature and described the "noble savage."

Many of More's ideals are reflected in the eminently practical framework of Karl Marx and Friedrich Engels's *Manifest Der Kommunistischen Partei* (1848; *Manifesto of the Communist Party*, better known as *The Communist Manifesto*). (*Utopia* forwards communist and socialist ideals, but because More tackles his subject so playfully, it would be stretching a point to link his ideas to those of any modern political party.) The philosophical system in *The Communist Manifesto* is referred to as Marxism, and the party that attempted to bring it into actuality was socialism; eventually, many of Marx's ideas were incorporated into the communism that defined the Soviet Union and its satellite nations. But that form of communism gave rise to a decidedly less than ideal situation for the governments and people of the Soviet bloc. Beginning in 1989, the Cold War (the battle between capitalism and communism for world dominance) ended because of the crushing failure of communism in its practical application.

Moby-Dick author Herman Melville responded directly to More in an unpublished poem written in the 1850s. *The Melville Log: A Documentary Life of Herman Melville, 1819–1891* (1951), by Jay Leyda, reports on a discarded manuscript page that includes this statement: "Observable in Sir Thomas More's 'Utopia' are first its almost entire reasonableness. Second its almost entire impracticability. The remark applies more or less to the Utopia's prototype 'Plato's Republic.' " The page also includes the four-line poem "A Reasonable Constitution":

What though Reason forged your scheme?
'Twas Reason dreamed the Utopia's dream:
'Tis dream to think that Reason can
Govern the reasoning creature, man.

A number of notable utopian and dystopian novels appeared in the late nineteenth and early twentieth centuries—a period characterized by alternating waves of optimism and fear in response to technological advances and the rise and fall of socialism. In Samuel Butler's influential *Erewhon* (1872; the name is an anagram for "nowhere"), the narrator comes upon the land of the title, which seems perfect in its contempt for money and machinery. First impressions give way, however, as the novel evolves into a clever satire of Victorian England that attacks, among other things, the nation's practices in religion and child-rearing, and its treatment of criminals.

Almost unrivaled among nineteenth-century novels in its public impact, Edward Bellamy's *Looking Backward: 2000–1887* (1888) tells of a young Bostonian who falls asleep in 1887 and wakes to a drastically changed society in the year 2000. This utopian romance describes a peacefully achieved new society whose socialist underpinnings and fair distribution of work and wealth eliminate all human ills. Immensely popular when first published, *Looking Backward* led to the formation of a Nationalist Party in support of Bellamy's views, which included the nationalization of public services.

British designer, craftsman, poet, and socialist William Morris's *News from Nowhere* (1890) describes an ideal rural society. Morris, who admired More, disagreed strongly with Bellamy's notion that a central bureaucracy was the ideal way to manage society. In Morris's novel, the Houses of Parliament are transformed into a "dung market" after a violent revolution overthrows the old ways. In the new society, natural brotherhood, respect for work, and love of art sustain humanity in the absence of laws and money. H. G. Wells, noted British author of science-fiction classics *The Time Machine* (1895) and *The War of the Worlds* (1898)—both satiric social commentaries in their own right—alludes to More's title in his *A Modern Utopia* (1905). A mix of, as Wells put it, "philosophical discussion on the one hand and imaginative narrative on the other," the work attempts to "clear up the muddle in my own mind about innumerable social and political questions, questions I could not keep out of my work." Wells presents an optimistic view of an ideal society in this surprisingly realistic book.

Russian author Yevgeny Zamyatin countered the socialist visions held by writers like Bellamy, Morris, and Wells. In the satiric *We* (1924), Zamyatin demonstrates how the socialist dream of equality for all men differs little from lifeless conformity. So powerful was the impact of his dystopian novel, which describes life under a strict totalitarian regime, that George Orwell credited it with inspiring *Nineteen Eighty-Four* (1949). (It is thought that *We* also influenced Aldous Huxley's *Brave New World* [1932], though Huxley denied it.) Together these three authors produced the strongest dystopian novels of the early twentieth century; each criticizes an excess of governmental control in the life of man. In *We*, the main character, D-503, enjoys material well-being but not freedom. His acceptance of consistency and sterility is so absolute that he even condemns ancient poets for being inspired by clouds, which mar the perfect uniformity of the sky. Residents of D-503's state live in glass houses in cities where all eating occurs on schedule and even sex is rationed— with pink coupons.

The futuristic society of *Brave New World*, which takes its name from a line in Shakespeare's *The Tempest* (act 5, scene 1: "O brave new world, / That has such people in't!") applies a rigid caste system to the residents of an imaginary island who are raised parentless in communal hatcheries and kept happy with psychotropics and sedatives. Discord erupts in Huxley's black comedy when an American Indian, unaccustomed to typical life in 632 A.F. (the abbreviation for After Ford—that is, Henry Ford, who devised the first system for mass production), clashes with World Controller Mustapha Mond over their differing views on freedom and passion. Huxley's *Island* (1962) was the author's earnest attempt to describe an ideal society.

A year after psychologist B. F. Skinner invoked Henry David Thoreau (see below) in the title of his utopian novel *Walden Two* (1948), an idyllic and scientific celebration of a fictional commune, George Orwell published *Nineteen Eighty-Four*—widely regarded as the most scathing and effective refutation of the utopian ideal. Following the success of Orwell's political satire *Animal Farm* (1945),

Nineteen Eighty-Four details a nightmarish society firmly ruled by Big Brother and the Party, who quash privacy, seek power for its own sake, and constantly rewrite the past to suit the present. Thought Police arrest dissenters, while the official language, Newspeak, diminishes the range of human thought. The slogans of the Party dominate the landscape: WAR IS PEACE, FREEDOM IS SLAVERY, IGNORANCE IS STRENGTH. The book's impact was so strong that its title and several of its catchphrases—including Big Brother and Newspeak—have become common parlance.

Notable dystopian writings of the second half of the twentieth century include William Golding's *Lord of the Flies* (1954), Anthony Burgess's *A Clockwork Orange* (1962), and Alvin Toffler's *Future Shock* (1970). In its depiction of the barbarity that erupts in a group of schoolboys trapped on a deserted island, *Lord of the Flies* viciously contradicts Rousseau's notion of the noble savage and Montaigne's ideal of the primitive state. In *A Clockwork Orange*, a critique of both excessive liberalism and unfettered police rule, a young hoodlum rapes and murders at will in a lawless futuristic city; when he is captured, his brainwashing is so inhumane that the police seem the greater criminals. Stanley Kubrick's 1971 film version of Burgess's novel attracted a large cult following. In the nonfiction *Future Shock*, an entertaining and prescient read, Toffler predicts the distressing effects of the rapid pace of technological innovation upon every aspect of human society.

Attempts at Utopian Living

Around the time of *The Communist Manifesto*, idealists in America were attempting real-life utopian living experiments. Nathaniel Hawthorne's pessimistic novel *The Blithedale Romance* (1852) was based on the author's involvement as an initial shareholder in the communal living experiment known as Brook Farm (short for the Brook Farm Institute of Agriculture and Education) in West Roxbury, Massachusetts, near Boston. A joint-stock, subsistence community that reserved time in each person's life for individual self-improvement, Brook Farm was designed as a retreat from increasingly complicated and commercial urban life. Frequent visitors to Brook Farm, which prospered from 1841 until 1847, included philosopher Ralph Waldo Emerson and woman of letters Margaret

Fuller, thought to be the model for Zenobia, the exotic, doomed feminist of *The Blithedale Romance.*

Brook Farm was founded on the ideas of transcendentalism, epitomized in the essays and poems of Emerson and the writings of Henry David Thoreau, who recorded his own idealized, if singular, living experiment in *Walden: or, Life in the Woods* (1854). That collection of essays records events in the two years during which the author retreated from city life to reside alone in a cabin he built on the shore of Walden Pond, outside Concord, Massachusetts. Thoreau promoted self-reliance, simplicity, and the idea that only in isolation will the individual fully develop.

In 1906 Upton Sinclair published the "muckraking" novel *The Jungle* and the same year formed a short-lived communal living experiment called Helicon Home Colony, in Englewood, New Jersey. Novelist Sinclair Lewis, who would win the Nobel Prize for Literature in 1930, was a member. Lewis's dystopian novel *It Can't Happen Here* (1935) lays out the author's vision of life in the United States were fascists to take over.

Popular Tributes to Sir Thomas More

The manuscript of the biographical play *Sir Thomas More*, written collaboratively by several authors in the 1590s, remains significant for containing, according to some scholars, the only extant handwriting of William Shakespeare. The world's greatest dramatist revised sixteen lines of the play. And although More never appears onstage in Shakespeare's *The Famous History of the Life of King Henry the Eighth*, the play contains a scene in which Thomas Cromwell informs Cardinal Wolsey that More will replace him as lord chancellor. Wolsey replies presciently: "That's somewhat sudden; / But he's a learned man. May he continue / Long in his highness's favour, and do justice / For truth's sake, and his conscience" (act 3, scene 2).

The life of a sixteenth-century Christian humanist and intellectual largely unknown to the American public may seem unlikely as popular entertainment. But Robert Bolt's play about More, *A Man for All Seasons*, after earning intense acclaim in London in 1960, was a smash hit on Broadway in 1961, winning five Tony Awards, including Best Play; it played to packed houses across the United States when it went on the road. The 1966 film version, directed by Fred Zinnemann with a screenplay by Bolt, won six Academy Awards, including Best Picture, and was a top box office grosser for several weeks. Paul Scofield portrayed More superbly in both the original play and the dialogue-driven, yet dynamic film. In the latter, Scofield's performance is restrained, wise, and good-humored. Orson Welles is featured as the malevolent Cardinal Wolsey; a diabolical Leo McKern is the King's cohort Thomas Cromwell, and Robert Shaw plays Henry VIII.

American poet Robert Lowell immortalized More and the well-known portrait of him (featured on the cover of this edition) by Hans Holbein the Younger in the poem "Sir Thomas More." Like More, Lowell was imprisoned for his beliefs; as a conscientious objector during World War II, he spent several months in jail. Versions of "Sir Thomas More" appear in two of Lowell's works, *Notebook 1967–68* (1969) and *History* (1973). The version in *History* opens with a description of the portrait: "the brow's damp feathertips of hair, / the good eyes' stern, facetious twinkle." The last lines paraphrase a passage from William Roper's *Life of Sir Thomas More* (page 161 of this edition):

> And you, "If it were a question of my head,
> Or losing his meanest village in France . . ."
> then by the scaffold and the headsman's axe—
> "Friend, give me your hand for the first step,
> as for coming down, I'll shift for myself."

Comments & Questions

In this section, we aim to provide the reader with an array of perspectives on the text, as well as questions that challenge those perspectives. The commentary has been culled from sources as diverse as reviews contemporaneous with the work, letters written by the author, literary criticism of later generations, and appreciations written throughout the work's history. Following the commentary, a series of questions seeks to filter Sir Thomas More's Utopia *through a variety of points of view and bring about a richer understanding of this enduring work.*

Comments

ERASMUS

[More] published his Utopia for the purpose of showing, what are the things that occasion mischief in commonwealths; having the English constitution especially in view, which he so thoroughly knows and understands. He had written the second book at his leisure, and afterwards, when he found it was required, added the first off-hand. Hence there is some inequality in style.

—from a letter to Ulrich von Hutten (1519)

EDWARD PHILLIPS

"Utopia," though not written in verse, yet in regard of the great fancy, and invention thereof, may well pass for a poem.

—from *Theatrum Poetarum Anglicanorum* (1675)

JOSEPH ADDISON

He maintained the same cheerfulness of heart upon the scaffold, which he used to show at his table; and, upon laying his head on the block, gave instances of that good humour with which he had always entertained his friends in the most ordinary occurrences. His death was of a piece with his life. There was nothing in it new, forced, or affected. He did not look upon the severing of his head from his body as a circumstance that ought to produce any change in the disposition of his mind; and as he died under a fixed and settled hope of immortality, he thought any unusual degree of sorrow and concern improper on such an occasion, as had nothing in it which could deject or terrify him.

—from *The Spectator* (April 10, 1712)

DAVID HUME

[Thomas More was] a man who, besides the ornaments of an elegant literature, possessed the highest virtue, integrity, and capacity.

—from *The History of England Under the House of Tudor* (1759)

JOHN ADAMS

Utopia, or the happy Republic, a Philosophical Romance, by Sir Thos. More . . . is very elegant and ingenious—the fruit of a benevolent and candid Heart, a learned and strong Mind. The good Humour, Hospitality, Humanity, and Wisdom of the Utopians, is charming—their Elegance, and Taste is engaging—their freedom from Avarice, and foppery, and Vanity is admirable.

—from his diary (November 10, 1771)

SHARON TURNER

More, who counteracted, if he did not curtail his own "Utopia," and whose other writings degrade him for their feebleness, their bigotry, their scurrility, and their persecuting tendency, below the educated men of his day, would have sunk into oblivion, except as a punster, as a worthy pattern of the domestic virtues, and as one who had been fond of literature, and had been famed for it, but who in its most important department, was also its unsparing persecutor; if the oppressive violence of his death had not imparted that sympathy and sanctity to his memory, which the human heart liberally bestows on the victims of power, who unite firmness of principle with moral rectitude and intellectual cultivation.

—from *The History of the Reign of Henry the Eighth* (1826)

LORD JOHN CAMPBELL

Since the time of Plato, there had been no composition given to the world which, for imagination, for philosophical discrimination, for a familiarity with the principles of government, for a knowledge of

the springs of human action, for a keen observation of men and manners, and for felicity of expression, could be compared to the "Utopia."
—from *Lives of the Lord Chancellors and Keepers of the Great Seal of England: From the Earliest Times till the Reign of King George IV* (1845–1869)

JAMES ANTHONY FROUDE

The philosopher of the "Utopia," the friend of Erasmus, whose life was of blameless beauty, whose genius was cultivated to the highest attainable perfection, was to prove to the world that the spirit of persecution is no peculiar attribute of the pedant, the bigot, or the fanatic, but may coexist with the fairest graces of the human character. The lives of remarkable men usually illustrate some emphatic truth. Sir Thomas More may be said to have lived to illustrate the necessary tendencies of Romanism, in an honest mind convinced of the truth; to show that the test of sincerity in a man who professes to regard orthodoxy as an essential of salvation is not the readiness to endure persecution, but the courage that will venture to inflict it.
—from *History of England from the Fall of Wolsey to the Death of Elizabeth* (1856–1870)

OSCAR WILDE

A map of the world that does not include Utopia is not worth glancing at for it leaves out the country at which Humanity is always landing. And when Humanity lands there, it looks out, and seeing a better country, sets sail. Progress is the realization of Utopias.
—from the *Fortnightly Review* (February 1, 1891)

H. G. WELLS

There are some writers who are chiefly interesting in themselves, and some whom chance and the agreement of men have picked out as symbols and convenient indications of some particular group or temperament of opinions. To the latter it is that Sir Thomas More belongs. An age and a type of mind have found in him and his Utopia a figurehead and a token; and pleasant and honourable as his personality and household present themselves to the modern reader, it is doubtful if they would by this time have retained any peculiar distinction among the many other contemporaries of whom we have chance glimpses in letters and suchlike documents, were it not that he happened to be the first man of affairs in England to imitate the *Republic* of Plato. By that chance it fell to him to give the world a noun and an adjective of abuse, "Utopian," and to record how under the stimulus of Plato's releasing influence the opening problems of our modern world presented themselves to the English mind of his time. For the most part the problems that exercised him are the problems that exercise us to-day; some of them, it may be, have grown up and intermarried, new ones have joined their company, but few, if any, have disappeared, and it is alike in his resemblances to and differences from the modern speculative mind that his essential interest lies. . . .

A good Catholic undoubtedly he was, and yet we find him capable of conceiving a non-Christian community excelling all Christendom in wisdom and virtue; in practice his sense of conformity and orthodoxy was manifest enough, but in his *Utopia* he ventures to contemplate, and that not merely wistfully, but with some confidence, the possibility of an absolute religious toleration.

The *Utopia* is none the less interesting because it is one of the most inconsistent of books. Never were the forms of Socialism and Communism animated by so entirely an Individualist soul. The hands are the hands of Plato, the wide-thinking Greek, but the voice is the voice of a humane, public-spirited, but limited and very practical English gentleman who takes the inferiority of his inferiors for granted, dislikes friars and tramps and loafers and all undisciplined and unproductive people, and is ruler in his own household. . . .

It is no paradox to say that *Utopia*, which has by a conspiracy of accidents become a proverb for undisciplined fancifulness in social and political matters, is in reality a very unimaginative work. In that, next to the accident of its priority, lies the secret of its continuing interest. In some respects it is like one of those precious and delightful scrapbooks people disinter in old country houses; its very poverty of synthetic power leaves its ingredients, the cuttings from and imitations of Plato, the recipe for the hatching of eggs, the stern resolutions against scoundrels and rough fellows all the sharper and brighter. There will always be found people to read in it, over and above the countless multitudes who will continue ignorantly to use its name for everything most alien to More's essential quality.

—from *Social Forces in England and America* (1914)

G. K. CHESTERTON

[More] was the founder of all the Utopias; but he used Utopia as what it really is, a playground. His Utopia was partly a joke; but since his time Utopians have seldom seen the joke.

—from *The Fame of Blessed Thomas More:*
Being Addresses Delivered in His Honour
in Chelsea, July 1929 (1929)

C. S. LEWIS

All seem to be agreed that [*Utopia*] is a great book, but hardly any two agree as to its real significance; we approach it through a cloud of contradictory eulogies.

—from *The Oxford History of English*
Literature, Volume 3 (1954)

SIR WINSTON CHURCHILL

More stood forth as the defender of all that was finest in the medieval outlook. He represents to history its universality, its belief in spiritual values, and its instinctive sense of other-worldliness. Henry VIII with cruel axe decapitated not only a wise and gifted counsellor, but a system which, though it had failed to live up to its ideals in practice, had for long furnished mankind with its brightest dreams.

—from *A History of the English-Speaking*
Peoples (1956–1958)

Questions

1. When Hythloday and the character "More" disagree, whom do you find more convincing?

2. If More's *Utopia* were to be established, would you want to live in it? Why or why not?

3. A "utopia" can be thought of as a standard or model against which we measure what is real, to determine its shortcomings. Measured against More's Utopia, what are the shortcomings of the typical Western state?

4. What do you think More would have replied to Thomas Jefferson's statement that there should be a wall of separation between church and state?

5. Do you see *Utopia* as essentially a historical curiosity? Or do you see it as a work that should be important to countries in turmoil looking for a sociopolitical model?

For Further Reading

Modern Biographies of More

Ackroyd, Peter. *The Life of Thomas More.* London: Chatto and Windus, 1998. The most thorough and dependable modern biography.

Ames, Russell. *Citizen Thomas More and His Utopia.* Princeton, NJ: Princeton University Press, 1949. A good but somewhat dated study.

Chambers, R. W. *Thomas More.* 1935. Ann Arbor: University of Michigan Press, 1958. The classic biography, still valuable.

Marius, Richard. *Thomas More: A Biography.* New York: Alfred A. Knopf, 1984. A readable, popular biography.

Modern Editions and Translations of Utopia

Utopia. Edited by Edward Surtz and J. H. Hexter. Vol. 4 of the Yale edition of *The Complete Works of St. Thomas More.* New Haven, CT: Yale University Press, 1965. This definitive volume contains More's Latin text, a facing translation, a long introduction, and an extensive commentary.

Utopia. Translated and with an introduction by Clarence Miller. New Haven, CT: Yale University Press, 2001. Although a bit less formal than the original, a fluent translation that makes More's work accessible.

Utopia. Translated by Edward Surtz. New Haven, CT: Yale University Press, 1964. A very readable translation of the work.

Modern Studies of Utopia

Baker-Smith, Dominic. *More's Utopia.* London: HarperCollins, 1991. A generally useful commentary.

Essential Articles for the Study of Thomas More. Edited by Richard Sylvester and Germain Marc'hadour. Hamden, CT: Archon Books, 1977. This volume collects the best articles on More's work, including important ones by Bevington, Elliott, Schoeck, and Sylvester.

Fox, Alistair. *Thomas More: History and Providence.* New Haven, CT: Yale University Press, 1982. A scholarly study that examines More's Latin works with special care.

Hexter, J. H. *More's Utopia: The Biography of an Idea.* Princeton, NJ: Princeton University Press, 1952. One of the most important studies of More's work and its context—indispensable reading.

Logan, George. *The Meaning of More's Utopia.* Princeton, NJ: Princeton University Press, 1983. A solid introduction to More's work.

McCutcheon, Elizabeth. *My Dear Peter: The "Ars Poetica" and Hermeneutics for More's Utopia.* Angers: Moreanum, 1983. A somewhat specialized study, but the best book on More's Latin style.

Surtz, Edward. *The Praise of Pleasure: Philosophy, Education, and Communism in More's Utopia.* Cambridge, MA: Harvard University Press, 1957. A learned study primarily of the philosophical context for More's work.

———. *The Praise of Wisdom: A Commentary on the Religious and Moral Problems and Backgrounds of St. Thomas More's Utopia.* Chicago: Loyola University Press, 1957. A useful investigation of the religious dimension of More's work.